# One Thousand Stars and You

## ISABELLE BROOM

PENGUIN BOOKS

PENGUIN BOOKS

UK | USA | Canada | Ireland | Australia
India | New Zealand | South Africa

Penguin Books is part of the Penguin Random House group of companies
whose addresses can be found at global.penguinrandomhouse.com.

First published 2018
001

Copyright © Isabelle Broom, 2018

The moral right of the author has been asserted

Set in 12.5/14.75 pt Garamond MT Std
Typeset by Jouve (UK), Milton Keynes
Printed and bound in Great Britain by Clays Ltd, Elcograf S.p.A.

A CIP catalogue record for this book is available from the British Library

ISBN: 978-1-405-93552-4

www.greenpenguin.co.uk

To all those who not only look up at the stars,
but have the courage to reach for them too.

# I

The scar started on Alice Brockley's left temple and ran down to her cheek, where it burrowed through the softness like a dimple. It had begun as an angry pink tear, and soon after the broken flesh had been stitched neatly back together. As the years passed, so the colour faded and became subdued. New cells were produced, and the ragged edges where the shard of glass had penetrated were little more than a blur – a hint at past mischief, an echo of the girl from before.

Alice was no longer *that* girl.

Alice had not been that girl for nineteen years – not since she was ten years old. Not since the accident that scarred her. Yet here she was, standing at the foot of the ladder that would take her up to the highest diving board. Reckless, dangerous, selfish, foolish – Alice ticked the scornful adjectives off one by one, her conscience doing battle with her determined limbs. She stared out across the pool for a moment, watching but not seeing the way the light filtered in through the tall windows. The tiles turned the water a rich, deep turquoise, but the sunshine left golden trails across its surface. She put a bare foot on the cold metal, then another. Her hands gripped the rail, which wobbled a fraction. It was slippery from the application of a hundred wet fingers, but Alice felt no trepidation. There was a hunger in the hollow of her stomach that she recognised as need – a desire to quench the tension that had been gathering over the past few days.

Alice's toes curled involuntarily around the steps, finding traction as easily as her lungs would seek out the air. With every inch that she climbed, she felt taller, braver, lighter; the reverberating sound of voices and splashing water were reduced to a hum, the fluorescent tubes of light on the ceiling now closer to her than the aquamarine tiles lining the pool.

What would he say if he could see her up here? What would they all say?

Alice hesitated, doubt calling a halt to her resolve. She made herself focus on the diving board. It quivered silently in front of her, ready to spring deliciously under her feet as she bounced, folded, and fell out into wonderful emptiness. It was the anticipation of that feeling, that rush, which drove her forwards.

Her heart pounded as she ran, soared as she jumped, and swelled as she dived, but with the embrace of the water came her rebellion's end, and Alice thrashed back to the surface.

It wasn't worth it, she thought, panting and breathless against the edge of the pool, her hair slicked back against her scalp and her eyes stinging with chlorine. The risk of being caught behaving in this way, and of causing pain to those she loved the most, far outweighed the brief respite from her anxiety – she knew it.

She brought up a practised hand and ran her fingers along her scar.

And damn, she was never allowed to forget it.

'Sri Lanka?'

Alice glanced from the brown bespectacled eyes of her boyfriend Richard to the steely pale-blue pair belonging to her mother. They had made the same exclamation of horrified disbelief in unison, as if Sri Lanka was a planet in the far reaches of outer space as opposed to an island in South Asia.

'What's wrong with Sri Lanka?' she asked, regretting the question as soon as she saw the grim expression on her mother's face. Richard had reached across the kitchen table for his phone, and now looked up at her triumphantly.

'According to this government website,' he said, raising his voice so that Alice could hear him over the scraping of her dad and brother's cutlery against the Brockley family china, 'the risks associated with Sri Lanka include drowning, drink-spiking and credit card fraud.'

'So, much the same as here, then?' she replied. Her attempt at humour caused her boyfriend to frown at her in the same way she imagined he might at one of his students. Richard was a history teacher, and often crossed the line from lover to tutor when he was talking to Alice. She knew that it wasn't deliberate, more a trait that had developed over the time he had spent in the job, just as her years working for the local council had filled her head with all manner of useless information about tax, rates and how much it cost to replace a cracked paving slab, so she had never resented it. On the contrary, she took a certain amount of comfort from knowing exactly how Richard would react to things.

As he floundered for a reply, Alice heard her mother sigh.

'Are you trying to give me even more grey hairs?' she groaned.

Alice appraised her mother's neat blonde bob and took a deep breath. Marianne Brockley rarely had a hair out of place, grey or otherwise. She was petite and neatly put together, and Alice, who was far more athletic in build, envied her slim ankles and small hands. She had inherited more traits from her father's side of the family, who were all broad-shouldered and knobbly-kneed, while her nondescript brown hair came courtesy of her paternal grandmother. It didn't help that her mother would often wring her hands and lament to her husband, 'Oh Peter – it's just so unfair that we had a daughter and she looks more like you than me.'

Alice's father, Peter Brockley – who towered over everyone else in their average-sized family from his formidable six-foot-five height – would simply shake his head and chuckle at his wife with affection, before pulling her towards him for a hug and meeting Alice's eyes over the top of her head. It was the same expression he'd been sending her way since she was a child, one that seemed to say, 'I know she's a nightmare, but isn't she adorable?' Alice wondered now if Richard ever did the same thing to her, but in

4

his case, it would be Alice's mum he'd share a knowing glance with – the two of them were as tight as wheel nuts.

'You're not remotely grey, Mum,' Alice told her obediently, and her dad grunted with approval from his seat at the head of the table.

'There's nothing wrong with going grey,' piped up Freddie, who could always be relied upon to wind up their parents just as much as Alice tried her best not to.

'Look at Helen Mirren, and Jamie Lee Curtis,' he went on, catching Alice's eye and grinning. 'I'm telling you, Mum, silver vixens are all the rage.'

Freddie wasn't eating as much as he usually did, Alice noted. He was probably hung-over after yet another night on the tiles with his City mates. Ever since he had abandoned his childhood plans of working for a charity in favour of a job securing rich and extravagant clients for a hedge fund, Freddie was out more often than in, and Alice was growing weary of getting his voicemail every time she called. Christmas had been over two months ago, but it appeared that the party season never ended for her brother. Freddie had always been the smarter, more capable, more popular and more adored sibling, and Alice used to hope that if she spent enough time with him, then some of her brother's magic would rub off on her. When they were both still children, they genuinely believed that they could tell what the other was thinking, and would spend hours nestled in the makeshift cave Freddie had carefully constructed from the sofa cushions, testing each other. Alice wondered now if Freddie knew just how excited she was at the prospect of a trip to Sri Lanka, and that she still wanted to go despite Richard and her mum's disparaging remarks.

'This poor bloke was killed by a crocodile over there not long ago,' Richard persisted, holding out his phone so that Alice could see. 'That definitely wouldn't happen down the River Stour.'

*That's because nothing ever happens down the River Stour,* Alice thought, but knew better than to say. Richard, who was a keen angler, had fallen in love with the waterway running through her hometown of Sudbury the very first time she brought him to Suffolk to visit, and there had never been any question of where they would settle once they had collected their university degrees.

'I promise not to get eaten by anything, crocodile or otherwise,' she said, placing a reassuring hand on Richard's jeans-clad knee. 'It's only two weeks – I'll be back before you've even noticed that I've gone, and then it's the Easter holidays.'

Richard made a 'pfft' sort of noise that very nearly made Alice grit her teeth. She must remember that he only reacted in this way out of concern for her – just as her mother did. Both had seen the boisterous version of Alice that was once an unstoppable force to be reckoned with, and both had gently shooed her away. She was grateful to them for doing so, too. That Alice had been nothing but trouble – a danger to herself and others. How much easier her life was now, and how secure and loved she felt.

The memory of that morning's dive off the highest board flashed through her mind, the image wagging a metaphorical finger as if to say, 'But what about me?' Alice ignored it.

'I assume this holiday was Maureen's idea?' Richard surmised, and Alice dipped her chin. Her boyfriend had never been the biggest fan of her feisty, dark-haired friend, believing her to be a bad influence on Alice.

'Well, yes – and Steph really wants to go, too,' she told him. 'She's been desperate to go there for years – she wants to see the elephants. The two of them ganged up on me, and you know I can never say no to them.'

The fib slipped so easily off Alice's tongue that it barely registered. She could not remember when her lies first began, only that they had always been there, protecting not only her, but also those close to her. She could no more stop herself from telling them than she could from breathing, and over time they no longer even felt deceitful, but rather a necessity. She told herself that she would never be dishonest about the big stuff, but what did the odd little yarn matter, really? Wasn't it better to gloss over the truth than risk hurting someone?

'Maureen is trouble,' Freddie said happily, sipping his glass of red wine. Alice chose not to comment. The fact that her brother hankered after one of her closest friends made her feel uncomfortable, but only because she knew how Maureen liked to share intimate details of the men she hooked up with. Alice loved her brother, but there were definitely a few things that she did *not* need to know about him.

'She is,' muttered Richard, Freddie's playful tone skimming straight over his head like a Frisbee. 'Can't you three celebrate all turning thirty together in London or something instead?'

'Yes!' Alice's mother clapped her hands together in delight. 'Why not see a show?'

It was not worth pointing out that the capital city, with all its traffic, pickpockets and smog, was in all likelihood far more dangerous than Sri Lanka, and Alice pressed her lips together in a smile.

'All we're going to be doing is sunbathing and stuff,' she said vaguely, wincing slightly at her own dishonesty, before adding, 'You know I would never do anything to put myself at risk.'

Marianne Brockley clasped a hand to her chest.

'It still feels like it happened yesterday,' she murmured sadly. 'I will never forget the scream, all that blood. I thought I'd lost you.'

'You didn't, though,' Alice reminded her gently, as she always did, shifting so her hair fell over the damaged side of her face.

'I still have nightmares about it,' her mum confided, looking haunted.

Alice saw Freddie roll his eyes as he drained what was left in his wine glass.

'Your poor face,' her mum was saying. 'I can't bear to think about it, not even now.'

'I'm sorry,' Alice said, feeling helpless. If she could go back in time and undo her actions, then she would – of course she would. But turning back the clock was not an option. All she was able to do was apologise, and be sure never to let anything bad happen to her again – even if it meant nothing exciting happened to her, either.

'Just promise me,' her mum insisted. 'Promise that you won't do anything silly when you're over there.'

Alice smiled now with more confidence – here was a vow that she could wholeheartedly make.

'I promise,' she said.

# 3

Alice and Richard met three weeks into their first term at Plymouth University. He was studying history, she had opted for sociology, and both had headed to the Student Union bar that Wednesday evening to watch the infamous initiation ceremony of freshers into the rugby team – a process involving wigs, boys with meaty thighs wearing tight dresses, copious pints of lager and a great deal of chanting.

Richard had stood out to Alice because he was one of the only males in the whole place not jeering along with the crowds, and he later told her that she had stood out to him because of how short her skirt was. This being Richard, however, he didn't mean it in a sleazy way – he was merely concerned that she might potentially freeze to death on the way home, and wanted to offer her money for a taxi.

Finally turning eighteen and living away from the protective folds of her mother's apron for the first time in her life had lit a fire underneath Alice, and during her first few weeks at university she had shed her timid Suffolk skin and reinvented herself as a girl who liked to party – much to the delight of her new friends in her halls of residence. The new Alice plastered make-up on over her scar, rolled her hems up and carried a lit cigarette through the quad between lectures. She never actually went so far as to smoke it, using it instead as a prop that declared, 'I'm normal. I'm cool. I'm just like you.'

It took Richard a matter of days to see through all of it.

'This isn't really you at all, is it?' he had probed quietly, as Alice downed yet another shot which one of her more exuberant friends had thrust into her hand. The girl had offered Richard one, too, but he had declined, confident enough in himself not to worry what anyone thought. For Alice, who had spent the past eight years hiding her scarred face and wishing with all her heart that she could be anything other than who she was, this self-assured trait was enormously attractive. Richard was solid and dependable, mature and sweet-natured, and utterly unfussed by the puckered trail of damaged skin on Alice's face. She quickly realised that if she was with Richard, then she would be safe and protected from her childhood self which had started to re-emerge. He would remind her of who she wanted to be, and help her not to waver. So, when Richard had asked her rather matter-of-factly a few hours later if she would like to go to the cinema with him that weekend, she had practically leaped into his lap with eagerness, and the two of them had been together ever since.

They had returned from Sunday lunch with her parents a few hours ago, and Richard had retreated to the tiny boxroom that they used as an office to mark some test papers. The landlord had advertised the flat as a two-bedroom, which was the first of his many bad jokes. Other gems included, 'Those cupboards aren't meant to have doors – it's a feng shui kitchen' and, 'Of course I'll have the place professionally cleaned before you move in.' They put up with it because it was cheap and close to the school, and all the money they saved in rental rates and commuting costs was being put aside for a proper deposit. Within the next year or so, they would finally be able to buy. Alice had enough in her personal account to more than cover the cost of her holiday to Sri Lanka, but she still felt mildly guilty to be splurging quite so much.

'For God's sake – you only turn thirty once!' Maureen had said, frustrated when Alice pointed out what she knew Richard would say as soon as she told him about the trip. Even Steph, who was a lot less feisty than Maureen and knew Alice's boyfriend far better, nodded her blonde head in agreement. By some strange twist of fate, Alice and her two best friends had been born on three consecutive days in April – the first, second and third – and this year they would all be turning thirty. Marking the occasion with something extra-special made sense, and if Alice was honest, Maureen's idea was a brilliant one. She had not been away with anyone other than Richard for years, and he preferred to stay closer to home. Sri Lanka sounded so exotic and exciting – a real adventure, and a trip they would never forget.

Alice had agreed with Maureen's plan, but it had taken her three days to pluck up the courage to tell Richard and her mother about it over the dinner table. Three days that had culminated in such a knot of anxiety that Alice had ended up needing to do something to release it – hence the dive. Now she felt silly. Of course, risk-averse Richard had not been thrilled about the idea, but he hadn't told her that she couldn't go. He would never do that.

She heard the office door closing across the landing and picked up the TV remote, pausing *The West Wing* just as her boyfriend appeared in the bedroom doorway. He looked tired, she thought – adorably so, with his caramel fringe askew and a gravy stain on the front of his grey T-shirt.

'Nice bath?' he asked, stifling a yawn.

Alice nodded. Her thick, light-brown hair still felt damp. She must plait it before bed, she thought briefly, her hand going to its silky ends. Once upon a time, Richard would have offered to do it for her, but those days felt like half a lifetime ago. Living together had undoubtedly changed the dynamic of their relationship – which Alice had known it inevitably would – but she reasoned that she had gained more than she had lost. Richard might not be as affectionate towards her as he once was, but sharing a home had made their intimacy feel cosier, somehow. Being with him was easy.

'I've been thinking,' he said, coming towards her and sitting down on the edge of the bed. 'I want to do something special for your birthday, too.'

'Oh?' Alice sat up straighter and crossed her legs. She was wearing the pyjamas Richard had got her for Christmas, which were fleecy and covered in polar bears. Perfect for the below-freezing temperatures that had arrived hand in icy hand with the first few days of February.

'I know we said that we'd wait until we bought a place, but . . .' He paused, watching her closely to gauge her reaction.

Alice knew exactly what he was going to say, and her heart began to pound against her chest. It was the same feeling that had sent her up those slippery steps at the pool, the fluttering that she associated with losing control. Alice opened her mouth to speak, but found there were no words. Richard's hand was on her cheek now, his thumb hooking her hair around her ear, his fingers brushing against her neck. Alice shivered.

'I think that when you get back from Sri Lanka,' he said softly, 'we should set the date.'

# 4

Alice slipped her Sri Lanka travel guide into the side pocket of her backpack and did up the zip, almost dropping her passport in the process. Her hands had turned clammy with nervous excitement from the moment the captain switched on the seat-belt signs and announced that they would soon be landing, and she now felt as if the dial controlling her senses had been cranked to its highest setting. Her eyes widened as they took in the joyful chaos of Bandaranaike International Airport, her nostrils flaring with delight as a host of new scents assailed her, and her ears rang with a cacophony of sounds.

'Wow,' breathed Maureen, her usual buoyant sweariness for once subdued by the mayhem unfolding around them. 'Bit lively in here, isn't it?'

Steph rubbed her eyes and yawned blearily, her cheeks pink beneath her blonde curls, which she'd tied up in a high ponytail. While Alice had spent the eleven-hour flight devouring first her book and then several movies, her oldest friend had eaten one meal, then pulled her pink satin eye mask down over her face and promptly fallen asleep. Maureen had followed suit, but not before taking full advantage of the complimentary wine on board.

'My head hurts,' Maureen groaned, and Alice chuckled in amusement.

'Come on,' she said, bouncing eagerly on the balls of her feet. 'Let's get through passport control and find a taxi.'

They made their way through the chattering crowds, pointing in wonder at the open-fronted shops in the arrivals lounge, which sold everything from elephant-dung notebooks to washing machines. Alice had never seen white goods for sale in an airport before, but nobody else seemed to be looking twice as they hurried past. Every local face Alice glanced at carried an honest and warm smile; dark-brown eyes crinkling with pleasure as she returned their grins of greeting. When they reached the end of the long walkway, the three girls found themselves face-to-face with an enormous statue of Buddha.

'Selfie!' cried Maureen, but Alice put a hand on her arm before she could reach for her phone.

'Don't,' she warned. 'You're not supposed to take pictures with your back to Buddha – it's disrespectful.'

Maureen nodded, and Alice felt the grateful gaze of the nearby security guard fall across them.

'You are good,' Steph remarked, as they waited in the passport control queue. 'Doing all the research so we didn't have to.'

Alice shrugged, uncomfortable with the praise. She didn't want to admit that ever since they had agreed to come to Sri Lanka, she'd been reading whatever material she could get her hands on in order to be fully prepared. She had written out her wish list of places to visit, underlined phrases in the back of the guide book so she could communicate better, and generally immersed herself in all things Sri Lanka, as if she was bathing in the country and its culture. She was very glad she'd done her research on what to expect at the airport, because as soon as they'd all had their passports stamped and were heading towards the exit, the locals descended en masse.

'*Ayubowan*, ladies. Hello, hello – you want taxi?'

'Tuk-tuk? I make for you a very good price.'

'I take this bag for you.'

While it was full-on, none of the hopeful taxi drivers were so pushy as to make Alice feel uneasy, and so she smiled but shook her head determinedly as she continued to walk through them, Maureen and Steph not far behind. One wiry-limbed man with a white beard and matted hair pulled at the straps of her backpack, gesturing to her that she should hand it over.

'*Néhé istouti*,' she told him politely. 'No, thank you.'

'Since when did you speak Sri Lankan?' called out Steph, her knuckles white on the straps of her own bag.

'It's actually Sinhalese,' Alice corrected, and Maureen whistled in approval.

'I always said this one was a dark horse,' she told Steph, narrowly avoiding elbowing another tuk-tuk driver in the face as she swung round. They had reached the doors at last, and Alice took a short, deep breath before stepping outside.

'Woof!' said Maureen, stopping in her tracks as if the sudden, oppressive heat was a real curtain that had just been pulled across in front of her. Now that they had moved into the area reserved for official taxis, the tuk-tuk drivers that had swarmed around them just a moment ago melted away into the crowds.

'Oh wow, I feel better already,' Steph said happily, closing her eyes and dropping her shoulders.

Alice looked at her phone to see if the time had readjusted. It was nine-thirty p.m. here in Colombo – four p.m. back home – and the sky was a hard, dense black above the white awning outside the airport. She had been awake for over thirty-three hours now, but she didn't feel even remotely tired. On the contrary, Alice felt as if she could take off and run along the cluttered roads of the capital city, just as she did across the water meadows at home, all the way to the hotel they had booked for the night. Tomorrow morning, they would drive up to the Cultural Triangle, where the real adventure would begin.

'Earth to Alice in Wonderland!'

Steph was calling to her from the open door of a taxi, bemused as always by her friend's ability to drift effortlessly off into a trance. Alice hurried over and handed her heavy rucksack to the waiting driver. Thanking him as he wedged it into the boot, she clambered into the car and sat down next to Steph.

Maureen, who had opted for the front seat, leaned around to face them.

'So, are you girls glad that I suggested this trip, or what?' she asked.

Alice beamed at her.

'Maur,' she declared, buckling up just as their driver started the ignition. 'I'm so happy I could kiss you.'

Maureen smirked. 'That reminds me,' she said, 'I never told you about my last date.'

Alice looked up as the car inched forwards and joined the flow of traffic.

'This was with the mechanic, right?'

Maureen nodded, although it was already clear from her expression that this latest Tinder tale was not going to have a happy ending.

'His nails were bloody filthy,' she chuntered, shuddering at the memory. 'And when I asked him what his hobbies were, he told me he played the accordion.'

'Random!' chimed Steph, chuckling and then swearing as she attempted to untangle her sunglasses from her unruly curls. The short amount of time they had spent in the savage humidity had already turned her into a tumbleweed.

'I know!' Maureen looked aghast at the mere thought. 'Why couldn't it have been a saxophone? Saxophone players are sexy as hell.'

Alice blushed as she met the driver's eyes in the mirror. For some reason, she felt uncomfortable with where the conversation was going – especially with their driver listening in.

'You're missing all the scenery,' she said, wincing as an overcrowded bus almost veered straight into them. Colombo was a riot of colour, noise and activity, with car and tuk-tuk horns blaring, bicycles weaving precariously between the traffic, and a huge number of stray dogs wandering along the side of the road. Everyone they passed on the lit-up city streets was dressed in shades of vibrant red, sunshine yellows or deep, bright greens. There was clutter and chaos and rubbish and shouting and music, but as Alice pressed her nose to the glass and took it all in, she could sense a harmony to the madness, too.

Maureen was now bemoaning her accordion-playing mechanic's persistent follow-up texts, which made Alice laugh. When it came to their love lives, her two friends were looking for very different things. Maureen wanted to go out and get herself a man with his own house, car, business and, ideally, children, because, as she bluntly put it, 'Pregnancy destroys your body.' Steph, on the other hand, was resolutely hoping to be found by 'The One', a mythical creature with apparently no bad habits, a keen willingness to have at least six kids and, as she sweetly put it, 'A schlong to be seriously proud of.' Alice, of course, had found her life partner when she was just eighteen, so she'd never really had time to wonder about anyone else. Richard had been with her through everything – he had stayed the course all through university, forgiven her when she needed forgiving, and even, on occasion, stuck up for her when her mother became too much. A life with no Richard in it was impossible to imagine.

'I wish we were travelling all over Sri Lanka in this,' sighed Maureen, who was settling into the taxi's leather upholstery like a blissed-out cat.

'What, and miss out on all those five- and six-hour train journeys?' joked Alice.

'Don't remind me.' Maureen screwed up her pale-green eyes. 'I can barely handle the ten-minute Tube journey from Stratford to my office, so don't be surprised if I just start crying about an hour in.'

Steph tutted. 'Don't be daft – it will be amazing. And

how would we ever meet men if we were trapped in a car with each other all the time?'

'There's more to life than men,' Alice jokingly reminded the two girls.

'That's easy for you to say,' Maureen replied, humour dancing across her features. 'You've got lovely Richard waiting for you at home. I haven't met anyone worth a second date for months.'

'Nor me,' said Steph. 'The man of my dreams could be in Sri Lanka right now, just waiting for me to find him.'

Alice, who did not view the dating game as a treasure hunt in which men were the prize, kept her mouth very carefully shut and let Maureen and Steph carry on their conversation without her input. To her friends, she knew it must seem that she had it all worked out. She was living with a man who was kind to her, loved her and, as yet unbeknownst to them, wanted to marry her – but what they couldn't see was the nagging feeling, deep down, that something was not quite right with her and with the life she had chosen. Ever since Richard had mentioned setting the date, Alice had felt as if each of her limbs had been tied to bunches of helium balloons. She could not find traction on the ground, no matter how hard she tried.

Breaking air-conditioned-car protocol, she wound down the taxi window so she could breathe in the fragrant air, and was assaulted with the sweet, rich scent of burning wood.

What she was feeling must simply be a case of cold feet. Getting married was the logical next step for her and Richard, and it was one she wanted, no matter how jittery it made her.

## 5

'Alice. Alice, wake up.'

Alice sat bolt upright as if shocked with a Taser to find that Steph was poking her on the leg.

'Wh . . .' she began, blinking the sleep out of her eyes. It was pitch-black outside the car.

'When did the sun go down?' she asked blearily, stretching her arms out in front of her and grimacing with satisfaction when she heard her stiff joints click. After the long flight, yesterday's taxi from the airport to the hotel and today's mammoth drive cross-country from Colombo all the way up to Habarana, Alice figured she had done more than enough sitting down.

'Oh, about an hour ago. Vidu says we're nearly there – isn't that right, Vidu?'

Their driver grunted in agreement.

'You drooled on my shoulder,' Steph added, pointing to a wet patch on her green vest top. 'But you looked so peaceful, I didn't want to move you.'

'Sorry,' Alice said, wiping ineffectually at the damp area with her fingers. 'I can't believe I fell asleep.'

'It was a nice sunset,' Steph admitted. 'But there'll be plenty more, so don't worry.'

'Mmm-hmm,' murmured Alice, still shaking her head to unstick the cobwebs of exhaustion. It was impossible to see anything through the window save for the moon, which was three-quarters full and bright enough to cause Alice's eyes to water as she gazed at it.

In the front seat, Vidu muttered something in Sinhalese and turned off the road abruptly, narrowly missing a rusty painted sign half hidden behind dense foliage and applying the brakes as the car began bouncing over the potholes.

'Steady on, Vidu!' laughed Maureen from beside him, making a show of clutching on to the front dashboard as if she was on a roller coaster. 'I'm too single to die!'

'Jumping road!' announced Vidu, grinning as he gripped the steering wheel, and soon Alice saw lights appearing up ahead. As they drew closer, a line of single-storey cabins came into view, each with a numbered door. A wooden veranda ran all the way along the outside, and there were small tables and chairs beside every entrance.

Vidu was unloading their bags when a tall and exceedingly thin man with a large nose appeared soundlessly from amongst the trees, and prowled over to greet them.

'*Sadarayen piligannawa*,' he whispered. 'Welcome.'

Alice put her palms together in greeting, and was gratified when he followed suit. The man was quite unlike any other Sri Lankan that she'd seen so far, and seemed to almost be shrinking in on himself as he stood beside them. His hair was completely grey, and he was dressed – uncharacteristically for a local – head-to-toe in black. He reminded Alice overwhelmingly of Lurch from *The Addams Family*, and she had to subdue a desire to giggle.

While Maureen sorted out a generous tip for Vidu, the

tall man beckoned Alice and Steph forwards with a slender finger and showed them into their room for the next two nights. It was basic, with one double bed and a small single, which Alice bagged straight away. She was a restless sleeper, her fizzing anxiety causing her to kick off covers and fidget most nights, so she always avoided sharing except with Richard. He, at least, had grown accustomed to it. There was also a hard-looking sofa in the room, one table and a rudimentary bathroom. Alice loved it. The modern hotel where they had spent the night back in Colombo had been nice, but it hadn't felt particularly authentic. This place, which the three of them had discovered in the depths of Booking.com, was exactly what she'd been hoping to find, and now that they were here, Alice discovered she couldn't stop smiling.

'Dinner?' rasped Lurch, hovering in the open doorway like a spectre.

'Yes, please,' Steph said, clapping her hands together at the thought of food. Breakfast from the hotel buffet felt like a very long time ago, and all they'd eaten for lunch were packets of crisps that they'd picked up from roadside stalls.

'At nine o'clock,' he told them in his strange, scratchy voice, before shifting away.

Alice walked across the room to where Steph was staring in horror at her humidity-fried hair in the mirror.

'Pinch me,' Alice instructed.

Steph didn't move. 'What? Why?'

'Because I'm pretty sure I'm still asleep and have just dreamt that man.'

Steph laughed, her expression transforming in the smudged glass.

'Did I hear the word "man"?' demanded Maureen, who had just walked through the door and was buckling slightly under the weight of her backpack.

Alice started to explain, but Maureen shushed her with a flapping hand. 'There's no time,' she told them, tossing her bag on the double bed and unzipping one pocket after another.

'Shit, where the bloody hell did I put it?'

'Put what?' Alice asked, bending down to untie the laces of her trainers.

'My make-up bag,' Maureen replied, as if that much was obvious. Alice thought about the lone mascara nestled in the bottom of her washbag. She rarely bothered with make-up these days. It reminded her of the time when her scar had ruled her life, and she had been too insecure to leave the house without plastering on several inches of Maybelline's finest. And anyway, she thought, dabbing at the moisture on her upper lip with the bottom of her T-shirt, it was far too hot for foundation in Sri Lanka.

'I look like Monica in that episode of *Friends* when they all went to Barbados,' wailed Steph, who was still at the mirror, and now pulling at her frazzled locks in despair.

Alice opened her mouth to protest, then shut it again. Steph's description was unarguably accurate.

'Here it is!' cried Maureen, holding her cosmetic bag aloft as if it was the FA Cup and carrying it reverently into the bathroom. There was no way that she could have the hots for Lurch, thought Alice, rubbing her head. None of this was making any sense whatsoever.

She was just scraping her hair back into a bun ready to wash the day off her face, when Maureen re-emerged from the en suite in her bra and shorts, reeking of perfume and wearing enough red lipstick to stop traffic.

'OK.' Alice held her hands up. 'I give up. What the hell is going on? Why are you getting all tarted up?'

'Do you think the lippy is too much?' asked Maureen, directing her question at Steph rather than Alice.

'That depends,' replied Steph, not turning to look, 'on what it's for.'

'Not what – who!' Maureen told them, clearly exasperated. 'What is wrong with you two – did you not see those two hotties when we arrived?'

'I only saw the butler from *The Addams Family*,' Alice informed her. 'Unless you persuaded Vidu to stay for a drink . . .'

Steph started laughing, abandoning her comb in her unruly curls.

'Trust me,' said Maureen, pulling a clean top out of her backpack and yanking it on. 'There are two gorgeous men sitting at a table just around the corner from us, and every moment that we spend in this room is a wasted one. Now come on!'

'But my hair . . .' began Steph, but Maureen was already thrusting a band in her direction.

'Tie it up,' she instructed, then turned to Alice.

'Aren't you going to get changed?'

Alice had pre-planned her outfit for each day of their

stay, and packed them in order in her bag. The thought of rooting through them all now looking for a dress seemed ridiculous.

'Nah,' she said, wriggling her hot toes into flip-flops. 'If I look like a tramp, then you two will look all the better next to me.'

'You couldn't look like a tramp if you tried,' said Steph loyally, but she, too, was now applying make-up. What a bloody palaver, thought Alice. All this fuss and preparation for two random blokes that they'd never met before and would probably never see again after tonight. The only holiday romance that she was remotely interested in having was with Sri Lanka, and she couldn't even begin to imagine meeting a person that would delight and enthral her as much as this country already had.

# 6

# Max

*If I should die,*
*Remember me whole,*
*Not torn and broken,*
*Robbed of my soul . . .*

Max had seen the girls arrive; had watched as the car headlights were distorted by the mass of undergrowth that lay between the cabins and the road. The wheels of the vehicle crunched over the gravel driveway, reminding him of a time now past – a time where a stony pathway felt treacherous, the sharp edge of each pebble a trap waiting to be sprung. Reaching instinctively for his wrist, he felt the thick rubber band between his fingers. It was always there, a comfort and a necessity, and it stilled his mind to feel it, taut against his skin.

He heard the car come to a stop and the sound of the doors opening. He could not see its occupants from where he and Jamal were sitting, two bottles of beer dribbling beads of condensation on to the wooden table top in front of them, but he could hear their voices. Three British females, he identified, one much more vocal than the others. And from the gentle grunts and groans, he'd be willing to bet they each had a hefty backpack in tow. Even Max had been surprised at the weight of his own bag, despite being well practised in the art of lugging kit around.

He wondered if it was the start of the girls' trip, or the end. He knew that some visitors chose to begin in the Cultural Triangle area of Sri Lanka, while others headed south and went straight to the beaches – a bit of rest and relaxation before tackling the climbs and treks further north. A beach holiday didn't interest Max in the slightest – he'd done enough lying down.

An image of his mother drifted into his mind unheeded, and Max reached for his beer and took a slug as he recalled, yet again, the tense conversation they'd had the morning he left. She didn't understand this need that he had, to come out to Sri Lanka and explore. He wanted to push himself as hard as he was able, but he also needed to get away – from her more than anyone. Being at home was slowly suffocating him, and only now he was here, did Max feel as if he could breathe again. Ironic, really, considering how wet the air was in Sri Lanka. He had known it would be hot, of course he had, but he hadn't factored in just how much the humidity would cause him to sweat.

He plucked at the damp material of his T-shirt, which had begun to adhere itself to his back, and grimaced. Jamal, sitting across from him, twitched a dark eyebrow of enquiry. Jamal never seemed to sweat, the lucky bastard.

'Getting all hot and bothered around me again?' Jamal joked, picking at the label of his Lion Lager.

'Well, I'm only human,' quipped Max, and was rewarded

with an easy smile. Jamal was always smiling – his grin was his greatest asset. Max could still remember the first time he'd seen it, back when there didn't seem to be anything left to smile about. Over time, of course, he learned that there was plenty. You just had to know where to look. Max knew that there was more good in the world than bad, and he'd seen some of the darkest acts a man can see. The trick was simply to focus on what was still in the glass – the fullness that remained even when what you believed to be the essence had been drained away. There was always tomorrow – hell, there was always right now.

Max heard a door slamming shut, and cocked his head towards the sound. Some habits die hard, he thought. Perhaps he should write about them, these well-worn instincts. Try to put into words the way they lurked like unexploded bombs through the unfolding path of his life. An unfortunate analogy, but an accurate one. What would Jamal say, he mused, if he pulled his notebook and pencil out of his back pocket and started scribbling down the verses of a new poem? Would his friend mock him? No. Max was certain Jamal would be nothing but encouraging. But he still wasn't ready to share that side of himself with anyone. Not yet.

'Eyes up,' said Jamal, letting go of his bottle so quickly that it spun slightly on the spot. 'We've got company.'

Max blinked, just once, although he would remember it as a far more profound pause later. Because later there would only be Before, and then forever there would be After.

# 7

Alice noticed his eyes first. They were deep-set, symmetrical, and looked almost black beneath his thick, straight brows. He had brown hair, perhaps a shade or two lighter than her own, and it was short all over save for a section at the very front that he'd swept up to one side. Alice imagined him in front of a mirror, gel between his fingers which he then transferred through the strands in a single, practised movement. His jaw was strong and set, his bottom lip full on a mouth that was slightly upturned at the corners. You couldn't call it a smile exactly, but there was an openness there, the hint of amusement, a laugh waiting in the wings.

There was a healthy amount of stubble across his jaw, but it looked deliberate rather than unkempt, and as Alice stared at him, the stranger brought up a hand as if to brush away an itch. He was watching her, too, she realised, dropping her eyes quickly and feeling the heat creep into her cheeks.

'Ladies.'

This came from the other man at the table, and Alice turned her head to see dark eyes, dark skin and a wide, warm smile.

An enthusiastic Maureen made the introductions.

'Hey, I'm Maur – well, Maureen, but everyone calls me

Maur – Maur, not less.' A cackle. 'And this is Steph, and Alice. Have you guys just arrived, too? It took us forever to get here. We drove all the way from Colombo, past the elephant orphanage – have you been? Oh, you have beers – thank God. I could murder a beer. Where's that man gone?'

Lurch appeared in the crack of the partially open doorway behind them so quickly that he could only have been lurking there in wait.

'Ah, there you are!' said Maureen happily, gesturing to the beers on the table. 'Can we order three more of these, please?'

Lurch nodded, before melting away once more. Alice fought the compulsion to laugh again. For some reason, she was feeling incredibly light-headed, and banged her elbow on the table in her haste to sit down.

'Shit!' she muttered, rubbing the spot. Why people referred to it as the funny bone when it was anything but, she would never understand.

'Squidge up,' said Steph, who wanted to sit beside her, and Alice shuffled along the bench seat until she was almost right next to the man she'd been caught staring at. He was wearing baggy blue tracksuit bottoms and a black T-shirt, which Alice couldn't help but notice clung to the muscles across his chest and upper arms.

'You OK there?' he asked, and their eyes met again. There was a directness in his that Alice had never encountered before, and she found herself absurdly unable to speak for a moment.

'Yes,' she finally managed. 'Thank you.'

The man responded with a half-smile.

'What are your names, then?' asked Maureen. She had chosen the only free chair, which was diagonally across from the man with the massive grin.

'I'm Jamal,' he said. 'And my boy here is Max.'

'How old are you both?' Maureen went on boldly.

'Maur!' cried Steph in amusement. 'You can't just ask a person their age like that.'

Max lifted and dropped his shoulders and Alice caught a whiff of peppery aftershave.

'Doesn't bother me,' he said. 'But if we tell, I reckon it's only fair that you ladies do, too.'

'You first,' demanded Maureen, her pale-green eyes narrowing flirtatiously as she ran them over him. Alice shifted in her seat, unable to find a comfortable position, suddenly aware not only of every limb, but the exact arrangement of her facial features. The top she'd been wearing all day felt itchy against her skin, her denim shorts too tight.

'Fair enough.' Max fingered his bottle of beer as he looked across at Maureen. 'I'm thirty-three.'

'And I'm thirty-seven,' added Jamal, grinning as they all looked at him in surprise. 'I know, I know, I don't look it. Must be all that Oil of Olay I pinch off my mum.'

'If that's what you use, I'm going to order in a lifetime supply,' said Steph, and Jamal beamed at her, his eyes, noticed Alice, lingering slightly longer than was strictly necessary. Maureen explained about the three of them all turning thirty being the reason for their trip, and as she was talking, Lurch returned with a tray of beers and some cutlery, which he laid out in front of them.

'I don't think there's such a thing as a menu here,' Max

explained, turning to Alice. 'I think you just eat what you're given.'

'Suits me.' She braved a glance at him. 'I've been looking forward to trying some Sri Lankan cuisine. The hotel we stayed at last night was nice, but they didn't have much traditional stuff.'

Max nodded, understanding. 'The food is all part of the experience.'

Alice relaxed a fraction.

'Have you travelled a lot?' she asked, even though the answer was obvious. There was something about this man that exuded worldliness – she could sense it in the creases around his eyes, and the rather pensive expression on his face as he considered her question.

'I guess so,' he replied. 'Although perhaps not to anywhere that you would choose to go.'

'Oh?' she began in response, but Maureen cut across her.

'Jamal's just invited us to go to Sigiriya tomorrow,' she told Alice. 'That's the place with the big rock, right?'

*It's slightly more than that*, thought Alice, but chose not to elaborate. They had planned to visit the cave temples in nearby Dambulla first, perhaps followed by a drive out to the ancient city of Polonnaruwa, but she didn't suppose it mattered what order they saw things. Sigiriya was one of the places she wanted to see most of all while they were here, second only to Adam's Peak, the mountain in the centre of the country which you traditionally climbed through the night so you could watch the sunrise from the summit. Alice had come across it during her research into Sri Lanka and persuaded Steph and Maureen that they simply must see it. The thought of being up that high made her heart lighten.

She heard herself agreeing wholeheartedly to the Sigiriya plan before her brain had proper time to think about how Richard would react. He trusted her, of course he did, but no man would be thrilled about the idea of his girlfriend spending time with strange men on holiday. Then again, she thought stubbornly, this wasn't like a normal package trip, with chartered flights and organised sightseeing – they were roughing it with backpacks, like proper travellers, so the rules were different.

Perhaps, whispered a voice from deep inside her, it would make more sense simply not to tell Richard about Max and Jamal. Not yet, anyway. What was the point in stressing him out when he was so far away?

'She does that,' Steph said with affection, snapping Alice back into the present moment. Her friend was leaning over her to talk to Max, who was in turn peering at Alice with amusement. 'Vanishes into her own little world in the middle of a conversation. Alice in Wonderland is what I tend to call her, because she's always off in one.'

'Alice in Wonderland, eh?' The corners of Max's mouth turned up. 'I like it.'

There was nothing Alice could say in her own defence; it was all true. Instead, she concentrated on drinking some more of her beer.

Lurch arrived with plates of food and glasses of papaya juice, which was thick and gloopy and unfortunately tasted a lot like Alice imagined stagnant washing-up water might, if you were ever inclined to sample it. They waited until he had gone back inside to exclaim in whispered voices how revolting it was, laughing as they all agreed they would have to force it down regardless, so as not to offend their host. Luckily, the home-made vegetable curry that came with it was delicate in flavour, and the fresh spices made Alice's taste buds zing with pleasure. Rather than the slop she was accustomed to from the local take-away back home, Lurch's curry contained crunchy beans, corn and wonderfully sweet tomatoes, and was flavoursome rather than hot.

Max ate quickly, one hand using a spoon to scoop up the rice and curry and the other resting in his lap. There was an elastic band around one of his wrists, Alice noticed, and a thin gold chain disappeared into the front of his T-shirt. She didn't often wear jewellery, didn't really own much save for a few pairs of plain stud earrings, and she glanced down now at the bare fingers on her left hand, trying to imagine how a ring would look there. A gold band with a diamond set into it – a piece of jewellery that announced to the world that she was spoken for, that she belonged to someone, that she had been chosen to become Richard's wife.

Alice blinked and looked away.

'Are you all right?' Max said it quietly enough that only she would hear. He had lowered his mouth to her ear and his breath felt hot on her cheek.

She nodded, overwhelmed suddenly with a bizarre compulsion to tell him exactly what she was thinking. Despite her unusual proximity to a man who wasn't

Richard, Alice didn't feel uncomfortable being so close to Max. She felt something, but it wasn't an emotion exactly – it was more a sense. Something inherent within her that felt inexplicably soothed and safe. How could it be possible to feel so at home with a total stranger?

'I was just thinking about Sigiriya,' she lied. It was always easier to lie. 'I hope I make it to the top.'

'Me too,' Max agreed, picking up his beer only to remember that he'd drunk it all.

Alice made a show of looking him up and down.

'You look in pretty good shape to me,' she said, blushing at her unintentional disloyalty to Richard. 'I bet you'll leg it up there in no time.'

Max smiled at that, but it didn't quite reach his eyes. Now that she was sitting so close to him, Alice could see that they were blue, just like her own.

'Appearances can be deceiving,' he replied, ripping a bit of label off his bottle. Alice sensed that she'd somehow caused him to close a door on her, but she couldn't be sure. Perhaps she was being over-familiar? She would have been offended if he'd commented on her physique, so why had she felt like it was acceptable to do the same to him?

'I didn't mean to . . .' she started to say awkwardly, stopping before she added the word 'upset'. How could she have upset him? She was being ridiculous.

'So, why Sri Lanka?' Max asked, wisely changing the subject. 'Of all the places in the whole world, what drew you here?'

'It was Maur's idea,' Alice said, gesturing towards her

dark-haired friend. 'And I have to admit, it was an inspired one. We've only been here since last night and I love it already.'

She scooped up another mouthful of curry and smiled at him. 'How about you guys?'

Max considered this momentarily, and as she waited for him to reply, Alice uncrossed her clammy legs under the table and promptly kicked him hard in the shin.

'Fu—I mean, oops,' she spluttered, cringing away from him. 'I'm so sorry.'

Max didn't even flinch.

'Didn't feel a thing,' he said, and smiled at her with such warmth that Alice couldn't help but return it in kind. The air between them suddenly felt to Alice as if it was crackling with energy, and she was relieved when Jamal distracted Max with a suggestion of more beers.

Maureen then took over the conversation where Alice had left it, and Max told them that Sri Lanka had been on his bucket list for a long time – mainly because he, too, wanted to scale Adam's Peak.

'We met a Sri Lankan dude called Senura at the last place we stayed,' he said. 'He told us that he climbs the Peak every year with his eighty-six-year-old grandmother.'

'Eighty-six?' exclaimed Alice.

'I know, right?' Max laughed. 'The Sri Lankans call Adam's Peak *Sri Pada*, which I think translates as "sacred footprint", or something like that.'

'It does,' Alice confirmed. 'Depending on which religion you follow, it is either the footprint of Buddha, Shiva or Adam.'

Max appraised her with new respect. 'You clearly know your stuff. Are you a historian?'

She shook her head, and was about to tell him what she actually did for a living, when Maureen interrupted.

'Funny you should say that,' she told Max. 'Alice's boyfriend is a history teacher. I bet we have him to thank for all her knowledge.'

'Oi!' Alice admonished. 'I found this out for myself, I'll have you know.'

She was struck with a mixture of guilt at not being the one who had brought Richard into the conversation, and annoyance towards Maureen for doing so. It shouldn't matter that Max and Jamal knew about her boyfriend, but for some reason Alice wished that they didn't. Not yet, anyway. At home, she was so accustomed to being one half of Ali and Rich, and part of her had been looking forward to simply being Alice for a while.

She glanced sideways at Max, scanning his face for a reaction, and when he felt her eyes on him and turned, Alice dropped her chin so that her hair fell over the scarred side of her face. Old habits die hard, she thought.

She distracted herself by picking up her beer, sipping it, putting it back down. She stretched out her legs, laughed at something Maureen was saying, fiddled with the cutlery on the scraped-clean plate. But, when she eventually sneaked another look back at Max, she found that he was smiling at her. He could tell that she was uncomfortable, and was doing his best to make her feel more at ease. And, to Alice's surprise, she found that Max had succeeded.

# 8

# Max

*If I should die,*
*Know it was in vain,*
*I would have suffered,*
*There would have been pain . . .*

The dream always started the same way, with light and with laughter, reeling him in with its uncomplicated promise of happiness. Max's limbs would settle, his heart would still, and he'd let himself go and float away into the moment, into the warmth of his untarnished memories of that time.

For a long while, Max hadn't been sure if he had any to venture into. It was as if what came later had eradicated all the goodness, like a fist brought down hard on a burning candle, all the brightness snuffed out. In time, however, he learned how to look back and find them, how to peer through the dark brambles of horror and find patches of clear, open joy. Because it hadn't all been terrible; it hadn't all been for nothing.

But as soon as he gave in, let go of the fear and waded out into the shallow water of the dream, Max's world would shift and spiral off in all directions. A red-hot flash, shouting, pain, so much pain, tearing through his body as if his very soul was on fire, throwing him up in the air before tossing him down in the dirt. More pain. Dust. A ringing sound loud enough to rattle his brain inside his head. Screaming, his screaming. Pain, pain, pain, pain.

'Come on, Max. Mate, wake up. It's OK, you're here. You're OK. I've got you, I've got you. Come on.'

Max moved to thrash his arms, his compulsion to escape far stronger than his vague realisation that Jamal was kneeling beside him, his big, solid hands on Max's shoulders.

'Come on, mate,' Jamal said again, his voice low and steady. 'It was just a dream.'

Max blinked and waited for his heart to stop racing. He took a deep breath, focused on Jamal, on his kind brown eyes and his smile.

'Shit,' he said at last. 'Sorry, mate.'

'Less of that,' Jamal released Max's arms. 'You know I don't like apologies.'

'I thought I'd . . .' Max trailed off, embarrassed by the sweat on his knotted sheets and the tears on his cheeks.

'I get it.' Jamal nodded in sympathy. 'You thought the dream was gone, right?'

'It's been months.' Max wrung his hands. 'I didn't even bring my tablets, because I was so sure that I—' He stopped again, angry with himself but knowing he shouldn't be. This was the life he had chosen for himself, and the consequences of that choice were his to bear. There was no point in piling extra pressure on himself. The pills he swallowed to help him sleep were for the very worst times only, and there had been fewer of those with every passing month. Max had thought being away from

41

home would help, that his mind would have so much to focus on, so many new sights, smells and sounds, that he would be looking only forwards, rather than back. But that was the morbid beauty of the mind: it didn't ever completely forget.

Jamal passed him a half-empty bottle of water.

'Here,' he said. 'It's a bit warm, but it's better than nothing.'

'Thanks.' Max took a slug and grimaced. It really was warm, like the bath water he used to swallow as a child, his head immersed beneath the surface as he listened to the strange sound of his heart thumping away in his ears.

Jamal sat back down on the edge of his own bed, his dark eyes searching Max's, enquiring but not fussing, happy to do whatever Max needed. It never failed to amaze Max just how generous his friend could be, and how patient. Jamal didn't so much wear his heart on his sleeve as carry it around in his open palm. He envied his friend for having found a job he was so passionate about. While Max had enjoyed elements of being a soldier, the army was never his passion, and now he worked in the office of his dad's construction company, chasing orders and organising staff rotas. It was about as uninspiring as Max could imagine a job to be, but he had found it impossible to refuse when his father offered. How could he turn his nose up at such kindness, after everything his parents had done for him?

'I'm OK,' Max assured Jamal. 'Really. Tip-top.' He tapped his chest as he said it, stirring up another memory in the process, one that was buried as far down as he could force it. There was more than one type of memory, Max knew, and this one straddled both mind and muscle. He wondered if he would ever leave it behind.

'Go back to sleep,' he told Jamal, a glance at his phone telling him it wasn't even six a.m. yet.

Jamal cocked his head to one side, a gesture that Max read to be gently mocking.

'I'm all right,' came the predictable reply. 'Slept like a log on the flight, didn't I?'

He had, it was true. Max had been unable to settle, his familiar aches intensified by the lack of movement and the pressure inside the cabin.

'So, what do you think of our new lady friends?'

Max looked up at Jamal, who was trying but failing to look nonchalant.

'I think that you would only ask me that question if you'd taken a shine to one of them,' Max replied, reaching for the small wooden box on the table beside the bed and sliding open the lid.

'Damn, you can read me like a Sunday tabloid,' groaned Jamal, folding his long legs back under his sheet with a grin. 'Am I really that obvious?'

'You like Steph, right?' Max prompted, deftly flicking the domino pieces he'd extracted from the box between his fingers. One was a two, and the other a five. Twenty-five – the same age he had been when it happened.

'She's definitely my type,' agreed Jamal, gazing up at the ceiling fan, before glancing back at Max. 'You know I can't resist a blonde.'

The same could have been said of Max, once upon a

time, but nowadays all blonde hair did was remind him of his ex-wife. Not that Steph seemed to be anything like her, which could only be a positive. Faye was a lot of things, but it had turned out that right for Max wasn't one of them.

'I think she likes you, too, you know,' he told Jamal. 'She laughed at your rubbish jokes, for a start.'

'Now, now,' Jamal tossed a pillow in Max's direction. 'We both know full well that I am the funniest person that either of us knows.'

'Which makes me, what, the funniest looking?' quipped Max, his laughter petering out almost immediately. 'Oh, come on,' he insisted, grinning at his friend's blank expression. 'Laughing at myself is a positive thing. Isn't that what they always said at Headley?'

Jamal tutted. 'They say all kinds of shit at Headley. But what's at stake here is who the funnier person is, me or you. And I'm saying it's definitely me.'

'Have it your way,' Max grinned. 'But you know I have the edge when it comes to the slapstick stuff.'

Jamal chuckled despite himself, leaning back on the pillow he hadn't thrown at Max and closing his eyes.

'You're a dickhead,' he sighed.

'Takes one to know one,' Max pointed out cheerily.

'So, come on then,' prompted Jamal.

'Come on what?' Max selected three more pieces from his box of dominoes and started constructing a miniature Stonehenge on the table top. He liked to build things; the methodical action involved helped to calm his mind.

'Which girl did you take a shine to?'

Max paused for just a second, but not so long that Jamal picked up on his hesitation.

'No, don't tell me,' Jamal went on. 'Let me guess. It's the little brown-haired one, isn't it?'

Max felt colour flood into his cheeks as he pictured her.

'Why do you say that?' he asked blithely, concentrating on his little black-and-white building blocks instead of his friend.

'Because she jumped about a foot in the air every time you spoke to her, mate,' Jamal exclaimed. 'And because I know you, and it would be too easy for you to go for Maur, who was making it pretty obvious how much she wanted to get to know you better.'

Max allowed himself to picture Maureen. With her shiny dark hair, alluring, cat-like eyes and easy confidence, she perhaps was the obvious choice, but there was something about Alice that had drawn him in. There was no space in his life for game players or attention seekers – he needed someone he could trust on a higher level than most people, and Alice, to him, had felt like she could be one of those people. He had spent less than two hours in her company, but he somehow knew he could trust her not to judge him. He felt comfortable, he realised, acknowledging as he did so just how rare a feeling it was. He didn't even feel that way with some members of his own family any more.

He didn't realise he was smiling until Jamal pointed it out, laughing as he did so and teasing Max that he must have it bad.

Whatever it was about this girl, Max mused, perhaps it

was a blessing that she had a boyfriend, and that anything romantic could be ruled out from the off. He had not experienced much luck when it came to finding a compatible partner, but he was always keen to make a new friend, and this girl, Alice, already felt like one.

# 9

Alice waited until Lurch had crept silently back to the kitchen before holding her nose and tipping down her papaya juice in one. Even when you couldn't smell it, the taste and texture were still disgusting, and she pulled such an expression of revulsion that Maureen started cackling and promptly spat out a mouthful of her own juice across the table.

'Bollocks!' she cried, grabbing a napkin. 'And I was so looking forward to drinking that, too.'

'You're welcome,' Alice deadpanned.

She had been sitting in the seating area for an hour now, scribbling down her first impressions of Sri Lanka in her journal and reading up on Sigiriya Rock again, just in case she'd missed anything vital. With every minute that passed, the temperature seemed to rise, and despite the early hour, Alice could feel sweat prickling the backs of her bare legs. A thin veil of cloud was just visible through the treeline to the east, the sky around it a pale, arctic blue.

Before going to bed last night, the five of them had arranged for Lurch to order a driver for the day, and they were all due to be collected in half an hour. If Max and Jamal didn't get a move on, they would miss breakfast – and so would Steph, for that matter.

'What *is* she doing in there?' Alice asked Maureen now,

who looked over her shoulder at the empty pathway leading from their room and shook her head.

'God knows. Her hair, probably. It was so frizzy this morning, I had to ask her if she'd plugged herself into the mains overnight instead of her phone charger.'

Alice snuffled with laughter.

'Harsh,' she said, 'but funny.'

She was just about to get up and go in search of her errant friend when a door banged shut and Jamal appeared from around the corner, a small rucksack in his hand and a wide grin on his face.

'Ladies,' he said in greeting, nodding at each of them in turn, before adding, 'Where's the other one?'

'We could say the same to you,' replied Maureen, reaching down to flick an insect off her ankle. She'd tied her hair up today in the sort of effortless chignon that Alice could only dream of creating herself, and her fake-tanned legs poured out of black denim hot pants. The red polka-dot scarf she was wearing as a hairband clashed merrily with her purple vest top, and diamond studs glittered at her ears. Maureen always looked so chic, and seemingly without putting much thought into it at all, whereas Alice looked the same as she had as a child, in clothes that didn't quite fit in colours that didn't quite suit her. It didn't help that she had been blessed with a disproportionately large bottom which made feminine little dresses the enemy, or that she had the stumpy, muscular legs of a Shetland pony. Today she was wearing a pair of khaki shorts from Gap and a grey T-shirt with a Ghostbusters motif on the front. Sexy was as far removed from Alice today as Land's End was from John o' Groats.

'Max is just booting up,' Jamal told them, giving Lurch a thumbs up as the willowy Sri Lankan deposited a plate of breakfast on the table in front of him. There were scrambled eggs decorated with tiny flecks of fresh chilli, bread rolls still warm from the oven, a small dish of fiery red sambal and a plate of sliced banana and pineapple. Alice, who had been tempted to lick the plate clean after finishing her own helping, gazed at the food with envy.

'Walking shoes really aren't attractive, are they?' mused Maureen, frowning down at her own pair. 'I feel like one of those elderly ramblers that invade Suffolk every summer.'

Alice, who loved her new walking shoes and was partial to the odd ramble, said nothing. She supposed she should get up and fetch her bag from the room, but she was anchored to her chair by the heat of the morning, the singing insects and the warm fullness in her stomach.

'Morning!'

Steph had finally joined them, looking typically adorable in red shorts and a pink shirt dotted with blue flowers. Her hair, as predicted by Maureen, had clearly been causing her some grief, because she'd uncharacteristically slicked it back into a tight bun. A few frazzled strands were still escaping around her face, though, and Alice wondered if her pink cheeks were the result of her battling with them for the past half-hour. Steph's flustered appearance didn't seem to register with Jamal, however, who grinned broadly at her and shuffled along the bench seat so she could sit beside him. Maureen took this in at the same time as Alice, and the two of them exchanged a knowing look.

When they'd returned to the room last night, Steph had coyly confessed to finding Jamal attractive, and it looked as if the feeling was mutual. Maur, meanwhile, had openly admitted that she much preferred Max, a revelation that had come as no surprise to Alice. Her flirtatious friend did not believe in playing it coy, and Alice doubted if anyone who was seated at their table last night could have been left in the dark about where Maur had chosen to focus her attentions.

Steph was now tucking into her eggs and ignoring the sambal, and both she and Jamal were pretending the papaya juice did not exist. Alice took out her phone. Ten minutes until the driver arrived, and a message from Richard which had just come through on the temperamental Wi-Fi, asking if she knew where he'd left his tackle bag. She sighed through a tolerant smile as she tapped out a reply – it would be where it always was, on the ledge outside the back door, with its wormy, maggoty contents as far away from Alice as she could get it. Richard had tried to get her into fishing many times over the years, but Alice had no patience for it. If she was outside, she wanted to be moving. She couldn't bear to be immobile, just waiting for something to happen. Richard and his dad could sit there for hours, passing the time with idle chat and eating the doorstep-sized cheese-and-pickle sandwiches she'd made for them. In the winter, they would take a thermos of tea each and spread a blanket out, their feet inside their wellies wrapped up in several layers of socks and their fingertips pink with cold. It was Richard's place, and his time, too – Alice would not have wanted to encroach on it even if she did have a burning desire to wield a rod and net.

'Here's the man,' Jamal suddenly announced through a mouthful of eggs, and Alice jumped so violently in her seat that she dropped her phone under the table. Bending to retrieve it, she saw Max's feet come into view, and realised that his walking shoes were the same brand as her own. Running her eyes up, she took in one hairy shin leading up to a thick, muscular knee and strong thigh, which disappeared into the bottom of dark-grey cargo shorts. On the other side, where his ankle should be, there was instead a thick silver bolt, and from there a metal rod went up into a hard-looking black plastic shell the same shape as a shin pad. The knee area was obscured by a shiny white socket, which was half-covered by the hem of his shorts, and as she stared, realisation trickling through her, it dawned on Alice that what Max had told her when she accidentally kicked him last night – that he couldn't feel a thing – was true. He really hadn't felt a thing, because the leg she had bashed against was prosthetic.

Alice sat up rapidly, her face aflame, putting her phone on the table as Max made his way towards them. He looked happy, and handsome and full of energy, and he smiled as their eyes met.

'You better have saved some papaya juice for me,' was all he said.

## 10

'I had no idea. Did you know? You must have, you were sitting right next to him all evening.'

'Maur!' Alice snapped, her tone uncharacteristically sharp. 'Keep your voice down.'

Maureen had managed to wait until the minibus arrived to blurt out what she was thinking – what, in truth, all three of them had been thinking since Max emerged from his cabin that morning.

'The poor thing,' Steph whispered, fiddling with her tangled seat belt until it lay flat. Outside the bus, Jamal was talking to Lurch and the small, wiry driver, while Max was hoovering up his breakfast at record speed. Neither seemed to be aware that Alice, Maureen and Steph were gossiping about Max, but Alice still felt guilty that they were.

'Do you think it was an accident?' Maureen mused, her eyes wide with imagined tragedy. 'It must have been. Maybe a car crash or something – a roller-coaster collision!'

'I don't think we should be speculating,' Alice told them, still speaking as quietly as she could. 'It's none of our business.'

'It's such a shame,' said Steph, looking genuinely forlorn, and Maureen nodded in agreement. Alice, however, felt herself bristle with irritation.

'Why is it a shame?' she hissed. 'What do you mean by that?'

Steph looked at her, taken aback.

'I just mean, he's such a good-looking guy, and it must have been so devastating for him and his family to—'

'He lost a leg, not his life,' argued Alice, her spark of genuine anger surprising even her. 'He's still exactly the same person we met last night.'

'I bet he's very different to the person he used to be,' put in Maureen, who at least had the grace to look slightly sheepish. 'You can't go through losing a leg and still be the same person.'

Alice remembered how the other kids at school used to cast enquiring looks her way in the months that her injury was still healing. They would whisper behind their hands, their eyes full of pity with a trace of disgust. Alice had hated it – had hated every single one of them.

'You're both forgetting about my face,' she pointed out. 'You sound like my mum used to when I was going back and forth to the hospital. She was all full of "you will never be the same after this", and "this is the worst thing that has ever happened". She made me feel like a freak.'

Steph chewed her bottom lip.

'You were never a freak, Alice – but your accident *did* change you, remember? You were a right tearaway when we were little kids.'

Alice hated being reminded of her childhood self and she was closer to becoming grumpy than she had been for a long time. The only person she ever really got angry at was herself, so she could understand why her friends were looking at her now with such bewilderment. She couldn't seem to put a lid on it, though, like she normally would. She was sure Max didn't need her fighting his battles for him – clearly, he had already been through some – but something in her was pushing her to protect him regardless. Seeing his prosthetic limb had been a shock, of course it had, but that had passed now and all Alice was left with were the same feelings she'd had the previous night. Max had not changed at all in her eyes; he'd merely peeled back a layer of who he was, and as a result Alice felt more connected to him, even though they had yet to utter more than a few words to one another.

'I think I'm just irritable because I need more sleep,' she said, making sure to sound appropriately contrite. Steph's expression changed at once from one of wounded child to concerned friend.

'Of course you do, you poor thing. Do you want to see if we can push back this trip by a few hours so you can have a nap?'

'No!' Alice shook her head rapidly. 'I mean, please don't worry. I'll be fine once we get moving.'

'If you say so,' replied Steph, but she didn't look convinced. Maureen was now leaning forwards in her seat to see what was holding up the two men, and before Alice had time to warn her friend off saying anything else inappropriate, Jamal was clambering into the minibus to join them, with Max close on his heels.

'All set?' Max asked, as he slid the door shut behind him, his gaze roaming across them before settling on Alice.

She looked at the creases around his eyes that hinted at humour, the new grade of stubble decorating his jaw and the wide, generous mouth, and felt her tension start to ease.

'Ready as I'll ever be,' she told him.

The compulsion to stare at the back of Max's head as they drove along was a strong one, but Alice forced herself to look through the window instead, towards where the colourful and cluttered Sri Lankan landscape was unfolding beyond the glass. It was nearing eight a.m., but every shop they passed seemed not only to be open, but also bustling with people. While it was far less chaotic here in Habarana than it had been down in Colombo, tuk-tuks still hurtled haphazardly in and out of the path of buses and cars, narrowly missing motorbikes piled to dangerous levels with passengers. Alice grinned in surprised delight as she saw an entire family clinging to each other on one – the father steering, his wife sitting pillion, two young girls behind her and a small boy propped up by the handlebars, the top of his dark head tucked under his dad's chin.

The roar of traffic mingled with the music coming from the tuk-tuks, each one decorated in a different style. Alice saw lurid pink canopies, golden tassels, painted fire stripes and lime-green quilted seats. The drivers were mostly rake-thin and clad in torn jeans, bright-coloured polo shirts and tatty flip-flops. While there was a lot of noise, shouting and blaring horns, it was all friendly in tone and manner, and after a few miles, Alice stopped cringing every time a bicycle veered too close, or a stray dog strolled out into the road in front of them.

Jamal was chatting away happily to Steph, who had leaned forward in her seat so she could hear him over the din, her chin resting on her hands, which were right next to his shoulder. They seemed so at ease, the two of them, more like friends who had known each other for years than strangers who had only met the previous day. There was something very open and approachable about Jamal, though. He seemed kind and so comfortable in his own skin – there was nothing fake or contrived about him. Steph deserved to meet someone like that, a man with a positive spirit rather than a nagging bore who would drag her down. She had been out with men like that in the past, her wonderful patience always persuading her to put up with more nonsense than she strictly should, and both Alice and Maureen were forever urging her to go for the sweet guys, rather than the lads.

The minibus had left the main road now and was heading down a narrow lane edged with vast trees. Alice had not expected Sri Lanka to be as green as this, or as lush, and she savoured the sweet, moist air as it cascaded in through the open windows. Max had propped his elbow up on the inner handle of the door, his fingers splayed to let the wind rush over them and his head resting back against the seat. His hair didn't have any product in it today, and several strands were sticking straight up on his crown.

She replayed the conversation they had exchanged the previous night, picking over the words in search of any clues that he might have scattered in about his injury. Alice never had to draw attention to her own scar or drop hints to people she had just met, because it was right there for the world to see. She had long ago grown accustomed to the lingering looks, the raised eyebrows of enquiry, the expressions of pity, intrigue and fascination. She wondered now if Max was used to them too, or if his prosthetic limb was a relatively new addition to his life.

Perhaps this was the reason why she felt inexplicably drawn to him – maybe a part of her had subconsciously recognised a kindred spirit. She had never met anyone with a scar as big or as prominent as her own, but Max's injury made hers feel like a splinter in comparison. She thought back to her teenage years, to the tears of frustration she had wept as she tried in vain to disguise the legacy left behind by her old self – that reckless, out-of-control child whom Alice had despised for so long. Now her histrionics felt utterly absurd. What she had been through was nothing compared to Max, yet here he was – chipper and healthy and bursting with infectious humour and energy. It was inspiring.

## 11

Sigiriya Rock loomed over the surrounding landscape like the lost child of a mountain range, out of place and sync with its setting, but all the more impressive as a result. At its top was what remained of an ancient fortress, once undoubtedly resplendent, but now a collection of crumbled foundations, worn stairways and dry earth. Foreign visitors and locals alike still made their way up the two hundred metres of rough-cut steps, ladders and walkways in their thousands, though, because the view from the peak was said to be one of the best in the world.

As Alice gazed up at the summit from the path hundreds of feet below, she already felt humble just to be there. Her guidebook estimated the original build happened between AD 477 and 485, which Alice found unfathomable. It was rare to be this close to a structure so imbued with history, and despite the furious heat of the day, she shivered as she thought about the things that must have happened here, and the tales hidden amongst the cracks in the weathered stone. Whispers of love and fear and death, her whole lifetime a mere pinprick in the fabric of this place and its past.

'Big old girl, isn't she?'

Alice turned to find Max right beside her, his eyes focused on the top of Sigiriya Rock.

'Oh, I dunno,' she looked sideways at him. 'It's no Adam's Peak.'

'True.' Max looked down at his shoes, then at Alice, as if daring her to point out the obvious – that climbing a mountain wasn't easy for the able-bodied, let alone him. But if so, he was wrong, because Alice wasn't thinking that at all; she was merely glowing with the anticipation of what lay ahead.

'Steph's still on the fence about tackling Adam's Peak,' she told him. 'I haven't managed to talk her into it yet.'

Max gestured ahead to where Jamal was walking between Steph and Maureen, a casual arm thrown over each of their shoulders.

'Leave it to Jamal,' he said, moving to follow them. 'He can be very persuasive, I assure you.'

They walked along in companionable silence for a while, Alice watching the strange red dust settle over her brand-new boots and Max ignoring the stares directed his way by the other groups of tourists they passed. To reach the bottom of the Rock, they had to first make their way through the Royal Gardens – a patchwork quilt made up from squares of well-tended lawn, water features and the rustic shells of once-grand pavilions.

'Bloody hell!' exclaimed Alice, pointing up to where a bright-yellow triangular sign warned of wasp attacks.

'"Keep still and silent",' Max read out. 'Fat chance of that if you're being stung half to death.'

A little way further, another, larger sign featuring an image of a man being chased by insects informed them: 'Noise may provoke hornet attacks.'

'Thank God I left my trombone at home,' murmured Max, and Alice giggled.

'You don't really play the trombone, do you?' she asked, trying but failing to picture it.

Max stopped and grinned at her wickedly.

'No – but who's to say I won't start? I reckon I'd be great at it.'

'I'm sure you would,' Alice agreed, humouring him. 'But if you really want to stir up a hornet's nest, I suggest the tuba.'

'Or the didgeridoo?' Max replied.

'Best name for an instrument ever,' Alice said, laughing.

Max raised an eyebrow. 'I always liked the organ, myself. A nice, big organ.'

'Now, now,' she chided in amusement.

There was a short moment of awkwardness when they reached the first set of steps, and Alice hesitated, waiting to see if Max would require any assistance.

'It's OK,' he assured her, bounding up them at speed, before turning back to face her. 'Steps I can do – just don't ask me to cartwheel, for God's sake. I could never do those, not even when I still had both my legs.'

'Cartwheels are easy!' Alice insisted, her foot already on the next set of steps. 'I bet I could teach you.'

'You're on!' Max hurried after her. 'But if anything happens to Mister Tee here, you'll have to piggyback me right to the top of Adam's Peak.'

'Mister Tee?' Alice queried.

'My leg,' he said, bending over and tapping it with

affection. 'The main man. Tee is short for Teetotal – the opposite of legless, you see?'

She pulled a face.

'That's awful!'

Max laughed easily. 'Humour is the best medicine,' he told her. 'Even if it is really terrible and teeth-itchingly bad humour, like mine.'

It occurred to Alice then, as she looked up at him, that there hadn't been nearly enough humour in her own life recently. When was the last time she and Richard had laughed at something together until their sides hurt and tears ran down their cheeks? She could remember doing a lot of that in the early days of their relationship, but along the way they had grown up, and become too serious around each other. Max was absolutely right, though – laughter was the best medicine. Nobody had been laughing in the aftermath of her accident, but Max had clearly found a way to joke about his own. It was a testament to who he was as a person, and convinced her of the presumption she had already made – that her pity was not something he wanted. He probably didn't want sorrow from anyone at all – but her heart still ached a bit for him then, for his loss and what he must have had to overcome.

Max, who was still looking at her, seemed to sense what she was feeling, because he dropped his eyes and turned away.

'Come on,' he said, snapping her out of her melancholy train of thought. 'If Jamal beats us to the top, I'll never hear the end of it.'

Alice led the way towards the next part of the ascent,

which was an extremely rickety spiral staircase. Max was much slower on these wobbly, narrow steps than he had been on the wider, stone ones, and Alice kept pausing to wait for him. She didn't want him to think that she was being patronising by doing so, but she also hated the idea of leaving him behind. When they finally reached the top and caught up with the others, Maureen rushed straight over to greet them.

'There you are!' she exclaimed, her cheeks pink. 'You'll never guess what we've found – come and see.'

'I hope it's not a hornet's nest,' muttered Max to Alice, causing her to snort with laughter which a few seconds later turned into a cry of delight, because there, sitting nonchalantly on the top of a wall just ahead of them, was a monkey.

'Oh, look at his little face,' Alice said, gazing at the creature in awe. The monkey was light brown all over save for its white stomach, and it had a long tail, narrow pink face and black, almond-shaped eyes. In one of its tiny, knobbly hands it clutched a half-eaten corn on the cob, while the other rested on the wall.

A crowd of overexcited tourists were aiming their cameras at the monkey, but it didn't seem in the least bit bothered. If anything, Alice thought, it looked rather bored by the whole charade.

She had never seen a monkey like this before except for in a zoo, and it was so wonderful to see the little mammal out in the wild, knowing that it had chosen to climb up here and hang out with them all. Of course, monkeys like food, and tourists must presumably equal lots of the stuff, but even knowing that didn't take the sheen off how it felt to be here in front of it. Alice pulled her phone from the back pocket of her shorts and took a tentative photo, doing her best to get as much of the amazing view in the picture as possible.

Jamal, who was far less cautious, walked boldly over to where the little creature was perched and attempted to get a selfie with it, only for the monkey to scowl at him and scamper off out of reach.

'Must be female,' he joked, staring after it sadly.

'Oh, stop fishing for compliments, you,' replied Maureen, and Max gave her a small cheer. A few of the assembled tourists had stopped taking photos of the monkey and were gawping at Max's prosthetic leg instead. They could at least try not to be so obvious, thought Alice crossly, stepping forward so that she was between the curious eyes and Max.

'Excuse me,' she said to the nearest woman in the group. 'Can you take a photo of me and my friends, please?'

The woman nodded, and Alice passed over her phone before calling out to the others to bundle together by the wall. The monkey had scarpered now, leaving its part-chewed sweetcorn in the dirt.

Jamal threw his arms around Alice and Steph, pulling them both against his chest, which left Maureen free to drape herself across Max. As he then wrapped his arm around her waist, his fingers brushed Alice's ribcage, and she was aware of a creeping heat spreading out from below his hand.

By the time the five of them had done the obligatory

cry of 'cheese' and Alice had taken back her phone, Maureen had laced her arm through Max's and was walking away with him towards the next set of steps. Alice's first thought was to hurry after them, but Steph appeared at her side before she had time to move.

'Will you walk with me?' she asked. 'I feel like I've barely spoken to you since we landed.'

There was an odd expression on her face that Alice could not quite read, but which felt loaded all the same. Was her friend concerned that she was spending one-on-one time with Max? Steph should know her better than that. After all, she was the first person Alice would call when she and Richard really did set the date. She had been there through all the ups and downs of Alice's relationship, had seen her grow up into someone reliable and stable, a girl who no longer took risks. Steph knew her better than anyone.

As they continued their climb, idle chatter filling the well of unspoken tension that Alice could sense had opened between them, she thought about that fact.

If Steph had cause to feel uneasy, should Alice be worried, too?

## I 2

# Max

*If I should die,*
*Wash off the dust,*
*Clean away blood*
*The colour of rust . . .*

Max found Alice sitting on a low stone wall on the west side of Sigiriya's summit, her legs dangling over the edge and a faraway look on her face. He remembered what Steph had said the previous evening about her nickname being Alice in Wonderland, and smiled to himself. The others were messing around taking silly photos up at the highest point, the girls shrieking when Jamal pretended to give chase. Maureen had insisted on having her picture taken with just Max, holding her phone at arm's length and telling him to smile. Not that she needed to. It was hard not to smile around Maureen – she was fun and feisty and full of wonderful energy, not to mention beautiful, and once upon a time Max would have flirted right back just as enthusiastically.

'Room for a Mister and his Mister?' he asked, noticing how Alice's face lit up when she saw him.

'Of course.' She patted the wall next to her and Max sat

down, using his hands to steady himself and being extra careful not to bang into her with his prosthetic leg.

'The view up here is quite something, isn't it?' he ventured, following her gaze out towards the horizon. Mountains were visible in the far distance, as well as hundreds of acres of lush vegetation, forests and a vast, light-dappled lake. A swell of low clouds sat like cappuccino foam just above it.

'You can see why King Kassapa chose it,' Alice said, gesturing to her open guidebook. 'Apparently he murdered his own father to take the crown, then built a palace all the way up here so he could hide from those seeking retribution.'

'You would definitely see them coming – it's a great vantage point,' said Max, rubbing the top of his right thigh with both his hands. The final climb up here had been quite tough going, and the scorching heat of the day was causing moisture to collect around his stump. What he should really do was take off his prosthesis and wash his residual limb with what was left in his bottle of water, but he didn't want to make Alice feel uncomfortable. She was undoubtedly a cool girl, he was convinced about that, but he had also witnessed even his closest friends and some members of his own family avert their eyes whenever Mister Tee came off. The staring didn't bother Max so much as the trying not to stare. 'Have a good old gawp,' he often told people. 'Get it out of your system.'

'Don't you want to know?' he asked Alice then, his thoughts tumbling from his mind and out through his mouth before he was fully aware of what he was thinking.

She turned to him, not immediately understanding the question. The sun had brought out a scatter of freckles across her nose and cheeks, and her top lip was dappled with droplets of sweat. At least it wasn't just him suffering in this heat.

'Know what?' she asked, banging her heels against the wall. There was something of the naughty child about Alice, Max decided. Perhaps that was another reason why he had taken to her – it was the rebel in him recognising a fellow comrade.

'What happened to this,' he replied, pointing down at where the bottom half of his right leg had once been. It had been almost eight years now since Max had lost it, but he was still occasionally surprised to look down and see it gone, even now. That was normal, though, he'd been assured. His central nervous system would still be playing catch-up for some time yet.

'I didn't want to . . . I mean, I don't need to . . .' Alice stopped, her features contorting.

'It's OK.' Max touched her arm briefly. 'I'm happy to tell you. Only if you want to know, that is?'

'I do if you want to tell me,' she replied. 'But don't feel you have to. It's really none of my business. I mean. Oh, you know what I mean.'

Max smiled, trying to reassure her with his eyes. A bright-blue bird with vibrant red plumage on its front landed on the ground a few feet away from them and cocked its head, as if waiting for him to continue.

'Well, this fella definitely wants to know,' Max said lightly, and Alice made a small noise of amusement. Max knew he was doing exactly what he hadn't wanted to do and making her feel uneasy, but he was here now. And anyway, he wanted her to know the truth. He wanted to share something with her, and it had been a long time since he'd had such a compulsion.

'It happened back in May 2009,' he began. 'I'd not long celebrated my twenty-fifth birthday. Well, as much as you celebrate anything when you're stuck out in a conflict zone.'

'You were in the army?' Alice asked, looking almost fearful, her blue eyes wide despite the glare of the sun. Max guessed that she must already have gone over all the possible reasons for his lack of a lower limb, and that the one he was about to tell her would have been the most horrific she'd come up with. People tended to opt for a car crash first, as if that was somehow an easier idea to grasp than the far more violent reality.

'I was, yes,' he told her. 'For a long time. Since I was eighteen, in fact. When all my mates went off to uni, I followed my big brother into the Welsh Gunners.'

'But you're not Welsh,' Alice pointed out, flushing when he laughed at her.

'You don't have to be Welsh to join,' he said. 'That's just a nickname the regiment had; we were part of the Royal Artillery.'

Alice nodded. 'Guns,' she said simply.

'There were lots of guns,' he agreed. 'Not that they made a difference in my case. The only thing that can arm you against an enemy buried under the ground is luck, and unfortunately for me and a few of my crew, luck wasn't in great supply the day we happened to drive down that stretch of road in Afghanistan.'

Alice had gone pale, and Max could see the hair standing up on her bare arms despite the heat. She didn't say anything, just waited for him to continue telling his story. He was trying to keep his tone as light as possible, but it was hard when he got to this part of the tale, it always was. For so many months, Max had been unable to even think about what happened, let alone articulate it, but as time passed, and he got the help he needed to accept it and move forwards, the words became less frightening. It wasn't talking about it that could hurt him, he had learned that, but he was still afraid of the unexpected triggers that could send him right back there. He knew it was only ever a matter of time before one caught up with him.

'It was an IED,' he said matter-of-factly, his voice calm in spite of the ugly tableau he could now see in his mind. 'That's an improvised explosive device, just in case you didn't know.'

Alice nodded again; her shoulders looked tense. There was a light breeze up here on the summit, and strands of her hair were being blown gently across her forehead. Max resisted a strong urge to reach across and tuck them behind her ear.

'We were in a convoy, me and three other guys in the Wolfhound – that's a big truck – transporting some ammo and kit, and we drove right over the bloody thing.'

He was close enough to Alice to feel her shudder.

'Made a right old noise and a right bloody mess, as you can imagine,' he went on, coughing to clear his throat. It was always the same when he told this story – his mouth would feel as if it was somehow full of the strange, thin dust that coated everything in that dismal place, and made its way into every crevice, nook and hole, filling up empty boots and destroying cameras, phones and portable radios. Max would often wake from one of his nightmares with the taste of it in his mouth – it was the flavour of death.

'It was a fairly sizeable bomb,' he went on, watching the clouds shift and billow above the lake. 'Parts of the Wolfhound came apart in the blast and there were bits of it embedded in my right foot and ankle. A flesh wound, the medic called it, but that basically translated into an injured leg that was too damaged to save. The docs did their best, but they had nothing viable left to work with.'

'I'm so sorry.' Alice looked as if she might cry, and Max was compelled to pull her against him in a comforting half-hug.

'Oh, don't be,' he said into her hair. 'I got off lightly. The two lads in the front cab didn't make it – and the other one still can't hear right. Like I said, a bloody mess.'

They sat there in silence for a few moments, Max soothed by the rhythmic pattern of Alice's beating heart, which he could feel through the arm that he'd wrapped around her. After the bomb had gone off in Afghanistan and the terrible, high-pitched screaming of his fallen comrades had ceased, Max had tried to focus on the beating of his own heart. Lying there amongst the mangled remains of the armoured truck, he'd known from his training that he must try to apply a tourniquet to his leg – or what was left of it – and he could remember reaching up towards his chest and the pocket where it would be, only to find that his hand was red and dripping. His fingers wouldn't do what he told them and the pain was too much. It was too difficult to be in the present, to manage that moment and pull a coherent thought out of pure feeling, and so he retreated inside himself to where his heart beat on like a clock – one-two, one-two, one-two – and stayed there, hidden, until everything went black.

He must have drifted off momentarily into his memories, because the next thing Max was aware of was Alice moving gently out of his embrace.

'I can't imagine how frightening that must have been,' she said, her eyes searching his. It was strange, Max thought, how unguarded he felt with this girl. He sensed that she was letting her guard down with him a bit now, too. She no longer looked uncomfortable, as she had when he'd started telling his morbid story. Her shoulders had dropped, and her expression was open. She was sorry for him, yes, but there was more there than mere pity or even misguided admiration – there was understanding.

'I thought that coming here to Sri Lanka was a scary thing to do,' she admitted, looking away from him as the blue-and-red bird in front of them shook out its feathers and took flight once again. 'To tell you the truth, I get scared all the time these days. It's ridiculous, really – you should have seen me as a child. I was a right nightmare.'

'Oh?' Max prompted quietly, pleased that his assumption about her had been correct.

'I used to get myself into all sorts of scrapes,' she told him.

71

'Even before I could walk, I would crawl so fast that my mum would lose sight of me in moments. I almost drowned when I was two, because I ran into the sea and didn't stop.'

Max laughed at that. 'You nutter!'

'I was,' Alice agreed, but Max noted that she didn't seem amused. 'I guess I thought I was invincible. I managed not to damage myself too often, so I had little incentive to stop.'

'Why did you?' he asked, his eyes flickering over the old injury on her face. It was neatly healed, but certainly noticeable, and he could tell that it must have been quite severe when it first happened.

Alice fingered her scar and stared straight ahead.

'I got injured,' she said simply, her tone sheepish. 'My parents' house has a flat ledge on the roof, and I used to climb out of my bedroom window to reach it. It drove my mum mad – the few times she caught me in the act, she would scream and yell at me to come down, threaten to ground me until my sixteenth birthday, that sort of thing. But I still didn't stop. I refused to listen to her. And I must have done it a hundred times, but this time it had been raining and I lost my footing.'

'Shit,' Max said, drawing air through his teeth in a wince.

Alice turned to him. 'The greenhouse broke my fall,' she told him, gesturing once again towards her face. 'Thirty-odd stitches and two skin grafts.'

'How old were you?' Max wanted to know.

'Ten,' she said. 'Right at that age when you start to care about your appearance, so not the best timing.'

'I bet you were straight back up on that ledge, though, right?' Max joked, and was surprised when Alice shook her head.

'God, no. My mum would have locked me up. After it happened, she barely let me and my older brother out of her sight. Poor Freddie – he went from having complete freedom to a strict curfew overnight, and he hadn't done anything wrong. My mum was so traumatised by what had happened to me, she made me swear on her life that I would never do anything stupid and reckless again, and I haven't – well . . .' She stopped, glancing over her shoulder as if to check that nobody else would hear her. 'What I mean is, I am far more cautious these days.'

'Well, you made it up here OK,' Max told her. 'You weren't scared on the rickety stairs, were you? Because I was.'

'No.' She smiled briefly. 'I don't feel at all scared here, but I do feel . . . different.'

She wrinkled up her nose as if confused by her own words. 'I don't mean that in a bad way. Sorry, I'm not making much sense, am I?'

'Not much,' Max replied, a smile playing around his lips. 'But it doesn't matter. You've got two more weeks to figure it out.'

She nodded, taking in a deep breath through her nose and looking down at their feet, side by side, the metal joint where Max's ankle used to be glinting in the mid-morning sun. He realised for the first time that she was wearing the same walking shoes as him, albeit far smaller and much cleaner. He liked sitting here with her; he liked the way she made him feel like himself. Not the Max who joined the army and got himself blown up, not the Max who was a burden to his family, but the real him, the one that barely anyone knew.

'We should find the others,' Alice said. 'Do you think they'll be wondering where we are?'

Just as she said it, Jamal appeared behind them, and Max noticed the look of relief cross his friend's face. It didn't matter how many years had passed since they first met that day at Headley Court, Jamal still felt the need to look out for him. And, as much as Max hated the fact that he was more vulnerable since his injury, he liked the security of having Jamal with him on this trip. He was one of the few people in Max's life who truly understood what he was going through, and he knew how best to deal with him. Friends and family tried, but they didn't really understand – how could they?

Alice was already on her feet and Max clambered up awkwardly after her, flinching slightly as his stump moved inside the socket. Jamal and Alice reached for him instinctively as he stumbled, their hands grasping him as he righted himself.

'Cheers, guys.'

Was it his imagination, or did Alice look almost sad to be letting go of his hand? As he watched her walk ahead to join her friends, he realised that a very big part of him hoped that she was.

## 13

The phone call came through not long after the minibus had dropped Jamal and Max back at the homestay. The cheerful driver had waited while Alice, Steph and Maureen quickly got changed, and they were now on their way to the cave temples in nearby Dambulla, leaving their new friends behind to locate some lunch. Food, on this occasion, had won the argument against further sightseeing.

'Hey,' Alice said as she answered, before adding, 'It's Rich,' to the other two.

Steph settled for waving, but Maureen leaned across until her mouth was next to the handset and trilled, 'Hi, Dickie!'

Alice heard her boyfriend sigh. 'Can you tell Maureen that Dickie is *not* my nickname? Never has been, never will be.'

'I think she already knows,' chuckled Alice, turning her back on her laughing friend. Maureen had never been able to help herself when it came to winding Richard up. She found his serious side endlessly entertaining, and liked to see how far she could push his boundaries. Not far at all, as it turned out.

'Tell her she owes me a pint to make up for it,' Richard added. Alice could hear a blender whirring in the background and guessed that he had called her while making one of his famous breakfast smoothies – one banana, three strawberries, a handful of spinach, one large spoonful of natural yoghurt and half a cup of oats. Then, if he was feeling extra adventurous, a dollop of honey, too.

'What have you been up to?' she asked, then listened politely as Richard relayed a story about a school trip he'd taken his students on the previous day.

'Caught a load of the kids smoking behind the museum,' he grumbled. 'Anyone would think they want to rot their lungs and end up prematurely impotent.'

'They're probably just doing it to look cool,' Alice said, and Richard grunted in disgust.

'Anyway,' he said finally, switching off the blender. 'What's it like over there? Have you been riding elephants? Oh, you haven't drunk any of the tap water, have you?'

Alice laughed. 'Of course not – who do you think I am?'

'I just worry,' he replied. 'It's my job to worry.'

Alice was about to reply, when it occurred to her that she never worried about Richard. Not ever. He just wasn't the type of person to get himself into trouble, so she had never had cause to feel concerned. Was she a terrible girlfriend? Rich was always saying that he worried about her – it must be exhausting.

'You don't need to worry about us,' she assured him, and saw Steph and Maureen exchange a glance. The minibus had come to a stop on the dusty road and was indicating to turn into a ramshackle car park.

'I think we're here,' Maureen said loudly, and Alice cringed into the phone.

'You girls sound busy,' Richard stated, doing his best to appear nonchalant but failing hopelessly. Alice's heart went out to him – he always had been a terrible actor.

'Listen, Rich,' she said. 'Let me call you back later when we're not on the move, and I'll tell you all about the monkey we saw today.'

'Were you looking in a mirror at the time?' he joked.

'Ha ha.' Alice couldn't quite bring herself to really laugh. 'Very clever. Now get to work – catch some more kids smoking. Put them all in detention. I'll talk to you later. Yes, you too. Bye.'

Maureen was still laughing at her 'Dickie' comment five minutes later, as they made their way up the steps towards the cave temples. Because it was a religious site, bare skin (other than faces, hands and feet) was prohibited inside the most sacred areas, and Alice was glad she'd packed a pair of lightweight trousers. Maureen and Steph, however, had been forced to wrap their beach sarongs around their middles, and both were now waddling through the open courtyard in front of the Buddhist Museum like awkward geishas.

High above them, a vast, golden statue of Buddha sat cross-legged on the roof, a stern and noble expression on his face and a tiny monkey scampering across one of his shoulders. Alice lifted up her large, expensive camera to capture an image. It still didn't feel real that she was here, in Sri Lanka, surrounded by all this incredible history, nature, and colour. She didn't know whether it was something to do with the perpetual sunshine, but the country seemed to virtually vibrate with the very brightest and

77

boldest hues from the spectrum. Yellows didn't just shine, they throbbed; reds weren't just powerful, they were passionate; and the endless blue of the sky above Alice's head hummed with an infinite beauty.

They had only been in Sri Lanka for a couple of days, but Alice already knew that she was storing memories she would revisit time and again, not just for their aesthetic value, but also because of the associated emotions. As she had admitted to Max on the summit of Sigiriya Rock earlier that day, being in Sri Lanka was making her feel different, in the best possible way. It was as if she'd been asleep inside herself for a very long time, and now she was waking up. Of course, Max probably thought she'd been babbling a load of old nonsense, but it had still felt nice to tell someone how she was feeling. Sri Lanka was too special to keep to yourself, she thought. The very nature of the place and its people seemed to Alice to be about openness, kindness and good humour.

'Wow, look at this ugly little fella,' exclaimed Maureen, coming to a stop at the base of a long flight of stone steps.

Alice blinked and looked away from the wise eyes of the golden Buddha and into the far less enigmatic face of a scrawny monkey. It was crouched on the bottom step, clutching a small banana and glaring at them with open malice.

'It looks like Donald Trump,' she said, causing Steph and Maureen to shriek with mirth.

'Oh my God – it really does!' Steph laughed, bending down to take a photo. 'It's got the same weird flat hair and everything.'

'Poor Trump-key,' Maureen lamented, peering up the hillside. 'And poor us, having more bloody stairs to climb.'

'Think of your glutes,' Steph told her, stepping warily past the grumpy monkey. 'You'll have buns of steel by the time we get back to Suffolk.'

The heat of the afternoon pressed down on them as they made their steady way up towards the caves, stopping every few yards to take photos of yet more monkeys in all shapes and sizes. Alice was enchanted to spot a mother with a tiny baby clinging to her front high up in one of the trees, its dark eyes shining with mischief and its soft hair a fluffy halo around her head. She marvelled at how quickly you could become accustomed to new things, realising that she felt quite happily at home amidst this platoon of monkeys.

It took them around twenty minutes to reach the very top of the steps, where the entrance to the cave temples was marked by a series of cluttered wooden shoe racks. Alice, who had a bag with her, slipped off her flip-flops and stowed them, while Steph and Maureen shoved their sandals on a middle shelf. The air felt fresher up here, the marble covering the ground pleasantly cool despite the heat, and Alice flicked through her guidebook to find out how long ago it had been laid.

Once inside the caves, they could smell the past. It was the same musty scent that Alice associated with churches and museums, as if the very particles in the air were steeped in the remnants of years gone by. Inside the first cave was an enormous statue of a reclining Buddha, which the sign informed them was fourteen feet in length and carved from solid rock. Walking down its length, they found themselves dwarfed by two huge feet, the soles of which had been decorated with colourful swirls.

'Reminds me of the Spirograph I had as a kid,' Steph said, coming to a halt beside Alice. 'Back in the days before computer games were a thing.'

'Urgh,' Alice groaned. 'Bloody computer games. I swear Richard has an addiction to *Call of Duty*.'

'You know who would be great at *Call of Duty*,' Maureen said. 'Max.'

'I guess he probably would,' Alice agreed, feigning nonchalance.

'Did he tell you?' Maureen asked.

'You mean about his leg?' Alice guessed, and Maureen nodded.

'He did, yes. It happened in Afghanistan eight years ago – a roadside bomb.'

'Bloody hell,' breathed Steph. 'The poor thing.'

Alice unscrewed the bottle of water she was carrying and took a sip. 'I know.'

Maureen was looking thoughtful.

'I think I still would. You know, with Max,' she said. 'At first it freaked me out a bit, the idea of it, but he's so fit.'

Alice stared at the patterned feet of the reclining Buddha, unsure of how to respond.

'Did you find out if he was single?' Maureen went on.

'No,' said Alice mildly, shaking her head. 'But he didn't mention a girlfriend to me, and he's not wearing a wedding ring. That doesn't mean he's not spoken for, though.'

'It must be hard,' Steph said. 'I mean, he's obviously

been through a lot. Dating is probably the last thing on his mind.'

'Pah!' Maureen laughed. 'He's still a man, and all men are lusty monsters deep down.'

Alice hated how clichéd they were all being, standing here like a flock of gossipy old hens and proclaiming that all men were the same, motivated by pure libido. Max didn't strike her as a man desperate to pull anything that looked in his direction; he was far less of a lad than Maureen was giving him credit for. Then again, Alice thought guiltily, she had rather been hogging him all morning. Perhaps if Maureen spent some more time with Max, then she, too, would notice the subtleties.

'I can find out from Jamal, if you like,' Steph offered, blushing prettily as she mentioned his name. 'But I can't promise he won't blab about it to Max.'

'I don't mind if he does,' Maureen said dreamily. 'I always find it's best to be upfront when you fancy a man – especially when time is of the essence.'

'Come on,' Alice told them, firmly changing the subject. 'No more man talk, if you please. There are one hundred and fifty-three statues of Buddha in these caves, and we've only seen one.'

Before Steph and Maureen could reply, she had headed past them and back outside into the sunshine.

# 14

# Max

*If I should die,*
*Don't say I was brave,*
*Duty was my armour,*
*And life was all I gave*

Max woke to the sound of his phone vibrating. Rubbing his eyes, he picked it up and squinted at the message on the screen. It was from his brother, Anthony, no doubt some terrible round-Robin joke that he'd picked up from the lads. Ant was not long back from leading a training exercise over in Gibraltar, and he always returned home with a full arsenal of dreadful humour after spending time with the young recruits.

Pressing his finger to the button, Max was pleasantly surprised to find instead a photo of Ant, his wife Tina and their five-year-old daughter Poppy, all beaming with joy at the apparent newest addition to their family – a floppy-eared springer spaniel puppy.

I finally gave in, said the accompanying message, and Max chuckled to himself. Ant Davis might be an army captain who could reduce a grown man to tears with a withering stare, but he was a total pushover when it came to the ladies in his life – both the older and the younger. Like Max, Ant also allowed himself to be bullied by the other woman in both their lives, too, because the next message that came through read:

Mum says, are you looking after yourself?

Ant had added an emoji of a monkey with its hands over its eyes, which was a standard choice. The fret levels of their mother were something he and Ant had joked about together since they were teenagers, and Max's injury had only exacerbated things. His mum would literally wrap him up in cotton wool if she could get away with it, and not a day had passed since he woke up in the hospital in Birmingham, his mum sobbing by his bed, when he didn't feel guilty for what he had put her through. Her need to check up on him and fuss around him had been one of the reasons that Max had been so determined to come to Sri Lanka – he needed to get away just as much as she needed a break from worrying about him.

Tell her my other leg's fallen off, he typed back, punctuating it with a laughing-face emoji. Then, noticing the time, added, Why the hell are you awake this late?

Bloody puppy doesn't sleep, Ant replied. I'm in the garden now, waiting for him to do his business and freezing my nads off in the process. You OK?

Max smiled as he pictured the scene. He loved going to his brother's place down in south-east London, with its long, chaotic garden and narrow Victorian hallways. Poppy was still young enough to be adorably frank with her uncle, and asked him endless questions about his leg.

When she was only three, Max had woken to find that she'd snuck into the spare room and stolen Mister Tee while he slept, dragging it off to her bedroom where she'd wrapped one of her mum's pashminas around it and renamed it Cynthia, before pretending to serve it tea along with the rest of her cuddly toys. Tina had been appalled and apologetic, but Max and Ant had laughed uproariously until tears ran down their cheeks.

He shuffled up on his elbows and arranged the pillow comfortably under his head, yawning widely as he sent a few more messages to Ant, assuring him that yes, he was fine, and that Sri Lanka was every bit as frenetic and beautiful as he'd hoped it would be. He almost added a final text about Alice, but decided against it. What would he say? That he had met a girl he liked and she had a boyfriend, but that didn't matter anyway because Max just wanted to be her friend? It sounded totally bizarre, and Ant would rib him about it for sure. His brother was all too aware of the issues that Max had when it came to relationships. It had taken him two years to get over the collapse of his marriage to Faye, and then another year had passed before he could face dating.

Max's main problem now seemed to be the type of girls he attracted. They were either morbidly curious about his leg and lost interest once they'd had a good look, or they were mothering types who saw him as some sort of injured puppy that must be mollycoddled. Max did not want a girlfriend who championed his missing limb or pitied him for losing it – he wanted to find a partner in crime, someone who would challenge him, make him laugh, tell him off if he complained too much and love him for the man he was. It was the simplest dream, but one that he was starting to think would never happen.

No, it was better that he focus on the real reason he'd come to Sri Lanka. This trip was never about meeting girls; it was supposed to be about Max proving something – to himself and to his family. Anything else would only muddy the waters. Yes, he had to admit that Alice was intriguing, and seemed to be neither overly curious nor cloyingly sympathetic – but she was spoken for, and Max respected that. He would not, and could not, be the reason that someone else's heart got broken. And that, he thought, lifting aside the sheet and reaching for his crutches, was simply that.

Once up, he made his way into the bathroom and carefully washed and dried his stump. The tall man who ran the place hadn't commented on Max's leg when he'd first shown him and Jamal to their room, but Max had been touched to discover that he'd moved a small plastic stool into the bathroom for him while they were eating dinner. It was far easier for Max to wash, shave and clean his teeth when he had something to sit on, even if he did pride himself on his ability to balance. It had been Jamal who insisted they bring the collapsible crutches with them on the trip, waving away Max's protestations that he didn't really need them.

There was no arguing with Jamal when it came to health – Max had learned that on his first day at Headley Court – and he reluctantly admired his physio friend for being so steadfast when it came to recovery. Jamal had seen Max at his lowest ebb, curled into himself on the floor having fallen yet again, howling tears of rage, pain and frustration, and he had taken it all in his faultlessly cheerful stride. 'I'll have you back up and running by Bonfire Night,' he had promised on that first June afternoon, his eyes meeting Max's as they both stood facing the large, wall-mounted mirror. Back then, it had felt like an impossibility, but Jamal hadn't been wrong. Max owed so much to his friend, and was so indebted, that on occasion he imagined that he could feel the sheer weight of it pressing down on him. He owed it to everyone who had patched him up and put him back together since that explosion to make the most of his future. Max was hungry for truth, for happiness and for an escape from the perpetual guilt that had spread like a stain across his life – and this trip was a big step towards achieving those goals.

By the time he had finished getting ready, Jamal was showered and dressed, too, his normal buoyancy subdued somewhat by the seven or so bottles of Lion Lager he'd sunk the previous evening. The five of them had headed to a nearby restaurant, but barely made it in one piece. After stumbling along the dark road leading away from the cabins in search of tuk-tuks, they had found themselves face-to-face with a cow that had presumably escaped from a field. Maureen had shrieked in fright, Jamal had screamed even louder, and the cow had fled in alarm, almost knocking Steph and Alice into a ditch of putrid water as it stampeded past. Max, who was a few feet behind them all having stopped to consult his compass, got away unscathed, and had very much enjoyed taking the piss out of Jamal all through dinner for yelping like a woman.

'Ready to go and visit an ancient city?' Max asked his friend now, as they locked up the room behind them.

Jamal grinned. 'You know me, mate, always ready for anything.'

'Except cows,' put in Max, ducking to avoid Jamal's friendly punch. 'You're not going to start crying if we see any, are you?' he teased, hurrying away towards where the girls were already sitting, each of them staring in abject horror at the full plates of papaya on the table in front of them.

'Very funny,' Jamal responded, bending over to kiss Steph in greeting. The two of them had finally had a goodnight kiss the previous evening, and now seemed unable to put each other down. Max pretended to his mate that his slushiness was revolting, but in truth he thought Jamal and Steph were adorable together. It was nice to see both of them looking so happy.

'What's so funny?' Maureen wanted to know, and Max glanced over to where she was sitting, her endless legs on show as always, smiling up at him. Her hair was down today and snaking around her shoulders like a glossy curtain. Alice had her walking shoes on again, as well as denim shorts and an oversized T-shirt with a gangster panda printed on the front. Max liked her tomboyish style – it suited her. It was rare to meet a girl whose clothes you could imagine borrowing, as opposed to vice versa. When he and Faye had got together in their teens, she'd raided his wardrobe to such a degree that he'd been forced to rely on Ant's oversized hand-me-downs.

'Just reliving Jamal's manly encounter with the cow,'

Max told them, taking a seat and pushing his plate of papaya firmly to one side. 'I wish someone had filmed it.'

Jamal scoffed. 'Whatever, He-Man, your time will come. I hear there's some really big lizards down in the south.'

'You'll fit right in then,' chuckled Max, not missing a beat, as Jamal picked up a bread roll and aimed it at his head.

'Now, now!' Maur scolded. 'Stop messing around, and eat up all my papaya like good boys.'

Laughing, Max pretended to stick two fingers down his throat in mock horror, only for Maureen to respond by blowing him a leisurely kiss.

Rather than returning the gesture in kind, Max glanced quickly at Alice. She was looking in the opposite direction, towards where Jamal, the soppy git, was feeding pieces of banana to Steph, so she could not have seen anything. Max was aware of the rush of relief that washed over him, and he knew what it meant, too. It shouldn't matter that Alice saw him and Maureen flirting with each other, but it did. The realisation made him feel guilty, with its implication that he was developing feelings he shouldn't for this girl, who was very much spoken for. Or perhaps he was simply overthinking it all, he decided, easing himself gently off the metaphorical hook. It had been a very long time since he had met a girl who felt instantly like a friend, so that had confused his feelings. But a friend was all she ever could be.

# 15

The bus to Kandy was scheduled to leave at eleven a.m., and despite giving themselves over half an hour to make the ten-minute tuk-tuk journey from the homestay in Habarana to the nearest stop, Alice, Steph and Maureen still only just made it. Their departure was initially delayed by Steph and Jamal's private farewell, which took place in the boys' room and went on for far longer than was comfortable for anyone left waiting. It reminded Alice of her heady first days with Richard, when the two of them would hole up in the bedroom of his shared house at university for days at a time, only emerging to make rounds of toast or use the bathroom. It had felt to her then as if every second with him should be treasured, and she would panic at the thought of leaving him – even for the short time it took her to venture back to halls for a shower and a change of clothes. That feeling had long since worn off, and nowadays it seemed to Alice that they both actively sought time away from each other, Richard with his fishing and Alice on her long runs. Not that it worried her all that much – the relationship they had now was much healthier, and she appreciated Rich more this way.

When Steph finally emerged, red in the face and with her shirt buttoned up all wrong, Maureen then insisted on saving her number into Max and Jamal's phones, and vice versa, even though they had already arranged a meeting place in Kandy.

'Just in case,' she told them, although Alice knew that what she was really doing was making sure she could contact Max at her leisure. They would only be separated from the two men for one night, but Maureen must have a seduction strategy formulating in her mind. The polite distance Max had been maintaining would only act like a bunch of bananas might to a hungry monkey – Maureen wanted her feast, and she would do whatever it took to get it.

'Don't meet any other girls and forget us, will you?' Maur called out of the open side of the tuk-tuk as they wobbled away, and Alice did her best not to cringe.

The next thing that held them up was the tuk-tuk driver. As was customary, he began to barter with them as soon as they got to the main road, telling them with confidence that it was 'much better' to stay in his tuk-tuk all the way to Kandy, and that he would give them a 'special price'.

'No, thank you,' Alice repeated, smiling as she shook her head to emphasise the point. He may have only been asking for 3,000 rupees, which amounted to around fifteen pounds, but the bus would cost only 400 rupees for all three of them – less than two quid. Plus, Alice had assured the other girls, taking the bus would afford them so much more in the way of culture and experience. She wanted to sit amongst the Sri Lankan people, talk to them and hear them speak to one another. She had watched the overcrowded buses hurtle by in Colombo and yearned to be a passenger – it felt like a far more authentic thing to do than hire a driver.

'Sorry!' Alice yelled back at the still-pleading tuk-tuk driver, her rucksack in her arms because she hadn't had time to put it on her back. The bus was sitting idle by the kerb, and the young conductor, who was dangling out on one arm from the open back door, was beckoning to them to hurry up.

'Come on!' she urged Steph and Maureen, who were still dawdling by the tuk-tuk. 'We're going to miss it!'

At last, sensing that Alice was going to get on this bus with or without them, the two girls hurried down the road after her, exclaiming in surprise as the conductor leaped down and tossed their backpacks unceremoniously into the luggage area, where they landed with a thud on top of some giant sacks of vegetables. The three of them thundered up the steps, only to almost fall back down them seconds later as the bus shuddered into life and sped off down the road, barely pausing to wait for a gap in the steady flow of traffic.

'Bloody hell!' shouted Maureen, laughing as the other two fell against her. 'This is mental!'

Alice knew at once that they had made the right decision. The bus was old and rickety, with rows of worn seats upholstered in cracked red leather. Sri Lankan music blared out of speakers that were fixed all along the walls, and at the front, a large TV screen hung precariously right above the driver's head. There were decorations inside the bus – colourful strings of paper flowers and posters of Buddha, and the atmosphere was one of joy and frivolity.

Alice pulled the other two towards three empty seats right at the back, then rooted around in her daypack for some fare money.

'Thank you, ladies!' the conductor yelled over the music, and they watched as he sauntered off down the central aisle with an easy swagger.

'I love it!' Alice declared, beaming at her friends. 'Isn't it brilliant?'

Steph was waving at a small child sitting across from them, the little girl's dark eyes serious above her shyly smiling lips. Two long plaits of shiny black hair fell over her shoulders, and her fingers were tightly entwined with those of an older woman who was wearing a bright-orange sari.

'It's nuts, is what it is,' said Maureen, but Alice could see that she, too, was captivated by the spectrum of colour and noise that was exploding all around them.

'Come on, girls,' she added, leaning her head against Alice's shoulder. 'Photo!'

Alice thought of the inevitable Instagram post, and how happy Richard would be to see a nice photo featuring the three of them. She smiled widely, even throwing in a thumbs up for good measure. It was a good photo – they all looked happy and kissed by the sun, so different with their blonde, dark and light-brown hair, but so in tune and comfortable with each other that they could be sisters. Alice had often lamented not having a sister. She loved Freddie fiercely, but she wondered if another girl would have changed the dynamic at home. Would Alice have been less of a tomboy tearaway if she'd had a sensible elder sister, rather than a big, strapping brother? Alice had to conclude that she probably would have been. Freddie had never scared his parents to the same extent that Alice had, though, and so he had grown up less mollycoddled. While Alice's mum had been thrilled to welcome her back to Sudbury after university, saying at the time that she relished the opportunity to keep a close eye on her daughter, she had encouraged Freddie to move down to the capital. His ambition and drive undoubtedly came from the same place as Alice's reckless tendencies once had, but while Freddie's urges led him towards success and financial security, Alice's had landed her in hospital.

Fishing out her phone from her bag, Alice fired off a quick message to her brother, telling him that Sri Lanka was wonderful and that she would be sure to bring him back something made from elephant dung. She missed her smelly-footed, kind-hearted, mickey-taking plank of a sibling. Freddie worked too hard these days. Aside from their monthly lunches at the family home, Alice barely ever got to spend quality time with him, and their sporadic phone calls were not enough. When she got home, she would go and visit him, she decided.

'Messaging your brother?' Maureen asked, her voice raised so that Alice could hear her over the chaotic combination of bus radio, roaring engine and bursts of the horn, which the driver was leaning on with rather alarming regularity.

'Uh-huh,' Alice confirmed, amused that her friend had blatantly been snooping.

'Is he still as fit as ever?' Maureen had a familiar glint in her eye.

Alice pictured her brother, with his straight teeth, short, tidy hair and wide, welcoming green eyes. He'd grown a beard last year, but then wisely concluded that it looked bloody awful and shaved it off again.

'It is never not going to be weird that you fancy Freddie,' she informed Maureen. 'It's just . . . wrong.'

'Oh, but he is so far from being in any way wrong,' Maureen went on. 'And he's rich, too, right? The dream.'

'I'd ask you to stop making plans to seduce and then fleece my brother,' Alice scolded jokingly.

'Boo.' Maureen stuck out her tongue. 'You're no fun!'

'On the contrary,' Alice grinned. 'You should be thanking me for saving you from the stench of his feet. Seriously! That man could give Limburger a run for its cheesy money.'

'She's not joking,' Steph put in, fanning herself with a folded map. The bus had braked forcefully to pick up more passengers, and the heat when the air stopped flooding in through the open windows was intense. It was another beautiful day, and Alice luxuriated in the patch of sunlight that was shining across her seat. The temperature here really did make it hard to feel too stressed. At home, Alice found herself on edge constantly, her sleeping often erratic and her head buzzing with an anxiety that could only be tempered by diving off the highest board, or by running down dark, wooded pathways so fast that her lungs burned in protest. Here, in Sri Lanka, she felt as if all the warmth and joy had enveloped her in a comforting hug.

Steph was now telling Maureen a story about the first time she ever stayed at Alice's house, and how Freddie had insisted on sticking his putrid feet in her face while they were watching *The Nutty Professor*.

'I almost threw up my Butterkist,' she said earnestly, her blonde curls bouncing up and down as the bus barrelled along at speed. Steph's hair was a bit less like Doc Brown's in *Back to the Future* now, mused Alice – her friend must be acclimatising to the humidity at last.

'I'd wear a peg on my nose,' declared Maureen, refusing to be dissuaded.

'Just what every man wants to see on a girl while they're having sex with her,' Steph deadpanned.

'Oi!' Alice clapped her hands over her ears. 'Do not talk about sex and my brother in the same sentence, please!'

'Do you think Max is still able to . . . you know?' Maureen pondered, just as Alice removed her hands.

'Have sex?' said Steph. 'I don't see why not.'

'Well, we don't know how badly he was injured, do we?' Maureen went on.

Alice's good mood evaporated like rainwater off a hot road.

'I don't think it's any of our business,' she told them, folding her arms. 'He's not exactly going to tell a bunch of girls he's just met all his most personal information, is he?'

'That is a good point,' Maureen allowed, before adding slyly, 'I'll let you both know if I find out.'

'Maur!' Steph chastised. 'You can't just sleep with him out of curiosity.'

'That's not the reason I want to,' Maureen insisted. 'I know you both think I'm some sort of sex addict, but I think he's cool. It's been ages since I genuinely felt a connection with a guy as well as simply fancying them, and I really do like Max.'

Alice turned to the window and watched as a stray dog lolloped along the pavement, one of its paws held up as if it was hurt. A coconut stall sagged under the weight of its load, palm trees swayed in the wind, and the dust from underneath the bus wheels danced in the air in between them.

'I asked Jamal,' Steph said then, lowering her voice conspiratorially. 'You know, if Max was seeing anyone.'

'And?' Maureen was practically foaming at the mouth.

'And he's definitely single,' Steph told her with satisfaction.

'Good work, Stephie!' said Maureen. She was clearly delighted. 'I have caught Max looking at me a few times, you know. I thought I might have been imagining things, but maybe not – maybe he has been checking me out.'

'I'm sure he would have,' Alice said. 'He's only human, after all.'

She hadn't meant to sound quite so sarcastic, and Maureen turned to her at once, confusion narrowing her eyes.

'I thought you'd be pleased,' she said. 'Better Max than Freddie, right?'

What could she say to that? Alice tried to laugh Maureen's comment away, but her insides churned as she realised that the thought of Maureen and Max hooking up was actually far worse than the idea of her and Freddie – and the implications of that were far too much for Alice to process.

'I think you should go for it with Max if you reckon he's up for it,' she said, her mouth dry. 'I'll even put in a good word for you, if you like?'

'You will?' Maureen kissed her on her rigid jaw. 'I do love you, you know, Alice – even if you won't let me shag your brother.'

Alice shook her head in mock despair, deliberately avoiding both of her friends' eyes.

She was doing it again, she thought. She was making promises that she had absolutely no intention of keeping. Lying to Richard and her mum was bad enough, and now she was telling lies to her friends, too.

# 16

Despite heeding the warning in their guidebook about the Goods Shed bus station in Kandy being one of the busiest stop-offs in the entire country, Alice, Steph and Maureen were still shocked by the scene that greeted them as they arrived.

'This place is absolutely bonkers!' Steph exclaimed, almost stumbling over sideways at the bottom of the bus steps as a surge of people pummelled her out of the way in their haste to board.

Alice didn't answer, because she was too busy legging it round to the back of the bus to collect their rucksacks, all three of which had been tossed on to the tarmac almost as soon as the driver applied the brakes.

'Give me a hand,' she called out to the others, dragging two of the bags and kicking her own forwards with one foot. There didn't seem to be a designated area for disembarking, and they were in genuine danger of getting flattened by whichever bus was due to arrive next. All the people who had been on the journey with them had vanished, and Alice looked around in vain for a sign that would tell them which way to go. The air was thick with the smell of diesel and the heat was stifling, and all Alice could hear was car horns, shouting and engines being revved. She had thought the capital Colombo was busy, but Kandy was something else. She could barely think straight, but rather than feeling wary, she found that she was exhilarated by all the unfolding chaos.

'Yes, please,' she heard Maureen saying, and she turned to find a Sri Lankan man standing in front of them, a grin on his face and a bright-red polo shirt straining over his round belly. He was already holding Maureen's rucksack, and now reached his hand out towards Alice.

'I carry for you,' he offered, but she shook her head.

'I can manage, thank you.'

The man nodded, the wide smile never leaving his face, then took off at speed in the direction of a tall, concrete clock tower.

'He's our tuk-tuk driver,' Maureen explained helplessly, before hurrying off after him through the crowds and leaving Steph and Alice with no choice but to follow in close pursuit. They weaved in and out of groups of schoolchildren, jumped over dogs, sidestepped sacks of vegetables and rice, and narrowly avoided toppling over a stack of cages containing cramped, squawking chickens. A thick wave of tuk-tuk drivers parted to allow them through, each one shouting out a greeting of '*Ayubowan*' and a rival fare price as they passed.

It only took them five minutes to reach their designated three-wheeled taxi, but it was long enough in the intense afternoon heat for Alice to feel her back dampen with sweat. It was such a different heat here in Sri Lanka from what she was used to on the beaches of Spain or Greece – it felt almost as if someone had shut them inside a vast sauna and cranked the temperature dial around to the highest setting. Out of nowhere, her mind went to Max – how would he fare in amongst all this pushing and shoving? Since he had told her how he lost his leg, Max had become more vulnerable in her eyes, the reality of what he had been through something that she could not overlook, however much she guessed he would want her to. He was a man who had been broken, both physically and mentally, and Alice's feelings of concern were only natural. What kind of person would she be if she didn't feel empathy towards him, if she didn't want to protect him from further hurt? Anyone who met him would feel that way, surely?

A prominent vein popped up across the forehead of the tuk-tuk driver as he attempted to squash their three huge backpacks into the small space behind the seat, but instead of swearing with frustration, he seemed to find the whole scenario hilarious.

'Too many shoes!' he laughed, pointing with spooky accuracy at Maureen's bag. 'Ladies always have many, many shoes.'

'We can have one bag under our feet?' suggested Alice, stepping forwards before Maureen had a chance to lecture the driver on the importance of having a pair of kitten heels for every occasion. This seemed to please him, and a few minutes later they were off, wobbling through the seething throng of traffic, Alice, Steph and Maureen all with their knees up to their chins.

'You like music?' yelled the driver.

'YES!' they all chorused, and the next second their backs were vibrating with the bass coming from a massive speaker hidden in the panel behind the seat.

'No wonder there's no room for our bags,' shouted Steph, over what could only be described as banging drums and chanting. 'He's got an entire Dolby sound system rigged up in here.'

'I like it,' declared Maureen, punctuating her comment with a yelp as they almost collided with a motorbike. The young guy steering it bellowed something friendly-sounding at their driver, flashed two rows of teeth, and zoomed off ahead. Alice's eyes widened as she peered around the edge of the tuk-tuk's black awning and saw the hairy face of a goat staring back at her out of an open car window. *I love this crazy place*, she thought, happiness tugging up the corners of her mouth.

The centre of Kandy was a hive of activity, but once they'd negotiated their way through and were chugging noisily up a steep hill, the whole atmosphere transformed into one that was far more serene. As there was so much of Sri Lanka to cover on this trip, the three girls had agreed to split the task of booking their accommodation between them, and the choice for the next two nights had been made by Steph. Like Alice, she favoured homestays over hotels, and Alice was pleased to see that her friend had clearly done her research on Kandy. As soon as they pulled up in a cloud of dust outside the beautiful two-storey house that they would temporarily call home, she breathed an audible sigh of relief. It was totally worth the money they'd have to spend on tuk-tuk trips to be staying this far out of the city. Down there was mayhem, while up here it was tranquil.

Alice paid the driver as the others dragged out their

wedged-in backpacks, her buoyant mood leading her to give him a huge tip.

'Thank you, thank you,' he said gratefully, putting his hands together. It was refreshing the way men spoke to you here. There was never a hint of flirtation or sleaziness, just pure friendliness with a hint of mischief – especially when it came to bartering down a price. Alice had not expected to feel safer here than she did back home – specifically on her rare trips into London, where she had been pummelled into by short-tempered, disdainful men too many times to recall.

'Shall we?' she said to Maureen and Steph, as the tuktuk wobbled off down the hill. Shouldering their packs, the three girls pushed open the white wooden gate and stepped into an immaculate garden. Flowers of all colours and sizes burst out of neat beds, an idle sprinkler sat mute in the centre of a pristine lawn, and above them tree branches groaned with the weight of ripe coconuts. Even the heat felt less oppressive up here, the air somehow cleaner and alive with the rich fragrance of nature. Down in Kandy, you were more likely to inhale petrol fumes than floral scents, and now Alice took deep, hungry breaths as they made their way along a stepping-stone path towards the front door.

'Shoes,' Maureen said, pointing down to a discarded pair of men's sandals and some smaller, more delicate slip-ons. Alice, who was wearing trainers, knelt slowly to untie them, careful not to let the weight of her backpack cause her to keel over sideways. Before she had time to stand up again and knock, the door was flung open in front of them and an elderly Sri Lankan man held his hands out wide.

'Stephanie, Melissa and Alison,' he declared, stating rather than asking.

'Good enough,' Maureen replied with a grin.

'Ah, you are early,' the man said, clapping his hands. 'Come, my wife is here. She will make you some food. Are you hungry? Did you come from the train? How many days have you been in Sri Lanka?'

Alice could only open and close her mouth uselessly as he led them through an incredibly tidy lounge area, chattering away without waiting for them to reply. The smooth white tiles felt wonderfully cool beneath her bare toes, and she pushed her feet down against them as she would have in a yoga class, encouraging the pleasant sensation to spread into her lower limbs. She had always considered herself a fan of the sunshine, but even Alice had to admit that it became overwhelming here – especially when carrying a dead weight on your back.

'I am Chatura,' the man told them, pausing by the bottom of a flight of wooden stairs and beckoning for his wife to come out from behind a beaded curtain that concealed the kitchen from view. She was tiny and softly rounded, with grey hair pulled back into a low bun and large, conker-brown eyes.

'This is my Monisha,' her husband proclaimed proudly, looking at the diminutive woman as if she was the most beautiful thing he'd ever seen.

Monisha smiled shyly and waved, before backing away again and disappearing behind the beads.

'She likes to hide,' Chatura said happily, giggling as he started up the stairs. 'She is scaredy like a cat.'

He seemed to find this hilarious, and bellowed with laughter as he padded barefoot along a narrow corridor. There were three doors, which he opened in turn – the first led into a bedroom containing two bunk beds, one small single, and a dressing table; the second was the bathroom, which was large, square and basic, and the third opened out on to a long balcony.

'Oh, wow,' Alice breathed, leaning over Steph's shoulder so she could see the view.

'The best view in all of Sri Lanka,' Chatura told them solemnly, his hand clasping the metal railings that ran all the way along the balcony's outer edge. Below Alice could see the sprawl of flowers that decorated their host's back garden, and beyond that the landscape tapered away downhill in a heady mixture of greens, yellows and reds. In the far distance, on the other side of the city, vast hills loomed, while above them lay a scatter of dip-dyed clouds, half white, half grey, the sky around them a freshly laundered blue.

'The sunset here is very good,' Chatura informed them, clearly pleased by their matching expressions of awe. 'Come back here at six. I bring tea, we watch the sun setting.'

'That sounds lovely,' Steph replied, looking at Alice and Maureen, who agreed. It was only just two p.m. now, so they would still have a few free hours to explore.

Chatura left them alone to settle in, but not before explaining at length and in broken English how to work the shower, how important it was that they bolt the balcony door every night before going to bed, and where the bottles of complimentary water were stored. Alice took it all in with a smile, then clambered on to the bottom bunk while Maureen headed for a quick freshen up and Steph popped outside to take photos in the garden. With every passing minute that they spent in this house – well, really in this glorious country – Alice felt easier and more relaxed, but also invigorated.

She knew she had allowed herself to settle into a rut of sorts back in England. Her job in the council office no longer challenged her, while her relationship with Richard ticked along pleasantly enough, but it had been a long time since Alice had needed to try. When she talked to Steph about it, confessing her concern that things between her and Rich had become all too predictable, her friend would roll her eyes and tell her not to be so silly.

As far as Steph was concerned, Alice was lucky to be in such a comfortable relationship, and she should feel blessed not to have any drama in her life, but Alice was beginning to wonder if the too little, in their case, might eventually lead to a too late. The spark that she saw so clearly between Steph and Jamal, the same one that Maureen imagined lit the space around herself and Max, was not one Alice could recall feeling for a very long time.

Well, she thought guiltily, extracting her phone from the top of her backpack – not with Richard, anyway.

Alice had expected a barrage of messages to appear as soon as she logged on to Chatura and Monisha's Wi-Fi, but the home screen remained stubbornly free of little grey text-message boxes. Nothing new from Richard, and she'd had no reply from Freddie.

Rearranging the pillow so that she could lean against the wall comfortably, Alice opened Instagram and clicked through to Maureen's account. The last photo her friend had uploaded was of the three of them on the bus to Kandy, all shiny faced and happy, and Alice double-tapped it and watched the little red heart appear below the image. Further down, she found a photo of some chunks of papaya on a plate, which Maureen had captioned with a green, about-to-be-sick emoji. Giggling, Alice liked that one, too, then scrolled down and felt the blood rush into her cheeks at the sight of Max. He was standing on the summit of Sigiriya, his arm casually thrown around Maureen's shoulder and his face upturned for the selfie. Alice could see the reflection of the sun and the trees in the lenses of his sunglasses, and his smile was wide below them. She used her fingers to zoom into the image, looking closely at his white teeth, at the stubble on his jaw, at the neat curve of his ears. Tapping her finger below, Alice saw that Maureen had done as she hoped and tagged Max in the photo. 'BoyBrooke,' she read, frowning slightly. She was sure Max had told them that his surname was Davis.

Abandoning Instagram and opening her Facebook app, Alice hurried through to Maureen's profile on there and checked her recent new friends. Yes, there he was, Max Davis, grinning as if he'd just been laughing in his profile picture. So, she wondered, what was the 'Boy-Brooke' all about? Perhaps an army nickname?

She returned to Instagram and searched for Max's

account this time, ignoring the creep of guilty sweat that was beginning to dapple her chest. She was only looking. There was nothing wrong with that. She wasn't even liking anything – and she hadn't started to follow him, either. And anyway, she reasoned, Max was her friend, so it was totally fine to scroll through some of his pictures.

Alice quickly discovered that a large number of his photos featured a cute, determined-looking little girl, who she worked out from reading the captions to be his niece, Poppy. There was a man in some of those photos who could only be Max's older brother. He looked a lot like him, but taller and broader with less symmetrical features. They had the same light-brown hair, the same intense gaze, and both seemed to spend a lot of their time pratting around, from what Alice could see.

Way further down, past family snaps, pictures of food, a Christmas tree and group shots of Max with a whole pile of muscular-looking mates, Alice discovered a photo of Max crossing the line of the London Marathon a few years ago, tears streaming down his face. There was another one of him sitting up in what looked to be a hospital bed, a wheelchair beside him and a drip trailing out from under the covers. He was giving the camera a thumbs up, but Alice winced at how sunken his cheeks were, and how pronounced the shoulder blades beneath his T-shirt. Max had added a caption to this one that read, '#TBT to when I woke up in Selly Oak. Putting on a brave face but shitting it (not literally, Mum!). Thanks again to the incredible team of doctors and nurses that I will never forget – and sorry for hiding that pilchard salad you tried to make me eat in the cupboard and forgetting about it. That'll teach you to dish out the pain meds like sweets!'

The post had over 200 likes, and so many comments that Alice had to scroll down to read them. Many were jokey ones from his mates, messages written in a military jargon that Alice didn't understand, but there were also expressions of love, and of pride from the medical professionals who had been part of the team that looked after him. An Instagram user called 'JayIsDaMan' had written, 'Milking it much?' and Alice grinned as she clicked through on a hunch and discovered that it was indeed Jamal.

It felt strange to see Max like this, when he was still unknown to her. He had occupied her mind so much over the past twenty-four hours that the idea of not knowing him at all seemed absurd. Even if she never saw him again after these two weeks – and, with a leaden heart, she accepted that this was the most likely scenario – Alice knew that it would comfort her just to know that he existed in the world. Him being in it made it better. She didn't know why she felt this way, or why she was so sure of it, but she was.

'Alice?' The bedroom door banged open to reveal Maureen, her wet hair dripping on to the tiles and her cheeks pink from what must have been a hot shower.

'Off in Wonderland again?' she joked, peering through the gloom. Alice had closed the wooden shutters, thinking that she would get changed, then been distracted by her phone.

'Chatura's brought up some banana cake,' Maureen

went on. 'And then he says he'll drive us down to the Temple of the Tooth.'

'Give me two minutes,' Alice said, thinking that she would fire off a quick message to Richard, telling him they had made it to Kandy safely. When she looked back down at her phone, however, she realised in horror that she'd accidentally liked the photo of Max in his hospital bed. A photo that he'd posted over two years ago.

It was only the knowledge that sweet little Chatura was just outside the door that prevented Alice from cursing very loudly.

# 17

# Max

*If I should die,*
*Don't bury what remains,*
*Turn my body to ashes,*
*And scatter me like rain . . .*

There was a dull, insistent pain in Max's stump. He had been aware of it for a few days now, and hoped that the long flight was to blame, but it was not showing any signs of abating. In fact, Max accepted with a grimace, it was getting worse. As a doctor at Selly Oak Hospital had explained to him right at the start of his long period of recovery, pain was a continuum with his sort of injury. The loss of a limb was never a simple snip, tie, stitch and then off you go; it was the beginning of a healing process that went on for the rest of your life.

Frustrated by the limitations that his predicament had forced upon him, Max was initially eager to crack on with his rehabilitation and get around without having to use a wheelchair. This determination, as well as sheer force of bloody-minded will, had him up on the comfy sticks within a fortnight, and from there it was only a matter of time before a cast was made for his first prosthesis.

Alas, as Max had learned early on, the smallest of changes or fluctuations in his still-healing stump could mean a hold-up of days or even weeks. It didn't matter how many times he was patiently told by the medical profession-als around him that he must allow for new rules when it came to his residual limb, that blood flow would be limited and so recovery would take five or six times longer, that his shattered bones could further deteriorate, that ulcerations could occur and damage the tissue inside his leg, that even the slightest change in his weight might cause his socket not to fit properly, and make getting around unaided impossible yet again. Despite all this, Max still battled.

There had been dark days and brighter ones – an infection had slowed the healing of skin grafts taken from Max's inner thighs, forcing him back into bed, but then, two weeks later, he felt like he'd conquered a mountain when he managed to climb a set of steps without using crutches. Every hurdle overcome, Jamal had told him, his serious dark-brown eyes on a level with Max's, no matter how small, was a triumph. But, and this was vital, if Max ever felt any sort of pain or even mild discomfort, then he must not keep it to himself.

Max knew this rule. He would go so far as to say it was a mantra, even – something that was so absolute in its import-ance that he should no more question his duty to obey it than he should to breathe in and out. But today, and with this pain, Max did not adhere to it. He was not an inherently stubborn man – far from it – but Max was tired of his body no longer feeling like his own. There had been so many doctors and nurses and physios, and for a long time, there had been his mother, helping him to wash, to pee, to shave, to do all the things she should not have to do. The only way Max could make peace with it was to disassociate himself from his physical form, close off that part of his mind that made him feel humiliated and small. Logic reasoned with him that this was his mother, the woman who had given birth to him, raised him, knew and loved him more than any other – but it was still close to being unbearable. The burden he had caused her haunted Max to this day, and there was no question in his mind that the blame was his and his alone. No mother should have to endure what Max's had. No father, brother, sister, child or friend either, for that matter. It was all so barbaric – the lifestyle he'd chosen, the injury that followed, and the trauma it left behind.

As the years had passed and the searing red-hot memory of that time had diminished somewhat, Max had learned to let go of a lot of the things that in the beginning felt so intolerable. He understood he had lost the ability to be as spontaneous as he once was, he recognised the need to keep his weight in check because of the effect any fluctuation would have on his stump, he accepted the mental trauma he'd been left with and coped with it as best he could, and he had persevered in the practice of self-examination, staring at himself in the mirror until his scars felt familiar.

It was a long time before Max felt comfortable enough to be intimate with anyone, but when that time did arrive – with a riding instructor called Eve at a uni mate's wedding – it went surprisingly well. Eve didn't seem repulsed or even curious about his stump; she'd simply had a quick look and said, 'Oh, it's lovely and neat,' before continuing to remove her bra. For Max, who had been building up to the moment for years, the encounter was a breath of relieved air.

He glanced across the bus now to where Jamal was sitting, his head resting against the dusty window, fast asleep despite the thumping music and the cacophony of traffic noise, and wondered why the hell he was being so stupid and not just talking to his friend about this pain. He would, Max decided, once Adam's Peak was out of the way. As soon as he had proved to himself and to everyone else that he could still scale mountains – and Max knew this was as important to him figuratively as it was literally – then he would give in and let Jamal take a proper look. It was only a few days away now anyway – how bad could it really get in that tiny snippet of time?

Max turned to his notebook, frowning as he read back over the beginning of another poem. He'd started his collection of work inspired by Rupert Brooke's 'The Soldier' while he was serving in Afghanistan all those years ago, and the tone was decidedly bleak. He had borrowed the late poet's infamous opener, '*If I should die*', to start each of his efforts, but he could never seem to continue past four lines. Being in the army had given Max a complicated viewpoint on death, insomuch as he'd had to make peace with the idea of it, but at the same time have a huge amount of disdain for it, too. Dying was losing, simple as that, and Max knew all too well that a wretched loss always accompanied death, that it would sit right beside death in its chariot as souls were snatched away. Max had no respect for either – life was what mattered.

What he wanted was to write poetry about beauty, and

love, and joy – but the words fell apart on the page when he attempted it. The truth was, and Max acknowledged it with a sad sort of reluctance, that when he reached down inside himself to pull out, explore and share what was in his heart, he could only ever find pain, hurt and bitterness. If there once had been love in there that was pure, he sometimes feared that it might be hidden too deep to recall. Perhaps his marriage to Faye coming to a messy end had chased it away, or maybe death carried it away along with his loss and fear. Max wasn't sure, but what he did know was that the idea of opening up to someone again, of laying his heart out on the line in pursuit of love, scared him. It wasn't that he had given up on love, more that he felt nowhere near ready to seek it out.

As he stared down with unseeing eyes at a blank page, Max thought about Alice, and the way he'd felt connected to her as they shared stories up on Sigiriya. They had not had any time alone since, and Alice merely said a brief farewell when the girls left for Kandy yesterday morning. Max had clocked the shifty way she glanced at the ground, up into the trees, down at her nervous fingers – at anything, it seemed, to avoid looking at him.

He was used to this reaction, because new people often acted strangely towards him to begin with, and Max would not have thought too much about it if he believed Alice was uncomfortable around him. But he didn't think it was because of that – there was something else going on that was making her feel uneasy. Perhaps he should just ask her straight. After all, he would be seeing her in just a few hours' time. The five of them had arranged to meet at the main entrance of the Peradeniya Botanical Gardens in Kandy just after lunch, with a plan to go for a stroll around, before heading towards the lake in the centre of the city. There was a bar not far from there called Slightly Chilled, which all the guidebooks recommended.

Max realised he was smiling when a small Sri Lankan boy beamed back at him from across the aisle of the bus, before pointing at Mister Tee and saying something to his father in Sinhalese. The older man glanced up and shook his head apologetically at Max, before whispering in the child's ear. It was only natural for children to be inquisitive, and actually, Max didn't mind it at all. His niece Poppy had even taken him into her primary school one day for show and tell, which Max had enjoyed enormously. Adults would always tiptoe around the difficult questions, misguided politeness and fear of being inadvertently offensive preventing them saying what they were really thinking – but the younger generation had no such qualms.

'Do you beep at the airport?'

'Would that melt if you sunbathed with it on?'

'Did it hurt when your leg was blown off?'

'Did you cry?'

'Do people laugh at you?'

'Are you cross with the men who made the bomb?'

Max had answered all their queries as honestly as he was able, admitting that yes, he had cried an awful lot, and that no, he wasn't cross, because being cross wasted too much energy, and he needed as much of that as he could get nowadays. He should do more of that kind of thing, he thought, watching in a half-trance as the bus braked hard to avoid a man who was casually towing a cow across the road. Visit more schools and educate more kids about the reality of living with a prosthetic limb. Curiosity was important, and he hated the idea of those same children growing up with a lack of knowledge that could so easily turn into disregard, or worse, judgement.

It was easier having a prosthetic now than it must have been even ten years ago, thanks to things like Prince Harry's Invictus Games, the Paralympics, and celebrities like Jonnie Peacock taking part in *Strictly Come Dancing*. People were generally accepting, and Max rarely if ever found himself heckled or reviled, but then again, he was uncomfortable with the notion of an artificial limb being worn like some sort of badge of honour. There was a lot more to being an amputee than overcoming a physical abnormality, and Max believed it was important to show people the whole story, not just the positive, attention-grabbing headlines. The public wanted a happy ending to their stories, a fallen hero winning a medal being just one of many, but the truth was far more subtle and complicated.

Max took a deep breath, stifling a yawn and stretching his arms up above his head. The traffic on the other side of the window was building, and he guessed they would soon be arriving in Kandy. Checking his watch, he calculated that he and Jamal would have perhaps an hour in which to locate and check into their hotel, before finding their way to the Botanical Gardens and the three waiting girls. He knew Jamal was buzzing at the thought of seeing Steph again, and there was a fluttering of sorts in Max's own stomach, too.

# 18

Alice sat down on a low bench just inside the entrance to the Peradeniya Botanical Gardens, waiting for Steph and Maureen to get back from the shop. Today was Good Friday in Sri Lanka, but the pace in Kandy didn't seem to have slowed down at all. Of course, Alice concluded, the majority of people in Sri Lanka – over seventy per cent, according to her guidebook – were Buddhists, while Christians only accounted for around eight per cent. Alice was not religious, had not been raised as such, but she had always respected individual people's faith. Buddhism, from what she had read, seemed very reasonable and moderate. She could get on board with the idea of not harming living things, not stealing and not becoming too intoxicated by drugs or alcohol – but she didn't think any self-respecting Buddhist would welcome her with open arms, either. Because, and it made Alice cringe inwardly to think about it, Buddhism strictly forbade lying of any kind.

How could people get through life without telling even a few white lies? Alice found it hard to fathom. Lies were necessary if you wanted to avoid hurting people. If Alice confessed to her mother that she still occasionally acted recklessly just to deflate the balloon of anxiety that built up inside her chest, it would only end in a row.

She had tried once to be completely, unflinchingly

honest about her behaviour. She had admitted to Richard that on the weekend she had vanished from university, on the pretext of doing some research for an essay, she had in fact gone on an intensive diving course. She had expected understanding – perhaps even admiration – but he had been appalled. Ever since then, the knowledge that she had misled him had spread like weeds through their relationship, strangling the freedom she craved and suffocating her aspirations to do anything that could put her at risk. Her need to be adventurous, and to let that younger and less trustworthy version of herself burst boisterously back into her life and lead her astray, had almost cost her Richard. Alice had been steadfastly trying to bury any remnant of that version of herself from that day until this. On the days she failed, such as on her recent trip up to the diving board at the pool, she simply kept the information concealed. It was easier that way, and better for everyone.

Earlier that morning, Alice had woken before the others and crept out on to Chatura and Monisha's balcony, settling herself down in one of the fold-out chairs and gazing across to where the sun was steadily rising behind the mountains. As the day slowly unfurled like spring blossom, she found that she could hear six or seven different birdsongs. A gentle and most welcome breeze was bothering the topmost leaves in the trees, and a fine mist sat suspended in the middle distance. Below her, the garden was a vivid jungle of colour – reds battled with yellows, while pinks caressed their purple neighbours, and insects buzzed with contentment as they made their way from petal to stem.

She had heard back from Richard late the previous night, his message pinging through as soon as they returned to the homestay and her phone picked up the Wi-Fi connection. It didn't say much, save for telling her the house was very quiet without her, and not to forget to call him on her birthday. This would be the first one Alice had not spent with him in over ten years, and it was an important one, too. She would be thirty – a real, unequivocal adult, eight years older than her mum had been when she got married, and five years older than Richard had once told her he wanted to be when he said his vows. She had been batting away conversations about marriage since they met – and for what? What was so terrifying about putting on the white dress and having what was essentially a nice party? Alice knew that it wasn't the separate elements of that one day which concerned her, however; it was what came next, once the confetti had been swept up and the champagne flutes returned to the caterers – it was the ever after that made her feel uneasy.

Steph would talk almost wistfully about the grand wedding she hoped to have one day, while Maureen seemed to view marriage as more of a business transaction, but there was no doubt in either of her friends' minds that it was something they both wanted – a goal to aim towards that must be achieved. Alice often thought there must be something intrinsically wrong with her, because she was no more desperate to get married than she was to fall through the roof of a greenhouse again. The idea of being Richard's wife was comforting, but it wasn't exciting. She knew that a wedding was supposed to be the happiest day of your life, second only to the moment you become a parent. That's what everyone said, and she understood why, but she had never genuinely longed for it.

Poor Richard, Alice had thought as she sat on that balcony, crossing her ankles in her chair and squinting as the sun clambered higher in the sky. The heat was winning the battle against that eerie morning mist, and as Alice stared, the view below her grew in clarity and richness. There were so many greens, blues and whites – she felt as if she'd strolled on to the set of a 1950s' technicolour movie.

If only a tornado would swoop down and pick her up, like it had done to Dorothy Gale in *The Wizard of Oz*. If only she could be carried away to a distant shore, where the real world no longer existed, and be left there, in that alternate reality. But no, she told herself sternly – that was a selfish wish. The allure of spontaneity might be a strong one, but it meant putting her own happiness ahead of everyone else's. As a child, Alice had approached every time adventure beckoned a finger, and look how that had ended up. She wanted to fight these thoughts and focus on the future that was already mapped out for her, however predictable it might be.

She looked up now from her spot on the Botanical Garden bench, and smiled as she saw who was approaching. They all must have bumped into each other outside. Jamal already had his arm around Steph, and she was glowing even pinker than Alice's sunburned knees, while Maureen was chatting away to Max, her flirt-o-meter cranked up to a strong ten as she flicked her dark hair over her shoulder and laughed at something he'd said. He was wearing baggy brown cargo shorts today and a Breton T-shirt, his hair hidden underneath a navy baseball cap and a pair of sunglasses in one hand.

Alice stood as they drew closer, and Max lifted his free hand in greeting, smiling at her with what felt to Alice like genuine affection. He was happy to see her, just as she was to see him.

'Nice top,' he appraised, and Alice looked down at herself.

'Nirvana have yet to be eclipsed musically, in my opinion,' she replied, stroking the printed image of Kurt Cobain.

'You're not a One Direction fan, then?' he asked, and Alice shook her head.

'Phew!' he laughed, pretending to wipe his brow. 'That could have been the end of our friendship right there.'

'What's wrong with One D?' Steph exclaimed. 'Zayn Malik is the prettiest man alive, if you ask me.'

'Ahem,' said Jamal, releasing her from his grasp. 'I think you mean *second* prettiest.'

Steph made a show of looking him up and down.

'No,' she said sweetly. 'Zayn still has the edge.'

'Well, you're off my Christmas card list, young lady,' he joked, then pulled her back against him and kissed her quickly on the lips.

Maureen began filling the boys in on their amusing morning in Kandy. Chatura had insisted on driving them into town via his friend's gem store, which turned out to have a mini museum in the basement, and all three girls had felt compelled out of politeness to buy some jewellery before they left.

'What did you choose?' Max asked Alice, and she reached into the front of her T-shirt and extracted her new purchase – a moonstone pendant on a silver chain. Taking a step forwards, he picked it up for a closer look, and Alice felt his breath on her throat.

'Pretty,' he said, glancing sideways at Jamal. 'Almost as pretty as Zayn from One Direction.'

'Watch it, Davis,' his friend replied, and Max laughed easily.

'I got a ring,' Maureen said, raising her right hand towards his face. Out of the three girls, Maur had spent the most – £200 on a pink sapphire ring – and it glittered in the sunlight as Max bent to examine it. Alice was not surprised to see her friend take advantage of the situation by slipping her fingers through his, but Max didn't take the bait. He merely complimented her choice, then squeezed her hand gently before letting it drop.

'Come on, then,' said Jamal, who now had his arm around Steph's waist. 'Let's go explore.'

He and Steph led the way along a gravel path towards a large greenhouse, which the sign outside informed them was full of orchids, and they all made their way inside.

'Ooh!' Maureen whistled, gazing around in awe. 'Look at all the colours.'

Alice peered at the peach and red blooms closest to her, and tried to inhale their scent through the thick, moist air. It was even hotter in here than it was outside, and an open pond ahead of her revealed a collection of fat but rather listless koi carp. She took her camera out to take a photo for Richard, knowing he'd be far more interested in the fish than he would the flowers, then turned and looked for Max, watching as he took off his cap and ran a hand through his hair. He was undoubtedly feeling the effects of the intense humidity, just like the rest of them, and Alice kept her eyes on him as he strolled towards the exit.

She hesitated, just for a second or two, unable to suppress the thought of Richard and what he would say if he was here, if he could see the way her eyes sought out this stranger again and again. Then she took a deep breath and followed him outside.

## 19

'Not an orchid fan?'

Max raised his shoulders in a shrug as Alice let the door shut behind her.

'Not a huge one – you?'

'I just get nervous around greenhouses,' she joked, and he chuckled.

'Alice the rebel,' he said lightly, almost wistfully, before adding, 'It's a bit hot in there for Mister Tee.'

They both looked down at his right leg. 'If this gets too sweaty,' he tapped the socket with a finger, 'I have to take the leg off and wash my stump, and that's a faff I could do without.'

'Oh,' Alice said.

'Imagine putting your foot into a plastic bag, then walking around with it on all day, in this heat,' he told her.

Alice made a face.

'Yep,' Max grinned. 'Pretty gross, right?'

'I bet you've got nothing on my brother,' Alice told him, gesturing towards the shaded area underneath a nearby tree. 'Shall we?'

Max nodded and went to follow her.

'Freddie's got the smelliest feet in the world – probably the universe,' she explained.

'Older brother?' Max asked. 'Aren't they just the worst?'

Alice thought back guiltily to the photos she'd snooped at on Max's Instagram account. He hadn't mentioned it yet, but surely he must have seen the notification by now?

'Freddie used to annoy the hell out of me,' she admitted, coming to a halt and looking up into the branches above them. She had conditioned herself to always check the trees in Sri Lanka for monkeys, but this one was sadly unoccupied. 'But we became better friends as we got older. I don't see anywhere near enough of him now that he's working in the City.'

'Me and Ant are the same,' Max told her. 'We served together once upon a time, too, but he wasn't on tour when I was injured. These days he trains the new recruits – poor buggers.'

'Is the training tough?' Alice wanted to know, and Max filled her in, telling her in detail about his own experience.

'It's bloody hard work, but at the same time it was the best thing I'd ever done, you know?'

Alice thought she understood, and said as much, but Max seemed to have become more pensive as he recounted his early years in the army.

'I still don't do so well on my own,' he admitted. 'I'm at my happiest in a team situation, so I guess maybe the army institutionalised me in a way.'

'I prefer being by myself,' Alice confessed, kicking at the dirt.

'Why is that?' Max asked, fixing her with his no-nonsense gaze.

Alice opened her mouth to lie, and found she couldn't. No words came.

'Is it because you're misunderstood?' Max probed, and Alice flushed in surprise.

'What do you mean?'

'I just mean that it's easier to be alone sometimes, because that's when you can really be yourself. Trust me, I spent years trying to be this tough army guy, just like my brother, but I couldn't keep it up. I was always the more sensitive one when we were growing up, but I've kept that side of myself very well disguised until . . . well, now.'

Alice pulled out her hairband and her hair fell around her shoulders. She felt suddenly agitated, as if the midges she could see hovering in the air around them were in fact underneath her skin.

'I guess I . . .' She stopped, unable to articulate what she was feeling. Max touched the back of her hand, just briefly.

'It's OK,' he said. 'You don't have to talk about it.'

'No.' She shook her head and kicked at the dusty ground. 'I want to, I just can't. I don't know where I would even begin.'

'Alice?' Max said gently.

Alice knew that he was looking at her, but she couldn't bring herself to lift her chin. She was afraid that if she did, he would see right through her. His words had got her thinking about her own childhood self. Max had been sensitive, whereas she had been foolhardy. Both had grown up doing their best to push aside that which came naturally, but while he had done so out of a desire to fit in, Alice knew she had followed that path out of fear. Fear and duty. She had always believed that her devil-may-care attitude belonged firmly under lock and key, but what if she had been wrong? What if all this inner turmoil was simply her real self, trying to smash its way back to the surface?

'I think there's an adventurous side to you that you try to repress,' he went on. 'I could tell how buzzed you were to climb Sigiriya – there was a fire in your eyes.'

Alice shook her head, muted into silence by his observation. There was no point denying it, because he was right. She had been excited.

'You know,' he said, plucking a small leaf off a nearby hedge and rubbing it between his fingers. 'So many people assume that if I could get in a time machine and go back to that day in Afghanistan – or even back to way before then, when I first joined the army – that I would do so in a heartbeat. I would make different choices and I would still have both my legs. But the thing is, I wouldn't. I'm proud to have been a soldier, and to have served my country – and for all the pain, there were some great times, too. If life hadn't unfolded the way that it has, then I wouldn't be the man I am today. I wouldn't be here today, under this tree, talking to you.'

Alice gazed at him. 'You really wouldn't change anything?' she asked. 'Not even the . . .'

'Injury?' he put in, and shook his head. 'No, not even that. If you'd asked me when I was going through rehab, then maybe, but nowadays I just accept it. It's not like I have much of a choice in the matter, and like I told you before, I was one of the lucky ones.'

Alice was astounded. She had spent years wishing that

someone would turn back the clock and let her live the day of her accident again. More than that, she had yearned for the chance to be reborn without that troublesome streak in her at all. She had always wanted to be someone else.

'I'm guessing you would get in the time machine,' Max said, reading her mind, but Alice shook her head.

'You know what?' she told him, letting herself meet his eyes for once. 'Five minutes ago, yes – but now . . .' She shrugged helplessly and grinned at him.

Before Max could reply, however, the door to the orchid house opened again and Maureen emerged, her eyes narrowing as she spotted the two of them standing so close together.

'Hey,' Alice called quickly, taking an unconscious step away from Max.

'It was too hot in there,' she told Maureen when her friend reached them, but Maur merely lifted her eyebrows in a 'whatever you say' gesture, then moved in beside Max and threaded her arm firmly through one of his.

'Kind sir,' she said coyly.

Max smiled. 'My lady.'

The others had now joined them, and they made their way as a group through the gardens, stopping to take photos of a huge circular pond covered in lily pads and delicate white flowers, cone-shaped evergreens moated by beds of fiery-red cypress vines, and hundreds of roses in a rainbow of shades. Max knew the names of many of the plants purely on sight, explaining that he'd developed a fleeting interest in botany when he'd been at Headley Court.

'It's part of the treatment, in a way,' he told them, as they paused to admire a long lane which was overhung on both sides by vast palm trees. 'It made sense for us lads to nurture something through from seed to sapling; it reminded us that life goes on, and that things take time. In the army, it's all so go, go, go, that when you get the rug pulled out, so to speak, it can be tough to readjust.'

'Couldn't have put it better myself, mate,' Jamal said, before telling the girls, 'The garden at Headley was extended the year Max and I were there – the whole centre was. There were so many blast injuries happening then, and me and Max here, we were both the new guys at the same time.'

'Is that what you bonded over?' Steph guessed, resting her head affectionately against Jamal's shoulder as they gazed up at the majestic trees.

'Well, yeah – that and the fact that he was drawn to my amazing good looks and sense of humour.'

Max laughed. 'Steady on, mate.'

'I've told you before and I'll tell you again,' Jamal replied. 'I just don't see you in that way, Max. You're in the friend zone.'

Max shrugged exaggeratedly. 'A man can dream.'

'I'm always having to put guys in the friend zone,' muttered Maureen. 'I go on a lot of first dates,' she explained to the boys.

'Why only first?' Max was intrigued, and Alice braced herself for the inevitable overshare.

'I'm fussy,' Maureen told him. 'I'm looking for some-one exciting, and all I ever seem to find are bores.'

'Poor guys.' Jamal laughed at Maureen's expression of mock outrage. 'I mean, speaking as a man, you can't win sometimes. Girls say they want a nice guy, but if you treat them nicely then you get friend-zoned. If you go the other way, and treat them mean, they can't get enough of you.'

'That's so not true!' declared Steph. 'I like nice guys.'

Jamal turned and kissed the end of her nose.

'You, Miss Winters, are a rare treat.'

'What about you, Max?' Maureen asked as they continued to walk. 'Do you prefer the nice, boring girls, or the naughty ones like me?'

Max considered this. 'A mixture of the two,' he said diplomatically. 'But I would argue that nice doesn't necessarily mean dull. Surely you can be fun and nice?'

'I would happily be whatever you wanted me to be,' Maureen told him boldly, and Alice turned as red as the flowers on a nearby Pride of Burma tree.

There was a beat of awkward silence, which Jamal then broke by bellowing with amused laughter, telling Maureen to 'stop making a move on my boyfriend – you know he only has eyes for me'. Alice did her best to laugh along with them, but her effort was half-hearted, and she looked around to find Steph staring at her in much the same way as she had halfway up Sigiriya.

'I've just remembered I brought a Frisbee with me,' Max said then, neatly changing the subject. He started to take off his backpack. 'Who's up for a game?'

They all chorused an enthusiastic 'me', and Alice dropped her own bag on the grass and took off across the wide lawn. Max's suggestion could not have come at a better moment – ever since their conversation outside the greenhouse, Alice had felt the familiar froth of anxiety starting to bubble, and it was a relief to run and jump it away. Despite the heat, she played with more gusto than she ever had before, and was still up on her feet long after the other two girls were lying on their backs, pink with exhaustion.

'You're a demon!' Max told her, almost toppling right over as he tried and failed to reach one of her angled throws of the Frisbee. 'You do know I only have one leg, right?'

'Excuses, excuses,' she said blithely, gesturing in the air. 'You're only playing that card because you're being beaten by a woman.'

Jamal cheered just as Max's mouth opened in flabbergasted amusement, and Alice lifted each arm in turn and kissed her biceps for good measure.

The sun was starting to sink when they finally reached the exit of the Botanical Gardens, all five of them sweaty, sunburned and parched from the game. Spotting an ice-cream shop on the opposite side of the road, Maureen headed across with Max and Jamal, leaving Alice alone with Steph.

'Don't fancy one?' Steph asked, nodding after the others.

'Not sure if I trust what they wash the scoops in,' Alice explained. 'Rich told me some horror story about a woman who ended up lactose intolerant after being exposed to contaminated water.'

Steph chuckled good-naturedly. 'That sounds like him.'

'He just worries,' Alice said automatically. 'Did I tell you that he's fitted a child lock on the medicine cabinet?'

'No!' Steph exclaimed. 'Who does he think he's protecting?'

'I have no idea,' Alice laughed. 'You know me – I just keep my mouth shut and let him get on with it.'

'I do know you,' Steph agreed, but the humour had slipped from her tone. She was looking at Alice thoughtfully now, as if debating whether or not to elaborate.

'How are things with you and Rich?' she asked, her attempt at nonchalance failing.

'Fine.' Alice heard his words again in her mind – 'set the date' – and nodded firmly. 'Totally fine.'

'There's nothing you want to tell me?' Steph pressed, and Alice looked at her, feigning confusion.

'Like what?'

'You two have been together for so long,' Steph began. 'It makes sense that the idea of someone new is exciting.'

Alice pictured Richard, with his collection of fishing rods and his glasses case labelled with his name, and suddenly felt like crying. She wanted to tell Steph not to be so stupid, but the lie felt like too much effort. She was beginning to learn that honesty, no matter how uncomfortable, was sometimes just easier.

'I'm being an idiot,' she said finally, her voice small. 'I think this is all just a reaction to Rich saying that we should set the date – for the wedding.'

'He said that?' Steph looked thrilled, but Alice could only nod.

'About time, too,' Steph added, grasping Alice's hand. 'That's amazing news, isn't it?'

Alice attempted a smile that turned into a grimace. 'I don't know. I mean, it should be.'

The others were making their way back across the road now. Alice could see Max's bright-blue ice cream through the throng of tuk-tuks.

'Just promise me one thing,' Steph said, her voice dropping an octave.

Alice turned to her. 'Go on.'

'Don't do anything that you might regret – something that you can't take back.'

Her meaning was clear, and as much as Alice knew she should be offended by the assumption, she had to admit Steph was right to make it. She had been straying back to her old self more and more with each passing day, her hot-headed need to push the boundaries now in danger of overruling her sensible side.

She knew what Max would say – he would tell her to go with it, to embrace it, to be herself and screw the consequences. She could so easily do that, Alice thought, but what would happen to her relationship with Richard if she did?

## 20

If the city of Kandy was an urban assault course, then its central lake was the prize at its end, and Alice felt soothed almost immediately by the sight of the gently rippling water. She, Steph and Maureen had seen the lake from a distance when they visited the Temple of the Tooth the previous evening, but they had not had time to stroll around its shores.

Stalls lined the road that hugged the water's edge, selling everything from ice cream to coconuts to fizzy drinks, water, nuts, popcorn and gifts, and Sri Lankans stepped regularly into their path, offering tickets to a dancing show, a tour of Kandy, or leaflets advertising a nearby bar. There were more local people sitting on stone benches, the men in their white shirts and dark trousers, and the women in their beautiful dresses, all quietly enjoying the view as the dipping sun cast an apricot glow across the buildings and treetops.

Shadows stretched and traffic rumbled, a man in tatty sandals led a pony down to one of the grassy banks to graze, and Alice let the others wander ahead as she stopped to take it all in. There might be confusion in her heart, but this was still an adventure, and Sri Lanka, with its beauty and its mystery, was keeping her spirits lifted. She couldn't help but be amused by the rowdy crows that were stripping twigs from the trees and dropping them in her path; nor could she fail to smile at the little girl who was feeding fish on one of the banks, her hand going again and again into her plastic bag of pellets, while an elderly woman stood next to her and pointed at the gaping mouths that kept breaking the surface below.

There were no monkeys here, either, but Alice started when she sensed movement below her and turned just in time to see an enormous water monitor lizard stalk past. It must have been at least two metres in length, with intricately patterned skin and small, hard eyes. Everywhere she looked, there seemed to be life, and as well as the lizard she could see Muscovy ducks, willowy white herons, tufty cormorants and even a lone pelican.

She caught up with the others at the northernmost tip of the lake, exclaiming over a red post box that was situated not far from the water's edge. It looked exactly the same as those back in England. Max was in the middle of telling Maureen how the post boxes in China were green, which prompted Jamal to start reeling off a list of countries, just to test his friend.

'What about India?'

'Red, I'm guessing,' Max chewed his lip thoughtfully. 'Same as here.'

'And Australia?' Maureen wanted to know.

'Red again,' he replied.

'Have you been down under, then?' Steph asked, and Jamal started laughing.

'Probably not for a while, eh, mate?'

Max blushed slightly at that, and Steph gave Jamal a playfully stern look.

'I went years ago, with my family,' he said, wisely choosing not to rise to Jamal's crass bait. 'But I want to go back.'

'It's right at the top of my bucket list,' Alice agreed. 'Australia and New Zealand.'

Steph looked at her in surprise.

'Since when?'

'Since forever. Rich was really keen on the idea until he did some research and realised just how many things can kill you over there. He's convinced that if we went, we'd end up with skin cancer, or eaten by a crocodile.'

'Your boyfriend is hilarious,' Maureen put in, turning to the others. 'Rich would literally keep Alice on child's reins if he could get away with it.'

Alice said nothing, but she felt Max's eyes seeking hers out.

They completed the circuit of the lake just as the sun was getting ready to turn in for the night, and found two tuk-tuks to drive them up the hill to the Slightly Chilled bar, which offered a stunning view of the city from its balcony and a mixture of Sri Lankan, Chinese and British cuisine.

'Will you all judge me if I order a jacket potato?' said Maureen, kicking off her flip-flops and resting her bare toes on the bottom rungs of Max's chair.

They had found a table right on the edge of the veranda, but it was a snug fit for five, and Alice pulled out her own chair only to accidentally bang it against the knees of another backpacker sitting right behind them.

'Sorry!' she said, but the blond, Nordic-looking guy barely batted an eyelid. The clientele in Slightly Chilled was an eclectic mixture of Sri Lankans, English, Aussies and more, ranging from eighteen to middle-aged.

Not long before she left to start university, Alice had planned a fantasy trip through Asia and Australia. It had always been her plan to take a year off after her studies, but Richard had proven to be a big distraction, and he didn't want to go. He had never told her outright that she should stick a pin in her plans, just as he would never tell her what to do now, either, but his implicit displeasure at the idea was obvious. Alice knew that to go would mean upsetting her mum, who still liked to keep her close, and jeopardise what she had with Richard. She did not want to risk losing him.

Sitting here now, though, surrounded by travellers, Alice felt a keen envy towards the seasoned backpackers at the other tables, with their six-month tans, beaded chunks of hair and weathered expressions. She didn't care that they probably hadn't slept in their own beds for months, or that they were, in all likelihood, wearing their smalls for the fourth consecutive day – what did it matter when they were doing something so real, and so fun? She remembered reading a quote once that had stuck with her: 'Travel is the only thing you buy that makes you richer.' If only Richard would agree to taking a year off work to explore the world with her. But he wouldn't. There was no point even asking.

Once they had all ordered food and there was a round of Lion Lagers on the table, Alice excused herself and went in search of the bathroom, stepping over two huge bulldogs which had fallen asleep on the stairs. She could tell from her reflection in the cracked mirror above the sink that she'd caught the sun, and her cheeks and forehead had turned pink, despite her careful application of factor thirty every few hours. Clearly, different rules applied here than in Europe, where a single dollop of lotion could see you through half a day at least.

She washed her face and hands with the rather dubious-looking nub of grey soap she found on the basin, before scraping the hair she'd pulled down back up into a ponytail. There were always bits that fell out and framed her face, and she flicked them away as she pushed open the door and almost collided with Max, who had his good leg extended over one of the dozing dogs.

'Whoa!' he said, using Alice and the wall to right himself. 'You almost had me A over T there.'

'Sorry,' said Alice, aware that she was blushing.

Max brought his other leg over and stood in front of her, making no move to go around to the gents'.

'You OK?' he asked. 'You seem, I don't know, a bit out of sorts this evening.'

'Just tired from thrashing you at Frisbee,' she said, and Max smiled, his head dropping slightly to one side.

'So, this bucket list of yours,' he began. 'What else is on there?'

Alice thought for a moment.

'I would love to go on a dive somewhere amazing,' she told him. 'Rich and I did a course once on holiday, years ago now, but he hated it, and I haven't been since. I loved being under the water, though – everything down there is so quiet and calm.'

'You don't strike me as the quiet and calm type,' he replied, leaning his shoulder against the wall. He was so close that Alice could smell the remnants of his deodorant mingling with the tang of sweat. It was a pleasant, musky smell, and she felt her senses reel.

'Not deep down, anyway.'

'I have my moments,' she allowed. 'But I am quiet and calm most of the time. Keeps me out of trouble.'

'More fool you,' he said lightly, and Alice cleared her throat.

'I guess you could say that.'

Very slowly, Max reached across and touched her scar, his expression unreadable as his thumb gently stroked. Alice froze, unsure of how to react.

'You've caught the sun today,' he said at last, his eyes searching hers. 'Pink as a flamingo.'

The larger of the two bulldogs chose that moment to wake up from whatever exciting and twitchy dream it had been having, then promptly started chasing its non-existent tail around in a circle. It was the most active behaviour Alice had seen a dog display since she arrived in Sri Lanka, and she laughed as Max dropped his hand from her cheek.

'Do you ever feel like you're doing that?' she asked.

'Doing what?'

'Chasing your own tail.'

*I feel like it's all I do*, thought Alice. *I go around and around on the same track and never get anywhere.*

Max chuckled. 'Sometimes, yeah – especially when I'm doing something really boring at work. You?'

'Constantly,' she admitted, and Max abruptly stopped laughing.

'You need what this fella here needs,' he said, looking at the dog rather than her. 'Someone to throw a ball for you.'

# 21

# Max

*If I should die,*
*And lose that fight,*
*Chase out the darkness,*
*Seek only the light . . .*

Max put down his pencil and reached for his cup of black tea.

His poems were less bleak now than they had been at the start of this trip. Where there had only been blackness before, now he was finding hope, and despite the nagging pain in his stump, he found that his mood was one of contentment. It was as if he knew, without any doubts at all, that everything was going to be all right – even though he had no idea why.

He had gone to sleep thinking about Alice, smiling to himself as he pictured her chasing after the Frisbee, so animated and full of energy. That side of her jarred with the one she seemed to cling to – the sensible, cautious one – and Max was beginning to realise that Alice was a bit of a lost soul. He wished he could lay out all the pieces of her that he had discovered – that way he might stand a better chance of putting them together and getting the real person, or at least a better understanding of her.

Max could no longer pretend that he wasn't drawn to Alice, but it wasn't just that he was attracted to her, or intrigued, or even perplexed. It was none of those things, but all of them, too.

The thing he had realised last night, when Alice had accidentally revealed so much of herself to him, was that she felt trapped by the routine of her current life. It was probably a large part of the reason why he was being reeled in – he wanted to help her break free. Max had been there, had spent years trying to be the person he thought he was expected to be, rather than who he truly was. He knew better than anyone how difficult it could be to be happy when a major part of your life felt like a lie.

But would Alice want his help? Did she even realise how destructive it could be to bury a side of yourself in the hope that it would just go away? It had always been in Max's nature to protect. He was the boy in the school playground who stood up for the bullied kids, the first of his mates to step in if a fight was kicking off on a night out and try to defuse it, and the lieutenant all his comrades would come to first if they were worried, or upset, or struggling with the unrelenting horror of life in a conflict zone. It was who he was, and the more time he spent in Alice's company, the more he sensed that element of him being called upon.

But Max was torn, because it wasn't simply that he wanted to prove to Alice that there was another way – a more honest way – to be happy; he also wanted other things from her, too. And he couldn't venture down that path, not even if he wanted to, not even if *she* wanted him to. She had never tried to pretend that she didn't have a boyfriend, but then she had been looking through his Instagram account. Max had been pleased to get the notification.

He had briefly considered broaching the subject of Alice with Jamal, but his friend was in favour of the idea of Max and Maureen hooking up. After they had bid the three girls farewell the previous evening, Jamal had begun trumpeting his approval. Max had nodded along and humoured him, but he couldn't lie and say that he liked Maureen as anything more than a friend at this stage. She was a gorgeous girl, so confident, fun and feisty, but the connection was not there. Max had paid attention when Maur admitted she was on the lookout for an exciting man, and it made him wary. While he loathed the idea of a girl disliking him because of his injury, he equally wasn't interested in being with someone who wanted him purely because they found his lack of a lower right leg alluring.

He had given up on sleep not long after sunrise, the pain in his stump winning the battle against slumber, and he was now sitting in the courtyard garden of the Sunflower Hotel in Kandy, bright-yellow breakfast pancakes on the plate in front of him. They had to leave to catch the early train to Hatton in less than an hour, and from there it was a bus or local taxi out to Dalhousie, the small village at the base of Adam's Peak. Whenever he thought about trekking up to the summit of that mountain, Max was assailed with a gut-churning mixture of trepidation and elation. It was going to be hard going, as much on the climb down those 5,500 steps as the trek up them, but he was adamant that it was another milestone he must achieve. He had set his mind on completing the London Marathon, and he had done it. This challenge should be more achievable, if anything.

Back at Headley Court all those years ago, stairs had been Max's nemesis. He had felt like a fraud when he struggled so much with his balance – especially when there were chaps with bilateral amputations making the task look easy. Again and again, he had fallen; time after time, he had felt as if half the world was made of quicksand. The ground seemed to fall away from him, and he would feel where he should not, hurt where there was nothing, and be bombarded by the nasty whispers in his mind telling him that he would never do it, that it was too hard, that it was easier to give up.

But Max had not given up – he had fought hard, and he was still fighting.

'You gonna eat those?'

It was Jamal, looking well rested and perky as ever. He was pointing at Max's untouched breakfast pancakes.

'Yes, mate – I bloody am,' Max told him in amusement. 'Get your own.'

'They any good?' Jamal asked, holding his nose before necking his waiting papaya juice in one gulp.

Max picked up his knife and fork and cut a slice off one of the rolled-up pancakes. It was moist and delicious and oozing brown sugar.

'Itsh gwood,' he said as he chewed.

'Bad night?' was Jamal's next question, but he said it lightly.

Max shrugged. 'Just a bad dream,' he lied. 'Nothing too sinister.'

'You should have woken me,' his friend replied, thanking the waiter who had just brought over another plate of pancakes, plus some traditional string hoppers, scrambled egg and a small dish of bright-orange sambal. The desiccated coconut and chilli pepper mix was as common on a Sri Lankan table as salt and pepper would be in the UK, and both men sprinkled it over their food with enthusiasm. As was the case in so many Sri Lankan hotels and homestays, there was no breakfast menu – you simply ate what you were given.

'I would have if it was a really bad dream,' Max assured him, but he could tell that Jamal was not thoroughly convinced by his casual brush-off.

'There isn't anything else, is there?' he pestered, his physio head firmly screwed on. 'Any pain or discomfort?'

'Right as rain.' Max tapped his socket under the table. 'Mister Tee here is fired up and ready to go, just like me.'

'It's not Mister Tee I'm worried about, mate,' Jamal said, scooping up a pile of eggs and dumping them in the middle of his string hopper nest. 'That's several thousand pounds' worth of engineering right there – he's built to endure. But your residual limb is another matter.'

Max took a deep breath so as not to betray his annoyance.

'Honestly,' he said, fixing his friend with what he hoped was a convincing expression. 'I'm fine.'

Jamal forked up a few more mouthfuls before replying,

sipping his tea and watching Max intently over the rim of his cup.

'Ulceration happens when a strained muscle can no longer recover on its own,' he began, and Max rolled his eyes.

'You don't need to lecture me on the details of broken tissue,' he insisted. 'I've been there and lived through all that, remember?'

Jamal shook his head, exasperated.

'I know that, mate – which is why I'm bringing it up now. I know you want to climb this mountain tomorrow, but it's not worth putting yourself at risk for. Pressure ulcers are like a sniper inside your stump – you know that. You won't even know they're there until they shoot you down, and by then it will be too late. Do you want to be laid up again?'

Max grumbled under his breath.

'You know I don't.'

Jamal abandoned his cutlery and started tapping his slender fingers on the table. Max could tell he was frustrated, but he also knew that this time Jamal was not going to talk him into wimping out. Walking was still possible, and so climbing would be, too. Max would not let a silly muscle cramp stop him from achieving the one thing he'd set his heart on when they booked this trip. And that was all the pain was, he was sure – just plain old muscle cramp.

'You'd better eat fast,' he told Jamal, motioning to the leftover pancakes. 'We've got to crack on and catch that train soon. You wouldn't want Steph to leave without us, would you?'

At the mention of his new favourite person, Jamal visibly cheered up, but Max sensed his friend's eyes watching him very closely as he got up to go and settle their bill.

Just a little while longer, thought Max, and then they would reach the coast and he could rest his leg all he wanted. He would simply have to prove to Jamal that there was nothing at all to worry about.

## 22

'Alice, give me a hand with this, will you?'

Maureen looked in genuine pain as she struggled to do up the waist strap of her backpack, and Alice let her own bag drop back on the bottom bunk before hurrying over to help.

'I ate too many bloody coconut rotis!' wailed Maureen, as Alice tried and failed to get the clip to snap into place.

Monisha had prepared them a veritable feast for their final breakfast at the homestay, and as well as the coconut rotis, they had also shovelled in white bread with the crusts cut off, apple jam, rolled pancakes, fried eggs and a vast platter of chopped fruit, all washed down with passion fruit juice and black tea sweetened with honey. Alice felt like one of the rotund Muscovy ducks that she'd seen waddling into Kandy Lake.

'I'm going to have to adjust it – hang on,' said Alice, bending over until she was eye level with the offending canvas strip.

Steph, who was all strapped up and ready to go, took out her phone and recorded a video, laughing the whole time as Alice and Maureen each gave her the finger.

'One final Instagram story before we lose Wi-Fi for the next God-knows-how-long,' she said, pressing a button with a flourish just as Maureen went to grab the phone from her hand.

'That reminds me,' said Maureen, almost purple in the face now that Alice had finally managed to strap her in. 'I need to check my emails before we go.'

'You've got five minutes,' Alice warned. 'Or we risk missing the train.'

'Are you really sure we have to climb this mountain?' Maureen checked, for what felt to Alice like at least the twentieth time. She had initially been keen on the idea, but since arriving, her enthusiasm had been swayed by the intense heat.

'It'll be fun,' Alice said. 'An unforgettable experience, I promise.'

'I'd rather find a man for one of those,' quipped Maureen, disappearing in the direction of the balcony too quickly to hear Alice's amused tut of disapproval.

Steph grinned at Alice.. 'She's just frustrated because nothing happened with her and Max last night. She never usually has to work this hard.'

Alice made a non-committal noise in response.

They had all stayed at the Slightly Chilled bar longer than perhaps they should have, given the long journey they faced today, but the warm evening breeze and the cold Lion Lager had been a very persuasive combination. After ten p.m., a live band had started playing inside the bar, too. Maureen had continued to flirt with Max like the future happiness of all humanity depended on it, but she had got nothing more for her efforts than a chaste peck on the cheek as they clambered into their separate tuk-tuks at the end of the night. Alice was trying not to think about how relieved she was that nothing had happened and focus instead on the next few days ahead.

'We beat you for once.'

Max stood up from where he and Jamal had been sitting waiting for them on a stone bench outside the train station, accepting Maureen's kiss hello and a hug of greeting from Alice and Steph, before producing three pink paper tickets from the back pocket of his tatty denim cut-offs.

'I hope second class is OK?' he asked. 'We thought we could all slum it together.'

'How much do we owe you?' Alice already had her purse in her hand, but Max shook his head.

'It's, like, three quid each or something,' he said. 'Call it my treat.'

He was wearing his baseball cap again today, and it made his eyes look more indigo than blue. Alice had pulled on her trusty denims, too, teamed with a plain black vest and the moonstone necklace she'd bought at the gem store. She'd opted for her walking shoes, simply because they were heavier to carry than any other footwear she had brought, and she predicted having to lug her rucksack further than usual today. It was a long way to Hatton, and the various travel blogs she'd read had warned that this route in particular was a busy one. There was no guarantee of getting a seat on the train, and Hatton was almost three hours away.

The rumours were proven true when the five of them clambered up the wobbly steps into the train carriage to find all but one lone seat full.

'Ladies.' Max extended an arm, but all three girls looked at him askance.

'I'm fine standing,' said Maureen.

'Don't look at me.' Steph raised both hands as Jamal slid his long arms around her waist and pulled her backwards to where he was already setting up a little area of piled bags by the doors.

Alice looked at Max.

'Don't be a hero,' she told him. 'Sit down for now, we can always swap later.'

She could tell he was not altogether thrilled by the situation, but he didn't argue with her. He did insist on stowing her rucksack in the luggage rack for her, however, and she stared unthinkingly at the muscles flexing along his arms.

Maureen had abandoned her bag with Jamal and Steph and was now halfway down the carriage, busy making friends with a group of young British lads who were passing a bottle of Jack Daniels around between them. The rest of the seats were mostly taken by elderly Sri Lankans, their eyes closed and their white hair lifting off their foreheads every time one of the large ceiling fans completed a rotation.

'Bit early for Jack,' remarked Max to Alice as the lads jeered, and she pulled a face.

'Tell me about it. I bet someone tells them off,' she added, thinking about Buddhists' strict rules when it came to drinking.

More passengers were getting on the train now, and soon every available standing space was full as well as every seat, leaving Maureen stranded with the British booze hounds and Alice's bare thighs pressed up against Max. He felt warm and solid and wonderfully present, and Alice's heart began to beat a touch faster than it should. When the train finally jerked and rattled away from Kandy station, there was a clammy film of moisture between the two of them where their skin had come into contact, and Alice had to repeatedly stop herself from falling over by putting her free hand on his shoulder.

'Sorry,' she kept saying, until the two of them were laughing and Max offered his knee as a seat, pretending to look hurt when she refused.

'I don't bite,' he said. 'Well, not hard, anyway.'

The Sri Lankan man sitting next to Max was staring with unashamed curiosity at his prosthetic leg, but Alice noted that Max didn't seem in the least bit bothered. He must be well used to it by now, she supposed, but surely it still irked him sometimes? Alice hated people gawping at the scar on her face.

They passed the time chatting about the upcoming climb and pointing things out to each other through the window. It didn't take more than a few minutes for the large buildings in Kandy to vanish behind them and the lush hillsides and forests to appear. They passed homes that were little more than ramshackle sheds, many with a dog or goat tethered to a post outside next to piles of dead or decaying palm leaves.

The train clattered along the tracks like something out

of an old film, and when Alice bent her head to look, she could see steam from the engine billowing out behind them. All the doors were wide open, and the air that rushed through the carriage was fragrant with the scent of earth, smoke and vegetation. The group of British lads were making short work of their Jack Daniels, and Alice could hear Maureen's peals of laughter floating over the seats. If Max was annoyed that she'd called a hiatus on her campaign of determined flirtation, he didn't show it – his demeanour was almost serene today, his eyes closed against the sun streaming in through the window and a contented half-smile on his lips. Alice envied him – she felt as if her whole body had been stretched out like rope and then tied into knots.

After half an hour or so, squealing brakes heralded their arrival at the first stop, and even more local people piled on to the train, some with young children and others with huge sacks that they balanced on their shoulders. There had been barely any space to move before, and now there was none, but again Alice shook her head when Max patted his lap in invitation. It wasn't that she didn't want to take him up on his offer; it was more that she did. She was so hyper-aware around him, and every morsel of physical contact sent a new tremble through her body. Now that the train was heading out into more open country and gathering speed, it was hurling everyone from side to side, and Alice's hands, legs and body repeatedly collided with Max.

'It must be your turn by now,' he commented mildly, after she'd lurched so far forward that she almost headbutted him.

What Alice wanted to say was that there was no way she was letting him stand, that it was hard enough to balance on this train when you didn't have to factor in an artificial limb, but instead she fobbed him off with a shake of the head.

'I'm enjoying myself,' she told him with enthusiasm. 'I'm getting the authentic Sri Lanka experience here.'

Max smiled. His hand kept going to the top of his prosthesis, and he kept stretching the foot out in front of him.

'Does it hurt?' she asked, flushing at the directness of her question as he looked up at her.

'Not so much,' he said. 'For a long time after it first happened, I would still feel my leg there, even though it was gone. That was pretty weird.'

'I can't imagine,' Alice said honestly, turning her head away momentarily as she heard Maureen emit a particularly loud shriek of mirth.

'It takes a while for your central nervous system to realise what's happened,' Max explained. 'I had spent twenty-five years with two feet, then suddenly one was gone. You know how people always say they need to get their head around things?'

Alice nodded.

'That's what my brain has had to do – get itself around this bizarre and unexpected turn of events.'

'You're amazing,' blurted Alice, before hurriedly adding, 'You know, I just mean because of how open you are about it all. I used to do anything to avoid answering questions about the wound on my face.'

Max thought before answering.

'I wasn't always so open,' he admitted. 'For years, all I wanted to do was hide in my bedroom, and the pain was a problem – it was chronic and there seemed no end to it, no respite. I drank too much as a way of dealing with it, then that became a problem, too. I'm a classic problem child.'

He smiled at that, but it didn't quite reach his eyes.

'What changed?' Alice asked, swearing and then laughing as the train rounded a corner at speed and she careered into him yet again.

'It was a combination of things, really,' he told her, helping her to stand up straight.

'My wife left me.' He took in Alice's stunned expression. 'Yes, I was married. I'm a divorcee.'

'Wow,' was all Alice could manage as a response.

'I know, right? As if anyone would be crazy enough to marry me,' he said, clearly entertained by Alice's instant 'oi' of disagreement. 'Me and Faye were childhood sweethearts, but she found it hard with me being away so much. In fact, I later found out that she was cheating on me long before that IED went off, and then afterwards she stayed out of guilt, rather than love. When I became unbearable to live with any more, she walked out. I guess I don't really blame her now, but at the time it was a shock. I knew I could either spiral down even further with the drinking, or I could use the break-up as a catalyst for sorting myself out. I chose the latter.'

'It must have been awful,' Alice said, mentally drawing comparisons yet again between Max's situation and her own. She had been through a dreadful time after her injury, but it barely registered on the scale when put up against his.

'It was actually Jamal who stepped in to help at that point,' Max continued. 'He put me in touch with a charity called Blesma, which supports limbless veterans like me, and through the people there I found help, and a network of men and women that I could talk to, people who were going through the same thing I was – or worse. They were a real light at the end of my tunnel for a good few years, and I'm still in regular contact with them now. If it wasn't for Blesma, I would probably still be where I was eight years ago – sitting in my bedroom feeling sorry for myself.'

'I think you're entitled to feel sorry for yourself,' she argued gently. 'What you've been through, it's just—' She stopped abruptly, surprised by the sudden emotion that had collected in the back of her throat.

'You sound like my mum,' he replied, looking out of the window. They were surrounded by thick forest now, on both sides of the train, and Alice could smell the moist scent of the trees through the open window.

She pictured her own mum, leaning over the side of her hospital bed, sobbing as she took in the damage inflicted by the greenhouse roof. It had alarmed Alice at the time, and later, as she grew up, it had made her feel increasingly guilty for being the one who had worried her own mother to such an extent that she wept tears of fright. Both she and her mum had ended up traumatised for different reasons, and it occurred to Alice now that neither of them had ever really moved past it.

'Your poor mum,' she said to Max, her knuckles white as they gripped the top of the seat behind his head. He had taken off his baseball cap now, and was turning it over in his hands.

'I know.' He turned to face her, his expression grim. 'I think that's actually been the worst thing of all, you know, seeing my mum upset. She never stops worrying – it feels like I can't breathe with the guilt sometimes.'

Aware that she'd inadvertently hit a nerve, and struck by just how similar the two of them were, Alice steadied her feet on the carriage floor and crouched down until her eyes were level with his.

'It's not your fault, you know,' she said, attempting to put a hand on his arm, but being thrown off balance by another lurch of the train and grabbing his left knee instead.

Max stared at her hand unseeingly.

'I chose to join the army,' he said simply. 'My decision.'

'So what?' Alice braved a laugh. 'I chose to wake up today – does that mean it's my fault if I trip over a loose paving slab and break my nose?'

Max raised an eyebrow. 'Yes.'

'OK, so that was a terrible example,' Alice exclaimed, repositioning the balls of her feet. 'But didn't you tell me yesterday that you wouldn't change the past, even if you had the chance? You could sit there all day trying to trace back who was really to blame for what happened – was it you, or the insurgents who planted the bomb, or the army, or the government, or the people in charge before them, or before them? You'll drive yourself mad doing that.'

'I very nearly did,' Max admitted, and Alice thought her heart would break at the solemnity in his eyes. She hated that he felt this way and would have said anything to alleviate some of his misguided guilt, but she also knew that she was being a hypocrite to even think it – after all, wasn't it guilt about the aftermath of her own injury that had kept her own wings clipped for so many years? Didn't she carry the weight of it around like a wet blanket?

'You know what, I'm full of shit,' she said, and it felt so good to say it that she laughed – really laughed, letting go of the tears that had been lurking and wiping them off her cheeks as Max gazed at her, clearly perplexed by her reaction.

'I think you might be mad,' he allowed with a sideways grin. 'But you're not full of shit, Alice.'

Alice couldn't speak, so instead she just shook her head.

'Most of the people I meet just pity me,' he went on. 'Some are full of morbid curiosity and want to hear all the gory details, then there are a few who just act as if nothing has changed, like my oldest mates from school. I can see why they do it, and I appreciate the sentiment, but the thing is, I have changed.'

Alice had stopped laughing. She could feel her knees tightening and knew she would have to stand up soon.

'But you,' Max said, his hand coming to rest on her upper arm. 'You are the first person, probably since Jamal, actually, to call me out on some of this stuff. You're very . . .' He frowned as he searched for the word.

'Honest,' he said. 'That's it – you are the total opposite of being full of shit. That's why I can talk to you so easily.'

Alice swallowed. If only he knew. Honest was not a word that she would use to describe herself, but then she was different with Max. There was a zero-bullshit aura around him that she respected and – she understood now – admired. Really admired. It was refreshing to be able to speak openly and without fear, and she loved that he had recognised that in her. Why was it so easy to be honest when she was with Max, when she could not do it with Richard, or her family, or even her best friends?

'I do enjoy talking to you,' she said, beginning to stand so that Max's hand fell away from her arm. The brakes of the train were squealing in protest as they pulled into another station, and the Sri Lankan family sitting closest were getting up to retrieve their bags.

Max waited until the curious man beside him had moved towards the door, then he glanced up at Alice and patted the empty seat.

'Come and talk to me some more, then.'

The train continued to trundle along, the rhythmic sound of the pounding pistons blown in through the open windows by the thick, wet air. Alice could smell pine, woodchips and smoke, and her T-shirt clung to her back, which was pressed against the seat. Maureen had joined them not long after they left the last station, half-cut and giggly from her share of the Jack Daniels. Steph and Jamal, meanwhile, were sitting in one of the train's open doorways, their legs dangling down side by side and their hands knotted together in Steph's lap. Alice had gone to see if they wanted two of the spare seats inside the carriage, but both assured her they were quite happy on the floor.

In normal circumstances, Alice would have been jealous of their plum position, but today she didn't mind. Mostly because, she admitted guiltily to herself, she had enjoyed having Max all to herself for a time. He was different when the others were around, and as far as Alice could tell, he seemed to save his serious conversations for her.

While Max turned over the domino pieces he carried everywhere in his hands, Maureen filled them both in on the anecdotes she'd heard from her new friends, all of whom were now slumped asleep in their seats further down the carriage, backpack straps twisted around their legs for safety. Not that anyone here would be likely to rob them, Alice thought. She hadn't felt under threat at any point since they arrived, except perhaps from the crazy traffic in Kandy.

'Baz, that's the ginger one, he says that Unawatuna is the best place to go on the south coast. There are bars all the way along the beach there, apparently.'

Max smiled politely, pretending not to notice the small belch Maureen only just managed to muffle behind her hand. Alice couldn't believe her friend had let herself get tipsy this early in the day. It was a bit much, even for Maur.

'I heard it's touristy,' Max replied, turning to Alice for confirmation. She had read the same thing, but didn't want to pop her friend's party balloon quite yet.

'There are loads of little places all the way along the

coast,' she said pragmatically. 'We can just go from one to the next until we find an area we like.'

The train lurched.

'I don't feel well,' muttered Maureen, and Max caught Alice's eye.

'Here.' Alice unzipped her daypack and retrieved her bottle of water.

'Urgh, it's warm!' moaned Maureen. She was being uncharacteristically whingey, and Alice suspected that the whisky was to blame.

'Take it or leave it,' she told Maureen simply, and Max coughed away a laugh.

Maureen took it, only to complain that it was like drinking bath water. Over her grumpy friend's hunched shoulders, Alice watched as more trees flashed past beyond the large windows, and then suddenly the landscape dropped away and a deep valley appeared below them, as lush and green as Middle Earth. Max, who had also seen it, made to stand up.

'I'm going to go and have a look out of the door,' he said, limping slightly as he moved away, and Alice fought the urge to spring up and race after him. She expected Maureen to leap in and start giving her the fifteenth degree about what she and Max had been talking about, but her friend had gone unusually quiet now – she really must be feeling ill.

'We should be there in less than an hour,' Alice said brightly, and Maureen responded with a limp half-smile.

'Cool.'

'Are you all right?' Alice asked. 'You seem a bit, well, not yourself.'

Maureen avoided her gaze and pulled a face.

'I'm fine.'

'Have I done something?' Alice pressed, wondering if her friend was annoyed with her for monopolising Max. 'If I have, I'm sorry.'

Maureen frowned.

'Do you think you've done something?'

'Um, no. Not really.' Alice laughed nervously.

'Well, then.' Maureen flicked a dismissive hand. 'Don't apologise. You say sorry too much, that's your trouble.'

'Sorry,' Alice said again, laughing as her friend groaned with exasperation.

'Ladies.'

Alice looked up to see Max, back from his little trip to the open doorway. He was holding his phone and baseball cap in one hand.

'There you are,' Maureen said sweetly, all trace of her strange mood gone. She copied what Max had done earlier and patted the seat next to her.

'Come and sit next to me – I feel like I've barely seen you today.'

Alice knew he would look at her, so dropped her eyes quickly to the floor of the train. She didn't want to antagonise Maureen when she was in this weird mood, and she sensed that Max paying her any direct attention would almost certainly wind her friend up. She was convinced Maureen had been lying when she said that nothing was the matter. Alice could see dishonesty in others as clearly as she could feel it smouldering away inside herself – she was an expert. But that still didn't explain what had soured her happy mood from the morning, or why she was unwilling to tell Alice the truth about it. If it was to do with Max, why didn't she just say so? It was very unlike Maureen not to speak her mind, and it was this that troubled Alice the most.

She spent the rest of the journey staring quietly out of the window, waving back at the small children who stood in clusters beside the tracks, waiting for the train to pass. There were always so many smiling faces here, every-where you looked. Being on this rattletrap of a train reminded Alice of watching *The Railway Children* as a kid, her and Freddie with their bare scuffed knees side by side under a blanket, and smells of baking coming from the kitchen. Whenever Alice pictured her mother from those days, she would always be wearing an apron, the smears of flour and butter as much a part of her as her soft, lined hands and her stern expression. Even then, Alice had felt like she was playing a part, agreeing to help mix the batter for some cookies and then pretending to enjoy it, when she would much rather have been crouching by one of the ponds down at the water meadows, trying her best to cap-ture a frog, or simply watching in awe as a water boatman skidded across the surface.

Alice often went on family picnics when she was young, and she could still remember how she would slip away to lie in the long grass as soon as she was able, daring herself to stay as still as possible, until she almost became part of the landscape. She would feel a thrill as passing insects walked across her bare arms, their faces so close that

Alice could make out the intricate patterns. On one occasion, she had wriggled on her tummy all the way across the meadow in pursuit of an army of ants, only to tumble accidentally down the muddy banks of the river. When her mother summoned her back to the blanket, and a wet Alice ventured sheepishly towards her with stains all over her dress, her mum had thrown up her hands in despair.

'Oh, Alice,' she had said, casting around for something she could use as a towel.

'Why must you always get yourself into trouble?'

This was years before that fateful day when she toppled off the roof, and Alice could still recall how confused she had been. Freddie was always getting mud on himself. He had even waded into the water and let it flow over the top of his wellington boots, and he still hadn't got told off. If Freddie's behaviour wasn't deemed to be troublesome, then why was hers?

Right up until her accident, Alice had ignored the scoldings that her mother dished out on a regular basis, and continued to get herself into all sorts of trouble. She probably would never have stopped, either, if it hadn't been for those slippery roof tiles. How different would her life have been? Would she have grown up to become a deep-sea diving instructor, or a soldier, or even just someone who lived a bit closer to the edge? The idea of it thrilled and frightened her in equal parts.

'I think we're here,' she heard Max say to Maureen, and her imagined life splintered into pieces as she blinked and turned, finding a smile waiting on her new friend's lips. Maureen was already on her feet, her face flushed.

As much as she had enjoyed this journey, Alice was keen to begin the next leg of their trip, and as soon as the brakes began to squeal, she stood up and reached for her bag, only to find that the straps had got caught in the luggage rack. She was still trying to untangle them when a high-pitched scream rang out through the carriage.

## 23

Maureen had landed on her back, her rucksack thankfully breaking her fall and preventing her head from smacking against the concrete floor of the platform. She had climbed down the train steps backwards, ironically to help her balance more easily, but slipped and managed to get her ankle caught in the process. It was the pain of that, rather than the fright of the fall itself, that caused her to cry out. Jamal, who had already been standing on the platform but had not managed to catch her in time, was now crouched at her feet.

'Does this hurt?' he asked, gently bending her left foot to one side.

Maureen yelped.

'OK.' Jamal slowly lowered the injured foot on to his knee, then moved his fingers around the joint, glancing up to gauge Maureen's reactions. She winced but didn't scream again, and eventually Jamal let go and helped her up into a sitting position.

'I don't think it's broken,' he told her, looking up at Alice, Steph and Max, who were all peering down at the two of them in concern. 'Badly sprained, for sure, but we won't have to amputate.'

'Very funny!' Maureen swiped at him as Max laughed, and again Alice marvelled at the two men's rather macabre sense of humour.

'Luckily for you, I have these,' Max said, pulling his retractable crutches out of his bag. 'My comfy sticks, here to serve in times of need.'

Despite her obvious pain, Maureen managed to smile at him.

'My hero,' she simpered, and then, 'I'm so embarrassed.'

'Don't be silly,' they all chorused, and Jamal moved to help her shrug off her backpack. The crowd of people that had gathered around them immediately after the fall had dispersed, and they were now alone save for a few curious locals. Alice couldn't be sure whether it was the mildly pissed, slightly hysterical girl on the ground they were staring at, or Max's leg, but she appreciated that the five of them had made quite an entrance.

'Are you sure you can spare those?' she asked Max, remembering the way his hand had kept straying to his leg on the journey.

Hatton was only the first stop on their way to Adam's Peak – from here they would somehow need to get to Dalhousie.

'She needs them more than I do at the moment,' he assured her, glancing away as Jamal headed off in search of a taxi.

'I'm sure there are some tree branches we could fashion crutches out of if we had to,' Alice said.

'You don't need to use me as an excuse if you want to go scampering up trees like a monkey,' he told her, a smirk playing around his lips.

'Me?' Alice feigned surprise. 'I'm a proper lady, don't you know?'

'Well, in the army, all the proper ladies can climb trees,' he countered. 'And I'd be willing to bet you're more one of those than the other sort.'

'Other sort?' Alice enquired.

'You know.' Max pulled a disapproving face. 'All fake nails, strings of pearls and shoes you can't walk in.'

'Strings of pearls?' Alice exclaimed. 'This isn't the eighteenth century.'

She stopped chuckling when she saw the look on Maureen's face.

'How is it?' she asked quickly, kneeling by her feet.

'Painful,' came the reply.

Steph looked at Alice.

'I've got some ibuprofen in my pack,' she said. 'As soon as Jamal gets back, we'll get you some water so you can have some. I'm sure it will feel better in no time.'

'Not in time to climb Adam's Peak, though,' Maureen grumbled, and Alice shook her head.

'Shit, I totally forgot. That sucks. Sorry, Maur.'

Maureen shrugged expansively.

'I'll get over it. One of the lads I met on the train isn't doing it either – told me he was too lazy. Maybe I can just hang out with him.'

Alice wanted to point out that their ascent would begin at two a.m., meaning that both this bloke and Maureen would most probably be tucked up in bed, but she thought better of it. Maureen's fuse had been frazzled by her fall, and Alice could practically feel the fury in the air around her. Her being pedantic about anything right now would not be well received.

'I'll stay with you, if you like?' offered Steph, and Alice reddened. She should have thought to say the same thing. The truth was, though, that it would take a train running right over Maureen to stop Alice going up that mountain.

Maur, however, was shaking her head. 'No, absolutely not. I'm not letting any of you babysit me. Well, unless you'd rather stay in bed with me than climb a big old rock?'

She looked straight at Max as she said the last part, but he laughed it off in good humour.

'No way am I missing out. Sorry, Maur.'

'Your loss,' she said jokingly, and Alice stared hard at her shoes.

Jamal was back and beckoning them to follow him, so Alice and Steph hoisted Maureen up between them while Max carried her discarded rucksack and his crutches. Outside in the station forecourt, predictable chaos was ensuing, with tuk-tuk drivers falling over each other to reach them and offer a fare, and buses and cars belching smoke as they stood idle in the dust. Somehow, in the midst of all this, Jamal had found them a real taxi with room enough for eight, and they all piled in thankfully. There was dirt on the floor and no air conditioning or seat belts, but it was certainly a step up from a three-wheeler, and Maureen was able to use a spare seat as a footrest.

'Now you're my hero,' she told Jamal.

'I'm a hero every day,' he joked, and Max started boo-ing loudly from the front of the van.

'Dalhousie, all?' checked the driver, who barely looked old enough to have a licence.

'Yes, please!' they chimed, and with an extra-long lean on the horn and a certain amount of friendly yelling by the driver out of his window, they were off, chugging through the traffic before turning off and winding along a narrow road overlooking a deep valley.

Alice's mouth opened in a perfect 'O' as she peered over the edge of the cliff and took in the wide blue lake hundreds of metres below, its surface the impenetrable blue of spilt paint. The towering hillside on the opposite bank was patterned with swatches of green, and intermittent flashes of bright-red leaves or fruit – Alice could not be sure from this distance – were visible in the treetops. The colours were achingly bright and rang with clarity, as if someone had taken a photo of the landscape and applied filter after filter, nudging up the contrast and saturation levels until the image looked more painted than real.

The road they were on banked and twisted, the loose stones on its dry surface crackling under the weight of the tyres. The young Sri Lankan drove with one hand on the wheel, nonchalant even on the tightest of bends, and Alice could only just make out what he was saying to Max over the sound of the rushing wind. He was explaining what Alice already knew, that today was Adhi Madin Full Moon Poya Day – the second of two full-moon days in the month of March, and a Buddhist holiday. As well as this, it was Easter Saturday, and Steph's last day as a twenty-something. There was an awful lot going on. She listened as the driver explained that their climb that night would be very busy, because many Sri Lankan people planned their visit to coincide with Poya Day, and advised that they set off in plenty of time.

'You can climb with this leg?' Alice heard him ask Max, but a tuk-tuk driver chose that moment to zoom past them beeping his horn, so she didn't catch the reply.

It was another hour's drive to Dalhousie, by which time Alice's limbs were beginning to ache from lack of movement. The combination of painkillers, Jack Daniels and humiliation had lulled Maureen into a snooze, and Jamal had dozed off on Steph's shoulder, but Alice was far too excited to feel tired. She was trying her best to take it all in, bank all the memories for a future that she feared would contain far less vibrancy, noise and energy. As they rolled into Dalhousie, however, her first impression wasn't one of captivated awe, as she'd hoped it would be. Straight away she understood that here was a place born purely out of necessity rather than anyone's true desire to make a home.

'Bloody hell,' said Max. 'This place reminds me of Afghan.'

The taxi pulled up in a makeshift parking area that was essentially a muddy field, and the five of them clambered out in turn, Maureen wobbling slightly on Max's borrowed crutches. Three paths led off in different directions, and a hand-drawn sign crudely informed them that the left-hand one was the start of the climb, while the one on the right took them to the hotels. The last pathway would take them back the way they came. All around the edges of the drop-off zone and stretching away along either side of the dirty roads were stalls of various shapes and sizes, selling everything from food and drinks to high-tech walking gear and camping equipment. Everything had been crudely constructed, as if it had been thrown up in a great hurry, and it was quiet here, too – so much so that it was almost eerie. Alice had never been to a shanty town before, but if she had to describe Dalhousie, those would be the words she would choose. With its muted palette of greys and browns, it was so unlike the rest of the country they'd seen so far that at first Alice was shocked into silence. She had never felt more like she was actually in Wonderland in her life.

'What a shithole,' proclaimed Maureen, and Jamal burst out laughing.

'I was going to say "rustic",' he replied. 'But you may have a point.'

'Look,' said Steph, pointing towards the nearest stall. 'You can even buy toys here.'

She was right. The pop-up shop was piled high with plastic dolls in boxes, buckets and spades, trucks, cars, teddy bears and even a small tricycle.

'Because toys are exactly what you need when you're climbing a mountain,' Jamal commented in bemusement. Sri Lanka kept the surprises coming, that was for sure, and now Alice realised why all the travel blogs she'd read before they came out here advised only staying in Dalhousie for a few hours at the most. It was merely an overgrown forecourt to the main event, but she had no doubt that Adam's Peak would more than make up for it. She could see the top of the mountain now, as they made their slow way towards Daddy's Guest House, rising out of the late-afternoon mist. It looked as if it was miles away, and was mind-bogglingly high, too.

'Starting to feel grateful for my swollen ankle now,' commented Maureen, who had fallen in beside Alice and was also gazing up at the peak. 'Is it really only seven thousand feet?'

'I think it's closer to seven and a half thousand, if memory serves,' Alice said. 'But what's an extra five hundred feet when you've already been climbing for three hours?'

'Rather you lot than me,' Maur replied.

Alice shook her head. 'I actually can't wait,' she said, smiling to herself as Maureen shook her head in disbelief and moved away awkwardly on the crutches. Alice liked that Dalhousie was strange and bewildering, because it was almost as if they had been driven right into the pages of a fairy tale. Nothing felt solid or tangible here at the foot of Adam's Peak, and the edges seemed to blur like those in a dream. Wispy fog swirled, the air was thick and made her ears hum, and tonight the moon was going to shine at its fullest and most bright. Alice knew with a sweet certainty that she was about to embark on a physical challenge like none other she had ever had the chance to try, and the knowledge alone was enough to thrill her. Not only that, but she was also going to share this experience with someone she had grown to care about, more than she knew she should. At least for a while, Alice thought, she would allow herself to believe the fable, and let herself be free. This was her time, and she wanted to look back and know that she'd spent every moment of it as her real self.

# 24

# Max

*If I should die,*
*Do not seek to blame,*
*I chose this adventure,*
*Made mortality a game . . .*

Max rubbed the sleep from his eyes before lacing together his fingers and pushing his hands forwards, feeling his joints creak and his ligaments burn with the effort of moving. A gaping yawn drew much-needed oxygen into his lungs and cleared his groggy vision, and he unscrewed his bottle of water to take another long drink.

Alice was next to him, her eyes shining with determination in the darkness, her gaze fixed firmly on the trail of lights that seemed to go right up into the heavens. Their pathway up Adam's Peak was lit; now all they had to do was follow the flickering golden stars to the top.

Jamal and Steph were here, too, hand in hand as they always seemed to be, so at ease with one another despite having met less than a week ago. It said a lot that his friend was being so attentive, because while Jamal was always unfailingly fair to the girls he hooked up with – and Max had known there to be rather a lot of those – he was usually casual, too. Steph had got underneath Jamal's skin in a way that Max had never seen any girl do before, and he worried what would happen when the two inevitably had to say their goodbyes. Then again, he chastised himself, Suffolk was not that far away from London – if Steph and Jamal wanted to keep on seeing each other, then he imagined they would find a way to make it work. Hell, if Jamal could get Max working again, he was probably capable of anything.

They had all headed to bed early the previous night, after a huge helping of kottu roti each, and were only mildly miffed to discover that beer was strictly off the menu because of the full moon. Being dehydrated would not serve the four of them well on this climb, and for Max it was an even bigger problem. The tedious pain in his stump was currently being kept at bay with a couple of aspirin, but he was nervous about them wearing off – especially now that he didn't have his sticks as a back-up. It hadn't occurred to Maureen to offer the crutches back to him when she limped off to bed, and Max had been too proud to ask.

Too proud and too stupid, he thought to himself now.

Dalhousie was even stranger at two in the morning than it had been in the daylight, with small pockets of people clustered around the stalls that remained open, and barely any sound save for the gentle scrape of their walking shoes on the muddy ground. It reminded Max unavoidably of going out on a mission in the early hours, his night-vision goggles making the barren desert surroundings look even more like an alien planet. He could recall the thump of his agitated heart in his chest, the throbbing of the veins in his temples as fear and adrenalin coursed through him, and the sound of his comrades in front and behind, their footfall steady and repetitive.

Max snapped his elastic band against his wrist and blinked himself back into the present.

'Chilly, isn't it?' said Alice. She had been quiet since they left the guest house, seemingly content to just take it all in as they made their way to the starting point of the climb, but now she brought her hands up to rub at the sleeves of her hooded top.

'I quite like it,' he admitted. 'It's helping to wake me up.'

Max had a spare jumper in the small rucksack on his back, but for now he was still in a T-shirt as well as long, baggy combat trousers. Alice was zipped right up to the chin in a plain purple top and black leggings, and she'd tied her hair back in a high ponytail. She looked about fifteen, thought Max with affection, save for a few fine lines around the corners of her eyes.

'It's going to be a hell of a lot colder at the top,' Jamal warned, and they all looked up to where the flickering lights gave way to real stars. Max knew the maths, knew that it was only four miles from where they were to the top, a distance that he could have done without breaking a sweat, once upon a time. But staring up there now, as Adam's Peak glared majestically back down at them, it felt far higher. He would make it up there, though, pain or no pain. He had to.

They passed a large statue of Buddha encased behind glass, and crossed a bridge over what sounded like fast-flowing water, but which they could not see through the gloom, before joining the back of a short queue of people waiting to start their pilgrimage. A Sri Lankan couple stood silently just ahead of them, a young boy between them who Max guessed must be their son. He couldn't be any older than six, but he looked just as pious and purposeful as any of the adults around him. All three were barefoot, and Max's eyes flickered to his own feet, one full of bones, muscle and flesh and the other an expertly crafted lump of wood and urethane foam. He was wearing a fresh prosthetic sock made of wool for the climb, which he hoped would help to ward off any excess sweat and keep the residual limb as comfortable as possible. Given the amount of work he was asking it to do, however, Max did not have as much confidence as he would have liked, and he knew that there would be some serious teeth-gritting to be done over the next six or seven hours.

'You OK?' Alice brushed a finger against his arm. She always seemed to know when he was experiencing discomfort – he must wear his worry like military stripes.

'Yeah,' he smiled at her, nudging her shoulder with his. 'Just keen to get going.'

They stepped forwards and slipped some rupees into a donation box. There was a monk dressed in orange robes standing off to one side, and as soon as the notes and coins had been dropped in, he tied a length of white wool around each of their wrists in turn. Max watched Alice's expression grow serious as she fingered hers, and smiled to himself. This climb clearly meant just as much to her as it did to him, and in that moment, he felt awash with happiness that they would be experiencing it together.

The dark pathway was already filling up with people,

but hardly anyone was talking. The atmosphere was one of silent contemplation, as pilgrims focused on the task ahead and saved their energy for the ascent rather than conversation. Large, wide steps were cut into the dirt, each one a simple hop upwards, but as they rounded a corner and passed a large stall selling plastic flowers, the going gradually became steeper and more taxing. Where before mouths had been closed, now they were open and panting and breaths could be heard. Max himself was not feeling the aerobic burn yet, but some of the elderly Sri Lankans making the climb were already beginning to slow their pace. Alice, who was keeping step with Max almost exactly, looked pumped, and was positively fizzing with energy. Max reckoned she could probably run right up to the summit if she wanted to.

'You seem pretty fit,' he said, shaking his head as a woman wrapped up in robes and a woolly hat offered him a cup of chai. There were vendors all the way along this section of the path.

Alice grinned at him. 'I run a lot,' she explained. 'And swim.'

'I used to hate swimming,' Max admitted. 'But I got really into it after . . . Well, what I mean is it's nice to do something where you don't have to rely too much on the leg, you know?'

She nodded again with that smile of hers that Max had come to love eliciting. Jamal and Steph were a few steps behind them now, and Alice turned furtively to look, almost as if she was checking that they weren't in earshot.

'I'd secretly love to try surfing,' she said quietly. 'It's one of the reasons I've always wanted to go to Australia.'

'Why do you keep that a secret?' Max asked, feeling his forehead creasing with a frown.

Alice walked up three more steps before replying, her expression unreadable.

'Honestly?' she said. 'Because my mum would hate the idea, and I reckon Rich would compile a dossier of every person ever killed or injured while cresting a wave.'

'Killjoys, both of them,' he declared, but Alice merely lifted her shoulders as if in defeat.

'Do you want to know a secret about me?' Max asked, and this time it was his turn to check over his shoulder to make sure Jamal was far enough away not to hear.

Alice was waiting, her cheeks aglow in the light coming from the torches. They had been walking for around twenty minutes now, and the curved pathway was still going steadily upwards.

'I write poems.'

'Oh?' Alice's surprise was evident in her expression.

'I know, right? I told you I was a sensitive soul.'

'What are they about?' she asked.

Max explained about his hero and inspiration Rupert Brooke, and how reading his work had led to Max picking up a pen and having a go himself. Alice nodded along in recognition – she had studied Brooke at secondary school.

'The content depends mostly on my mood,' he admitted. 'They used to be quite dark, but since being here they have actually become a bit less depressing.'

'That must be a good sign,' she stated, and Max nodded in agreement.

'Maybe I'll show you some one day,' he said. 'But that's a big maybe. I have never shown them to anyone before, and if you laughed, I'd probably never get over it.'

'You worry too much,' Alice replied good-naturedly. Her breath was beginning to shorten now, but her pace was increasing, and Max lengthened his stride to keep up. Behind them, Jamal called out something that sounded a lot like, 'Wait for us!'

Max could not quite believe that he had just voluntarily admitted this to Alice. Writing poetry was not a particularly unusual thing for a person to do, but it meant a great deal to him. For a long time now, it had been the primary outlet for his emotions, and writing about the way he was feeling helped him to make sense of it. During long nights in Selly Oak Hospital, when he couldn't sleep because of the pain in his stump, Max had scribbled away in the patient diary beside his bed – the same one that had come with him all the way from Camp Bastion, where first the Medical Emergency Response Team, and then the medics on the ground, had added updates on his condition.

Writing about his agony had made it more tangible somehow, something to be overcome rather than a state of being. Then later, after he had struggled through the early stages of rehabilitation, Max began to deal with the resentment that had clobbered him, and the impotent rage he had been left with. Every emotion he felt, he tried to put into words, and when Faye left he took strength from raging against both her and himself in his poetry.

As well as being a useful tool, Max's poetry made him feel like his old self again, the version he had tried to grind down in favour of becoming a tough guy. He had not realised how much he needed that old Max until he got him back again.

However, at no stage during any of this had it occurred to Max to show his work to anyone. It had always been a very private and personal thing. Today, after all this time and for no other reason than the simple fact that he wanted to share something truly meaningful with her, Alice had become the very first person to find out his secret.

## 25

Alice lifted her chin and squinted up at the twinkling pattern of lights above her. They had been climbing for over two hours now, but the top of Adam's Peak never seemed to get any closer. After a moderately easy start, the pathway had narrowed and the steps had become steeper, with each one now knee-height or higher. It was still pitch-black everywhere but the few metres ahead of and behind them, and Alice could not tell how far they had come up the mountain, or what was in the undergrowth on either side of the path. One thing was certain, though, and that was that the only way was up. There would be no quitters on this trail – no matter how hard it got.

Max was still with her, but the last flight of steps had been tough enough to quash their conversation with exhaustion. Alice could feel her knees shaking, and the muscles in her thighs and bottom screamed with fatigue, so she could not even begin to imagine how much tougher it must be for Max. It had only really dawned on her when they were well on their way that he should have brought his crutches with him just in case, and she cursed herself for not having the foresight to ask Maureen to give them back.

'Shall we rest for a bit?' she said through her gasping breaths, and Max nodded, looking thankful. They had reached a natural stopping point, and found a clear space on a low wall opposite a small wooden refreshment stand. The gentle breeze felt cool and fresh up here, and there was a lingering scent of spices. No sooner had Alice stripped off her hooded top than she needed it back on again to stay warm. Max, meanwhile, was still wearing his grey T-shirt, and she could see a trace of goosebumps on his arms.

'What's that smell?' he asked, sniffing the air.

Alice pointed across the path. 'Chai tea,' she said. 'Do you want one? I brought my purse.'

Max shook his head. His short hair was plastered to his forehead with sweat, and he brought a hand up and wiped his brow.

'I might wait until we get higher. There's bound to be a tea shop near the summit.'

'Can you see the others?' Alice asked then, peering downwards into the shadows. Every now and again, another head or two would emerge through the darkness, as more people struggled up the mountain.

'Not yet.' Max shrugged off his rucksack and lifted his feet to let a stray dog wander past. Alice had been surprised to see so many of them at first, but now she'd grown used to it. She imagined there would be monkeys, too, hiding out of sight in the surrounding trees. She was sure that she'd heard one an hour or so ago. It felt as if they were in their own little world up here, so far removed from their everyday lives.

She shivered, and Max leaned his body against hers for warmth. He felt solid and real and comforting, and she pressed herself back into him, all the while listening to her heart as it beat loudly in protest.

'Do you mind sitting here for a bit longer?' Max asked, unzipping his bag and taking out a large bottle of water.

'Of course not.' She shook her head and checked the time. 'We still have at least an hour and a half until the sun comes up.'

'I think I need to give my little fella a wash,' he said, and Alice blushed.

'Your who?' she exclaimed, and Max looked momentarily puzzled.

'Oh, no! I don't mean *that* kind of little fella. Not that he's little, or unwashed.'

Alice put her hands over her ears. 'Stop!' she cried, closing her eyes. 'I get it!'

Max laughed as he bent down to roll up his right trouser leg.

'I'll try not to be offended by that reaction,' he joked, bending over again and easing down what looked like a long sock. Alice heard a click, and then Mister Tee was off and in Max's hands.

'Do you want to hold him for me?' he asked, and Alice nodded without hesitation, holding out her hands as if he was about to pass her a baby.

'Wow, he's really heavy,' she said, wobbling on the wall as she repositioned the leg in her arms.

'He has to be,' Max said. 'He's supposed to be the same weight as my real leg would have been. That way my central nervous system has a better chance of getting used to him.'

'Makes sense,' said Alice, turning the leg around so she could examine it in more detail. Any awkwardness she had felt when she first caught sight of Max's prosthetic leg days ago had long since passed, and now she was genuinely interested to find out more about it. She watched as Max removed another white wool sock, laying it over his shoulder, before finally easing off the last part of the prosthetic by rolling it neatly over his knee.

'This is the liner,' he explained, holding it up. 'It's a bit sweaty, though, so don't get too close. Remember what I told you about the plastic bag?'

'You don't need to tell me twice,' Alice assured him, hugging Mister Tee tightly against her chest. The bottom of Max's trainer was covered in the strange red dust of the path, and it had wiped off all over her leggings.

'Shit,' Max swore as he realised, pausing with the water bottle in his hands. 'Sorry.'

'It's only dirt,' she said, nonplussed. 'Don't worry about it.'

Alice found that she couldn't stop looking at his stump, which Max had elevated so it pointed straight out in front of them. Several people who had also stopped to catch their breath were staring, too, and one old woman even gasped in surprise.

'Nice scar, isn't it?' said Max, pointing so that Alice could see. The neatly puckered line ran all the way along the bottom of his stump and up either side.

'It's the shape of a smile – much better than mine,' she said, and he grinned.

'I draw eyes and a nose on it sometimes to make my niece laugh,' he admitted, lowering the leg again and dousing it with water.

'Don't you need soap?' Alice wanted to know, but Max shook his head.

'Nah, it irritates the skin. Plain water is the best thing, but I forgot a towel, so I'll have to let it air-dry for a bit.'

'Does it still feel weird?' she asked when he had finished washing. The few climbers who had stopped to gawp were now sitting on the wall next to them, sipping chai tea and pretending not to stare.

Max ran his hands over the stump as he considered her question. 'Sometimes,' he allowed. 'Learning to drive with it was weird, and finding out how I could . . .' He stopped, coughing with what sounded like embarrassment.

'What?' Alice asked, even though she could sense where he was going.

Max brought his head down until it was close to hers and whispered.

'Have sex.'

'Oh, I see.' Alice's cheeks burned with mortification.

'It can get a bit hairy,' he added. 'When the girl on top gets carried away. It's not always possible to balance.'

'And the driving?' she said firmly, changing the conversation before she fell off the wall.

Max laughed, delighting in her bashfulness.

'I can show you,' he said. 'Give me that.'

Alice handed back Mister Tee, and Max propped it carefully against the wall.

'Now bend your right knee and sit on your foot – that's it. Sit hard on your foot until it starts going numb.'

Alice did as she was told, trying not to think about the red dust that would now be all over her bottom.

'OK, now imagine that you're at the wheel of a car.'

Alice held up her hands and gripped an imaginary steering wheel.

'Right, now accelerate.'

Alice looked at him, then down at her bent knee. The lower part of her leg was still pinned underneath her bottom.

'I can't,' she said, feeling stupid.

'That's because you're using your eyes,' he said. 'Close them and try again.'

Alice couldn't see how it would make any difference, but she shut her eyes anyway and tried to imagine her foot pressing down on the pedal, how the vibrations would feel against the bottom of her shoe.

'Can you feel it?' Max said, his voice low in her ear.

Alice smiled. 'I can. I think I get it!'

When she opened her eyes again, Max was looking at her so intently that Alice found she couldn't meet his gaze.

'Of course you do,' he told her. 'And I think you get *me*, too.'

Alice opened her mouth to reply, to tell him that he was right, that he could see in her what she never showed to anyone – not even the people who meant the most to her – but her words were lost as Jamal and Steph clambered up the steps below them and cheered.

'About time,' Max teased, rolling his liner back over his stump so quickly that Alice didn't even see in which order the socks went. 'I got so bored waiting that I took my leg off.'

'Attention seeker,' countered Jamal, who bizarrely didn't even seem to be out of breath.

Steph could only mouth uselessly, she was that knackered, and Jamal plucked Max's water bottle off the wall and gave what was left of it to his ailing partner-in-climb.

'Drink up, beautiful,' he said sweetly. 'There's a long way to go yet.'

Max met Alice's eye before standing up with renewed energy.

'Bloody physios,' he told the girls. 'Slave drivers, the lot of them.'

'I think I might die,' panted Steph, her cheeks obviously pink even in the darkness. Alice remembered Max's tale about Senura the Sri Lankan waiter, and how his eighty-six-year-old gran scaled this beast of a rock every year.

'Come on, birthday girl.' She offered Steph an arm, hoping as she did so that her friend would be far too tired to probe her about her alone-time with Max. 'Last one to the top of the next flight has to buy the other a tea.'

She turned to begin a count of three, but Max and Jamal had already scarpered, leaping up the huge steps as if they were mere cracks in a pavement.

'Why wasn't it me that fell off that bloody train?' wailed Steph, as the two of them watched the boys disappear in a cloud of dust, but she managed to crack a smile nonetheless.

'That's fate for you,' Alice replied, taking a deep breath as they tackled the first step. Had it been fate that had led them here to Sri Lanka? Put them in that homestay in Habarana at the same time as Max and Jamal? Had fate thrown Maureen off the train so she couldn't be here with them on this mountain? Had fate planted the bomb that robbed Max of his leg? There were some things that happened in life which nobody could control. But there were also, Alice realised, gritting her teeth as her thighs burned in protest, decisions that you were in charge of, actions that you chose to make, and feelings that you allowed yourself to develop.

The way she was beginning to feel when she was with Max could not be blamed on fate – the truth was as hard and as undeniable as the ground beneath her feet. But what she chose to do with those feelings could affect the fate of so many others.

# 26

# Max

*If I should die,*
*Let it be said,*
*He fought with his heart,*
*Stood strong, never fled . . .*

Max lowered himself down gingerly until he was sitting beside Alice on the step. The summit of Adam's Peak was now just a stone's throw from where they were, packed in amongst all the other people who had made their pilgrimage on this Poya Day. Steph and Jamal were lower down, having waited a bit longer in the relative warmth of the mountain's highest tea shack, which was at the base of the steps. When they had all staggered up half an hour ago, a beaming Sri Lankan man in earmuffs and a quilted jacket had given them each a high five and announced that there were 'only three hundred and sixty-five steps to go'.

'Only!' Alice had repeated in mock glee, and Max had laughed despite the pain in his leg. It was difficult not to think about it constantly now, but Alice being here was helping. She turned to him now, a look of enquiry on her face.

'Tell me more about your poems,' she prompted,

wrapping her arms around her raised knees. 'Are they all about your time in the army?'

Max frowned. 'Most of them, yeah. And, if I'm honest, they're all a bit depressing, too.' He attempted a laugh, and Alice jabbed him gently with her elbow.

'I bet they're not as depressing as you think,' she said. 'Maybe they're just sad. There is a difference, I think.'

Max thought about his sadness, about how confused he had been when he began writing his poems, and how afraid. The concept of death had become so real to him while he was still serving, and it made him want to lash out – to kick and scream and hold fast to the frame of his bed at Camp Bastion, so as not to be put in harm's way again and again. But there was no room for cowardice in the Armed Forces; you just had to crack on and get the job done – even if that job turned out to be dying.

'Well, I suppose sad is better than cheesy,' he allowed. 'The last thing I want is to be corny. There is nothing romantic about war. If your lenses are at all tinted, it's from the blood of your fallen comrades, not roses.'

'Now that really is poetic,' Alice said, and Max chuckled in appreciation.

'Clearly, I don't know my own talents.'

'Have you written any poems about Sri Lanka yet?' she asked him now, her eyes flickering away from his and towards the deep navy curtain of sky above them.

Max looked up, felt her shoulder warm against his own.

'Not yet,' he replied. 'But if ever a view was going to inspire me . . .'

'I've never seen so many stars before,' she said. 'It's like we're on a different planet.'

Max took a moment to absorb the view.

'What were the skies like in Afghanistan?' Alice asked, clamping her teeth together in a contrite grimace as soon as he looked at her. 'Sorry. You probably don't want to talk about it. Forget I asked.'

But Max looked amused. 'You apologise too much,' he informed her. 'And I'm happy to talk about it – especially with you. The thing is,' he said, 'Afghanistan *is* a beautiful country.'

Alice pulled a disbelieving expression, and Max nodded. 'Honestly! It gets a bad rep, for obvious reasons – and OK, there were times when it did feel bleak and barren – but there were other times when I appreciated it. I can remember sitting outside the mess tent in Camp Bastion, drinking a brew and watching two birds playing in the dust. All these terrible things were happening all around them, but those two little souls were totally sheltered from it all. It reminded me that even in the darkest of corners, there's always light – there's always hope.'

Alice nodded. She appeared to have been struck into silence by the thought.

'When we would go out on missions,' Max continued, 'sometimes we'd be stationed in the arse-end of nowhere, with just the distant ridges of the mountains and the stars to keep us company. The dust was always up, and it made everything appear sepia, like a photo taken in another century or something. I loved it and I hated it, and it scared me and exhilarated me, all at the same time.'

He paused, aware that he had begun to ramble.

'You must think I'm talking nonsense,' he said.

Alice sat up straighter. 'Don't be daft,' she told him. 'We're human beings, not robots, so of course we're capable of feeling a plethora of emotions all at the same time. I know I do.'

Max wanted to ask her for an example, but Alice was looking up at the sky again.

'How many stars do you think there are up there?' she asked after a few moments, her voice low.

'Let's see.' Max lifted his finger and pretended to count. 'At least a thousand.'

'One thousand stars,' she breathed, her words almost a poem on their own, mesmeric as they were. It felt to Max as if they were alone up on this mountain, in a bubble of their own making, where it was safe and always would be.

'And you,' he said, smiling as she turned to face him.

'And me what?' she asked, her expression open.

What could he say? That he felt as if she was the only thing that mattered to him right now, just her, on this step, beneath those stars? Of course he couldn't.

'I'm just glad that you're here,' he said instead, trying to convey through his eyes what he was incapable, suddenly, of saying with words. Max thought that whatever he chose to say in a moment like this would be wrong, either inappropriate or simply banal.

While he was still chasing this conundrum around in his mind, Alice put her hand tentatively over his.

'I'm glad that you're here, too.'

They stayed where they were and watched as the sky

turned from the deepest blueberry to the faintest azure. As the night lifted, the landscape began to emerge below them. Max could see the tips of smaller mountains and the tops of distant trees, each mysterious shape revealing itself inch by slow inch, with the morning mist hanging over the view like finely spun silver. At exactly six-thirty a.m., the throbbing red line of dawn appeared on the horizon, chased up by the sun, and shafts of brilliant light raced across the wild terrain to greet them.

Behind them, up on the summit, bells began to ring, and there was a collective sigh of joy as everyone stood to watch the sun rise. Bunting strips of colourful Buddhist flags fluttered and snapped in the wind above them, the sound adding a tender percussion to the ethereal bells and the whispered messages of love that Max could hear being exchanged.

Alice was still holding his hand, and when Max looked down he saw that her cheeks were wet.

'Hey,' he murmured consolingly, wrapping his arm around her shoulders. 'What's the matter?'

'Nothing.' Alice shook her head, only to screw her face up as more tears followed.

'It's a bit overwhelming, isn't it?' he said gently. 'All this. The sunrise, the temple, all these monks.'

Alice pulled her mouth into a smile, and rubbed at her eyes.

'It's just so beautiful,' she said, again shaking her head as if she could not quite believe what she was seeing. 'It makes a mockery of all the other stuff, all the shit, all the nonsense.'

She had to pause then to allow a small sob to escape, and Max tightened his grip on her.

'This is one of *those* moments,' he told her. 'You don't get many of them in a lifetime, but you know when you do. It will never leave you, this feeling, the one you're experiencing right now.'

Alice made a small snuffling noise.

'Just enjoy it,' he urged. 'Take it all in, bank it. Be comforted by it.'

'You really are a poet,' she muttered, squeezing his hand. 'And in no way corny at all.'

'Thanks,' he said, but it was almost more of a sigh. Shifting a fraction closer to her, he rested his cheek on the top of her head.

The sun was almost full now, and the temperature was rising with every breath that Max felt Alice take. Everyone around them was busily taking photos, but the two of them had yet to move. Max did not want to break the spell that they were in, and he did not want to let go of Alice either. He could feel that her sobs had stopped, but she seemed content to still be wrapped up against him.

'We should get moving,' he heard her say, and Max lowered his ear towards her mouth just as she turned her head. Before he could register what was happening, their lips had brushed softly together, his top against her bottom.

Alice pulled away, her eyes dropping to the dusty ground just as Max mumbled out a 'sorry'. All he could think was that he wasn't sorry – not in the slightest. The encounter had been so brief, over in less time than it took to blink, but he had felt it everywhere – he could still feel it now, in the raised hairs on the back of his neck and the juddering percussion of his heart.

He watched as Alice stretched out her arms, closing her eyes as sunlight bathed her face.

'Ready to go?' she asked, turning to look at him.

'No,' Max replied honestly, thinking about how many steps awaited them. 'But what goes up and all that . . .'

She smiled at that, in what looked like relief, and Max gritted his teeth as he took his first step downwards. The pain ricocheted through his stump, more insistent than ever, but it was no longer the only thing giving Max pause for thought. Because as sure as he could feel the sun warming his cheeks, hear the flapping of the flags in the wind and smell the sweet aroma of chai spices in the air, Max knew the bright spark of affection that had been ignited inside him the day he met Alice had just burst into flames – and he had no idea how he was going to put them out.

## 27

Alice could not remember ever feeling so worn out. The muscles in her thighs were tremoring with fatigue and her ankle and knee joints felt stiff and brittle, as if they could snap with ease. The climb up Adam's Peak had been arduous but fulfilling, while going back down simply felt endless. Even the monkeys, which she had finally spotted peering down at them through the branches of the surrounding trees, did little to perk her up. But Alice knew that it was not only her frazzled body causing her to feel on edge; it was everything spinning around in her head as well.

Max was finding the descent difficult, too. He had not uttered a word of complaint, but she had noticed him wincing as he tackled the steepest steps just below the summit. Moving across to offer him her hand, Alice had been surprised when he shook his head wordlessly to refuse her help. It was ridiculous of her to feel so stung, but that's what his rebuttal had felt like – the sting of a whip, lashing across her throat and causing it to thicken with hurt. After that she had maintained a small distance, hurrying down the steps until she was twenty or so paces ahead of him.

Had she imagined that moment up on the summit? Did she conjure up the feeling of Max's lips brushing against her own, and the look in his eyes when he'd held her in his arms? She knew she had not, but now everything between them felt so entirely different, and Alice could not understand what it was she had done wrong.

'Wait up!'

She turned to find Steph, pink in the face and panting as she jogged down the steps towards her.

'Sorry.' Alice waited for her to catch up. 'I was in the zone, there.'

'Not like you,' Steph joked, smiling despite her heaving chest. Then, 'Do you have anything to tell me?'

Alice frowned.

'Um . . .'

Steph folded her arms across her chest.

'A secret that you've been keeping?'

Had she seen Max hug her at the top of the Peak? Could she see inside Alice's head?

'No,' she said, shaking her head. 'What do you mean?'

'Oh, I dunno, like the secret of what amazing present you've bought me!'

Alice laughed in relief, picturing the tickets to the West End show Steph had wanted to see for months, which were tucked into a side pocket of her backpack back at the guest house.

'Oh, that. Well, I thought the birthday bumps for starters,' she said. 'Unless you'd rather get those from Jamal . . .'

'Well, I wouldn't say no,' Steph replied, a coy look on her face. 'And this is already turning into a birthday I will never forget.' She gestured around them. 'I mean, what a place to turn thirty.'

'One of Maur's better ideas,' agreed Alice. 'I feel so bad for her that she's missing this.'

*But thankful, too*, she acknowledged guiltily.

'I thought it would feel weird, you know, reaching the big three-O,' Steph admitted, following Alice as she started down the next flight of wide steps. 'I thought I would be sad, that it would remind me of the fact that I'm single and childless. But actually, I feel quite happy. Relieved, even.'

'You're not strictly single any more,' Alice pointed out slyly, and Steph blushed even pinker.

'Nothing is official,' she said.

'The way Jamal looks at you is official,' Alice assured her. 'The boy has got it bad.'

'Do you really think so?' Steph sounded genuinely hopeful – so much so, that Alice had to laugh.

'You know he has,' she told her. 'Sometimes these things are as clear as cling film.'

Steph didn't say anything to that, and for the next few minutes they continued to descend in companionable silence. Alice's thoughts strayed yet again to Max, and she sneaked a look backwards over her shoulder to make sure he was still behind them, letting out a breath that she had not been aware she was holding in as he came into view. She had been worried that his injury could cause him to stop altogether, but he still looked as determined as he had on the way up.

She only realised she had stopped walking when Steph tapped her gently on the arm.

'Clear as cling film, was it?' she teased, following Alice's gaze, but there was an undeniable hint of warning in her tone.

They reached the ramshackle hotel just before ten a.m. and found Maureen waiting for them on the wide terrace, a pot of coffee on the table and Max's crutches propped up against a chair. When the food arrived, they all fell on it gratefully, and Alice was so thirsty that she even necked the papaya juice without complaint. They filled Maureen in on the events of the night, both girls being careful to play down just how incredible it had been to watch the sunrise. They didn't want their friend to feel even more hard done by than she already did. Maureen, however, seemed to be back to her carefree and buoyant self, and was soon insisting that Steph have a birthday beer with her breakfast.

Max seemed in better spirits, too, Alice had noted with relief as she returned the smile he offered her when they first sat down. Whatever had happened to sour his mood up on Adam's Peak, it seemed to have been forgotten now, and again Alice was left wondering if she was inventing things. She must stop being so oversensitive.

Max and Jamal had just headed off to get showered when her phone lit up with a call.

'Dickie!' cried Maureen delightedly, but this time Alice had her hand firmly over the handset.

'Hi,' she trilled, her voice uncharacteristically high-pitched. 'You're calling early.'

'Couldn't sleep,' Rich muttered. A disgruntled sigh came down the phone. 'How are things?'

'Yeah, great!' Alice garbled exuberantly, then paused to

clear her throat. 'I just got back from climbing a mountain, actually.'

'Mountain climbing?' Richard was aghast.

'No, no – not that kind. I mean it was more of a hill, really. A peak. It was perfectly safe.'

'Says the girl that fell off a roof,' he joked stiffly, and Alice chuckled far too hard in response. Usually she could tolerate his overprotectiveness, but today it rankled. Why must he always assume the worst when it came to her? She turned around and caught Maureen's enquiring eye, shaking her head slightly to communicate that now was not the time for jokes. She could tell that her boyfriend had something on his mind, and she braced herself.

'So,' he began, his tone studiedly casual. 'Have you three met anyone over there?'

Alice shook her head redundantly. 'Not really.'

'Who are those two guys on Maureen's Instagram then?' he went on, and Alice cringed into the phone.

'Oh, you mean Jamal and Max. They stayed at the same place as us in Habarana, and so we all went to Sigiriya Rock together, and Jamal fancies Steph, so, you know . . .'

'Jamal is the black guy?' Richard guessed, and Alice confirmed that he was. 'So, I'm guessing that if he's after Steph, Maureen's after the other one?'

'You know my friends too well,' she said, a mixture of guilt and relief flooding through her when she realised he did not suspect her of liking either of the two men. Steph and Maureen were both watching her now, their eyebrows hitched in interest at the mention of their names.

'Can't be much fun,' Rich went on. 'Playing gooseberry. I thought this was a girls' trip?'

'It is!' Alice assured him. 'It's not like we're in each other's pockets all the time.'

'Certainly seems that way,' Rich said. Even though he was arguing with her, the pitch of his voice hadn't changed. He was using his history teacher voice on her, and yet again she felt irritation begin to prickle.

'How is everything there?' she asked, choosing to ignore his last comment, and his frosty mood thawed a fraction as he told her about a perch he'd pulled out of the River Stour the previous day.

'Have you heard from your brother?' he asked after a while, and Alice conceded that she had not, remembering as she did so that Freddie had never replied to her message. It had been two days now.

'We were supposed to meet up this weekend,' Richard was telling her. 'It was only a loose arrangement, but he might have texted me to let me know he'd changed his mind. I waited around at the flat all morning.'

'I'm sorry,' Alice said automatically. 'You poor thing.'

It wasn't fair, but suddenly Richard's story about the fish and his grumpiness towards her brother and his predictable passive-aggressive line of questioning about Max and Jamal felt ridiculous. He was so predictable – she had always known that. It used to comfort her, but today she just felt weary of it. And of him, if she was brutally honest. It felt horribly disloyal to compare Richard to Max, but Alice couldn't help it. The two men could not have been more different. And now Rich was chuntering on about Freddie and time-wasting and rudeness, and she simply could not be bothered to listen to it.

'Rich,' she said, her tone just as stern as his had been a few minutes ago. 'I have to go. We have to catch a train soon.'

'It never seems to be a good time,' he complained, and Alice gritted her teeth.

'I'm sorry about my brother, but it's really nothing to do with me. Just call him yourself and sort it out.'

There was a silence as Richard digested her words, as well he might struggle to, given the fact that she rarely, if ever, told him off. Alice didn't know if it was her exhaustion from the climb or the fact that Richard had pulled at the Max thread, but whatever it was, she was fed up.

'You obviously don't want to talk,' Rich stated, and Alice could picture the hurt look on his face.

'Rich, sorry. I'm just—'

'Don't worry,' he said flatly. 'Get back to your friends.'

He had put so much sarcastic emphasis on the last word that he could only have been referring to Max and Jamal, but before Alice could come up with a suitable response, Rich had gone.

# 28

Less than a full day had passed since the five of them had been on the train, but Alice felt as if it had been weeks. Max had been spot on that morning, when he had told her that she was experiencing a moment that was special, unforgettable, even magical – and now she was sitting in one of the train's open doorways, staring far into the distance at the very same peak she had stood on just hours before. Speeding away from it like this made it seem as if the moment had been fleeting – a mere page in her story. But to Alice it had felt like much more than that. Being up there, so separated from the rest of the world and everyone in it, had reminded her of just how much beauty there was in the world, and how much she desperately wanted to see more of it.

They had departed from Hatton on a packed train at around lunchtime, passing through Nuwara Eliya station an hour or so later, where enough people had disembarked to free up some seats inside the carriage. Exhausted from the climb and their lack of sleep, Jamal and Steph had soon nodded off with their arms draped across one other, while Max shuffled down and rested his head against the window and Maureen disappeared behind the hardback shell of the latest Marian Keyes novel. As the Sri Lankan eagle flew, it was only fifty-four kilometres to Ella, where they would stay for the night, but the train would take at least a further three hours to get there because of all the mountain ranges it had to pass through on the way.

Alice had struggled to settle on her plastic seat, fidgeting in a hopeless effort to get comfortable and chewing at her already bitten-down fingernails. That morning's disastrous phone call with Rich was preying on her mind, along with a host of other things she dared not analyse, and after a while she had come out to sit in the doorway, her plan being that the view and the breeze would chase her discombobulation away.

She lifted her camera and snapped a few frames of the peak, zooming in but finding it impossible to focus as the train swayed and clattered beneath her.

'Room for a little one?'

Alice turned to find Max standing over her, his expression unreadable and his hair standing up on one side where his head had been resting against the train window. She shifted wordlessly to one side, and waited as he slowly lowered himself, before bending over to prop his prosthetic foot on one of the wooden steps leading out of the carriage.

'How are you feeling?' Alice asked, recalling how he had winced as they made their way back down Adam's Peak.

'Like I haven't slept for about three days,' Max said, yawning widely but turning it into a smile. 'But it was totally worth it.'

'I can't believe I cried,' Alice said now, turning red. 'I'm blaming my impending old age.'

'Hey!' Max nudged her with an elbow. 'Less of the old. I've got over three years on you, remember?'

'You don't look a day over fifty-eight,' she retorted, and he laughed.

'So,' he began, pausing to wave at two young children as the train trundled past a tiny village. 'It's your birthday in two days' time – what do you want?'

Alice inclined her head, puzzled by the question.

'Come on – we can't let you turn thirty and not mark it somehow. How about a coconut carved to look like a monkey? Or a year's supply of papayas?'

'Both sound incredible,' she said, unable not to grin at him. She was glad they were back to taking the mickey out of one another again.

'But what is it that you really want?' he asked, and this time Alice found that she could detect no humour in his expression. His eyes beneath his light-brown fringe were tinged pink with fatigue, but they were serious.

'I have no idea,' she said quietly, unnerved slightly by the sudden intensity in his eyes, and the possible weight of his question. 'I don't know what I want any more.'

'I gave my ex, Faye, a ring on her birthday,' he said, raising his voice so she could hear him over the sound of the train.

Alice felt something twist inside her guts.

'I was young and infatuated,' he told her with a sad sort of smile. 'Twenty-two, for God's sake. I had no business getting married to anyone at that age.'

'What made you do it?' Alice asked.

'I thought I was in love, is the simple answer,' he replied, chewing thoughtfully on his thumbnail. 'I was going away with the army, and I thought I was being romantic.'

'I'm sure you were,' Alice assured him, but Max pulled a face.

'I was a wet-behind-the-ears boy, then,' he insisted. 'Faye and I had been together since school, I didn't know any different.'

'At least you weren't afraid to try,' Alice said, leaning back quickly to avoid being whipped in the face by a thicket of bushes beside the track. They could no longer see Adam's Peak in the distance, and were instead skimming past dense forests. She took a deep breath and detected the fresh scent of eucalyptus underneath the more overpowering pine.

'Was it a big wedding?' she asked, but Max shook his head.

'Nah, we did it at Islington Town Hall, in London, then went to the dogs for our reception.'

'The dogs?' Even Alice was surprised by that revelation.

Max chuckled. 'Faye's dad was into dog racing, and he was paying. Plus, neither of us were too fussed about having a big fancy ceremony, so . . .'

'Do you still see her?' Alice asked, and Max's smile slipped down at the edges.

'Not since we split,' he said. 'She's still with the guy she cheated on me with, so I guess he was the one for her.'

'I'm sorry.' Alice knotted her fingers together in her lap.

'Don't be,' Max sounded resolute. 'She did me a favour by leaving. It meant there was one less person I had to feel guilty towards. If she had stayed out of some sort of perceived duty, then our marriage would have been bullshit, if you'll excuse the term.'

For a moment, he looked uncomfortable, and Alice nodded to reassure him.

'Nobody wants bullshit in their life,' she sighed, then stopped as a local seller of 'short eats' edged behind them on the train, shouting about his selection of wares over the din from the overhead fans and busy pistons.

'You don't strike me as someone who puts up with any bullshit,' Max said, and Alice laughed, because he was so far off the mark.

'What?' he pushed. 'What's so funny?'

'I don't know why I'm laughing,' she said, turning her head away. 'It's in no way funny.'

'You've lost me,' Max told her, sounding bewildered.

'The thing is—' Alice took a deep breath, then continued before her nerve got the better of her, 'I'm the one who is full of bullshit. Just this morning, I lied to my boyfriend for no reason. No reason at all.'

There was a short silence as Max took this in. Alice expected him to ask for details, or even look at her with disappointment, but he didn't. He simply sighed deeply, then reached up as if he was going to tuck a strand of her hair behind her ear, before thinking better of it.

'Have you ever told me any lies?' he asked.

Alice moved her chin slowly up and down.

'Probably.'

'I see.'

'But not about anything important,' she added hastily, anxious that he not misread her meaning. The truth was, she had been more honest with Max than she was with a lot of people, and it felt important to her that he know that. 'It's weird, but the truth is that I can't lie to you – not about the big stuff.'

Now Max looked as if he didn't believe her, and proved it a moment later by asking, 'How do I know you're not lying right now?'

'You don't, I suppose,' Alice said, frustrated by how inept she was at getting her point across. 'But it's true.'

Max considered her, his head on one side. The sunlight filtering in through the trees was casting stark shadows across his face.

'I've got an idea,' he said at last. 'How about I ask you some questions, and you answer each one of them truthfully?'

Alice felt a cold touch of dread.

'OK,' she croaked, not wanting to appear a spoilsport. He must have an agenda here – or perhaps after his ex lied to him so catastrophically, he simply preferred people he could trust to tell him the truth?

Max lifted an eyebrow. 'Right, we'll start with an easy one. What do you want most in the whole world?'

'That is *not* an easy one,' Alice joked, frowning at him.

'Come on,' he urged. 'If I was to sprout wings and magic a fairy wand out of my backside, what would you wish for?'

'More adventures,' Alice said, her smile matching his. 'And travel. Sri Lanka has officially given me the bug.'

'See,' Max gave her a slow smile. 'Not as hard as you think, is it?'

'I guess not,' she allowed. 'But what I want and what I can realistically get are two very different things.'

Max ignored her last comment, tapping the fingers of his right hand on the hard socket just below his knee. He was in shorts, Mister Tee uncovered and glowing in the sunlight.

'I'm thinking,' he said, and Alice pulled her mouth into a tight line of amusement.

'Right,' he said after a beat. 'Question two: are you happy with your boyfriend?'

Alice flushed with surprise. She had guessed that he might venture down this path of enquiry, but she had not yet had time to prepare a response that felt both honest and neutral enough not to scare him off from talking to her again.

'I don't see why,' she began, shaking her head. 'I mean, I think it's silly to . . .'

'It's a yes or no question,' Max pointed out gently. 'Just pick one.'

'I don't like this game,' she said, trying to joke her way out of it, but Max remained steadfast.

'You agreed to the terms,' he said plainly. 'And I have lost serious man points by telling you about my ex-wife doing the dirty behind my back. This is just to even the balance, so please humour me. And anyway,' he added, 'there's nobody here except you and me – nobody else can hear you.'

What he didn't seem to understand, thought Alice, was that she was here. She would hear the answer that came out of her mouth, and she wasn't sure she was ready to. There shouldn't be a pause between his question and her affirmative 'yes', but here it was, gaping open in her mind like a cavern.

'I think,' she began, and Max looked at her with encouragement. Alice stared at his thick, straight brows, his blue eyes above that neat nose and the swell of his lips, and tried to draw out the strength in herself that she could see within Max.

'I think my answer is going to have to be yes.'

# 29

'*Ayubowan*! Daughters, daughters, welcome! And sons, come in. You are welcome, all very welcome.'

'Thank you.' Steph spoke first, grasping the outstretched hands of the diminutive Sri Lankan man standing on the steps in front of them. There was a small yellow stain on the front of his white shirt and his red-and-gold trousers were turned up at the bottom.

'I am Doctor Perera,' he announced. 'This is my home, but you are very welcome. Very welcome.'

Alice removed her dusty trainers using only her feet, and pushed them neatly to one side. Max and Jamal were just behind them, having taken a separate tuk-tuk from Ella's train station up to the Sunshine Lodge homestay, and as soon as their enthusiastic host had ushered Alice, Steph and Maureen inside, he spotted Max's prosthetic leg and beamed.

'Come, come,' he beckoned, so eager to get Max on his sofa that he didn't seem to care about his grubby shoes on the white tiles. Everything in the wide open living space seemed to be white, from the walls to the large ceiling fan to the leather settee and matching chairs – even the cushions were white. Alice, who felt hot and dust-covered from the long journey, perched awkwardly on the edge of a hard-backed wooden chair that was pushed up against the wall.

'You were in the army, yes?' the doctor stated without preamble, and Max nodded in good humour.

'Good guess.'

Without waiting for an invitation, Doctor Perera knelt on the white rug and began rolling up the bottom of Max's shorts with both his tiny hands.

Maureen giggled nervously, while Jamal arched a bemused eyebrow.

'Ah, yes,' the doctor said, frowning as he examined Mister Tee in more detail, then started muttering away to himself in Sinhalese.

Steph and Alice exchanged a look.

The doctor seemed lost in thought, his grey head tilted slightly to one side and a faraway look on his lined face. When it became clear that he wasn't going to let go of Max, Jamal stepped forwards and waved a friendly hand.

'Can we check in?' he asked, sounding more entertained than anything else. 'We've been on a train for about a week, or so it feels like.'

'Seven days, yes,' bellowed the doctor, roaring with laughter as he sat back on his haunches.

What was it with middle-aged Sri Lankan hosts? Alice wondered. Chatura back in Kandy had been the same – always smiling and ready with a laugh. It was endearing.

'A very long way. Did you come from Kandy?'

'Hatton,' Max told him. 'We climbed Adam's Peak this morning.'

'You?' Doctor Perera exclaimed, and Max nodded.

'Yes, even me.'

'But not me,' put in Maureen, who in contrast to Alice

had already made herself at home by snuggling into the armchair. 'I hurt my ankle when I fell off—'

'Very good,' shouted the doctor, interrupting her. 'Tea, yes?'

They all said 'yes, please', guessing that to refuse would be futile, and as soon as Doctor Perera had vanished from view, Alice let go of the laugh she had been suppressing.

'He's brilliant!' she whispered as loudly as she dared. 'What a character.'

Max went to roll his shorts back down over his stump, but then thought better of it.

'I doubt he's finished with me,' he said, catching Alice's eye, and she grinned back at him.

'Tea. Very good,' said Doctor Perera, emerging back through an open doorway a few minutes later. The tray he was carrying was almost as big as he was, and Jamal hurried over to help him.

'Thank you, son.'

He sat down on the sofa and smiled widely at them.

'Shall I pour the tea, then?' said Steph, and again Alice had to cover her mouth to keep her snuffle of laughter inside.

Doctor Perera was looking at Max as if he was Buddha himself, and as they each took a dainty china cup and sipped the black, vanilla-scented tea, he explained in broken English that he was a retired surgeon, and that he had worked on many amputations.

'Sri Lanka has many landmines,' he said sadly, gesturing beyond the windows with the hand that wasn't holding a cup. 'We try to clear all, but many are hidden.'

He tapped Max's right knee.

'Landmine?' he asked, and Max nodded.

'IED,' he said. 'Do you know what that is?'

'Yes.' The doctor nodded forlornly. 'Very bad.'

Max shrugged with one shoulder. 'It's OK,' he said. 'It happened a long time ago now.'

'Shall I take a look for you? Check everything is well after the climb?' Doctor Perera questioned hopefully, and Alice became immediately aware of Max's discomfort.

'Maybe later,' he said. 'After a shower.'

Presumably thinking that Max was worried about getting dirt on the white sofa, the doctor started shaking his head and smiling, telling him not to worry and that it was not a problem. Max looked towards Jamal for help, but his friend merely widened his eyes in defeat.

'We can go to our room if . . .' Alice began, making to stand up, but the doctor was already feeling his way along Max's thigh to where the top of the liner sat taut against his skin. There was a fine line between being charmingly eccentric and a pain in the behind, and right now, thought Alice, Doctor Perera was walking right along it.

'Fine.' Max gave in. 'Jamal, can you grab my crutches, mate?'

Alice watched as Max quickly removed his prosthesis, not missing how intrigued Steph and Maureen were by the whole thing. Of course, neither of them had been there when Max had removed Mister Tee halfway up Adam's Peak, so it made sense.

Once the leg was off, the doctor knelt again on his pristine rug and ran his finger across Max's smile-shaped scar.

'Very good, very good,' he said, his ears lifting with his grin. He then ran an exploratory hand around the stump and patted it on each side, before letting it rest in his open hand. It was at that moment, when the base of Max's residual limb came into contact with Doctor Perera's palm, that Max flinched. It wasn't a jerk or even a wince, but it was something – and Alice was not the only person who had noticed it.

'Everything all right there, mate?' said Jamal, kneeling next to Doctor Perera before Max had time to react.

'Fine.' Max swung his stump to one side, but Jamal was too quick for him, reaching out and squeezing the base with his fingers.

There it was again, that flicker of discomfort. This time on Max's face as well as in the movement of his body. Jamal, whose own expression had now lost any trace of humour, lifted the limb to get a better look.

'Shit,' he said, letting go before turning to Max. 'How long has it been hurting?'

'It's not.'

Alice shifted on her chair. She could tell that Max wasn't being honest.

The doctor, apparently realising that a disagreement of sorts was brewing in his living room, scuttled off in the direction of the kitchen, muttering something about biscuits.

'Please don't do this,' Jamal said with a sigh, sitting back on his heels as Max collected his crutches.

'I'm not in any pain.'

'Really?' Jamal looked incredulous. 'Really, mate?'

'Look, it's nothing, just a bit of cramp,' Max said now,

his face beginning to colour. Alice wished she could get up and give the two of them some privacy, but with no room yet to go to, they were stuck.

'I wish I could believe you,' Jamal sighed. 'But we've been here before, remember?'

'Leave it out, all right?' Max was starting to get fed up now, and the stricken look on his face was enough to convince Alice to get up from her chair and hurry across the rug to the sofa, where she sat down next to Max and placed a comforting hand on his shoulder.

'Don't worry,' she told him, not knowing what else she could really say, but wanting him to know that she was there, that she was on his side.

'There is plenty he should be worried about,' Jamal said, turning to Alice. 'If he's been keeping his pain from me, then it is very much not all right.'

'I just think we should all take a breath here,' Maureen suggested. 'Let's not start accusing or snapping at anyone.'

'How long?' Jamal asked again, ignoring her, and Alice saw Maureen narrow her eyes.

'Just drop it, OK?' Max said shortly, his obvious anger making Alice go cold. Jamal moved out of his way as he used his crutches to stand up.

'Doctor Perera,' Max said loudly, and the door to the kitchen opened a crack. 'Can we see our rooms, please?'

'Yes, yes – sorry. I am coming.' The doctor was beaming his head off again, determinedly oblivious to the frosty atmosphere that had settled in the room.

He jangled a set of keys in his hand.

'Daughters,' he said, beckoning for Alice, Steph and Maureen to follow him back out of the front door.

Alice hesitated. Max was standing with his back to her, while Jamal was shaking his head. There was nothing more she could do here – they didn't need her.

'Will we see you for dinner in a few hours?' she asked Jamal, and he nodded, barely registering her words.

Whatever it was that Max had been hiding, it must be serious to have upset the affable Jamal to this degree. The thought of him being in pain made Alice's stomach twist into knots of misery. She knew then that if she could, she would take away his pain – every last atom of it.

# 30

# Max

*If I should die,*
*I will not be gone,*
*My body may be absent,*
*But my soul will live on . . .*

Max sat on the low stool in the shower, the warm running water flattening his hair and filling up his eyes. He blinked rapidly to clear them, raising a hand to wipe the droplets from his nose. His shower gel's frothy lather had collected in the dark patch of hair on his stomach, and below that his legs stretched out above the tiles, one whole and strong and thick with muscle, the other misshapen and swollen and reduced. In this moment, and for the first time in a very long while, Max hated his physical impairment with a burning rage that made him want to yell with the unfairness of it all.

Jamal was pissed off with him, and Max could appreciate why. His friend understood better than anyone how devastating it would be for Max if he ended up back in hospital, and really, Max thought with a sigh, it wasn't rocket science, was it? Listen to your body, watch out for irregularities and don't, under any circumstances whatsoever, ignore pain of any kind. Max had broken the rules, and now he was paying the price.

As well as the tingling pain in the end of his residual limb, there was also a soft area of what felt like swollen tissue, and a small red patch that looked like a splatter of ink. Max did not want to think the worst, that the awful bleeding into the skin that he'd had years ago had returned, along with what could very easily be an ulceration. The latter was by far the more serious problem of the two, and Max hoped that instead, the swelling was merely a temporary irritation that would return to normal with a few days' rest.

He could already hear his mother's voice in his ear, her reactions so predictable.

'I said you should never have gone on that holiday . . . Why did you have to climb a mountain? . . . My poor baby!'

Max knew that if he did end up back in hospital, then no matter what he said and how much he pleaded, his mum would be there, from minute one until he was discharged, and then she would insist on taking time off work to become his nurse again. It was bad enough that he was still living at home – albeit in the specially adapted granny annexe at the end of his parents' garden – but now, Max accepted with reluctance, he would be causing the family even more worry and trouble. If the pain was what he feared, then it could mean further surgery on his stump and Mister Tee might no longer fit. And that wasn't even the worst-case scenario.

It had taken him so many years and so many reassurances – to his mum, in particular – to get to the point where his parents didn't fret about him almost constantly. Anything serious enough to land him back in hospital would undo all that progress, and he would have to start right at the beginning again. His mother was still, after eight years, constantly researching new surgeries that he could have – private procedures that cost enough to warrant remortgaging their house. It was utterly ridiculous and Max was not in the slightest bit interested in any of them, but what rankled the most was his mum's sole reason behind it – she wanted him to be 'back to normal again'. As far as he was concerned, he was more himself now than he had been before his injury – and wasn't that just as good as normal? And what did 'normal' mean, anyway? For his mum, it meant whole again, and that was never going to happen.

Max had tried many times to explain to her that he may have lost a limb, but that in the years since he'd gained so much more, and grown so much more. He was more of a man now than he'd been when he left for Afghanistan, back when he was putting on a tough-guy act the whole time, and he was still her son. While she would listen and nod and pat his hand, his words never seemed to sink in. His mother's favourite phrase had always been, 'I'm your mum, I know what's best for you.' She had been parroting that line since he was a little boy, and he feared that in her mind, at least, he still was one, and a broken one at that. She seemed unable to look at him without zoning in on what was physically missing, and he longed for the day she would be able to move past that ridiculous mental roadblock.

Max knew that his mum blamed herself for what had happened to him, even though it made no sense. She had never tried to talk him out of joining the army, and so therefore she carried the burden of blame for what came next. Part of the reason he had come away to Sri Lanka in the first place was to show her just how 'normal' he was still capable of being, and now, thanks to this wretched new pain, his plan had been ruined.

The shower had started to run cold as he sat there contemplating, and Max leaned across guiltily and turned it off. Jamal would have even more reason to be annoyed with him now that he'd inadvertently nicked all the hot water. When he emerged from the bathroom in a cloud of steam a few minutes later, however, his friend was nowhere to be seen. Jamal's rucksack lay open on one of the twin beds, its insides spewed out across the top sheet and the floor below, and his phone was plugged into a charger on the bedside table. He had probably gone to spend some more time with the birthday girl.

Max was just rooting through his own bag for some clean clothes when he heard a tentative knock on the door.

'Max?' a girl's voice called.

'Hang on,' he called, rearranging his towel around his waist. 'Come on in.'

He had assumed it would be Alice, so when the door opened and Maureen stepped boldly into the room, he raised his eyebrows in surprise.

'Oh, hello.'

'Sorry.' She looked suddenly unsure of herself. 'You hoped I'd be Alice.'

'No, no.' Max was contrite. 'Not at all. What can I do for you?'

'Now there's a loaded question,' she replied, flashing him that flirtatious smile he'd become so accustomed to seeing. Max couldn't help but feel flattered that she liked him – Maureen was a beautiful girl, and seriously sparky, too. He could do a lot worse.

'I actually came to check on you,' she went on. 'Is your, erm, leg really OK?'

Max took a long breath in through his nose.

'Not really,' he admitted with a frown, realising that there was no point in lying any more. 'But it will be, hopefully. It's just a bit swollen, that's all.'

Maureen glanced down to below Max's towel, to where one wet foot glistened. He'd used his crutches to get from the bathroom to his bed, and was balancing on them now, as he stood in front of her.

'You're in great shape,' Maureen pointed out, and Max laughed.

'Cheers.'

He didn't feel embarrassed at all, Max mused, even though they were both very aware that he was naked save for his towel. While he felt hyper-awake whenever Alice was with him, Maureen brought out his more light-hearted side. She radiated fun and frivolity, while Alice was often quiet and came across as more thoughtful. He supposed that was why the two girls' friendship worked, because they were able to balance one another out. If Max was to guess, he'd say that Steph was the mother hen of the group. There was something very grounded and calm about her – she and Jamal had that trait in common.

'I have to stay relatively fit,' Max told her, sitting down

on the nearest bed and gesturing to Maureen that she should follow suit. 'Boring, but true. If I put too much weight on, or lose too much, I risk my prosthetic leg not fitting. It can take months to get a replacement socket from the clinic, and they don't come cheap. I don't want to be more of a burden on the NHS than I have to be.'

'Well,' she said, looking at him from under her eyelashes. 'It looks good on you.'

'I could bore you all day long about calorie content,' Max told her, picking up a second, smaller towel, and using it to dry his upper body.

'It wouldn't be anything I hadn't heard before,' Maureen assured him. 'I think I've been talking about calories since I was about twelve – depressing but true.'

Max regarded her through narrowed eyes.

'You look good too, you know,' he said, returning the compliment.

Maureen didn't blush at his words, as he guessed Alice would have; she merely flicked her dark snake of a ponytail off her shoulder and smiled.

'It's because I'm so busy all the time,' she explained. 'I do yoga, but that's about it.'

Max listened as she chatted for a while about the merits of Downward Dog and meditation, pulling a T-shirt over his head and rubbing the second towel through his wet hair. He wanted to put his pants on, but didn't want to appear rude by asking Maureen to give him some privacy. As much as he liked her, there was a certain amount of effort behind their conversation – the chatter didn't flow like it did when he was with Alice. Maureen was regaling him now with stories about the various dates she'd been on, and men she'd rejected for being too needy, too poor, too possessive, or – in one puzzling case – too nice. It was the same topic that she'd chosen before, when they were exploring the Botanical Gardens in Kandy, and he assumed it must be her go-to option when talking to members of the opposite sex. Max knew he wasn't contributing much to the conversation, but he couldn't quite muster up enough energy to try.

'What have you got Alice for her birthday?' he asked, picking a subject he could at least be enthusiastic about.

Maureen pulled a face.

'It's my birthday first!'

Max held up his hands in mock surrender. 'Sorry – of course it is. What have you got planned?'

'Well, that's kind of what I wanted to talk to you about,' Maureen began. 'I was wondering if you wanted to do something, you know, just the two of us.'

Her expression made Max become even more aware that he was naked under the towel.

'Like what?' he said, rubbing his hair again so he wouldn't have to look at her.

Maureen hesitated.

'Aren't we all going to Pudumayaki National Park tomorrow?' he said. 'Wasn't that the plan?'

'Yes, but . . .' Maur stopped again, her cheeks reddening slightly. 'I meant in the evening. Dinner, maybe, or just a few drinks.'

'That is . . .' Max trailed off. He wasn't sure how to say no without sounding rude, and wondered if he should just agree. It was only dinner and drinks, after all. It wasn't as if he was going to do anything. And even if he did, why did it matter?

But it was hopeless. He knew why.

'Listen, Maur,' he said, making himself meet her green eyes with his own. 'I'm really flattered, but I don't think it would be fair on the others. It's your thirtieth birthday – Steph and Alice would never forgive me if I stole you away for the evening.'

'Well, that's a load of crap,' she replied, her expression turning hard. 'If you don't fancy me, you can just say so.'

'It's not that I don't. I mean, you're great – any man would be lucky to . . .' He realised that his words were doing the very opposite of appeasing her. She seemed angry now.

'Is this because of Alice?' she asked, and Max coloured despite himself. He realised her anger wasn't directed at him.

'No, of course not.'

'Did she warn you off me – is that it?'

Max actually laughed at that, because it was so unlike anything he could imagine Alice ever doing. Maureen stood up abruptly, her eyes flashing with hurt.

'You know what,' she said, her voice choked with bitterness. 'I think Alice has been with Dickie so long that she's forgotten what it's like to be single. Just because her own relationship is boring, she sees fit to mess around with everyone else's.'

'Alice hasn't said anything to me about you,' Max told her honestly, quickly swallowing the question he wanted to ask, about Alice's relationship with Richard apparently being tedious. She had told him on the train that she was happy, but Alice did not seem like the type of girl who would be satisfied with stagnation. 'Honestly, this is all me. I'm just not looking to meet anyone at the moment – not as anything other than a friend, anyway. I'm sorry,' he added, as her forthright temper dissolved into humiliation, and she cast her eyes to the floor.

'We can still go out,' he went on. 'I could use a big night out, truth be told – something to take my mind off the old leg.'

Maureen stared down at the space below the bottom of his towel, almost as if she had forgotten all about his missing limb, and for a second Max's heart went out to her. Before he could open his mouth to try to fix things, however, Maureen had turned and was walking away towards the door.

'We could go out tonight.' She paused, her manner softening. 'All of us, I mean. But only if you're feeling well enough.'

Max thought about his swollen, painful stump. The sleep he'd missed over the past twenty-four hours and the cluster of red dots spreading across the rippled join of his scar.

Then he pictured Alice, smiling at him.

'I wouldn't miss it for all the tea in Sri Lanka,' he said.

## 31

It was dusk by the time they left Doctor Perera's homestay and made the short tuk tuk journey down the hill towards Ella's rudimentary village centre. The sun that Alice and Max had watched rise together that morning was almost ready to slip away behind the distant mountains, and its fiery orb was now the dark-gold colour of lentil curry. The scenery in this part of Sri Lanka was dramatic, with sweeping, shamrock-green valleys, hillside tea plantations and the occasional glisten of a river far below the roads. The evening air was damp and a good few degrees cooler than it had been up in the Cultural Triangle.

Alice had left her hooded top on her bed in the girls' room, and she shivered as the air rushed through the open sides of their tuk-tuk. It was nice to feel a chill – it reminded her of being back at the top of Adam's Peak. The experience already felt as if it had happened days ago, rather than hours, and she was seized with fear that soon the memory would fade, and she would forget how it had felt to reach that summit and see the daylight pouring like bright treacle over the landscape. She knew that for the rest of her life, she would think back to the month she turned thirty and have not one single regret about the adventure she had marked it with.

Alice had never done anything as special and meaningful as that uphill trek, not even during all her years with

Richard. She tried to imagine how it would have felt to scale the peak with him, rather than Max, and the contrast saddened her. Rich would not have enjoyed himself – he would have been far too concerned about the probability of them both contracting a bacterial infection from the rudimentary bathrooms en route to appreciate the beauty of the place, and of the people. It had never used to bother her too much that she and Rich had vastly different interests – she had merely accepted that while he was her boyfriend, that did not mean he had to be by her side all the time. But what she was beginning to realise now, was that she wanted to share experiences with someone. She could easily have climbed Adam's Peak by herself, but would it have felt as magical? Wasn't that the whole point of relationships – and of love? Having someone there to share your adventures with, and knowing they wanted to be in that moment with you?

Rich would not dive with her, or climb with her, or travel the world with her. But he did love her – of that, at least, Alice was certain. If anything, he loved her too much. It was why he felt such a strong need to protect her, from herself more than anything else.

She was snapped back from Wonderland to reality as they rounded a corner at speed, and she promptly fell against Steph, who in turn squashed Maureen. Jamal and Max were in the tuk-tuk behind theirs – Alice could just about hear the nasal purr of its engine. She was relieved that Max was coming with them, but this was making her suffer a two-pronged attack of guilt. Firstly, because she was worried about the pain in his right leg, and knew he should probably be resting, and secondly because she shouldn't, in all honesty, be craving his company as much as she was. She had wanted to go and check on him earlier, following the confrontation he'd had with Jamal, but Maureen had insisted that she go instead, telling Alice that she could have first dibs on the shower. Doctor Perera had installed better showers than Alice had seen anywhere – not just in Sri Lanka – and it had been blissful to step underneath the hot flowing water and feel the aches and pains of the arduous climb easing away.

Steph had played the birthday girl card and persuaded Alice to wear a far tighter dress than she usually would, while an oddly distracted Maureen had helped coerce her stubbornly straight hair into messy, beachy waves, which Alice was continually fiddling with now as they drove. She had never really been a girl who dressed to impress, but today she had wanted to look different, more grown-up. She felt different, too, but she knew it was not solely because she was nearing an age milestone. Her rebellious and reckless side, which she had successfully, for the most part, trapped under a tight lid since her accident, was making a concerted bid for freedom. She could feel it there, just under the surface, and was rapidly losing any inclination she had to stop it. Just the fact she had agreed to wear one of Steph's tightest and shortest black dresses for their night out was proof that sensible Alice had been left on the train somewhere between Hatton and Ella. Bad Alice was out to play tonight, and the thought of her taking hold of the reins once again was exciting, even if she knew deep down that it was probably a knee-jerk reaction to the row she'd had with Richard over the phone. He would not be impressed to see her with this much foundation caked on, and he would tut at the high hemline of her dress. His argument would be that this wasn't her, that she didn't need either of these things to look nice – and he might be right on both counts. But tonight, for some reason, Alice felt as if she did need them. She wanted to plaster over her confused emotions with metaphorical Polyfilla.

The tuk-tuk driver dropped them off halfway along the main road that snaked through the heart of Ella, making sure they took one of his little business cards so that they might call him later for a lift back. Alice had quite a collection of them now, and she stowed this new one in the zip-up pocket of her bag with the others. There were bars, restaurants and shops dotted all the way along the street, most with thatched roofs and wooden floors, and most of the people Alice could see strolling past appeared to be tourists rather than locals. Ella was a popular stop-off point for anyone making the journey down to the south of the country from Adam's Peak or Kandy, and she was looking forward to exploring. Maureen was adamant that they make time for shopping, while Alice was eager to go on safari the following day. Steph, as always, was happy simply to tag along with whatever excursion they chose, although Alice suspected what her besotted friend really wanted was some proper alone time with the new object of her affection.

She watched Jamal now as he clambered out of the second tuk-tuk, holding out his hand to grab Max's crutches. The two men seemed to be back on speaking terms, but Alice hadn't managed to get Max alone yet to ask him if he was OK. Maureen had assured her that he was, but the appearance of the crutches could not be ignored. She hated the idea of him being in pain.

'Shall we just head over there?' Maureen suggested, tugging down the bottom of her denim hot pants. She, too, had left her warmer top back at the homestay, and Alice could see goosebumps on her arms.

They all looked across the road to where a two-storey bar called Kamikaze glowed with inviting light. It was open-fronted with a treehouse-like terrace as its top tier, and music filtered out from amongst tables cluttered with young travellers. After wandering up the steps, they were quickly ushered to a large circular table by a bearded waiter wearing gold trousers and a red shirt. Alice, who was determined to eat only local food while she was in Sri Lanka, was dismayed when the waiter reeled off a list of Western dishes, including beef burgers and pasta carbonara.

'Do you have kottu roti?' she asked, smiling as the waiter nodded at her, 'with eggs, chicken and extra chillies, please.'

'Remind me what that is again,' said Steph, her blonde hair a halo of frizz.

'Chopped bread – well, flatbreads,' Alice replied. 'Then it's fried, and you add toppings.'

'Yum,' Steph said, always easy to please. 'I'll have the same.'

Maureen was just in the middle of ordering a fish curry when Alice's phone lit up with a message. Distracted, she picked it up and swiped her finger across the screen, only to roll her eyes.

'Who is it?' Steph asked.

'My mum,' Alice informed the table. 'Checking that I'm still alive, as per usual.'

'Oh, bless Mrs Brockley,' Steph said kindly, but Alice wasn't listening.

'Freddie still hasn't texted me back,' she said, hearing the concern in her own voice as the realisation sunk in.

'I'm sure he's just busy and forgot,' Steph was quick to offer, adding, 'Freddie's her older brother,' to Jamal. Max finished giving his order of Ceylonese spit chicken and touched Alice's arm.

'Men are useless at replying to texts,' he assured her, but Alice shook her head.

'Freds never forgets – he makes a massive deal out of it if I ever leave him hanging. Maybe it just didn't deliver or something – I might message him again,' she decided.

'You had better be trapped under something heavy, unable to reach your phone,' she read aloud as she typed, 'or there will be hell to pay, Mister.'

Steph giggled.

'There.' Alice stowed her phone in her bag and clasped her hands together. 'That ought to do it.'

Maureen sucked at her teeth in what sounded like irritation, and Jamal glanced her way.

'Everything OK?' he asked.

'Fine,' she said, tossing her mane of dark hair around like a stroppy pony and picking up the bottle of Lion Lager that the waiter had just deposited in front of her. 'Now, are we going to get drunk, or what?'

## 32

It was a subdued group of five who tossed their backpacks into the minibus the following morning, and Alice clutched her head with both hands after she clambered into the seat by the window. Getting absolutely hammered when you had to be up at six a.m. the next day was not the best idea Alice had ever had – but then it had been a lot of fun. Well, the parts of the night she could remember, anyway. She knew there had been singing, and a copious amount of beer, and quite possibly a game of I Have Never.

'I feel sick,' muttered Steph from behind her, and Alice hid her laugh behind her hand. Maureen, who was up in her habitual spot next to the driver and wearing a 'birthday girl' badge pinned to her vest top, wound down the window to allow some air into the van, then let out a long, hung-over groan.

Doctor Perera had come out to wave them off, having insisted that they all have a photo taken with him for his guest book. 'All my sons and daughters,' he told Alice proudly, tapping the book's brown leather front. She wondered what had encouraged him to open the doors of his beautiful house to foreign strangers after what she guessed must have been a long and hectic career. But then again, she was learning that this was the Sri Lankan way – all the people she had encountered so far were as open with their homes as they seemed to be with their hearts.

It would take them at least three hours to reach Pudumayaki National Park, by which time Alice hoped that her lingering headache would have lost the battle against the two paracetamol she had taken after breakfast. She had noticed Max swallow what looked like painkillers, too, but guessed that his were more to combat the pain in his leg than the after-effects of too much alcohol. In fact, he didn't seem to be suffering much at all in that regard, and had assured her that he was 'peachy, thanks' when she asked if he was OK.

As the minibus continued to wind down through the hills, Alice's beer-sozzled mind began to feel soothed by the scenery. They left behind the deep valleys and dark shiny leaves of the tea plantations and drove past plains flooded with water. The mountains were still visible, but far away now, in the distance, their irregular outlines blurred by the dancing heat. The further south they journeyed, the more traffic they encountered, and the thicker and more humid the air pouring in through the open windows.

Jamal opened a packet of crisps and passed them round, feeding some straight into Steph's open mouth. He had presented her with a beautiful sarong as a birthday gift the day before, and promised to treat her to dinner on the South Bank in London when they met up back in England. It had made Alice mull over what present Rich would have bought her this year. In the past, he had nearly always forgone romantic gestures in favour of practical offerings, bestowing her with such treats as a NutriBullet, new brake pads for her dilapidated old Mini and a year-long membership to English Heritage. They were useful gifts, if a little unsexy, and Alice appreciated the thought that he put into them. However, she had, on occasion, wished that he would buck the trend and pick her out some lingerie, or even just choose her some perfume. That wasn't Rich, though. If it wasn't a useful, everyday item, then he did not see the point in wasting his money. Alice, who knew herself well enough to realise that her desire for frivolous goodies came from the side of her personality Rich did not like to see, had always done her best to ignore the cravings.

They finally arrived at Pudumayaki National Park a little before their booked safari slot of ten a.m., eager to get out into the sunshine and stretch their legs after the long journey. Max used his crutches to lever himself down to the dusty ground, only to chuck them back on to the mini-bus floor afterwards. Alice saw Jamal shake his head, but he chose not to comment.

It was an excursion that they had all been looking forward to, and Maureen was adamant that they would see not only the promised elephants, but also leopards and sloth bears, too – purely because it was her birthday. Alice privately hoped that they would, if only to cheer her friend up a bit. While Maur had not actually said as much, Alice noticed that she was not her usual feisty self – hadn't been since the train journey from Kandy to Hatton – and she still had no idea why.

As soon as the minibus doors were locked and their driver

had settled himself down on a nearby deckchair, Steph and Maureen scampered off to the ladies' – unfortunately little more than a few holes in the ground surrounded by flimsy fences and no roof – while Jamal headed to the ticket hut to find out which jeep they would be in. Alice and Max were left alone, save for an inquisitive monkey, which was peering down at them through the branches of an overhanging tree.

'How's the head?' Max asked, nudging her foot with his.

Alice squinted at him through her sunglasses.

'Better than it was. Yours?'

Max tapped his knuckles against his temple. 'Not even a whisper of a hangover,' he said, sounding proud. 'All those years of heavy army drinking turned my liver to iron.'

'What a legacy,' she joked in reply.

'Or a leg you no longer see,' he quipped, and Alice chuckled as she mischievously kicked a clump of dust at him.

'Bad news.' Jamal was back, and he waited until the approaching Steph and Maureen were within range before continuing. 'There's two big groups of German travellers arriving any minute, and they've pre-booked, too, apparently, so we have to share with them.'

'That's all right,' Max began, but Jamal shook his head.

'We can't all fit in one jeep – the guy says it's three in one and two in the other, so . . .'

'Girls and boys?' suggested Maureen, not looking too thrilled about it.

Steph just about managed not to pout at the prospect of being separated from Jamal.

'I don't mind, either way,' Alice said pragmatically, looking at Max, who shrugged.

'Why don't we draw straws?' Jamal declared, pulling some twigs off the lowest branches of the monkey tree. 'Shortest two in one, longest three in the other?'

It seemed fair, but Alice had to roll her eyes when she saw Jamal wiggle one of the twigs he offered to Steph. Why he hadn't just said from the off that he and Steph would go together in one jeep, she didn't know. Men were baffling sometimes.

Maureen, somewhat predictably, positioned herself between Max and Alice when they finally climbed into their jeep, but whether it was because of a desire to be close to him or as far away as possible from the large, hairy German guy bringing up the rear, Alice couldn't be sure.

They set off along a muddy track peppered with potholes, Maureen, Alice and the hairy German all standing up and holding on to the metal bar in the centre of the jeep, and Max sitting down with Mister Tee outstretched, his sunglasses over his eyes and a contented smile on his face. The wind lifted his short fringe, blowing the light-brown tendrils up and to the right, and Alice stared at his muscular forearm, which he had angled out of the open side of the truck. The veins in his hand bulged with the effort of holding on, his knuckles white beneath his skin, and his daypack, which he'd propped up against the outer wall, slid to the floor between his trainers as they accelerated.

'Look,' said Maureen, and Alice raised guilty eyes just in time to see a large lizard vanishing into the treeline ahead of them, its tail swinging like a rudder.

'I think I dated him once,' Maureen added, and Max snuffled with laughter below them.

After the lizard, there seemed to be living creatures everywhere they looked, from boisterous families of monkeys to brightly coloured birds to intricately patterned butterflies, all of which seemed duly unfazed by a jeep full of gawping tourists crashing past them. Birds that were little more than a blur of colour in the tallest treetops were transformed through the viewfinder of Alice's camera into regal kingfishers, emerald bee-eaters and beady-eyed fantails. They spotted green parrots, peacocks, and hundreds of tiny, flat-footed lizards, which moved so fast that Alice would be left wondering if she had seen them at all.

The two-jeep convoy continued along the edge of a wide and boisterous river, which was lined on either side by trees, their branches knotted together tightly as if they were grasping hands. In places where the dense thickets thinned, Alice glimpsed small meadows dotted with flowers, or sparse trees the shape of mushrooms. Life appeared to be thriving here, and Alice found herself buoyed by the sheer amount of growth, and scents, and nature. Again and again, she snapped away with her camera, trying to capture through images what she knew she would be unable to recall once she left Sri Lanka – the euphoric feeling of experiencing something completely new.

Finally, just as Alice was starting to worry that her battery would soon run out, the jeep swerved off the rough pathway into a clearing and there, standing not twenty feet away from them, was an elephant.

The driver braked and turned in his seat.

'Ah,' he told them proudly. 'Elephant! A male – young bull.'

The elephant looked over in their direction, his trunk poised below a half-stripped branch, ready to tear off more leaves. With his smile-shaped mouth and doleful eyes, he seemed to Alice to be more like a giant toy than a wild animal, but he was majestic, too. Seeing him standing there, in his natural environment, having a spot of lunch while they stared at him like the unwanted intruders that they were, felt both miraculous and treacherous at the same time. Alice didn't know whether to be wowed or ashamed.

'He's quite something, isn't he?' whispered Max, who had stood up beside her. Maureen, who had just finished filming a video of them for her Instagram story, was using her fingers to zoom in on the elephant with her iPhone camera.

'Here,' Alice offered him her camera. 'You can see him really well through this.'

Max thanked her and squinted through the viewfinder. The camera strap was still around Alice's neck, so he was forced to shuffle even closer to her, and she felt tingles shooting through every part of her body that was touching his. She felt so alert when she was with Max – alert and alive. Maureen was always lecturing her and Steph about the benefits of mindfulness, of being in the moment and savouring it, appreciating it. That was how Alice felt around Max, as if every single separate moment could be stretched out like bubble gum. She wished she could pick one and stay in it, suspended in time, safe in the knowledge that she would not have to go back to the reality of her everyday life.

They were only halfway through their time in Sri Lanka, but already Alice felt panicked at the thought of the holiday ending, and of having to go home.

## 33

After leaving behind the lone male elephant in the clearing, Alice, Maureen and Max's driver happily informed them and the German passengers that the next stop would be one of the park's central tanks, a huge lake where much of the wildlife would congregate to bathe, drink and, in the case of the elephants, socialise. As they bumped slowly closer, however, it became clear very quickly that it was also the spot where all the jeeps converged, too, and Alice was shocked to see so many vehicles in such a relatively small area. She had imagined that the safari would be a more timid and reserved experience, and that the jeep they were in would always stay a safe and respectful distance away from the animals, but it was becoming horribly clear that this was not the case with every driver in the sanctuary.

It was easy to understand what drew them all here, though, because there were at least sixty to seventy elephants in the area, ranging in both age and size, not to mention a vast colony of painted storks, large-bellied pelicans and hundreds of bandy-legged egrets. Alice thought they looked like miniature doctors in their feathery white coats, and she said as much to Maureen and Max as the three of them watched the birds tiptoe on their spindly black legs around the groups of enormous grazing elephants.

The driver parked a discreet distance away from the

water's edge, before explaining in broken English that the egrets were in situ to catch the falling insects from the mouthfuls of grass pulled up by the elephants. Alice watched entranced as a mother elephant gathered one heap, shook it gently up and down to remove any bugs, then passed it into the waiting mouth of her offspring. The baby elephants stuck close to their mothers, while the older females in the group formed a protective outer ring around them. *Just like me*, thought Alice, amused by the image of herself as a baby elephant – except she had not grown up as a clingy child; she had been mollycoddled into one.

On the surface, the scene was almost tranquil, but there was another feeling, too – an edge that Alice could sense rather than see. Glancing down instinctively to see what Max's take on it was, she found that he, too, seemed tense, his eyes wide and his fists clenched. She put a tentative hand on his shoulder.

'Everything all right?' she asked quietly.

Max nodded once, but didn't smile, and Alice saw beads of perspiration amongst the stubble on his upper lip. He was radiating nerves, and knowing it made Alice nervous, too. Maureen, on the flipside, was back in good humour and in her element, asking the driver endless questions and pleading with the Germans at the front to take photos of her with all the assorted wildlife visible in the background.

'You want to go closer for pictures?' asked the driver, eager to please, and Maureen clapped her hands together with a 'yay' of relish just as Alice shook her head, her protestations drowned out by the engine restarting. They rolled slowly across the grass, inch by stealthy inch, Alice cringing inwardly with discomfort as they drew almost level with three rather wizened-looking elephants, before continuing towards where the lake curved down into a shallow spoon shape. There must be at least thirty jeeps here now, Alice counted roughly, the guilt of being there now far bigger than the joy she'd felt at seeing such incredible animals up close. Too many. Some were bonnet-to-boot, too, with elephants from the same family group trapped on either side, unable to get through. She could see that many of them had begun tossing their trunks and swaying from side to side with agitation.

'I don't like this,' she said aloud, and Max stood up again, his hand clammy as it fell across hers.

'Me neither,' he agreed, his expression grim.

Maureen looked at the two of them, seemingly bemused. 'Don't worry,' she said. 'The elephants must be used to these jeeps. They come through here every day, after all.'

It was a fair point, but it did little to quell the unease pricking at the back of Alice's neck. Max didn't even reply, merely frowned in concentration at the back of the driver's head, as if willing him to steer them away through sheer force of will. Unfortunately, however, the driver was enjoying keeping his passengers happy too much to notice, and was now pointing out a new group of elephants that had just emerged from the undergrowth and were heading straight for them.

'This one, the big lady,' he said, gesturing to the mighty elephant at the rear of the pack. 'She is Kane Hila. It is meaning "hole in the ear". She get this after she was injured by a train one day. It struck her baby.' He slapped his hands together. 'Bang. Dead. No more elephant.'

'That's awful,' cried Maureen, and the driver nodded.

'Yes, very sad. Since that day, Kane Hila is very much not liking people and the trains,' he added, glancing at the approaching elephant before continuing. 'She is sometimes becoming angry and making threats – this is why you must always stay here, in the jeep. Do not get out.'

'Bloody hell,' Max muttered under his breath, his gaze never leaving the approaching herd. Alice could tell that he was on high alert – she could almost hear the hammering of his heart against the inside wall of his chest – and she longed to reach out and reassure him with a touch.

'Why is she doing that?' Maureen murmured, turning to Alice and then back to where Kane Hila was now standing, not ten feet away, swaying her body from side to side with alarming regularity.

'She's upset,' Alice replied, even though that much was obvious.

'Erm, excuse me,' Maureen called out to the driver, her usually calm voice wobbling with trepidation. The driver didn't hear her; he was too busy taking photos of the Germans and telling a story about how he'd seen an eagle attack a fox on the shore of the lake.

'He pick him up – whoosh – up in the air, and the fox he screams and cries, and I scream, but then the—'

Alice never got to hear how the story ended, because the next thing she was aware of was a loud shriek of terror in her ear, followed by a crash. The floor seemed to disappear from under her, and she was thrown sideways hard, her head snapping forwards and connecting with Max's. There was a second crash, followed by a bellow and the sound of car horns, lots of them. Alice felt wetness on her face and brought up her hand to discover blood. Her nose throbbed, and she let out a sob of terror as she looked to her right and saw the enraged elephant, Kane Hila, glaring straight at her with her trunk raised. She had barged into the jeep and almost knocked it clean over. The realisation hit Alice hard, and she reached unthinkingly for Max, her hand slapping instead against the metal floor of the truck.

The driver was shouting at the elephant now, a large wooden pole in his shaking hands, but Alice didn't want to watch. She could see that Maureen was being shielded by the hairy German, her hands clamped over her face, while everyone else in the jeep and those surrounding was screaming and yelling.

'Max!' Alice said urgently, shuffling up into a kneeling position and leaning over him. At first, she thought she must have knocked him clean out when she fell, because he wasn't moving, but on closer inspection she found that he was shaking violently, almost convulsing. He'd wrapped himself up into a tight ball on the floor, his face hidden from view inside a twisted nest of arms and his knees pulled into the foetal position.

'Max,' she said again, more gently this time, awkwardly patting his hair, his shoulder, his tightly coiled forearm.

'It's OK,' she soothed, even though she wasn't sure it was. Braving a look, she was relieved to see that Kane Hila was backing away from the jeep at last, her trunk still swaying. All the women were crying, and a few of the men, too, and the driver looked ashen as he clambered back behind the wheel. A few seconds later, Alice felt the engine roar into life beneath her and they began to move rapidly away.

Max was still silent, still shuddering, and Alice rubbed away tears of fear and relief.

'Hey,' she said, wrapping her arms around him as best she could in the cramped space. 'She's gone. It's over now. You're safe.'

Unsure what to do, Alice simply repeated the same words over and over, feeling silly but knowing, somehow, that Max needed to hear them. She remembered an article she'd read once about PTSD – post-traumatic stress disorder. Was this what she was witnessing now?

'You're safe,' she told him again, her mouth close to his ear. 'You're in Pudumayaki National Park. An elephant charged into our jeep, but you're OK. Everyone's OK. It's safe now.'

Max didn't move, and Alice felt tears begin to threaten again. She felt so stupid now for hankering after adventure, for chasing the illicit high that came from relieving her own anxiety. Not every experience was a good one, and Max had been through the very worst that a human could endure. She wished she could take all the hurt and fear and pain away from him, to have it for herself, even just for a single day, so that he could have a break from it all. It made no sense, she knew that, but it also wasn't fair that Max should have to deal with it all by himself.

She heard another commotion and froze in fear, but it wasn't an elephant charging towards the jeep this time, it was Jamal.

'Alice,' he said, out of breath, his dark eyes serious as they took her in, saw her arms around Max. 'Your nose . . .'

'I'm fine,' she said, meaning it. She had forgotten about her nose completely in her keenness to look after Max, but looking down now she saw that she'd bled all over her T-shirt.

Jamal had climbed over the side of the jeep and was crouching beside her.

'Can I?' he asked, tipping his head towards the huddled shape of Max, and Alice moved slowly out of his way, her arms reluctant to let go.

Jamal found Max's wrist and pulled at the elastic band he always wore there, letting go so it snapped back hard against his skin.

'Max,' he said loudly. 'You in there, mate?'

Another snap.

'Go to your place, mate. Just go there until you feel safe. I'm here. I'll be waiting for you.'

Alice felt a hand on her shoulder and looked up to find Maureen, her eyes wet with recent tears and her face flushed. She didn't say anything, but her concern was painted across her features. Alice smiled to reassure her, then glanced back just as Max finally began to uncurl. Jamal was on his haunches, talking to his friend softly and with authority, but Max was staring past him with unseeing eyes.

Whatever horror he had relived in these past few moments, Alice knew with a sobering certainty that it was one she would never be able to comprehend – not fully. She might have scars of her own, both mental and physical ones, but they were nothing compared to what Max had endured. He was always so ready to play down the incident that had cost him his leg, and had talked about it so matter-of-factly that he'd almost had Alice convinced. Now, however, she knew better. Max was still hurting, he was still suffering, and to know it so unequivocally made her heart feel as if it had been torn in two.

They had opened up to one another so much, the two of them, but so far, Alice had been able to kid herself that what drew her towards Max was simply the things they shared – the wounds they wore, the misplaced guilt they shouldered, and the drive they had to set themselves challenges to overcome. But what Alice was feeling now, as she stood with trembling legs and watched as the light slowly came back into Max's eyes, was a lot more complicated than that.

# 34

# Max

*If I should die,*
*Let go of your sorrow,*
*My life was but a gift,*
*That I was lucky to borrow . . .*

Max knew that he was staring into the kind, dark eyes of his friend, but he still couldn't see Jamal, not in the whole sense of seeing. He couldn't feel him, or smell him, or hear him. It was as if his ears were full of water, as if the blast wave was back and ricocheting through his body, causing the tissue in his lungs to convulse and his eyeballs to bulge inside his head. He opened his mouth to speak, to tell Jamal that he was OK, but the words were buried beneath piles of dust, sand, grit and shrapnel – all the detritus that the IED had sucked in and spat back at them, covering Max and his fallen men with destruction and despair.

The blackness was better, easier. Max closed his eyes and tried to dive down beneath the waves of darkness, to where it was safe. A muffled voice was telling him to move, to leave that place and find another, where he could sit bathed in sunshine, his brother by his side, the two of them just children, bare knees scuffed from fun, a shoelace unknotted and trailing, laughter and innocence warming the air. A stream trickling by below them, light dancing like merry jesters on its surface.

*Go there*, he urged himself. *Sit until the noise fades, until the pain recedes, until fear is chased away.*

He could hear the running water now, and the sound of his brother, Ant, laughing in his ear as he reached over and plucked a sandwich out of Max's hand. Max tried to imagine how it would taste, how the bread would feel as it squeezed into the gaps between his teeth. He had a missing tooth. That was it. The tooth fairy had left a shiny pound coin under his pillow the night before. The memory of it made his shoulders relax, and the corners of his mouth twitch into a smile. *It's OK*, he thought. *Everything is going to be OK.*

Max opened his eyes.

'You all right, mate?' Jamal asked, placing his warm hands on either side of Max's face.

Max swallowed, aware as he did so that there was a stinging pain on the crown of his head. Reaching up a hand, he rubbed at the spot.

'What happened?' he croaked, looking past Jamal to where Alice and Maureen were sitting on the bench seat of the jeep, staring at him with wide eyes. He had seen those same expressions many times before, and recognised the pity in them.

'Bloody elephant charged at the jeep,' Jamal told him lightly. 'Looked pretty hairy from where I was, so God knows how it felt for you lot.'

'Horrible,' Maureen said dryly, and Jamal braved a chuckle.

'Bit bigger than a cow, eh, mate?' he said, nudging Max. 'Now, shall we get you up off the floor?'

Max grimaced. 'I can do it.'

He hoisted himself back on to the seat using his hands and elbows as leverage, trying not to wince at the pain in his leg.

'Bollocks,' he said, looking at each of his three friends in turn. 'Sorry for freaking out.'

Jamal opened his mouth to reply, but Alice got there first.

'Don't be silly,' she said. 'There's nothing to be sorry about. It was bloody terrifying.'

'Where's our driver?' Max wanted to know, and Jamal laughed.

'Getting a rollicking from one of the rangers. And quite right, too – he basically drove you over that poor elephant's feet.'

'Poor elephant?' Max managed a laugh that turned into a gaping yawn. 'What about poor old crippled me?'

'Playing the sympathy card, are you? Nice,' Jamal replied, catching Max's eye and grinning. 'Don't you think you've had enough attention for one day?'

'Dickhead,' Max replied.

'Knob,' said Jamal happily.

Max tried to see past his friend to Alice, realising now that he hadn't even asked her and Maureen if they were all right. Fat lot of good he was in a crisis – he should have been the one protecting them, not curled up in a ball of fear on the floor. Max knew that these reactions were things he could not fully control, and logic told him that there was no blame to be laid, but that didn't stop an ugly flush of humiliation spreading across his cheeks. He didn't want Alice or Maureen to think of him as weak.

'Is everyone else OK?' he asked, and Alice nodded.

'Everyone except Aurik here, whose shirt has been snotted all over by Maur,' she joked, nodding in the direction of the hairy German man.

'Shit!' Max sat up straighter as he clocked the splatters of blood on Alice's face and T-shirt. 'You're hurt!'

Alice looked down at herself.

'I banged my nose on your head when I fell over,' she explained. 'Sorry about that, by the way. It all happened so fast, and I was on the floor before I had time to react.'

Max held up an unsteady hand. 'Please, no apologies. My head is just fine. Is your nose OK – is it broken?'

'She's fine,' Maureen put in, sticking her head around Alice's shoulder. 'Nothing broken.'

'Here.' Jamal shuffled around to face Alice. 'Let me have a look. I may only be a lowly physio, but I do know a smashed nose when I see one.'

Max watched as Jamal examined her quickly and efficiently, peering up her nostrils and making her follow his finger with her eyes as he moved it from side to side.

'You're all right,' he concluded. 'That nose will live to headbutt Max another day.'

'I didn't mean to!' protested Alice, her voice high as Jamal laughed openly.

Max stifled another yawn. He felt exhausted, as if every last ounce of energy had been drained out of him. It was always the same when he experienced one of these episodes – the catastrophic upset to his mental balance left him reeling. Jamal, who had seen Max through many of these panic attacks now, would be fully aware of this, too. And, as Max had predicted, his friend was soon leaning over to talk to the rather shamefaced driver, telling him in that no-nonsense but polite way of his that they must head back as soon as possible. Under usual circumstances, Max would have stepped in and assured them all that he was fine, but he was too tired. He knew the only way to feel even halfway back to normal was to rest, and he'd learned long ago that there was no point fighting the need to completely switch off after suffering an episode.

He wished Alice would sit down beside him so he could rest his head against her shoulder. He had a vague recollection of having her arms around him, and guessed that she must have tried to comfort him before Jamal reached the jeep. Whatever it was that he felt for her, Max could feel this complex tangle of emotions gaining weight. He was starting to feel as if the two of them were attached to one another with string, and the further away she was from him, the tighter it pulled around his heart.

Max was not going to get his wish this time, however, because the other jeep carrying Steph had just pulled up alongside them, and Alice was clambering across to take Jamal's place. Max stared at the back of her head, willing her to turn, and then, just as the vehicle's engine roared into life and they bumped off across the park, she looked back at him and smiled.

## 35

Almost as soon as they had checked into the modest hotel in the centre of Tissamaharama, Max made his apologies to the girls and headed straight to his and Jamal's room. Alice could see that he looked almost grey with fatigue beneath his tan, the episode in the jeep having stripped away his last vestiges of energy, and she hoped that he would be OK by himself. She could not deny that she was disappointed he wouldn't be spending the evening with them, but equally she appreciated his need for rest. In fact, he was so befuddled that he didn't even seem to register when she said a rushed goodnight – and that wasn't like Max at all.

They were only staying in the town for one night, before heading down to the south coast the following morning, but it was still Maureen's birthday, and so another session on the tiles was non-negotiable. Alice privately wanted nothing more than an early night. It had been a long day, and the scene she had witnessed in Pudumayaki National Park – not to mention how she felt afterwards – had left her reeling. The elephant charging into their jeep had been terrifying, but what scared Alice more was her immediate reaction. Her automatic and overwhelming concern had not been for her own safety, or even for Maur's – it was purely focused on Max. She was also struck by how little Richard had factored at that moment – or indeed after it. Surely her response to near-death-by-elephant should have been to call her boyfriend and tell him about it, reach out to the person she loved to let him know that she was still there. But Richard had not even crossed her mind until the point, hours after, when she was wondering why he hadn't.

The hotel was close enough to the town centre not to require a tuk-tuk ride, and Alice found that she and the others were all very content to stroll along the crowded streets past the edges of the reservoir, watching as spindly-legged birds picked their way daintily through the reeds. The vast white dome of the Raja Maha Vihara Buddhist Temple lay like a fallen moon in the distance, and Alice looked up to see a swarm of tiny bats burst out from the topmost branches of a nearby tree. The humid evening air was as thick as soup, but the weight of it was helping to temper the familiar fizz of uncertainty in Alice's chest. She took a deep breath, then another, doing her best to ignore the urge she had to run until there was no room for thoughts.

What was it about this place? Why had it begun by soothing her, but was now bringing her angsty side back to the surface?

'Alice in Wonderlaaaand!'

Steph was shouting back to her through the crowds of bustling locals.

'Coming!'

Every warning that Alice had read about avoiding restaurants with a buffet evaporated as soon as the four of them crossed the threshold of Ran Simhaya and smelled the food on offer. There was a barbecued meat area shrouded in deliciously fragrant smoke, vats of rice in various shades of red, yellow and green, and a more eclectic selection of desserts than Alice could ever have imagined existing.

'Bang goes the diet,' announced Maureen, her nose twitching with appreciation.

'Diets are boring,' Steph replied. 'And anyway, it's your birthday.'

'I can't believe I'm thirty,' Maur groaned, sitting down heavily on a wicker chair and thanking the waiter who had held it out for her.

Alice opened her mouth to protest, but Maur cut across her. 'And single!'

There was nothing much she could say to that, so Alice picked up the drinks menu instead.

'I wish they had Prosecco,' sighed Steph, as Jamal ran a casual finger along her bare arm. 'I don't think I can drink beer again so soon – not after last night.'

'What are you?' Jamal said. 'Woman or wimp?'

'Oi!' she grinned, before leaning across the table to kiss him.

Maureen pulled her own menu up over her face.

'Enough already!' she muttered. 'You two are making me feel even more single.'

Steph reddened. 'Sorry, Maur.'

'It's OK.' Maur waved a hand vaguely in her direction. 'I just wish Max was here to style me out – it's no fun being the only spinster at the table.'

'You're not a spinster!' Alice exclaimed. 'You're just picky, that's all.'

'Like you are, you mean?' Maur replied, and Alice smiled, although she wasn't quite sure what her friend had meant by it.

'I'm not at all picky,' she said tentatively, testing the mood waters.

'Only when it comes to me, then,' Maur retorted. She sounded combative, and Alice reddened as she wondered if her friend was referring to her failed campaign to ensnare Max. Was Maur angry with her for spending time with him? Surely it could only be that.

'I just want you to be happy,' she said quietly, but Maur would not meet her gaze.

They took it in turns to head over to the buffet and load up their plates, before ordering a round of rather dubious-looking bright-green cocktails and raising them in a toast to the birthday girl.

'May all your wishes come true!' said Jamal, clanging his glass against hers.

'Fat chance of that,' grumbled Maureen in reply, but necked half her cocktail anyway.

They chatted about their plans for the next few days as they ate, Jamal confirming that he and Max had now altered their itinerary so it would match that of the girls. Steph reached under the table and put her hand on his knee, her smile of contentment matching the one that Alice was doing her best to subdue. She was thrilled that the two men were staying around for longer, but she didn't want to make it too obvious – especially when

Maureen was being so tetchy. Her friend had merely reacted to Jamal's news with a non-committal 'cool', so clearly she, too, was dampening down her true feelings.

Tomorrow, all five of them would drive down to Tangalle, before moving west along the coast and passing through Mirissa and Unawatuna, before finally ending their trip in the port town of Galle. All of them agreed that they were looking forward to some beach time, with Maureen, in particular, going into near ecstasies at the thought of how great her tan would soon become.

'Is Max a beach fan?' Steph asked Jamal, and he finished chewing his mouthful of vegetable rice before replying.

'Not really,' he said. 'But rest is the best thing for him at the moment, what with this pain in his stump. He's been pushing himself too hard since we've been here – that's why I was so pissed off with him yesterday. Any pain at all, even a slight amount, can be a warning flag for something serious.'

'Like what?' Alice asked, her mouth engaging before her brain had time to wade in.

'Well, let's see,' Jamal began, putting down his cutlery so he could tick things off on his fingers.

'There's ulceration, purpura, bone fractures, infection . . .'

'But those are all treatable, right?' she asked.

'They are easily treated, if they're caught early enough,' Jamal assured her. 'But ulceration can have devastating effects if it's left to fester, and infection can be very dangerous. Being so close to a blast will have affected Max's immune system, too. An injury as bad as his always has a catastrophic effect. When it comes to blast injuries, what you can't see – the stuff happening on the inside – that's often far worse than the physical ailments.'

'How dangerous can it be?' Alice prompted, her need to know all the facts outweighing the small internal voice that was urging her to shut the hell up and stop making it obvious just how invested she was in Max's well-being.

'Well, the worst-case scenario would be sepsis,' he said matter-of-factly. 'The infection spreads into the blood and the internal organs begin to shut down.'

It was a sobering thought, and Maureen put her third cocktail firmly down on the table.

'Well, this is cheery talk we're having,' she drawled. 'Honestly, with the elephant trying to take my head off and now you lot talking about death, it really does feel like a special birthday.'

Jamal let out a low rumble of laughter.

'She has got a point,' he said. 'OK, let's change the subject. Maur, what would you like to talk about, as it's your birthday? At least, I think someone mentioned that once or twice,' he added, laughing again at her outraged expression.

'I dunno.' Maur took another sip through her straw. 'What does it matter now, anyway? We only have, oh, five minutes until midnight.'

'Is it that time already?' Alice gaped at her phone, noticing as she did so that a message had come through – from Richard.

Trepidation crept through her like a stealthy cat. Would

this be another reprimand about her spending time with Max and Jamal? A snarky remark about Maureen's latest Instagram story? Maybe he had delved far enough to see the 'like' she had left on Max's hospital photo – the one she had never meant to leave? She felt her hands go clammy as she picked up the handset, and it took her two attempts to enter the passcode correctly.

'Who's that?' Steph enquired from beside her, seemingly tuned in, as ever, to any changes in Alice's mood.

Alice didn't reply; she merely closed her eyes for a second before pressing to open the message that Richard had sent.

Happy (early) Birthday, she read. I bet you can't guess what this is! He had added a winking emoji face and two kisses, but it was the attached image that made Alice's breath catch in her throat.

It was a photo of a small jewellery box, exactly the right size for a ring.

## 36

Alice waited until the following morning to reply to Richard's message. Having agonised over what response would be the most suitable, she opted in the end for a simple, Oooh! and a smiley face. Rich had never been too great at the big romantic gestures, which had never bothered Alice in the slightest, so she was not surprised that he had chosen to send her a teasing photo of what she guessed must be an engagement ring. They had been together for so many years now, perhaps he felt that rose petals on a bed or a diamond ring buried in the middle of a chocolate fondant pudding would be a waste of time. They had already discussed that marriage was the next step, and they had both been in agreement about the fact. Well, they had until Alice had come to Sri Lanka. Now, the prospect of saying her vows made her feel decidedly uneasy, and she was very glad that she had insisted to Rich that they wait until after the holiday to break the news of their plans to her family.

She headed down to breakfast later than the others, struggling to fit everything into her backpack and swearing with uncharacteristic fervour when the straps failed to meet around the middle. Steph had given her a card with a picture of a polar bear on the front, its paw over its eyes and a message that read, 'You are HOW OLD?', while Maureen's featured several half-naked men standing over some felled trees, and a joke about big axes. They had clubbed together and got her a spa day voucher as a gift.

Alice had also got an oddly perfunctory text from her mum, wishing her all the best and telling her she could have her present when she got home, which Marianne made it clear she was looking forward to. Alice wasn't expecting anyone else to mark the occasion, so she was very surprised when she pushed open the door to the hotel breakfast room and found it empty save for Max, a mischievous-looking smirk on his face.

'Morning,' she said suspiciously.

'Happy birthday!' Max stood up to greet her, his stubble brushing against her cheek along with his lips.

'Where is everyone?' Alice asked, her face tingling with pleasure as she lowered her bag from her back and sat down.

'On their way to Tangalle,' Max informed her cheerily, sitting back down beside her, and Alice almost dropped the teacup she was about to fill.

'What? Why?'

Max smiled easily, his eyes crinkling with amusement.

'Don't worry,' he said. 'I told them to go. I have a birthday surprise for you, but it's strictly for two people only.'

'A surprise? For me?' Alice grabbed his lower arm impulsively. 'What is it?'

'If I told you,' Max said, 'it wouldn't be a surprise, now would it?'

Alice's mind raced through several possibilities. A tea

plantation tour, perhaps? A trek up another mountain? Whatever it was, she was sure she would love it – being singled out by Max felt like a gift in itself.

'Are you really serious?' she checked. 'You're not just winding me up?'

'I'm really not,' he assured her, picking up a piece of buttered toast and biting into it. 'Now eat up – you're going to need your strength.'

Feeling utterly perturbed but unquestionably happy, Alice did as she was told.

There was a taxi waiting outside the hotel, and it was a nice one, too, with air-conditioning and leather seats.

'Where are we going?' Alice asked Max, for at least the seventh time, as they settled into their seats. He waggled a finger at her.

'I told you – no clues. You only have to wait an hour or so to find out.'

He seemed back to his old self today, full of infectious energy and a determination to wind her up. If his leg was still causing him a problem, then he didn't show it, and she hoped that a good night's sleep had done the trick. Jamal's horror stories about blood poisoning and multiple surgeries had given her nightmares. The thought of something bad happening to Max caused her genuine physical pain, which mildly surprised her. Richard was far too careful to ever cause himself an injury, but the one time a few years ago he had got hurt – by an impatient driver who failed to brake in time when Rich was waiting to pull out at a roundabout – she had felt quite relaxed about the whole thing. Rich had called her from the A&E department of the local hospital, saying he had suspected whiplash, and she could distinctly remember finishing her cup of tea before driving over to sit with him. She wasn't sure whether it was because Max seemed more vulnerable than her boyfriend, or that she felt more protective of him than she did of Rich, but the question was troubling enough for Alice to push it to the back of her mind almost as soon as she considered it.

The driver nipped in and out of the Tissamaharama traffic like he was a skier on a slalom slope, and in no time at all they were clear of the town and heading south on a narrow highway. The usual cacophony of tuk-tuk engines, barking dogs and blaring horns was muted behind the taxi's closed windows. Alice stared out at the long shadows stretching across the green mosaic of the landscape, turning patches of undergrowth from emerald to pine, and the gold of the rocks and tree branches to a rich burnt amber.

'It's so beautiful here,' she murmured, turning to find that Max was looking at her rather than the view. He cleared his throat before replying.

'You're right about that.'

'I can't believe I'll be back in Suffolk this time next week,' she said. 'I wish I could have stayed for a month. Six months, even.'

'I'm not looking forward to going home much, either,' Max admitted, turning his navy cap over in his hands. His white T-shirt was pulled taut across his chest, and Alice let her eyes linger there for a hungry few beats before glancing away and looking out through the front windscreen.

'Back to the grind.'

Alice nodded, picturing her little desk in the council office, with its straggly old spider plant and hole punch with stuck-on boggly eyes.

'At least we'll be taking back some good memories,' she said, trying her best to sound enthusiastic.

Max chuckled. 'Yep, that's right. I will particularly treasure the memory of an angry elephant charging at us.'

Alice swivelled her head around to face him.

'That was so bad. We could have been killed, for God's sake! But I get what you mean – it was certainly unforgettable.'

'There are plenty of moments in this trip that have been unforgettable,' he said softly, and this time Alice could only nod.

'You never told me what it is you do for a job,' she said, manoeuvring the conversation back on to safer ground. 'You said you work for your dad?'

'That's right,' Max confirmed, his hand sneaking to the top of his socket as it so often seemed to do. 'He owns a construction company, and I work in the office, raising orders, dealing with invoices – that sort of thing.'

'Oh, right,' Alice said brightly, casting around for something more intelligent to say.

Max pulled a face. 'You don't have to pretend,' he stated. 'It really is as boring as it sounds. It would be fine if I was out on site, actually getting my hands dirty and helping with the building work, but my dad won't hear of it. I think just doing admin tasks is causing my brain to shrink.'

'I know exactly how you feel,' Alice agreed, her voice going up an octave. 'There are only so many times you can explain the process of setting up a direct debit for council tax payments before you start to go completely bananas. I don't even know why I've stayed there so long, to be honest.'

Max eyed her. 'Why have you?'

She picked at a flap of loose skin beneath her thumbnail. 'I guess, because I know it. It's close to home, the pay isn't too bad. I've been saving to buy a house for what feels like forever, so it's not like I can just up and quit.'

Max considered this for a moment. 'You can do whatever you want,' he told her. 'But then I'm a good one to talk. I can't stand my job, but I feel like I can't leave either, not when my dad basically created the role just for me. I think he likes keeping me close by, you know – both him and my mum like to know where I am. It's their hangover from what happened. If I left, I'd feel like I was throwing it all in their faces – everything they've done and all the things they've had to sacrifice since I got myself blown up.'

'It makes sense,' Alice said sagely. 'I know exactly what it's like to have overprotective parents, too, trust me. But you can't live your life for someone else.'

'No,' Max said, his tone quieter now, and more solemn. 'You can't, can you?'

Alice flushed as she realised she'd just parroted his own advice back at him. The two of them were their own worst enemies when it came to doing what was expected versus doing what they wanted. Unwilling to admit as much to Max, however, she diverted the conversation on to less uncomfortable turf.

'What would be your dream job?' she asked him, before lurching over and almost landing on top of him as the taxi overtook an overcrowded bus.

'I would love to do something more creative,' he said, looking almost wistful as he met her eyes. 'And I'd like to do more to help people in my position, you know? Lads that are struggling to cope with what they've been through. Finding an outlet for all that trauma is so important.'

'That sounds amazing,' Alice told him honestly. 'I say go for it.'

'Maybe I will.' He smiled at her.

'Maybe it's about time we both went after what we want.'

## 37

Alice's first thought when they turned off the road and drove past a sign that read *Ratu Hadavata Skydive Centre*, was that the driver must be lost.

She turned to Max, a mixture of panic and elation filling up her chest when she saw his expression.

'You haven't?' she gasped, and he grinned triumphantly.

'I have.'

'But . . . But . . .' Alice sat bolt upright in her seat, her fingers on the window. 'You can't be serious?' she managed at last, turning back to Max as the car bounced clumsily over potholes and came to a standstill beside a small, shed-like building.

'I am very serious,' Max assured her. 'You, Alice Brockley, are going to jump out of a plane.'

She wanted to say that she couldn't, it was too dangerous, the parachute might not open, Richard and her mum would go spare when they found out. But no words came. Instead, she found herself clambering out of the taxi as fast as she could and bouncing up and down on the spot with excitement.

Max took a few seconds longer than Alice to get himself into the right position to lever himself out of the taxi, but now he laughed as he spotted her.

'Come on, you bloody monkey,' he said, strolling towards the door of the little building. Alice ran after him, her heart pounding. Now that they were out of the car, she could see an aircraft hangar on the far side of a wide open field, and beyond it, the distant shapes of mountains. There were trees clustered together by the entrance to the hangar, and every branch seemed to twitch with life.

'Why a skydive?' she asked as they walked. 'It's such a random choice.'

Max paused and glanced at her in surprise.

'Not random at all,' he said. 'I already knew you were into diving, remember? And diving doesn't get much more extreme than this.'

That did make sense, she allowed – but there was a big difference between slipping off the edge of a boat into the water and flying up multiple thousands of feet in a plane.

'Look,' Max said then, pointing upwards, and Alice squinted through her sunglasses just in time to see a parachute emerge through the clouds, two people in red jumpsuits riding tandem at the end of its ropes. There was a whooshing sound and a strong gust of air, and before Alice knew what was happening, the skydivers had landed neatly on the open field just beyond the shed, the chute fluttering down after them like a dropped tissue.

'They came in so fast,' she said to Max, her eyes wide, and he laughed.

'You think that's fast,' he said. 'Just you wait for the freefall.'

Alice said nothing to that, but she was immediately

aware of a large balloon of nervous anticipation expanding right up to bursting point inside her chest.

After heading into reception, they were weighed, and each signed a form to say that they understood all the risks of what they were about to do, then a young Sri Lankan who introduced himself as Pamu led them along a pathway at the edge of the field towards the hangar. Once there, they were ushered into a room with a pull-down screen fixed to one wall, and shown a video of what to expect from the skydive, and which film and photography packages were available.

Max turned to Alice. 'Do you want one? I'm happy to treat you.'

She shook her head, almost laughing at the thought of what her mum and Richard would say if she casually played them a film of herself risking death after one of their Sunday roasts. Because that was what she was about to do – she was about to hand her life over to a stranger, and trust that fate was on her side. She should be terrified, but instead all she could feel was a humming buzz of anticipation. Max, who admitted he had skydived multiple times before, seemed totally relaxed, but Alice could tell he was thrilled that she was enjoying herself so much.

'I can't believe this is happening,' she said, not for the first time, wriggling her way into the flight suit she had been handed by another, wiry Sri Lankan. Max had booked them a jump from a height of 12,000 feet, which meant a full forty-five seconds of freefall. Whenever Alice looked up into the clouds high above them and tried to imagine hurtling through them at speed, she started laughing at the sheer ridiculousness of it all. There was no way, no possible way on earth, that she ever would have got herself to this point. To Alice, diving off the high board at the swimming pool back home had felt like a risk, but here she was, suited and goggled and about to dive out of a plane. It was mind-boggling.

'Are you sure you're OK?' Max asked, pulling a white leather skullcap down over his hair and snapping the clasp shut. 'You can still wimp out, you know. I won't tell the others.'

'No way!' Alice shook her head firmly from side to side as a smiley dark-haired man strapped her harness into place around her legs and back. 'Wild elephants wouldn't stop me.'

Max grinned wryly. 'Be careful what you wish for,' he said.

There wasn't much more time to dwell on what they were about to do, and after a quick and reassuring chat with her tandem master, Diyon, who checked and rechecked her harness, Alice found herself walking on unsteady legs towards where a small plane was waiting, the side door pulled open. Max strode next to her, a grin on his face, and they each turned to look at the other at the same moment.

'Thank you,' she whispered through her smile, and he picked up her hand and squeezed it.

They had got lucky in that they were the only two booked to jump in their timeslot, and once they had both slithered backwards along the parallel benches on their bottoms and were being clipped on to their tandem masters from behind, Max reached across and held Alice's hand once again. He was warm and solid to the touch, just as he had been when he pulled her into his arms at the top of Adam's Peak, and even though she was about to throw herself out of a plane, thousands of feet from the ground, Alice felt safe beside him.

The engines rumbled beneath them and the propellers whirred into action. Alice drew air into her lungs, watching wide-eyed through the tiny oval window as the prop plane gathered speed and then took off into the blue. She gripped Max's hand a notch tighter, and he returned the pressure in kind. Again, Alice imagined the two of them in a bubble, untouched and untouchable by the mundane realities that they each faced back at home. This was their time up here – their world. She all at once never wanted the moment to end.

'OK?' said a voice in her ear – Diyon. Alice nodded, and he tapped her lightly on the shoulder. 'You see up there, the light?' he asked, pointing to a red bulb above the closed hatch.

'Yes.' Alice's heart was racing.

'When it goes green, he will go,' he said, gesturing towards Max. 'Then we wait for a minute or two, and we will go after.'

'OK.'

Alice's jaw was beginning to ache from smiling, but her knees were trembling. Again she pushed her palm against Max's, and again he returned it with a squeeze. An image of Richard flashed into her mind, his glasses on the end of his nose as he read something aloud to her from one of the weekend papers – a book review, perhaps, or a recipe for sweet potato curry. He seemed so far away from her now, like a memory rather than someone who should be the most present person in her life – the man she was going to marry.

The light turned green.

'I'll see you on the other side,' Max called out, letting go of her hand as his tandem master pushed them both forwards. Another man, who was clipped to the wall of the plane, had hoisted open the hatch door, and cold air rushed in.

'Wait!' Alice went to say, but any sound she made was whipped from her lips by the wind. Max turned back to look at her, just once, winking as he arched his back and looked up towards the roof of the plane. Then suddenly, as if a hole had opened up in the space around them, Max and his partner fell forwards into the emptiness and were gone.

'Shit!' Alice shouted, elation mingling with terror as she watched the light go from green back to red. 'Shit, shit, shit!'

'You say shit!' Diyon said, chuckling as the plane soared higher. He carefully lowered Alice's goggles over her eyes and tightened the strap, tucking the end of it under her cap behind her ear, where it dug in. The pain made her feel more alive, somehow, her anxiety now a hive full of agitated bees. *Any moment now,* she thought, *I will burst. There will be bits of me all over this plane.*

The light turned green again.

'Ready, Alice?' Diyon checked, pushing her gently

forwards until her feet were poking out of the hatch. 'Now, make your body into a banana.'

Alice bent backwards as she had been instructed on the ground, tucking her feet on a strut outside the plane and grasping the straps on either side of her chest. She felt a tug somewhere in the small of her back, and then she was out, tearing through the air and watching the plane diminish rapidly above her.

Opening her mouth to scream, Alice almost choked as it filled immediately with air. Wind ripped past her ears, and she looked down to where the landscape was spread out below her like a patchwork quilt. The mountains looked tiny, the trees mere matchsticks, and a wave of dizzying realisation swept through her. She was really doing this. It was really happening and there was no going back now.

Diyon tapped both her shoulders to signal that she should lift her arms out to the side, and Alice let go of the harness and folded herself open, a smile anchoring itself yet again on her face as the world danced and rippled around her. She looked down again, hoping to see Max, but there was nothing below them save for the smudge of fields and forests, and a tinsel-line of river snaking out from beneath the treeline.

She felt another tap, this time just on one shoulder, and sensed Diyon move behind her. There was another hard tug from the harness around her legs and chest, then Alice felt herself soar upwards as the parachute opened. Almost immediately, the roar of rushing air ceased, and Alice laughed out loud. On and on she laughed, gazing all around them as Diyon used his handles to steer them from side to side, pointing out the white tips of faraway temples and the spot on the horizon where the Indian Ocean lapped at the shore. Alice had never experienced a sensation so liberating, or so exhilarating, and now that the dangerous portion of the initial jump was over, she found that there was an incredible sense of peace up here. The only sound now came from the rhythmic flapping of the open parachute high above them, and the occasional comments she and Diyon were exchanging. She could remember so acutely how it had felt to climb and explore as a child, how untethered she had been to fear, or guilt. Before the accident had stolen that innocence away and replaced it with fragility, she had been free. The thought brought tears to her eyes, and she was glad when Diyon lifted her goggles away and pointed towards the ground.

'Look there,' he said. 'Your boyfriend is waiting for you.'

He meant Max, of course, but Alice did not have the heart, or the inclination, to correct him. Max was still wearing his red jumpsuit, but he'd pulled off his cap and goggles. Alice could tell even from here that his hair was sticking up in all directions, and that he was smiling. A great, big, proud and happy smile, and he was directing it at her.

As the field rushed up to greet them, Alice lifted her legs and let out a comedic whoop as her bottom bounced off the ground. As soon as Diyon had unclipped himself from her harness, she allowed herself to lie down on the grass, her limbs splayed out sideways like wings.

'Oh my God!' she breathed, beaming up at him. 'That was . . . Oh my God!'

She sat up to find Max walking in her direction, his smile still fixed in place, and before she could talk herself out of it, Alice was on her feet and running his way, her arms ready to be thrown around him. At the last minute, she jumped up and wrapped both her legs around his waist, clinging to him like her life depended on it.

Max, who had stumbled on impact but managed to stay upright, tightened his arms around her body and pulled her against him. For a few seconds, they simply embraced, both lost in the moment as their hearts beat against each other's chests. Alice pulled back first, but only so she could look him in the eye – she wanted him to feel how happy she was; she wanted to show him how much this had meant to her, how it had reminded her of who she was, and of the person she now knew she was happy becoming. She wanted him to know all of it, but how could she even begin to put it into words?

Max waited, his blue eyes so kind and so sincere. Alice opened her mouth, determined that she must say something, but her words were swallowed as Max's lips pressed gently against her own.

# 38

## Max

*If I should live,*
*Let my heart find love.*
*Seek out the one*
*For whom I am enough . . .*

Max brought his arm up and folded it behind his head, his elbow creating a makeshift pillow in the cocoon-like shape of the hammock. He had taken off his prosthetic leg to shower, and used his crutches to travel the short distance from the treehouse bathroom to the wooden-floored veranda at its front. Despite his indifference towards the beach earlier in their trip, he was glad they were here now. Just the sight of the gently lapping turquoise water when they arrived a few hours ago had soothed him, while the warm salty air stirred up memories of childhood holidays spent digging in the sand around the south coast of England, he and his brother Ant doing their best to create a better castle than any of the other kids.

Ant had always been military-minded, insisting on tall battlements and a deep moat around their creations, and Max would habitually rebel by patting a drawbridge into place, and poking holes in the structure to make doorways and windows. A castle, to Max, should be a home full of people going about their lives, while Ant saw it as a fortress, put there to protect only an important few.

Tangalle had not been included on their original itinerary, but Jamal had been keen to spend an extra few days with Steph. Plus, his friend pointed out matter-of-factly, the coast would be the perfect place for Max to rest his leg before the long journey home at the weekend. Max looked down at his stump, frowning as he examined the inflamed area around the puckered edges of his scar. He had put on a good show at the skydiving centre that morning, convincing Alice and almost himself that the discomfort in his leg was receding when it was, in fact, getting steadily worse.

He probed the swollen flesh now with his forefinger and winced, sucking air through his teeth as a dart of pain shot up his thigh and into his lower back. This was not good. Nothing about this was good. A bead of sweat trickled down from his hairline to his jaw, and Max flicked it away, irritated suddenly by the humidity. Why did it have to be so goddamn hot here? He felt as if the heat would drown him sometimes.

He groaned and let go of his stump. Being in a hammock reminded him unavoidably of Afghanistan, although in contrast to Sri Lanka, the air over there had been acrid and dusty, the scent carried on the wind metallic. Some of the lads had strung the rope beds up inside the large tents at Camp Bastion, preferring to sleep even higher off the ground than the bunks would allow. Monstrous camel spiders were a very real fear, as were scorpions, and discarded boots, helmets and bits of kit had to be shaken out in the mornings to make sure nothing had crept in and set up home while their owners slept. There had been something inherently comforting about the rocking motion of a hammock out there, Max recalled, lowering his left leg to the ground to steady the swinging. Perhaps that was really why so many of the men favoured them – it helped them feel as if they were being swaddled and soothed to sleep, just like they would have been as babies. And if ever there was a place where a person needed to be comforted, it was Afghanistan.

Max heard a distant door creaking open, and lifted his head until he could see out and across the sand to the next treehouse along. The Cinnabar Resort where they were staying was set just back from the beach, close enough that guests could see and hear the Indian Ocean from every room. The accommodation was made up of a combination of wooden cabanas and tall, thatched structures – he and his friends had opted for the latter. Each one had a different name, which had been carved neatly into a wooden plaque and hung at the top of the rustic steps. Max and Jamal were staying in Wood House, while Alice, Maureen and Steph were in Palm House. He had thought that all three girls were already down in the beachside bar with Jamal to watch the sunset, but clearly not. Alice had stayed behind.

Max watched from his hidden position in the hammock as she wandered to the edge of the adjacent veranda, her hair wet and slicked back into a low ponytail and a towel in her hands, which she shook out and hung over the outer wall to dry. She was wearing a simple blue sundress with a halter-neck strap, and Max could just make out the faint white marks on each of her shoulders where her vest top had blocked the sun. His heart swelled, as it always did when he watched her, and he resisted the urge to call across and get her attention.

It had been so nice having her all to himself that morning, and treating her to an experience that he knew she would never forget. What had begun as an inkling of a wild soul buried somewhere deep inside had bloomed in the time Max had spent with Alice, and the skydive that morning had only confirmed it. Alice was a risk-taker, she had an adventurous soul, and he had seen – hell, he had felt – just how alive she had been after jumping out of that plane. When she had leaped off the ground and into his arms, kissing her had felt like the most natural and right thing in the world, but afterwards she had gone quiet. Not in a rude or even an embarrassed way, just contemplative, as if she was trying her best to work out the answer to a tricky riddle in her head.

Despite this, Max knew the experience had brought the two of them closer. When Alice had refused the chance to have her skydive filmed, or to have any photos taken, he had known that she was planning to keep the whole thing a secret – from her boyfriend and parents at least. How sad, he thought now, that the two of them felt duty-bound not to share such exciting moments with the people closest to them. At least they could talk about it together – it was done now, and could never be undone.

They had spent much of the taxi journey down to

Tangalle in companionable silence, Alice occasionally turning her head to smile at him, her cheeks still rose-tinted with exhilaration, while Max struggled to keep his game face despite the throbbing pain in his stump. He knew time was ticking now, and that soon he would not be able to ignore what was happening inside that leg, but he wanted to wait until he was home and could see his own doctor. It was only a few days, he thought – if he could just keep whatever this was at bay for a little while longer.

Max was still contemplating this as he watched Alice go back inside the cabin, only to re-emerge less than a minute later armed with a small bag and her camera. She was going to join the others in the bar area, and Max waited until she was down the treehouse steps and half-way across the wooden stepping stone path below before reaching for his crutches.

What he should do was stay here – rock himself into a lull in this hammock and allow his stump to recover. The thought of putting Mister Tee back on made his jaw tighten with dread, but he did not want to go down to the bar without it, either. It was difficult using the crutches on the soft, thick sand – and anyway, Jamal would know as soon as he saw him that something was still going on. Max twisted his elastic band around his wrist, cursing as it snagged on the fine hairs.

He didn't see that he had much choice.

'There he is!'

Maureen called out a greeting to Max as he made his slow way towards them through the tables, doing his best not to limp on his sore leg. The beach bar was rustic in style, with driftwood furniture and an abundance of candles. Two puppies of unspecified breed wrestled in the sand beside a stack of giant Jenga, and he could hear the ocean as it swished and rumbled just out of sight.

'The man of the hour,' Maureen said sweetly, using her bare foot to push out the empty chair next to her own.

Max lowered himself rather gingerly into it, feeling sweat dapple his back. It seemed to be growing warmer the later it got today. He had hoped it would be cooler by the coast.

'Thanks,' he said, looking round at each of them and catching Alice's eye. 'Why am I the man of the hour – surely that accolade belongs to the birthday girl?'

'I'm not a man,' Alice reminded him, and Steph giggled.

'You're the man that treated her to a skydive, though,' Maur said, the edge in her voice unmistakeable. Max chose not to rise to the bait.

'What did you lot get up to today?' he asked, and Steph immediately started telling him about their kayaking trip to the nearby lagoon.

'We saw an eagle catch a fish out of the water, right in front of us,' she said. 'It was amazing!'

Max smiled, accepting a beer from Jamal, who had nipped to the bar and back. 'Sounds it.'

He glanced up again to gauge Alice's reaction, but she was staring down at her phone, concern etching grooves across her forehead.

'Is everything all right?' he asked after a minute, cutting right across Steph's story about holding a baby crocodile.

Alice looked up, distracted.

'Is it Dickie?' said Maureen, snatching up her own bottle of Lion Lager.

Alice shook her head, starting to say something, but Maureen talked over her.

'Didn't Alice tell you?' she asked, her attention back on Max. 'I thought she would have, given that you spent all day together.'

'I don't really think that—' Steph began, but there was no stopping Maureen. Max wanted to hear what she had to say now, too, and looked at her with encouragement.

'Tell me what?' he said, watching a deep flush spread across Alice's cheeks.

'About the engagement,' Maureen continued, as if it was the most obvious revelation in the world. 'Dickie's bought the ring and everything – he sent her a photo of it last night. Show him, Alice. It really is rather sweet. I didn't think Dickie had it in him.'

Jamal coughed awkwardly as Max gazed across at Alice. He thought back to the events of that morning, to their conversation in the car about their aspirations to escape their boring jobs, to how she had gripped his hand as that plane took off and how she had jumped into his arms with delight once they were back on the ground, accepting his kiss without hesitation. Not once had she mentioned a ring, nor for a moment had she acted like a girl who had just got engaged.

Although Max had no right, and although he knew he was being far too sensitive, Maureen's words stung. It hurt to hear that Alice belonged to someone else, even though he had known it almost as soon as they had met. She had not tried to conceal the fact that Richard existed, but she had not brought him up willingly in conversation, either. Max accepted that he had – perhaps rather foolishly, as it transpired – taken those small observations and built them up in his mind until he was almost convinced that Alice's relationship with her boyfriend was not a very serious one. When Richard was simply the boyfriend she barely mentioned and openly kept secrets from, the extent of her feelings towards him had been an unknown quantity, as far as Max was concerned. Now, however, this engagement ring had landed smack-thud in the middle of his hopes.

'I was just . . .' Alice lowered her phone into her lap. She wouldn't meet Max's eyes, and looked almost stunned, as if she had been slapped. When her mobile then started ringing a split second later, they all jumped.

Alice snatched it up.

'Hey,' she said, her voice soft but laboured. 'I'm sorry I didn't call earlier. I was—What? What do you mean? What about Freddie? What's happened?'

Max saw Maureen and Steph exchange a look.

'She was telling me just now that she was worried about Freddie,' Steph hissed. 'He still hasn't replied to her text from a few days ago, or sent her a birthday message.'

'Shit.' Maureen ran an agitated hand through her dark hair and Max caught a whiff of apples as she tossed it over one shoulder.

Alice had got up from her chair and wandered over to where a set of small wooden steps led down to the beach.

Her shoulders were hunched, and she had wrapped her free hand around her middle. As Max stared after her, his heart telling him to get up and follow her but his head reminding him about the development in her relationship, Alice turned towards the light, and he saw tears coursing down her cheeks.

## 39

Alice had known almost immediately that something was seriously wrong. She knew Richard well enough to recognise even the slightest change in his tone, even when he was thousands of miles away in a different time zone. And his manner wasn't stilted because she hadn't called him since he'd sent the text message containing the ring box – this was something else, something far more important than any of the unspoken drama between them.

When Rich had taken a deep breath and said, 'It's Freddie,' a tumble of panic had engulfed her. She immediately assumed the worst – that her brother had been in an accident, or that he was gravely ill, and she fired questions at Richard as she stumbled away from the table and headed blindly across the sand-covered floor of the bar.

'I wasn't sure if I should call you,' Richard said, sounding torn. 'Your mum said not to, given that it was your birthday, but I thought you would want to know sooner rather than later.'

A plethora of horrible images flashed through Alice's mind. Her brother trapped in a burning car, or wired up to some machine that was keeping him breathing, the stoic expression of a doctor as he broke the news of a terminal illness.

'For God's sake, tell me!' she cried, not caring if her impatient tone annoyed him.

'Freddie has had . . .' Richard began.

Oh God, it must have been an accident. Alice clutched the back of an empty chair.

'Had *what*?'

A mosquito buzzed towards the candle on the table below her then promptly flew away. Alice stared at it distractedly. Not her brother, not Freds. She was aware of a sob building like lava in her throat, constricting her airways until all she could do was croak down the phone.

'Just tell me,' she said. 'Is he hurt?'

'He's safe,' Richard assured her, and Alice let go of the enormous breath she'd been holding in.

'Thank God,' she exclaimed, but the fear was still holding her frozen limbs to ransom.

'He's had . . . Well, I guess you would call it a breakdown.'

Alice's hand was over her mouth now.

'It all happened not long after you left, apparently,' Richard went on. 'I only found out this morning, but it's been eating me up, you not knowing, and I knew you would be wondering why he hadn't messaged you for your birthday.'

'I *was* wondering that,' Alice said, her voice small. There was a needle of guilt threading its way through her as she realised just how much she had been distracted that morning, and how little her mind had strayed to her brother's unusual lack of communication. 'I haven't heard from him once since we got here.'

'He checked himself into a rehab facility in Essex,' Richard told her. He sounded flustered, and Alice pictured the redness in his cheeks, and his hair askew where he'd run his hands through it. She knew how much he cared about her big brother.

'It turns out that he lost his job months ago,' Richard explained. 'He had been pretending to go into work, when in reality he was at home, drinking himself into a stupor most days. And that's not all.'

'Shit.' Alice sighed, an acidic taste rising in her throat. 'You mean drugs?'

Richard took a deep breath. 'Yes.'

'Oh no,' she managed, tears now snaking their way down her cheeks. Freddie was the rock against which Alice had always been able to bash, her myriad follies balanced out by his uncomplicated strength. She could not fathom that this had happened to him – or that none of them had noticed it.

'Your mum hadn't heard from him in a few weeks, so she went over there to surprise him one evening and found him and the flat in a right state. The only reason I even found out is because . . .' He stopped, and Alice gripped the phone.

'What?' she demanded, hearing the muffled footsteps of someone approaching. The next moment, Maureen was standing next to her, her face etched with concern. Alice shook her head and held up her hand to shoo her friend away.

'Because I wanted to tell your mum that we were setting the date,' he said, and Alice only just caught her huff of exasperation in time. She thought they had blooming well agreed to wait until after she got back from Sri Lanka.

'Your dad let me in,' Rich continued. 'When I asked where your mum was he just lost it. Alice, it was horrible. He was crying and everything.'

'Oh shit,' Alice said soberly, wiping her eyes as she pictured the scene. 'Bloody hell.'

'I can't get my head around it,' Richard admitted. 'Freddie always seemed so together, and so sensible, you know, just like you. I can't believe he let things get this bad.'

'I need to call home,' Alice said, sniffing away her sobs. Maur was still behind her, but had at least moved a discreet distance away.

'OK.' Richard did his best not to sound put out at her hurry to get him off the phone, but Alice could tell he was miffed.

'Don't be like that, Rich,' she sighed. 'I'm grateful that you told me, and I'm sorry you had to deal with my dad by yourself – but I need to know what's going on. I need the whole story. I'll call you back afterwards, I promise.'

'You can't.' He sounded exhausted. 'I've got six kids coming in for detention in five minutes.'

'Tonight then,' she said, and heard the click of a car door shutting. He must have gone outside to the school car park to call her from the privacy of his Renault Clio, and Alice closed her eyes against the inevitable waves of guilt.

'Tonight's fine,' he said, his tone now more conciliatory. 'Talk to you then. Oh, and Alice?'

'Yes?' Her voice was barely a whisper.

'I love you.'

Alice imagined that she could feel Max's eyes boring holes through her back.

'You, too,' she said.

Maureen hurried back over as soon as Alice lowered the phone from her ear, and listened with increasing shock as she was brought up to date with what had happened.

'Fuck,' she pronounced, and Alice nodded weakly.

'I need to call my mum.'

'Of course.' Maureen held her by her shoulders. 'It will be all right, you know. Freddie's done the right thing, he'll be getting the help he needs now.'

Alice pictured her brother's kind eyes. She thought about all the times he had defended her, encouraged her, teased her and offered her his shoulder when she had messed up. He was one of the good guys – one of the best people in the world – and the thought of him being so hurt, and so alone, and so afraid, made Alice want to lie on the ground and cry.

'I must call home,' she said again, and Maureen let her go.

'Go ahead,' she urged kindly. 'Me and Steph will be waiting. We can talk it all through, or we can just get drunk and forget about it – or maybe not,' she added, seeing the look on Alice's face.

'Thank you for being so nice,' Alice mumbled, and Maureen gave her an uncharacteristically timid smile.

'Well, durr,' she said gently. 'You're my friend, even if you do think I'm a terrible person. And it really will be OK, I promise. We all care about you – and Freddie, too – and we'll get you through this.'

Alice watched her walk back towards where the others were still sitting, and registered Max's worried gaze. She could not believe that while her poor family had been dealing with the shock of Freddie's illness — and he clearly was very ill — she had been throwing every caution to the wind. Quite literally, in fact — she had thrown *herself* into the wind. What if there had been an accident? What if her actions had landed her in hospital — or worse? As if her parents didn't have enough to worry about without her behaving like a child, a reckless and stupid child. Alice had been here before, and she knew how the story ended — with pain and regret and horrible guilt. What the hell had she been thinking?

She turned her back on Max as she scrolled through her phone and found her mother's number. Freddie was the only person who mattered now — that fact was as big and as clear as an elephant in the road. Everyone else would have to wait.

## 40

After speaking to her mum on the phone for almost an hour, Alice felt utterly drained. The giddy high of that morning's skydive and the rush she had felt upon seeing the ocean when they arrived in Tangalle had long been chased away by worry and guilt, and her neck and back felt stiff with tension. It had been difficult to hear her mother so upset. Freddie was the centre of her parents' world, the compass point of strength upon which they had always relied, and for him to fall so spectacularly apart had hit them very hard.

Alice had been assured by first her mum, and then her dad, that her brother was perfectly safe, and that he had agreed to get help as soon as the true extent of his problems had been discovered. While this made Alice proud of her brother, it also broke her heart to know that there wasn't anyone in his life who was close enough for him to confide in them. Freddie had loads of friends, but most of them were people he worked with in the City. They weren't old friends like Steph and Maureen were for her, and clearly, they didn't know Freddie very well at all – or, if they did, then they did not care about him enough. Rich and her brother got on well enough, but her boyfriend was not the type of person to pry into other people's lives or suggest a deep and meaningful chat. She supposed that not many men were that type, although she wished they would be. Max and Jamal seemed like they had that closeness – but then, even Max had kept the pain in his leg a secret from his friend.

Alice's initial instinct on speaking to Richard had been to try and change her flight home, and hurry back to Suffolk to help in any way that she could, but her mum told her tersely not to bother.

'Of course, it would have better if you were here,' she had snapped. 'I knew this holiday of yours was a bad idea, but it's a bit too late to start fretting about that now, isn't it, Alice? And anyway, your brother is not allowed any visitors for the first week. What could you do for him that I can't?'

Alice hadn't meant her offer to sound like an affront to her mother's capabilities as a parent. She bit her lip. Her mum was hurting, that was all. It was only natural that she was going to be feeling defensive and sensitive – something terrible had happened to one of her children, and she had not been there to catch Freddie before he fell, just like she had not been there to catch Alice, either – that was why she was lashing out. Alice taking offence wouldn't help matters.

'We just need to get him through this rehabilitation programme,' her mum had added. 'As soon as you're home again, you can help out and look after your dad, while I spend time with Freddie. He may be out next week, and we'll be looking after him here.'

Alice thought privately that her dad, a grown man, was probably capable of looking after himself, but again she said nothing and listened while her mum continued to talk.

'This is just a blip, that's all – a bump in the road,' Marianne said. 'He'll be back to normal before we know it.'

There was that word that seemed to keep cropping up, Alice had thought coldly: normal. For Freddie, normal had become a litre of vodka before lunchtime and a gram of cocaine to chase it down. Alice wondered just how sad her brother must have been in his so-called successful life to have sought such an extreme escape. She considered whether he might have been in a relationship that had ended badly – Freddie would usually tell her about a new girlfriend, but maybe this time he had chosen not to, for whatever reason. Alice wanted nothing more than to see him, to speak to him, to tell him that she was here – would always be there for him. Where before, the miles of distance from home had felt like a blessed relief, now they frustrated her – she was needed at home, where she could become the voice of reason to temper her mother's despair. She knew her mum wanted her there really.

'I just don't understand,' Marianne had wailed. Alice had left the bar area to sit on the beach, where she stared numbly at the repetitive motion of the dark waves as they scurried up the shore, only to hurry out again a moment later.

'He had everything he ever wanted,' her mum went on. 'A beautiful flat in London, a sports car, a great job.'

*All the trappings*, Alice had thought, but had not said.

'And now he's going to lose it all. Everything he has worked so hard to achieve. If I wasn't so bloody worried about him I would be furious!'

And at that, she had started crying again, great wracking sobs that made Alice cry again, too.

'Mum,' she tried to soothe. 'Mum, please don't cry.'

Eventually her mother had been unable to speak through her misery, and Alice talked briefly to her dad instead, who sounded shaken but determined.

'You just concentrate on having a nice birthday, darling,' he had said, and Alice had barked out a hard laugh, hearing her mother doing the same in the background. How could she possibly even think about something as pathetically unimportant as her birthday?

When she had finally said her goodbyes, Alice made her way back to the table. Steph, who knew Freddie almost as well as Alice herself, was in tears, leaving Alice full of remorse, on top of her worry, for being the one to bring a downer on everyone's day.

'Nonsense!' Maureen said, flapping her hands at Alice's mumbled apologies. 'You haven't ruined anything. It's still your birthday and we're still going to celebrate.'

Alice could think of nothing worse. She didn't have the energy to pretend that everything was going to be OK, or that she was fine.

Jamal and Max had both offered their commiserations as soon as she sat back down, but she wished they would leave. Her guilt about the skydive was making it impossible for her to even look at Max, who now felt absurdly like an enemy. She knew she was being unreasonable, but it was all too much; the thoughts were all too much. They were racing around in her head, and she was struggling for the self-control simply not to fall apart. She wished they would all just disappear.

'Why don't we leave you girls to it?' Max said suddenly,

and Alice glanced at him in surprise. He wasn't looking at her, though. His eyes were on Jamal.

'Um, sure.' Jamal reached for Steph's hand across the table and squeezed it. 'We'll be up in Wood House if you need us, yeah?'

Alice opened her mouth to say sorry, but her throat felt as if it was full of earth.

The three girls watched the two men leave in silence, and Alice's heart went out to her friends, for the sacrifice they were both making to stay and support her. It was their holiday, too, and Steph was missing precious time with Jamal. When she said as much, though, the words muffled by the curtain of her hair, they both told her not to be silly.

'To be honest,' Maureen confided, a smirk on her face, 'I could do with a few hours where I don't have to watch those two lovebirds pawing at each other.'

'Oi!' Steph braved a laugh. 'I would hardly call it pawing.'

Alice listened to their clumsy banter with envy. She felt wholly detached from the situation, as if her body was sitting there but her mind had long since departed. Her friends were already trying to distract themselves from the unsettling news – and she didn't blame them – but Alice could not simply place her brother's plight on a shelf and forget about it. She ordered a Lion Lager without really thinking, but found that she couldn't bear to drink it when it arrived. She closed her eyes against the image of Freddie sipping neat spirits at his desk. Alice's mother had told her that he'd filled his water bottle with vodka every day – that he had needed to in order to make it through the working day. Why hadn't he just talked to her? Was she such a bad sister that he didn't trust her?

She was vaguely aware that she would have to call Richard back soon. It was nearing four-thirty UK time, so he would be on his way home from school. For the first time since the plane had landed in Sri Lanka, Alice felt a pang of yearning for their little rented flat, for the comforting familiarity of the faded old sofa Richard's parents had given them, and her clothes neatly folded away in the chest of drawers that they had picked up at the second-hand furniture store in Cornard. She was missing the stoic presence of Richard, too, who she knew would stay calm and pragmatic throughout all of this. Alice used to assume that she would be strong in the face of a crisis, but she had been wrong. On the contrary, she now felt as if she was crumbling into pieces.

She kept wondering if things would have been different if she had never come to Sri Lanka, if she had done what her mum wanted – and what Richard wanted, really, even if he had pretended otherwise – and stayed behind, celebrated her thirtieth birthday with a pub quiz in the Black Boy and a Chinese takeaway in front of the telly. But there was little point in speculating. She was here now – what had happened had happened; there could be no changing it. She could only attempt to rebuild things.

Alice had also been worried that her mum would be cross with Richard for telling her about Freddie after she had forbidden it, but again her assumptions had been way off the mark.

'Oh, I completely understand why he told you,' her

mum had declared, her voice wobbling. 'He's practically part of the family, and you know how I feel about secrets.'

Alice's mother hated secrets. It had begun as a knee-jerk reaction to Alice's accident, which her mum blamed in part on her daughter's perpetual need to sneak off and get herself into trouble. There had been no locks on any of the doors in the family home – save for the front and back ones – since Alice got her scar. Even the bathroom door didn't have a bolt. In her mother's mind, secrets were things that shifty, untrustworthy people kept, and liars were even worse. The irony was, of course, that Alice had begun lying to her mum about some of the riskier activities she still indulged in purely because she had grown up with her cut-and-dry, black-and-white, right-and-wrong way of viewing the world. As far as Marianne Brockley was concerned, there were no grey areas, and so Alice had no choice but to create them herself.

Steph tapped her arm and offered a sympathetic smile.

'You were off in Wonderland again,' she said. 'Do you want to just call it a night?'

Alice looked at the two full drinks on the table in front of her friends, and shook her head.

'I might go on up, but you two should stay – get some dinner. I'm just not in a very fun mood, sorry.'

'Don't be sorry,' exclaimed Maur. 'We totally get it.'

'But we don't want you to be alone,' added Steph. 'If you're going to bed, we're going to bed, too.'

Alice tried her best to smile with the gratitude that she was feeling. She appreciated what they were trying to do, but she wished they would understand that she didn't want her dark mood to impact on their holiday. It was hardly fair.

Pushing her full beer across in Maureen's direction, Alice stood up.

'Don't,' she said, as Steph made to follow suit. 'Please stay. I'll be fine – just need to lie down and make sense of it all, you know. I promise you that I'll be absolutely fine.'

They let her go, albeit reluctantly, and Alice reckoned that she had about ten minutes before Steph would finish her cocktail and come to check on her. There was so much she could have talked about with her friends – not just concerning Freddie, but also Richard, and perhaps even Max, too. Alice knew she was confused about how to feel and what to think, but she also knew that she must get it all straight in her own mind first, before sharing it with anyone else. She had always been that way – prone to secrecy and quiet contemplation – but tonight, for the first time in a long while, Alice wished she was not.

Her mind strayed back to Richard as she made her way towards Palm House. She had never found out if he had got as far as actually telling her parents that they were setting a date for their wedding, but she had to assume that he would not have done something quite so crass – especially when she had made it so clear before flying out to Sri Lanka that she wanted them to share their news together. Richard was prone to putting the occasional size nine in his mouth before thinking it through, but he was also a sensitive soul.

Alice cast her mind back to that morning, before the news about Freddie had crashed into her world and made everything rain down like collapsed scaffolding, and recalled the kiss she had shared with Max. He had caught her completely by surprise, but then, she had surprised herself by leaping up into his arms like that. The kiss may have only lasted for a second or two, but in that brief moment when she kissed him back, she had felt it everywhere.

The truth was, Alice realised – sadness at the thought of losing that closeness between herself and Max making her breath catch – she could still feel it now.

## 41

A storm arrived during the night, so wild and angry and relentless that Alice wondered if her shattered emotions had somehow affected the weather. Thunder loud enough to shake the wooden bedframes reverberated through the treehouse, rain lashed in through the open partitions under the roof and lightning scored across the night sky as if flung there by an enraged sea god. Alice left her single bed, lifted the edge of the large mosquito net, and got in the double with Steph and Maureen, each of them still awake and wide-eyed with a mixture of terror and awe.

She hoped all the crashing thunder wouldn't cause Max to suffer another episode like he had in the jeep. Jamal was with him, though, and that had to be enough to comfort her. As much as Alice wanted to rush down the wooden steps, hurry across the wet sand and clamber up into his treehouse, she knew she could not. She could sense that a line had been drawn between the two of them now, and she had been the one to put it there. Maureen had been right to raise the subject of the ring. Alice should have told Max about it – of course she should. The reason she hadn't was purely a selfish one: she didn't want him to know. She had been enjoying the closeness building between them and was worried that it would be lost. Now, not only had he found out the truth, but he also knew she had kept it from him. No wonder he had taken the first opportunity to make his escape after the call came through about Freddie. He must think she was a terrible person, and right now, Alice would agree with him.

Talking to Richard again last night had only increased her sense of self-loathing, because she'd had no choice but to lie to him. She could not very well admit to jumping out of a plane – he would go berserk – and she'd had to swear Steph and Maureen to secrecy, too. How had she got herself tangled into so many knots? She knew how – by letting the old Alice surface from the depths where she had long since been banished. Sri Lanka had been a catalyst for this change in her, but she knew that meeting Max had also been a big part of it.

She waited in the treehouse while Steph and Maureen went down to have breakfast, telling them she wasn't hungry when in truth her stomach was grumbling in earnest. She had not eaten dinner the previous evening, because she hadn't been able to face the normality of sitting down to a meal. Alice still felt that way now, and she also wanted to avoid Max. Either he would have retreated from her and would be politely distant, or he would be so kind to her that she would fall apart again. Alice could not face either scenario – not yet. She simply did not have the strength. When the girls returned, bringing with them some bread rolls and jam for Alice, Steph informed her rather sheepishly that she was heading out for the day with Jamal – adding that she would of course stay behind if Alice would rather she did.

'Go!' Alice said, waving a hand at her friend. 'I'm fine!'

'Max is off to some turtle sanctuary or something,' Maureen added. 'So I thought we could have a beach day, if you're up for it?'

Alice smiled with genuine relief. She was pleasantly surprised that Maur had chosen to spend the day with her rather than insisting that Max let them tag along with him. Alice had kept her true feelings about Max hidden from both her best friends, but perhaps Maureen had worked out enough to know that Alice needed some space from him.

'That would be great,' she told Maureen. 'Thank you.'

They each packed a bag and smeared sun lotion over their exposed skin, waving goodbye to Steph before wandering out to the main road and flagging down a tuk-tuk.

'Can you take us to a nice beach?' Maureen asked the driver, who nodded with enthusiasm, and off they went, wobbling along the dusty road beside the beach before taking a sharp right and heading through Tangalle's typically chaotic town centre. It was clear straight away that this area of Sri Lanka was more geared up for tourists than the villages they had visited further north had been. There were inflatable beach toys, lilos and buckets and spades in neat stacks outside the shops, and many of the guest houses and bars they whizzed past had English names. There were surf shops, too, and Western tourists wearing board shorts or Billabong bikinis, their hair long and matted and their tans as dark as syrup.

Despite the ferocious rain that had been pelting the ground only hours ago, the tarmac of the road was dry and cracked, and the sunlight felt abrasive, like scratching fingers against Alice's skin. The tuk-tuk continued through town until they reached the head of a long, sloping pathway, which was shaded by overhanging palm trees.

'Down there, Goyambokka Beach,' the driver informed them cheerily, holding out his hand for his rupees.

'Time to get our tan on!' declared Maur, skipping off ahead of Alice down the path. She was being unusually cheerful, even if you took into account the allure of sun loungers and fresh coconuts. Alice thought it was almost as if her friend was putting on an act – albeit a very convincing one. Just as she had when she'd received that birthday text from Richard, Alice felt a creep of unease, and, as it turned out, she did not have to wait long to have her suspicions confirmed.


'Earth to Alice.'

Maureen brushed a finger across Alice's bare arm, causing her to shiver.

'Sorry, I was miles away.'

Maureen put her head on one side and pushed her sunglasses up off her nose. They were lying side by side on two raised beds, Alice under the shade of a large umbrella and Maur fully exposed in the glare of the sun. She had untied the halter straps of her red bikini and tucked them away to avoid getting white marks, and although they had only been on the beach for twenty minutes or so, Alice could see that her friend was already beginning to colour.

'Standard,' Maureen said. 'Where were you this time?'

Alice tried to smile, but it turned into a frown.

'Oh, you know, nowhere in particular.'

She turned away briefly and stared out across the Indian Ocean, listening to the gentle crackling sound of palm fronds coming from behind them. The whole of Goyambokka Beach was lined by trees, and the sand beneath their loungers was soft and white, like caster sugar. Alice could hear strains of reggae music filtering down from the lone bar, and in the distance, a little boy shrieked with delight as a wave rushed across the shore and filled the hole he'd dug with frothy sea water.

'I have a confession to make,' Maureen said, and Alice felt the knots pulling tighter in her stomach.

'Go on,' she said.

'I brought you here under false pretences,' Maur continued. 'I wanted some time to talk to you alone about something.'

'I see.' Alice wriggled up to a sitting position and reached for her bottle of water. She had never seen Maureen look like this before, almost as if she was afraid, and it immediately put Alice on edge. Was her friend about to confess her adoration for Max? Or had she somehow found out about their shared kiss after the skydive and wanted to tell her off?

'Whatever it is, you can tell me,' Alice went on, swallowing the nervous lump in her throat. 'After last night, I doubt anything would shock me.'

'I shouldn't have landed you in it with Max,' Maureen began, before talking across Alice's automatic protestations. 'No, it was wrong of me. It was your news to share with whoever you chose to – I had no right to tell him.'

'Why did you?' Alice asked, her curiosity outweighing her desire to reassure.

'Because I wanted him to know that you weren't perfect,' Maur blurted out. 'And because I was pissed off with you. I know you don't think that I'm good enough for him – or for anyone, really. I guess I just lashed out because I was angry with you for judging me. But then you got that call about Freddie and I felt like the biggest bloody bitch in the world. I'm so sorry.'

'I don't think you're not good enough for anyone!' Alice exclaimed, feeling totally bewildered. There was a pain in her temple that had been throbbing away since the previous night, and she rubbed at it now, trying to make sense of what Maureen was saying.

'You do!' Maureen was exasperated now. 'You don't think I'm good enough for Freddie, and you don't think I'm good enough for Max, either.'

The knot twisted apart inside Alice with a rush of relief, only to be replaced a moment later by guilt. She could not believe that one of her best friends could think that she would judge her in this way. It was awful, but equally ludicrous at the same time – and thankfully there was an easy way to solve it.

'Oh, Maur,' she said, starting to laugh. It felt good. 'Is this why you've been so weird with me over the past few days?'

Maureen inclined her head, looking at Alice with a puzzled expression. 'Maybe.'

'You are silly,' Alice went on. 'The only reason I'm squeamish about you and Freds getting together is because, well, let's just say you do have a tendency to overshare.'

'Oh.' The truth dawned on Maureen and the edges of her mouth twitched into a grin.

'You mean when it comes to sex and stuff?'

'Yes!' Alice laughed.

Maureen looked mollified. 'What do you take me for?' she asked. 'Do you really think I would tell you how big your brother's—'

'STOP!' Alice held up her hands. 'Don't even say it! And as for not being good enough – to be honest, he would be punching above his weight if he managed to pull you. I honestly had no idea you liked him all that much – I thought it was just you trying to wind me up.'

Maureen was laughing now, in relief as well as amusement.

'Does that mean I have your blessing?' she checked, suddenly looking much younger than her just-turned-thirty years.

'Of course!' Alice crowed. 'He will be over the rings of Saturn, let alone the moon, when he finds out you like him.'

'What about Max?' Maureen said gently, catching Alice unawares. 'What's the deal with him?'

Alice took a deep breath and stared again at the quivering blue line where sea met sky. Sunlight danced on the surface of the water, and a light breeze chased a rogue napkin across the sand.

'I haven't been trying to keep you and Max apart,' she said honestly. 'Me and him, we just understand each other.

308

I guess I got carried away with that connection, and I let it go too far. I let myself do something that I promised I never would again.'

'Shit!' Maureen's eyes were on stalks. 'Did you and him . . . ?'

'Oh God, no!' Alice shook her head firmly. 'Nothing like that. I mean the skydive. I promised my mum that after my accident, you know.' She touched the scar on the side of her face and Maureen nodded. 'I told her that I would never put myself in danger again.'

Maureen was quiet for a while, concentration making her squint even more than the sun was.

'Did you enjoy it, though?' she said finally.

'What?' Alice asked.

'The skydive. Was it fun?'

Alice drew her mouth into a line of reluctant concession.

'I guess so.'

'Well, then – stop beating yourself up about it. What's done is done.'

Alice nodded to show she agreed, even though her heart was not fully on board. She could not help but imagine how her family and Richard would feel.

'And as for Max,' Maureen added, sitting up to apply more sun cream to her reddening legs, 'he is no Freddie Brockley, but he is pretty special – you both are. You shouldn't feel bad for having a connection with someone, because that kind of thing is unavoidable. Sometimes you meet people that you just click with, and there is no rational explanation for it – it just is. Life would be pretty bloody boring if we didn't come across these kindred spirits from time to time.'

Alice put her head on one side as she considered Maureen's words. She was right, of course – the connection Alice had with Max did feel like something tangible – a solid fact that could not and should not be overlooked or undervalued. What she hadn't told Maur, however, was quite how strong she had allowed this inherent feeling of rightness to become.

'You and Max haven't done anything wrong,' Maureen continued. She had finished her legs and was now spreading sun lotion across her stomach. 'You haven't acted on the attraction you feel, so there's nothing to feel guilty about.'

'Do you really think that?' Alice persisted, and Maureen stopped rubbing for a moment and turned to face her.

'I do,' she confirmed. 'And I also think that whatever Richard doesn't know can't hurt him. If you're happy with him and you and Max are just good friends, there is nothing to worry about.'

She was right, conceded Alice, smiling at her friend. She could still get out of this whole mess without Richard getting hurt at all. It was, however, far too late for her.

# 42

# Max

*If I should live,*
*I will seek and explore,*
*I shall never let up,*
*I will strive for much more . . .*

Max had lied when he told the others he wanted to visit a turtle sanctuary. There was one not far from the Cinnabar Resort, but he had no intention of venturing even that distance. Instead, he had hobbled as far as the next beach bar along and sat in the shade with a glass of lemonade, swallowing down a couple more painkillers and doing his best not to panic about the increased swelling and localised pain in his stump.

He saw Alice and Maureen trundle past in a tuk-tuk on the main road, and Jamal and Steph followed shortly afterwards on foot. Max pulled his cap down to cover his face, but they were so lost in each other that they did not see him. Struggling to his feet again once the coast was clear, Max limped unsteadily back along the sand and hopped up the wooden steps of his treehouse, using the rails to balance. The storm had woken him from a fretful dream, in which he was trapped in a hospital bed, unable

311

to move and speak, while his family all stood around him, discussing whether to switch off his life support. Max had opened his mouth again and again to shout at them that he was there, that he could see them and hear them, but nothing had come out but a gasping wheeze.

It was hot inside the treehouse, but Max could not settle in the hammock just outside it either, plagued as he was by memories of Afghanistan. He checked his watch. Another hour until he could take anything more for the pain.

Stretched out on the bed with the overhead fan switched up to its fastest setting, he tried to count his breaths as he had been taught during meditation classes – something his mum had signed him up for and which had actually helped for a while. There was one particular sequence that was supposed to ensure you dropped instantly off to sleep, but Max could not seem to dredge it up from the dark folds of his mind. Eventually, he gave up and let his thoughts wander instead, allowing himself a small smile as they inevitably floated towards Alice. He pictured her face when they had pulled up at the skydive centre, the genuine tears of overwhelmed awe that she had shed as the sun rose at the top of Adam's Peak, and the kindly concern that had radiated out of her as he sat, shaken, on the floor of that jeep. She had been covered in blood but thinking only of him then; she had reached for his hand on that summit; and she had thrown herself into his embrace on that airfield.

The next thing Max was aware of was the treehouse door creaking open, and Jamal peering through into the gloom.

'Sorry,' he whispered, a huge smile on his face. 'Didn't mean to wake you.'

Max stretched, then winced as the pain registered once again.

'What time is it?' he asked blearily. 'It's so hot in here.'

Jamal walked into the bathroom and Max heard the sound of the toilet seat being propped up.

'Almost seven,' he called through the half-open door. 'How long you been back?'

'Not long,' lied Max, heaving himself up. He had forgotten to pull the mosquito net down around the bed, and he could see three new bites on his stump. He had dreamed about Alice this time as he slept, though, and the thought made him smile despite his discomfort.

'Where are the girls?' he asked as Jamal re-emerged, flicking water at him with a laugh.

'Stephie and Maur are in the bar, and I think Alice went for a walk on the beach,' he said. 'You coming down?'

Max nodded, pushing back a strong urge to grit his teeth as he swung around so his thighs were facing over the side of the bed.

'I'll meet you down there in a bit – there's something I need to do first.'

## 43

Alice walked along the beach until she had put a good distance between herself and the Cinnabar Resort, feeling troubled yet still enjoying the simple pleasure of fine sand slipping between her toes and sea air tickling at her senses. The sun sat low and heavy, the sky above it a stained-glass window of golds, lilacs, pinks and reds, while the shifting ocean below was transformed into a molten lake of whispering beauty.

There were bars dotted at regular intervals along the beach, each with their own set of staff preparing tables for the evening. Alice watched as one boy raked the sand flat and another lit several lanterns made from large wooden stakes. She could smell the citronella coming from the candles, but there was another scent, too, and squinting down at the curling smoke, Alice realised there were incense sticks poking out of the sand around the chairs. The mood was ambient, but her own inner turmoil still raged as wildly as the storm had the previous night.

She wandered a bit further before settling down on the rapidly cooling sand, staring at a fixed point on the horizon as she picked absent-mindedly at the scab of a shaving cut on her knee. She should feel unshackled here in sleepy Tangalle, with all this space and nothing in the distance but the blur of possibility, but on the contrary, it felt to

Alice as if the world was snapping shut around her like a magician's box.

It had been nice to spend the day with Maur at Goyambokka, but Alice had found it almost impossible to relax. She was worried about Freddie, she was concerned about her parents, she felt confusion when it came to Richard, and an emotion she was too afraid to examine surrounding her feelings towards Max. What she wanted to do was run away from all of it, but she was trapped. It would not matter how far or how fast she fled; the jumble of anxious gnawing thoughts would follow.

'Mind if I join you?'

Alice twisted around to see Max walking slowly across the sand towards her, limping slightly on his prosthetic leg. She hadn't heard him approaching, and told him as much as he covered the last few metres of beach that lay between them.

'That'll be all the years of stealth training in the army,' he joked weakly, lowering himself down close enough to Alice that their bare knees touched.

'How were the turtles?' she asked, and Max looked at her, confused.

'Turtles? Oh, yeah – um, they were fun. Did you have a nice day?'

'It was great, thanks,' Alice replied, hating how stilted and polite they were being with one another. She and Max had not had a moment alone together since Richard's call about Freddie, and he wasn't being his normal, energetic self. There was a dullness to his blue eyes, and he couldn't seem to get comfortable, no matter how he positioned himself on the sand.

'Listen, I—' she began, just as Max said her name, and they both laughed in mild relief that the strange tension had been broken.

'You go,' she said, and he smiled at her.

'I was just going to ask after your brother,' he said. 'I know how I would be feeling if it was Ant, so I thought I would come and check on you – see if you were coping all right with it all.'

'My mum wants me home,' Alice admitted. 'She won't say as much, but I can tell that she's angry with me for being here. I did look at booking an earlier flight, but something stopped me. I'm all over the place, to be honest. I've got all this nervous energy rattling around inside me – so much that I feel like I could dig my way through this beach and all the way back to Suffolk if somebody handed me a big enough shovel.'

'You would probably make it there, too,' he allowed.

He looked tired, Alice realised. The lines around his eyes were more pronounced and there was an extra sweep of stubble across his jaw.

'Are you OK?' she asked, putting a tentative hand on his arm.

'I'll live,' he said evenly, and Alice was reminded of what Jamal had told her about possible infections, and – what was it? – ulcerations. She was just about to move her hand instinctively to his forehead to check his temperature, when Max continued to speak.

'You know, before this,' he said, tapping the upper part of Mister Tee, 'I was a lot like you are now.'

Alice frowned. 'In what way?'

'Well,' he said. 'You know I told you before how I used to pretend to be a tough guy, just like my brother?'

She nodded. 'I remember.'

'I think you do the same thing, except with you, it's not so much tough as mousy.'

'I am not mousy!' she exclaimed, and he gave her a half-smile.

'I know that. You are probably the least mousy person that I've met in ages – you're the opposite.'

Alice felt like she had been caught out in a lie, but wasn't sure how.

'What are you trying to say?' she asked, taking her hand off his arm.

'We have both had things happen to us,' he said. 'Things that changed us.'

Alice's hand went automatically to her scar, then she let it fall.

'But whereas my accident,' he continued, emphasising the last word to make it clear that it had been anything but, 'encouraged me to drop the act, yours convinced you that you must put one on.'

'You think I'm full of shit,' she muttered, but Max shook his head.

'No, I don't – not with me, anyway. With me you're that brave little girl who climbed up on the roof and said to hell with the consequences. You're the girl who jumped out of a plane without a moment's hesitation – the girl who scaled a mountain just so she could watch the sun rise.'

Tears filled Alice's eyes and she blinked them away, stung suddenly by his words.

'That girl is trouble,' she said coldly. 'She will only end up hurting people.'

'Oh, Alice,' he said, staring at her with such dismay that she had to look away. 'I think you're wrong, you know. I think the only person you're really hurting by pretending to be someone else is yourself.'

'That's not true.' Alice was shaking her head so vigorously that her view of the sea became distorted. The crashing of the waves now seemed to match the pattern of her beating heart inside her chest. 'I put my mum through hell before my accident, then even more after it happened, and . . .' She ran out of steam and dug her bare feet through the sand in frustration.

'I get it,' Max said, his tone light. 'I put my parents through the mill, too. I still do, and I feel crap about the fact most of the time. I do know how you feel, I really do. But I also can't pretend to be the man I used to be. Truth is the foundation that I have been trying to rebuild my life on ever since I left the army. I accept who I am, and every day I get closer to being free because of it. Part of the reason I came here is to prove to my family that I am content, and that I don't need to be fixed.'

'You don't always tell the truth,' Alice said quietly. 'What about the pain in your leg?'

Max took a sharp intake of irritated breath.

'Forget my fucking leg for a second.'

She stared at him, wide-eyed with surprise at his sudden change in tone.

'I do forget it,' she argued. 'I don't even think about it – but I worry about you being in pain, of course I do.'

He softened immediately, his expression now one of regret that he had snapped at her.

'Sorry,' he mumbled. 'I just get sick of everything coming back to my blasted leg – my literal blasted leg.'

'That's not funny,' she sniffed, and he braved a short laugh.

'Alice,' he sighed. 'I almost died.'

He said it simply, yet with feeling, and Alice felt the hair on her arms prickle despite the heat.

'People always use that saying, don't they?' he went on. '"You could get hit by a bus tomorrow." I really did get hit by that bus, so to speak, only I got the chance to get back up again. Me. When so many others did not. It was just a single moment, that IED going off, but it changed everything in my life – everything except who I really was underneath that soldier persona. I'm the same person I always was, only now I embrace it.'

'So, you changed for the better?' Alice said, and he nodded, just once.

'I did.'

'Perhaps I did, too,' she insisted. 'Maybe I needed to have my accident to stop me being so reckless, to learn there was a better way to live.'

'That's all well and good.' He shifted on the sand until his body was angled towards her own. 'As long as you're happy. Are you?'

Alice nodded. She could feel him looking at her, but she didn't say anything.

'You told me that before, when we were on the train,' he said. 'But I still don't believe you. I still think you could be so much happier than you are – or claim to be,' he added, and she pressed her heels further through the sand.

'It makes me happy to know that my family are happy,' she explained, stumbling a bit at the half-truth. Because he was right, wasn't he? She was not as happy as she could be. 'They're only happy when they can trust me not to do anything stupid, or take risks,' she went on, now trying to convince herself as much as him.

'OK.' Max paused, his fingers on his chin. 'If that's really the case, answer me this one question: is your brother happy?'

Alice felt as if she had been slapped.

'No,' she mumbled.

'My guess is that your brother has been putting on a very good act, too,' Max continued. 'And he is now having his own moment – the one that will change everything for him.'

Alice did not even bother to catch her tears this time, simply letting them slide down her cheeks and drip on to her T-shirt. For a moment she thought that Max was going to carry on talking, that he would continue to push her in a direction she did not feel ready to go, but something stopped him. Seeing her so upset had bruised him into silence, and for a few minutes he simply sat and let her cry, staring ahead at where the sun was still sinking. And then, with a movement so small that Alice did not even sense it, he came towards her and pulled her tightly against his chest.

# 44

'I'm sorry.' Alice sniffed and rubbed at her eyes. She had wept a large wet circle on to the front of Max's navy blue polo shirt. 'I'm not usually this pathetic – it's just because it's Freddie. I feel like I should be there.'

'It's OK.' Max squeezed harder. 'It's best to let it all out.'

'Spoken like a true tough guy,' she joked half-heartedly, and felt him chuckle. 'You know me so well.'

They sat for a while not speaking, and Alice listened to the sound of Max's heart beating against her ear. It was fast and urgent, almost as if he was running up a mountain as opposed to sitting here on the beach. She was aware that if she lifted her face up towards his, then their lips would be level, and the thought was enough to make goosebumps appear on her arms and across the back of her neck. Being this close to Max felt miraculous, like the final piece of a jigsaw puzzle slotting into place, and again the need to flee tore through her. It wasn't him she wanted to escape from, though, it was everything else.

'Can I ask you another question?' he said eventually, and Alice pulled gently away until she could sit back up and look at him properly.

'As long as it's an easy one.'

He glanced down at his hands. 'It's not, I'm afraid. But it is a yes or no one.'

Alice scrunched her fingers through the sand.

'Go on, then.'

He took a breath, opened his mouth, then shook his head. 'No, I shouldn't. I mean, I don't know if I . . .'

She waited, not speaking, wanting him to tell her but also terrified of what he might say.

Max brought his eyes up once again.

'Do you want to marry Richard?'

Each word hit Alice like a punch.

'I . . .' she stuttered.

Max put a steady hand on the crook of her elbow.

'Yes or no?'

'It's not that simple,' she mumbled. 'With everything that's happened with my brother, I haven't had time to think about it. I mean, it's just not important – not at the moment.'

'Surely there isn't anything more important,' Max pressed, his voice still low but the meaning behind his words un-equivocal. 'If you really loved Richard and you were happy, then the answer would be as clear as the sky above our heads.'

Alice looked up.

'There are clouds,' she told him sullenly, and he fol-lowed her gaze without smiling.

'Yes,' he said. 'So it would appear.

'When I heard about that message,' he went on, 'about the ring, I felt . . . Well, it felt horrible, if I'm honest. It made me realise something – and that something is the reason why I just asked you that question. I know it's wrong of me, Alice, but I would never be able to forgive myself if I didn't ask, if I didn't make absolutely sure.'

Alice felt something shift deep inside her chest. She suddenly felt unsteady, as if the possible repercussions of what he was telling her were strong enough to cause the very ground to tremble. She was afraid to look at him, but unable not to meet his eyes, which were wide and open and sincere.

Max reached across and took her hand in both of his.

'I'm not usually this guy,' he said. 'I hate people who cheat. Those idiots who allow themselves to fall for a person that they shouldn't – I always believed that they were weak. But this doesn't feel like cheating, Alice – it would feel like cheating not to.'

'Not to what?' she murmured, and he smiled a little sadly.

'To hold your hand, Alice. To sit beside you, not just here on this beach tonight, but on every beach, on every day and night, for always.'

Blood rushed into Alice's cheeks. She thought she might stop breathing. Or cry. Or both.

'I didn't come to Sri Lanka to meet someone,' he continued, almost with a laugh, as if he could not believe, just as Alice could not, what he was confessing to her. He had become so convinced that the kind of connection he wanted to find was lost to him, and that he would never again allow himself to fall in love – not after what had happened.

'But then, there you were, so bright and shining with all your goodness and rightness. You became one of my best friends before I even realised what was happening, and now I don't want to ever spend a single day without you in it. I want us to climb more mountains, jump out of more planes. I want to teach you to surf, and for you to take me diving. We could take on anything, I know we could – the two of us together would be invincible. And I know it's crazy and I know I have no right to even be saying these things to you, but Alice,' he said, squeezing her hand, 'I think that you . . .'

He stopped, his eyes searching her face.

'What I mean is, I hope . . . I hope that you feel the same way as I do.'

Alice found that she couldn't speak, opening her mouth only to emit a gasping sound. All his words, all these emotions and promises – it was all too much, it was overwhelming.

She dropped her eyes from Max's and stared down at the sand between her feet, forcing herself to picture Richard's smile, the way his face was always half-crumpled when he woke, the way his fishing tackle piled up by their back door, and his clumsy and unromantic but totally sincere proposal. What would happen to Richard if she tore apart everything that they had built together? And what would her parents say if she betrayed him like this, in the same week that their son's so-called perfect life had fallen apart? There would be so much hurt and pain and for what – for a man she had known less than a fortnight?

Alice thought about what Steph would say – she would be kind and understanding, but also sensible enough to point out that perhaps a person's feelings cannot always be trusted. That Alice was away from home in an amazing place, having an adventure that she now knew she had been craving for so long. She and Max had shared experiences together that felt special, and it had happened at the same time as Richard started pushing her to set a date for the wedding. Her mum would say that Max was simply Alice's escape route, that her feelings felt real but that they weren't. Because how could they be? How could she love a man she barely knew, and how could he really love her?

Her largest stumbling block, however, was her fear. When Alice was with Max, she could not repress that childish nature she possessed, which made her push boundaries. He had booked a skydive – something that carried a risk far greater than the climb which had resulted in a short stay in hospital and a nasty scar – and she had run willingly to that plane without letting herself think about the consequences. She had, in short, put herself and Max before everyone else. The fact was, Alice could not trust herself with Max – and with Richard she knew that she would be safe. Who she was with Max frightened her just as much as it thrilled her, and Alice had learned a long time ago that chasing a risk often ended with a big fall.

Very slowly, she removed her hand from Max's grasp, knowing that it was probably the last time she would ever feel the warmth of his touch, or the comfort of him being so close to her, and wanting to be even closer. She made herself look at him, properly this time, and was greeted with an expression of such unwavering devotion that her resolve almost crumbled away like the red dust up on Adam's Peak.

'This isn't real, Max,' she said softly. 'How can it be? I can't trust it – and what if I'm wrong, and you're wrong? It would fall apart. And it's not fair on Richard, or my family.'

Max's expression cracked. She could almost see his hope begin to shatter.

'I understand all that,' he said sadly. 'But what about you?'

'What about me?'

'What about what's fair for you?' he asked. 'I know you don't want to hurt anyone – hell, neither do I. But sometimes you should be that reckless person; sometimes there is no easy option,' he insisted. 'You won't ever reach the potential you have for real happiness unless you take some risks in life – and I know you, Alice. I've seen you come alive in front of my eyes.'

'But I can't trust that person – the version of me that I am with you,' she said, her frustration at hurting him causing her voice to come out high and desperate. 'Sooner or later, I would make another mistake. And then what?'

Max shook his head. 'You are a person, Alice,' he said. 'You're not a mistake waiting to happen. And of course I can't promise you that things will work out, and that you will never get hurt again, even. That's the pain and beauty of life – none of us know what will happen; all we can do is ride the waves that life throws at us. And I want to ride them with you.'

Alice opened her mouth to argue, but Max held up a hand to silence her.

'All I know is that I have never felt this way before,' he said, his eyes now pleading. 'Not ever. Life is too short to ignore feelings like this. I could have left Sri Lanka and never said anything, but I didn't want to do that. I wanted to be honest, because I owe that much to myself, as well as to you.'

'I should never have done that skydive,' she muttered. 'It was selfish of me, and stupid.'

326

Max gaped at her.

'But you loved every second of it,' he said. 'I saw you. I saw how much it meant to you.'

'You saw what you wanted to see,' she replied, more snappily than she had intended. 'I'm not some problem that needs fixing, Max. I'm an adult and I can make my own decisions about who I want to be and who I want to be with.'

'OK.' Max held up both his hands. Alice could tell that she had hurt him, but she didn't seem able to stop. It was almost as if someone really had given her a shovel, and now she was using it to determinedly dig her way into a hole too deep to come back from.

Max had fallen silent now, and this time when she looked at him, Alice could see the defeat in his eyes. She wanted nothing more in that moment than to crawl across the sand and into his arms, to give in to the want that was tearing through her and let him kiss away all her fears. But she needed to be more sensible than that. She had to be.

'I'm sorry,' she said redundantly.

Max's mouth was set in a thin, hard line and the colour had drained from his cheeks. He looked hot and agitated.

'Don't say sorry to me,' he said abruptly. 'Save the apologies for yourself – you're going to need them when you wake up one day and realise you've thrown your life away, all because you were too scared to face up to who you really are and what you really want.'

What could she say? Alice had a terrible feeling that he was right, but the fear was too great. It had anchored itself inside her, and was holding her to ransom now, so that she was unable to speak or move or do anything other than stare at him. She watched in helpless anguish as Max got slowly and clumsily to his feet, wincing as the weight went down on to his prosthetic leg.

'I'm not even upset for myself,' he said grimly, looking down at her with what Alice took to be disgust. 'I'm upset for the girl that you turned your back on. She is the real you, and you will never be happy until you come to terms with that.'

He turned and began to walk away, leaving Alice alone on the sand. A big part of her wished that he would storm back over and shout at her, order her to stop being such a coward, because knowing that she was about to lose him for good was making it hard for her to breathe. How could she let this man go? How would she live with herself?

She started to get up, ready to chase after him, but then a thought stopped her.

How could she ever be happy with Max if he became the reason for causing so much pain to the people she cared about the most? She would only end up resenting him, and everything would fall apart.

She picked up a handful of sand, and then another, hurling clumps of it into the air over and over until trenches appeared on either side of her. While the two of them had been talking, the dark mass of the ocean had finally swallowed the sun, and the moon had crept up to replace it.

Alice got to her feet and started to hurry down the beach, reluctant to spend another moment in her own, cowardly company, but the soft sand fell away with each step, slowing her progress until she began to swear with frustration. She could see Max up ahead, not far from the beach bar, but as she stared at him he vanished. Alice blinked, squinting into the distance as terror hammered through her. Then she began to run.

Max had fallen, and he wasn't getting back up.

# 45

The events of the next ten minutes sped by in such a blur that Alice would later find that she could never recount each one separately. After she saw Max collapse, she ran as fast as she could along the beach, shouting his name as she went, followed by Jamal's, and punctuating each one with the word help, yelled as loudly and as urgently as she could muster. She reached Max at the same time as Jamal emerged from the beach bar, his brown eyes widening as he took in the scene.

'Shit!' he swore, almost losing his footing in his haste to reach his friend. Alice, who had dropped to her knees in the sand beside Max, leaned over to check if he was still conscious.

'He's breathing,' she told Jamal, putting a shaky hand across Max's clammy forehead.

Jamal was kneeling down now, too, the upper half of his body bent over Max as he attempted to rouse him.

'What happened?' he asked, looking sidelong at Alice.

'I don't know,' she cried. 'We were talking, and then he left and I was following him and he just . . .' A sob broke noisily through her words. 'He just fell over. I don't know.'

Jamal didn't reply, instead turning to Steph, who was now making her way across the sand towards them, a shocked hand covering her mouth.

'Can you get me some water?' he asked, and Steph hurried back the way she had just come, only to return half a minute later with a full bottle and Maureen hot on her heels.

'What the hell?' Maur exclaimed, looking first at Max then at Alice, who was still struggling not to cry.

Jamal unscrewed the bottle and poured some of the water over Max's face, being careful not to get any in his airways. There was a pause of a few seconds, in which nobody spoke, and then Max blearily opened his eyes, causing Alice to choke out a strangled sob of relief.

'I've got you, mate,' said Jamal, hoisting Max up until he was in a sitting position. 'Can you try to drink some water for me?'

'Has he got sunstroke?' asked Maureen, as Steph put a comforting hand on Alice's shoulder.

'He was fine,' Alice said. 'I mean, he did seem a bit like his leg was hurting, but he didn't say anything about feeling ill.'

Jamal's eyes darkened. 'His leg was hurting?' he checked, and Alice nodded numbly.

'Yes. He didn't say as much, but I could tell.'

Jamal chewed his bottom lip for a moment, thinking. Max had sipped the water, but his eyes were closed again, and Alice could see the sweat pooling on his upper lip. He looked sick, she realised, as if he had flu. Why hadn't she noticed earlier? Why hadn't she done something?

'Can you go and ask one of the lads behind the bar to come and help me?' Jamal said to Maureen. 'I need to get him back to the treehouse. He needs rest and fluids.'

Maureen did as she was told, and within a few minutes, Jamal and two of the Cinnabar Resort staff had half carried and half dragged Max across the bar and up the steps to Wood House. Alice heard the word 'doctor' as she trailed miserably behind them, and a cold hand of fear clutched icy fingers around her heart.

Steph followed the men up the stairs, only to return a few minutes later shaking her head.

'Jamal says we should stay down here,' she said. 'Max is OK, he's talking and making sense, but he needs some rest.'

'Does Jamal know what the matter is?' Maureen asked.

'It's his leg,' said Steph, glancing over her shoulder towards the closed door of the treehouse. 'It's in a right state. Jamal thinks an infection may have set in, but they're waiting for a doctor.'

'Shit,' said Maureen, her expression grim. 'Poor Max.'

Alice didn't say anything; she couldn't say anything. She felt like she had swallowed a fistful of broken glass. All she seemed capable of doing was crying.

'Hey.' Steph attempted to give her a hug, but Alice pulled away. 'I'm sure he'll be OK,' she went on. 'Try not to worry.'

'He just fucking collapsed!' exclaimed Alice, her voice rising. 'Of course I'm bloody worried.'

Steph's eyes filled with tears.

'I'm just trying to stay positive,' she said, and Maureen stepped forward before Alice could snap again.

'Clearly Alice is very worried,' she said calmly. 'She doesn't know what she's saying, do you, Alice?'

Alice sighed, weariness setting in just as rapidly as her anger had a moment ago. 'Sorry for snapping.'

'It's OK.' Steph, always so reasonable, managed to smile at her. 'Forget it.'

'Come on,' said Maur, gesturing back towards the bar area. 'There's no point standing here like a bunch of coconuts all night. We'll be able to see from the bar when the doctor turns up, and after he's gone we can find out what's going on, OK?'

Alice could not think of a reason to disagree, even though the thought of sitting still made her limbs itch with frustration. She knew that she couldn't do anything for Max, but she wanted to stay as close to him as she could, just in case he needed her, or asked for her. Then again, she thought forlornly, following the other two into the bar, after what she had just said to him on the beach, Max would probably never want to see her again.

## 46

The three girls sat in the bar until the staff began to close it down around them, sweeping sand off the wooden stepping stones and blowing out the candles that had been keeping the mosquitoes at bay. A doctor had arrived several hours ago by tuk-tuk, staying up in the treehouse for around ten minutes before re-emerging with a grim expression on his face. For Alice, who had become accustomed to seeing a smile on the face of most Sri Lankans she encountered, witnessing the doctor look so ashen was akin to a shadow falling across her hopes.

They dithered for a while, debating what to do, and then Steph's phone pinged with a message from Jamal, telling her not to worry and that they should turn in for the night.

'But what did the doctor say?' Alice demanded. 'Is he going to be all right?'

Steph shrugged. 'He doesn't say. I guess Max must be OK, or they would be going to hospital or something.'

'Can't you ask him?' Alice was exasperated.

Steph pulled a face. 'I don't want to start bombarding him with twenty questions, not when he's got Max to worry about,' she said. 'I'm sure we'll see Max in the morning and it will all be fine. He probably just got dehydrated or something. Maybe the leg is just a red herring?'

She really was taking her positive nature to the extreme, Alice thought.

Eventually they could ignore the pleading stares of the bar staff no longer, and even Alice conceded that the best thing to do would be to retire for the night. She had no intention of sleeping, however. She wanted to stay alert in case anything happened.

'You can't sleep in the hammock,' Steph said gently, watching Alice with sad eyes as she clambered into it. 'You'll get eaten alive out here.'

'I don't care.' Alice was resolute. As far as she was concerned, she deserved to be dinner for a thousand insects.

'Well, at least use this, then,' said Maureen, tossing her a can of repellent spray. 'There's no point contracting malaria because you were too bloody-minded to sleep under a net.'

After they had closed the treehouse door behind them, Alice settled back in her canvas cocoon and stared up through the wicker roof of the balcony to where the stars were twinkling beyond. Thinking about Max was too painful, so she thought about Freddie instead, wondering how her brother had got himself to such a dark and lonely place, and why he hadn't felt able to confide in her. For as long as Alice could cast her tired mind back to recall, Freddie had been the cherry on her parents' Bakewell tart, but she remembered now how odd his choice of career had seemed to her when he first broke the news.

They had both been sitting at their parents' kitchen table at the time, Freddie opening the bottle of red wine he had brought to go with Sunday lunch.

'You're going to be a banker?' she had scoffed. 'You? Mister scuffed trainers and three-day-old stubble? I don't think so.'

Freddie had shrugged. 'It's good money,' he had said.

'And?' Alice could remember that she had actually laughed at him. 'Since when do you care about money?'

It was at that moment that their mum had interjected, kissing Freddie on the top of his head as she wandered from the fridge back to the stove.

'Since he wanted to make us proud,' she had said warmly. 'Someone has to keep us in our old age, you know.'

Alice had frowned at her brother, finding him all of a sudden a person she did not know as well as she had thought. Freddie had always told her that he wanted to work for a charity, that he liked the idea of starting something non-profit that would benefit others. This new direction seemed out of character for a man who could never go past a donation box without emptying his pockets of change. Freddie cried at the Comic Relief films on the telly, and bought dog food and cups of tea for the homeless – he had never been the type of person to chase profit for a big, faceless corporation.

'This isn't you,' she had said, making sure their mum did not overhear, and Freddie had simply nodded, his expression resigned.

'I know,' he'd whispered. 'But at least she's happy.'

Alice hadn't needed to ask who he meant by 'she'. Like her, Freddie did everything he could to keep their mum happy. Alice understood that her accident had been traumatic for her mother – perhaps even more so than it had been for Alice – and so she kept trying to make up for it, time and time again.

Freddie had been caught up in it all, too, of course. He had been a teenager when Alice fell off the roof, and all his own freedoms disappeared overnight, even though he had not been the one who was hurt. Even when Freddie went away to university in London, he had to call home each night to let their mother know he was safe – a routine that lasted his entire first year. How smothered he must have felt, Alice realised now. And it was all because of her.

Max was right, her brother was not happy. He had never been happy – not really. The life he was living was one he had constructed out of a desire to please other people, and maintaining that lie had cost him everything – almost his life.

Alice closed her eyes, shutting out the stars, only to jump violently as the treehouse door creaked open and Steph emerged, her frizzy hair askew. She was wearing pink denim shorts and a vest top with a picture of a cat wearing a tiara on the front. Seeing that Alice was still awake, she tiptoed over.

'Jamal just texted,' she said, keeping her voice low so as not to wake Maureen. 'I'm going over to see him.'

'I'm coming with you.' Alice was already on her feet. She hadn't bothered to get changed when they returned from the bar, and had just pulled on a Harry Potter T-shirt over her black playsuit.

Steph threw her a slightly puzzled glance, but didn't

argue, and the two of them hurried quickly down the wooden steps and across the sandy pathway that separated the boys' treehouse from their own.

Jamal's expression softened as soon as he saw Steph at the door, but his eyes narrowed when Alice came into view behind her.

'Is Max OK?' Alice asked, choosing to ignore the obvious frostiness. She tried to peer through the gap in the door, but all she saw of Max was a section of his bare chest on the double bed.

Jamal pulled the door shut behind him. 'He needs rest.'

'Can I see him?' Alice asked, hearing the pleading tone in her own unsteady voice. 'I could sit with him for a bit if you need a break?'

'I don't need a break,' Jamal said, all trace of his usual good humour absent. 'And, to be honest, I think you are the last person that he needs to see right now.'

Alice recoiled as if she'd been struck, and Jamal rolled his eyes.

'I'm sorry, I don't mean to be rude, but he's been talking a lot in his sleep and well . . . I just think that whatever was said between you two earlier has upset him. I don't want him getting all worked up.'

'OK.' Alice's voice was small. 'I'll go.'

She turned and hurried away from them, her eyes stinging with unshed tears. She just wanted a chance to say sorry, to tell Max that he had been right about her, about Freddie, about everything. She was a coward and he had every right to hate her, but that didn't stop the knowledge hurting like hell.

When she reached the base of the Palm House steps, Alice turned and looked back up to Max and Jamal's balcony. Steph was still up there, her arms around her new boyfriend's waist as he leaned in and whispered in her ear. She was nodding, but not smiling, and Alice watched as Jamal handed her friend a small piece of folded paper, which she slipped into the back pocket of her shorts.

They kissed then, and Alice dropped her eyes to the floor, not wanting to intrude more than she already had on their happiness. All she had ever done, since she was ten years old, was try to make those around her happy, yet for some reason she kept messing it up. If Richard was happy, then Alice was not. If her mum was happy, then Alice was not. There was a pattern to this that should have been glaringly obvious – and so it had been to Max, who had seen it all and understood it, yet still let himself like her – really like her. And what had she done? She had thrown all of it back in his face. Every single word.

## 47

Despite the harassed thoughts chasing through her mind and the persistent roar of the ocean, Alice eventually dropped off to sleep, only waking when a fully dressed Maureen gently nudged her with a finger. She screwed up her eyes as soon as she opened them, putting out a hand to block the sun.

'What time is it?' she muttered, her voice gravelly.

'Almost nine.' Maureen suppressed a yawn. 'But checkout's at ten, so I thought I'd better wake you.'

The events of the previous evening landed like a thump in the middle of Alice's chest.

'Have you seen the boys?' she gabbled, sitting up so fast that she almost fell out of the hammock.

Maureen clamped her teeth together.

'Um . . .' she said, and Alice grabbed her arm.

'What? What's happened?'

'They've gone,' said Maur, looking at Alice with genuine pity. 'Jamal managed to get them on a new flight, but it was leaving this morning, so they got a taxi at about four a.m.'

'What?' Alice was aghast. 'Why didn't someone wake me?'

Maureen lifted a single shoulder in a half-shrug. 'I don't know. I only found out this morning myself. I think Steph said goodbye to Jamal earlier than that. He texted her or something. Max has got an infection – the doctor confirmed it – but he refused to go into hospital. Said he wanted to see his own doctor when they went home, so I guess the earlier flight is a compromise between the two.'

'I should be on that bloody flight,' wailed Alice. 'I should have changed my flight the minute I heard about Freddie. Why didn't I?'

Maureen was looking at her with increasing alarm.

'You said your mum told you not to.'

'Screw my mum!' Alice growled, finally climbing out of the hammock and running an agitated hand through her hair. 'I'm sick of doing whatever she says all the bloody time.'

'OK . . .' Maureen sounded on the verge of a nervous laugh.

'I mean it!' Alice went on. 'I'm done. I've had it with her trying to control my life.'

'Does she try and control your life?' asked Maur, and Alice nodded.

'Yes! But I'm not going to let her do it any more. I'm going to call her right now and tell her. I'm going to . . . Where is my phone?' she demanded, patting each of her pockets and then flipping the hammock over in a temper.

Steph opened the treehouse door.

'It's in here,' she said. 'Charging. Exactly where you left it last night.'

'Right,' Alice stormed, barrelling her way inside. 'Good. Right.'

She made it as far as the edge of the bed before folding over on herself in misery, biting her lip until she tasted blood. When Steph ran over to comfort her, Alice shrugged her away.

'I'm fine,' she said, although not one of them was in any doubt that she was not.

The journey from Tangalle to Mirissa passed without incident. Alice sat hunched on the left-hand side of the tuk-tuk, staring at but barely seeing the coast as they hurtled through the villages. The smell of the morning's catch hung thickly in the air, and she counted twelve makeshift stalls piled high with a variety of sea life. Not even the sight of a stray dog stealing a squid could raise a smile to her lips. All Alice could think was that she wanted to go home, but she had missed that morning's flight due to her own inability to make a decision, and now there were no more that would get her back to the UK any earlier than originally planned.

She was trying not to be sullen – if not for her own sanity then for the sake of Steph and Maureen, who still had holiday time which they deserved to enjoy. Alice figured that she had already caused distress to enough people that she cared about, without adding her two best friends to the list.

Steph was quieter than usual, presumably sad at having to say goodbye to Jamal so abruptly, but Alice had no doubt that they would see each other again within days of the three of them returning home. That piece of paper Jamal had given her last night could only have been his contact details, written down so that she could not forget them, even if she lost her phone. It was romantic, really. She was trying not to be cross with Steph or Jamal for allowing Max to leave without giving her the chance to see him – she knew that they each had the best interests of their separate friends at heart. But then, neither of them had been on the beach with her and Max – they hadn't heard what he had said or seen the look on his face as he said it. Alice could not believe that Max would have chosen to go without a single word, but perhaps she was being naïve. She had sat there and listened while he laid himself and his feelings out for the taking, and then she had tossed them away like sand into the air. She could not stop picturing the look of bewildered hurt on his face when she had cast scorn on the skydive – the skydive that he had thought of and arranged as a gift. He had done that, and she had chewed it up and spat it back at him. She had never felt more ashamed.

They checked in to a clean but very basic hotel in Mirissa, then spent the afternoon exploring. Similarly to Tangalle, the small town had an island feel, with souvenir shops, numerous bars and a plethora of travellers sporting tie-dye harem pants and dreadlocked hair. People were more relaxed on the coast, and everything seemed to move at a much slower pace than it did in the cities.

Alice asked Steph every ten minutes if she had heard anything from Jamal, but no messages were forthcoming. She had even switched on the roaming on her phone in order to check Max's Facebook and Instagram accounts, in case he had added an update before boarding the flight, but there was nothing new there, either. His last Instagram post was a photo he had taken of the elephants in Pudumayaki National Park. He had added something humorous below about it being 'the calm before the storming elephant', and all Alice could think was that she missed him so much it hurt.

After returning to their hotel to change and collect their washing – which the kind lady owner had laid out, knickers and all, across the roof of a small shed that was in full view of every single guest staying there – Alice, Steph and Maureen headed to the beach for dinner. There were restaurants dotted all the way along it, and Alice meandered behind her friends on purpose, content to let them decide where to eat. Soon, they were seated on squashy beanbags watching the sun set behind the ocean, Steph and Maureen toasting the various highlights of their trip and agreeing on all the things they would miss most about Sri Lanka, while Alice sat mutely beside them. When a message came through from Richard, she barely glanced at it, hating how unfair she was being to him but powerless to do anything about it. The sadness was just too heavy, her regret solidifying around her like wet cement.

Darkness seemed to arrive suddenly, as if the day had been turned off with a switch, and waiters hurried amongst the tables lighting candles. The stout palm trees lining the edge of the restaurant had been dressed in fairy lights, and small tortoiseshell cats picked their way between the holidaymakers' feet, rubbing their fragile bodies against bare shins in the hope of a morsel or two. Piles of brightly coloured fish were proudly displayed on a table mounded with ice at the front of the seating area, but Alice found she felt only pity when she stared into their shiny, unblinking eyes.

In the end, she ordered her favourite kottu roti, opting for vegetables rather than meat, and switched from water to beer once the food had arrived. She knew alcohol would only make her feel worse, but she craved the momentary escape from despondency that it offered. Maureen had spotted a sign advertising a party further along the beach, and was adamant that they must all go. Alice nodded along with the plan as she pushed her dinner around on her plate – she would go through the motions for the final three evenings of their holiday. She owed her friends that much.

'Isn't this fun?' Maureen slurred an hour later, grabbing Alice's hands and attempting to spin her around in a circle. The DJ at the beach party was playing club tunes that Alice had not heard since the late 1990s, but if anything, this seemed to spur Maureen on even more. The crowd dancing out on the sand next to them were mostly young backpackers, but there was a healthy number of Sri Lankans here, too.

Despite pulling off some seriously impressive moves and swinging her long dark hair around as if she was a moshing Rapunzel, Maureen had failed to get the attention of any men. A fact that she was now lamenting to Steph and Alice at some length.

'What does a girl have to do?' she shouted over the music. 'I mean, what is the secret?'

Steph thought for a moment.

'I think it's cartwheels,' she said, and Alice frowned in amusement. Steph was clearly a lot tipsier than she looked. Alice had not been paying attention to the amount any of them had been drinking.

'Cartwheels?' Maureen squeaked. 'But I can't do a cart-wheel.' She was speaking so fast and with such drunken indignation that all her words were running together.

''Tis easy,' Steph assured her, waggling a finger. She was wearing her pink denim shorts again, this time with a plain black vest top, which she was now tucking in with one hand.

'Hold this!' she instructed, thrusting her cocktail towards Alice before limbering up on the spot. Maureen, who was so drunk that she could not stay still, jumped up and down on the sand in anticipation.

'Geronimo!' yelled Steph, lurching forwards and man-aging to complete a rather bandy-legged cartwheel. Maureen began applauding loudly.

'See!' she declared. 'This is why you have Jamal and I am going to die alone!'

She staggered forwards a few steps as she said it, kick-ing sand over Alice's feet, then promptly bent down to pick something up.

'What's this?' she said, peering at the folded piece of paper. 'I think it's for you,' she added, handing it to Alice.

Steph stepped across to look, her hand immediately fly-ing up to cover her mouth.

'Oh bugger!' she swore, inebriation making her giggle. 'That must have fallen out of my pocket. Jamal gave it to me for you, but with everything that happened, I must have forgotten about it. Sorry, Alice.'

Alice wasn't listening. She was staring down at the piece of paper in her hands – a piece of paper that had her name written on it.

'Who's it from?' said Maur, but Alice did not reply. Instead, she unfolded the note and began to read.

# 48

*First comes love*
*I saw it shining there*
*Reflected in her eyes*
*And in the strands of her hair,*
*First comes love*
*A leader, a thief*
*Breaking through the surface*
*To my heart underneath,*
*First comes love*
*It was sought unconsciously*
*I did not know I had it*
*Until she looked at me,*
*First comes love*
*Bright as those stars*
*We gazed upon together*
*As if the world was ours,*
*First comes love*
*Truth follows behind*
*Courage must be third*
*As hope feels blind . . .*

# 49

## Max

*If I should live*
*I will strive to learn*
*What life is without her*
*And how not to yearn . . .*

The vibrations came first, the rumble of heavy tyres against the dry earth. Everything was bright and hot, and Max could feel the weight of his body armour pulling against his shoulders and pressing hard on his chest. Dust swam in the air, swirling insects darted from person to person, and from somewhere at the front of the convoy, a shout rang out.

Max tried to blink, knowing he was dreaming yet unable to wake up. '*Open your eyes,*' he urged himself, fearing what would happen if he did not, dreading the pain that he knew would soon reach up and drag him back to that place of terror and darkness.

He felt his body lurch downwards, then off to one side, his stomach disappearing as if thrown into a deep gulley. Sweat began to run down his face. He was not wearing his helmet. Why wasn't he wearing his helmet?

'Max.'

It was Jamal. But that couldn't be right. Jamal had not been in the desert with him.

'Max, it's OK. It's just turbulence. Go to your safe place. Can you hear me? Shit. Max, come on, wake up. You need to wake up.'

His safe place. Yes, that was it. Max could not wake himself up from this nightmare, could not open his eyes and banish the taste of death from his lips, but he could use what was left of his strength to take himself somewhere else, where it was not as hot, where he could breathe. But what was that place?

He could see a tumbling stream, and his bare knees as they had been before, when he was a child, stretched out in front of him, and he became aware of the comforting presence of his brother, Ant, beside him. For a few moments, the image swam around Max, and he reached out with his fingers, trying to draw the separate elements towards him, or haul himself into the image with them, into the place where he would be safe. But the picture was dissolving, a painting held under a faucet, a dream splitting open at the seams. Darkness crept in on the edges, black spots of despair that gave way to red.

Red was bad, red meant pain.

Max ignored the voice that he could hear urging him to wake. It was shouting at him over and over. He did not trust it – waking was a trap. There was nothing there for him but more pain. He screwed his eyes tightly shut and imagined that he was on a journey; that he was going to travel right down inside himself to where his heart sat beating, its rhythm shallow and irregular. What would he find inside it, he wondered, if he could only open the door?

Max pushed further, reached ahead of himself towards the light that glowed there, waiting for him. The redness began to darken. It was no longer the colour of fear, but the soothing shade of night. A night with a wide, clear sky, dappled with stars. One thousand stars.

She was here. Alice. Max could not see her, but he could feel her as she reached for his hand and he knew that she would not leave him. That she would keep him close beside her for always.

Max felt the fear flood out of him, and joy burst through in its place. Alice was his safe place, and now that he had found her, he could let go.

## 50

Richard answered on the second ring.

It was Alice's final evening in Sri Lanka, and she, Steph and Maureen were spending it in the south-west port town of Galle. The area had been colonised at different points in history by the Portuguese, Dutch and British, the influence of each still apparent through the area's European-style architecture and fortifying sea wall. Maureen had finally been granted her wish to shop, as the town centre was a warren of boutiques, cafés and ice-cream parlours. Traffic was not permitted through the heart of the city, and it meant that Galle had a quiet and almost timeless atmosphere, one which felt utterly at odds with the rest of the country. Wild peacocks strutted across rooftops, popcorn vendors wheeled their carts along the seafront, and children chased one another through cobbled squares.

It was quaint, but also tranquil, and Alice tried her best to draw as much peace from it as she could, drinking in the view across the water as she made her way along the city's outer wall, looking for a place to sit down. Galle's lighthouse stood proudly at the end of the pebble-strewn walkway, and Alice was reminded yet again of Max. He had acted like a guiding light in her life, had shown her the way towards real happiness, and now it was up to her to finish what he had begun.

'Thanks for agreeing to talk,' she said, pulling her mind away from Max and back to Richard. It had swung so often between the two men over the past couple of days that Alice felt as though her brain was a pendulum. As soon as she had read Max's poem, she had known what it was she must do, but she had still given herself time to come to terms with her decision, to let the idea and all its consequences sink into her conscience until she could be sure it was not simply a knee-jerk reaction.

She lowered herself down on a patch of sparse grass and swung her legs over the edge of the sea wall. In the distance, she could see the sun as it sank steadily behind the vast expanse of the ocean, taking the final day of her holiday with it.

'Is everything all right?' Richard asked warily. 'To be honest, I didn't quite know what to make of your message.'

Alice had texted him in advance, asking him to make some time for her. She hadn't said much more, other than telling him that it was important they speak to one another.

She took a deep breath. Now that she was here, speaking to him, her careful plan of what to say had crumbled into dust. She, Steph and Maureen had talked it all through the previous day, and it had all made sense then – she had been confident that it was the right thing to do. But now that it had come to saying the words to Richard, knowing full well the effect they would undoubtedly have, Alice found herself stuttering.

'Has something happened?' Richard continued, when it became clear that Alice was not going to say more than five coherent words.

How could she even begin to answer that? Yes, something had happened – so many things had happened. Deciding which one to begin with was the reason she had become suddenly inarticulate.

'Sorry,' she muttered, taking off her sunglasses and folding in the arms. 'This is hard. I don't know where to start.'

'Alice, what the hell is going on?' Richard sounded fed up now, but also fearful, and Alice waited a moment, breathing hard to halt her tears.

'I . . .' she began, staring at the throbbing semi-circle of red sun on the horizon. 'I don't think I can marry you, Rich.'

There was a silence, during which Alice tried not to picture the look of bewildered hurt that her boyfriend must now have on his face.

'Right . . .' he replied eventually. 'And are you going to tell me why?'

'Because I would be doing it for the wrong reasons,' she said, hearing the emotion in her own voice. It was so hard to do this, to hurt him when for so long, she had done everything she could to make him happy. But now that she was staring down the barrel of a future with Rich, she knew that it was not the right one – and it wasn't because she had met and connected with someone else; it was simply because she needed to accept who she was – really was – and that person was not ever going to be happy becoming Richard's wife. Alice hated that she had to be so brutal to do the right thing, but she also knew that she must.

'Surely, the reason to get married is just to be happy?' Rich argued. 'Are you saying that you're unhappy?'

Alice chewed her bottom lip.

'Yes.'

Richard sighed at this, but did not reply straight away. Alice could feel tension mounting in her shoulders and causing her arms to stiffen. The need to get up and release the awful anxiety – run away both literally and figuratively from this horrible situation – was almost overwhelming, but she forced herself to stay where she was. She needed to see this through, even if it was difficult – even if the easy option would be to take it all back and pretend to Rich that she had been pulling a terrible prank on him.

'Since when?' he demanded. 'How long have you been feeling like this, and why?'

Alice considered the question, not wanting to tell him the truth but also knowing that she needed to do so. Rich had done nothing wrong – he deserved her honesty at the very least.

'I think we've been content to just, you know, pootle along,' she said, and he sniffed in annoyance. 'You know what I mean,' she pleaded. 'You have to admit, it has felt as if we're going through the motions lately. When was the last time we laughed together? Or did anything together that wasn't dinner with my parents or yours? Everything feels like it's stagnated, Rich, and I know I should have said something to you earlier, but I guess I didn't dare. I kept hoping that I would wake up one day and feel differently, but it hasn't happened.'

Rich didn't answer, and Alice clutched her phone against her ear, waiting. She knew she was pushing him now, trying to convince him that he was as unsatisfied as she was, purely because it would make things easier. The truth was, she hadn't considered until now that he, too, might be genuinely disillusioned with the state of their relationship, and that perhaps the reason he was so keen for the two of them to get married was because he hoped it would act like a refresh button on their feelings towards one another.

'Does anything that I'm saying make sense?' she asked him now.

'I'm still trying to make sense of it,' he snapped, and then added, 'Is this all Maureen's doing? Has she been filling your head with nonsense? I knew it was a bad idea for you to spend too much time with her – she's never liked me.'

'This has got nothing to do with Maur!' Alice exclaimed. 'And she does like you – she always has. This is one hundred per cent to do with me, and how I feel. The thing is, Rich, I have worked something out while I've been here.'

'Oh, here we go,' he said, and Alice clenched her teeth.

'When you sent me that photo of the ring, I should have been over the moon, but I wasn't. It just made me feel sad and guilty, because I realised it wasn't what I wanted.' And it was true, too – she hadn't felt much of anything. When she thought about the elation that had surged through her when Max surprised her with the sky-dive, it was impossible not to compare the two.

'Well, we don't *have* to get married,' Rich said hurriedly, his tone all of a sudden placatory. Alice steeled herself against the predictable wobble that ricocheted through her. Rich was not unhappy; he wanted to save their relationship and was willing to compromise to keep her – did that mean she was making the wrong decision after all?

'If that's the problem,' Rich went on, 'then let's wait another year. We couldn't have done it this summer, anyway, not with your brother . . . Well, you know.'

'That's another thing,' Alice said, her resolve hardening once again as she seized on the mention of Freddie. 'If I go ahead and marry you, then it would be a lie. I think Freddie has been living in a lie for years, and look where he's ended up. I won't let that happen to me, or to you.'

'Oh, charming!' Rich said furiously. 'You think being married to me would turn you into an alcoholic? Thanks, Alice. Thanks a lot.'

'I just think we want different things,' she explained. 'And it's all my fault, because I didn't ever let myself tell you what I wanted before. I told myself that we wanted all the same things, because it was easier that way. It made you happy, it made my mum happy – I thought that was enough to make *me* happy.'

'Well,' Rich interrupted. 'What *do* you want, Alice? Why can't you tell me now?'

Alice cast her mind back to that open train door, Max by her side as forests and mountains flashed by, the half-smile on his lips as he asked her that very same question.

'I want adventure,' she said softly, her heart racing with nerves as she properly opened up to him for the first time in as long as she could remember. She wanted Rich to know her – *really* know her – and part of her even hoped that he would care enough to cheer her ambitions and champion her dreams.

'I want to travel the world,' she went on fervently. 'I want to dance on beaches and swim in the ocean and bungee off bridges and—'

The sound of Richard's laughter pulled her up short.

'You are funny,' he said.

'I mean it,' she told him. 'I'm not trying to be funny here, I'm telling you what I want.'

'This is all just talk, Alice. Once you're back home with me and your family, you'll forget about all of this. I know you, remember? I know how timid you are. There is no way you would bungee off the sofa, let alone a bridge.'

'I did a skydive,' she informed him.

Richard stopped laughing abruptly.

'You did what?'

'I jumped out of a plane,' she said. 'And do you know what? I loved it. It was the best and most exciting thing I have ever done – and I didn't hesitate. I wanted to do it.'

'You could have been killed!' he exploded. 'Did you not think about me? Or your mum?'

It was Alice's turn to sigh then. She looked again towards the sun. It was almost gone now; there was only a sliver of red visible.

'I probably should have done,' she allowed. 'But I didn't – not until afterwards. The news about Freddie threw me a bit, and I felt bloody terrible about the skydive then, if you must know. But then I remembered how alive it had made me feel – and how happy.'

'Who did you do it with?' Rich wanted to know, and

Alice furrowed her brow in annoyance at his attempt to derail the conversation.

'I can't see Steph jumping out of a plane somehow,' he said in a hard voice. 'And Maureen would probably be too worried about messing up her hair.'

Alice chose not to rise to his childish sniping. He was angry; he was allowed to throw a bit of scorn around. Maureen had predicted his reaction, too, telling Alice as they ate lunch earlier that day that Richard would inevitably blame her.

'I did it with a friend,' she said, and she heard him huff in infuriation.

'So, *that*'s it? You've met someone over there, have you? One of those blokes in the photos. You've had a sordid little holiday romance and now you think you're a different person. Well, I hope it was worth it, Alice, I really do, because it's going to take a bit more than a kiss-and-make-up to put this right.'

'You're wrong, Rich,' she said gently, closing her eyes as a warm evening breeze blew strands of hair across her face. He was angry with her, that much was apparent and totally understandable – but she felt no animosity towards him. In fact, it was quite the opposite.

'I did meet someone on this trip,' she told him calmly. 'I met me. The real me. The me that I've been hiding since my accident because I was so scared of getting hurt again, of hurting anyone else. But I can't pretend any more. Not for you, not for my mum. It's my life.'

Richard made a noise that told Alice he was less than impressed.

'It's not about you,' she said. 'This is all me – and I'm sorry that I've changed into a different person, but wouldn't you rather be with someone who wasn't having to pretend?'

Richard cleared his throat.

'So, you're saying you don't even want to try?' he asked. 'After everything? All we've been through and all the plans we've made for the future.'

'For your future,' she amended matter-of-factly, her tone soft. 'I was only ever tagging along with your dreams.'

'I still love you,' he said then, his voice cracking just as Alice felt her heart do the same.

'I love you, too, Rich,' she said. 'Just not in the way that I should, or the way that I want to. You deserve to be with someone who loves you because of who you are, not in spite of the differences the two of you may have. Our love has been back-to-front from the start.'

'Do you really believe that?' he said, and Alice knew that he was crying now. Should she have done this face-to-face? Once she had made up her mind, it had felt vital that she make the break – she did not want to draw it out any more than she had to, and she had wanted to capitalise on the courage that arrived along with her determination. She was conscious of Rich's feelings, too. It wasn't fair that he be kept in the dark when she had seen the light.

'I'm going to stay with my parents for a bit,' she said, by way of reply. 'I'll keep sharing the rent, of course, until you decide what to do.'

'This can't be it,' he mumbled, his voice broken by the

emotion he was trying his best to disguise. 'This can't be the end.'

'I am sorry, Rich. I truly am,' Alice said, smiling despite the tears that had begun to course down her cheeks. 'But this is not the end at all – it's the start of a new beginning.'

## 51

'You have done *what*?'

Marianne Brockley gaped at Alice in horror.

'Broken up with Richard,' Alice said again, her voice steady. She was standing in the front porch of her parents' house in Sudbury, her rucksack on her back and a bunch of daffodils in her hand, which she now thrust towards her mother.

'These are for you,' she said, and stepped around her into the hallway. 'Is Freddie home yet?'

'I'm sorry, but . . .' her mum began, following Alice into the kitchen. Freddie was propped up on a stool by the breakfast bar, eating a bowl of cornflakes, and Alice went straight across and hugged him, pressing her face against his bony shoulder. He had lost so much weight since the last time she had seen him back in February, and she was afraid he might break under the strength of her embrace.

'I'm sorry it took me so long to be here,' she said, her voice muffled by the fabric of his T-shirt. Freddie leaned back until he could look at her properly.

'Don't be daft,' he said, his eyes shining. 'I only got out of the rehab centre yesterday afternoon. But I'm glad you're here now.'

'Me too,' she said, relief that he was all right rippling through her. Aside from the dramatic drop in weight and a slight shake in his hand as he picked up his cereal spoon, Freddie still looked like her brother. She could tell from the mischievous glint in his eye that his sense of humour was still intact, and the way in which he regarded her with such easy affection was wonderfully Fred-like. Over the past few days, Alice had allowed herself to go to hell and back by wondering what state he would be in when she got home, but seeing him had allayed her fears. This was Freddie, her brave big brother – he would be OK, and so would she.

Alice looked round to where her mum was waiting, arms folded across her chest. She looked neither angry nor upset, which surprised Alice. She had steeled herself for a row as soon as she broke the news about Richard – perhaps even tears – but her mum was not saying anything at all. It was more than a little unnerving.

'Mum,' said Freddie. 'Weren't you saying something about putting the kettle on before this one turned up? That is, unless you're sick of tea after being in Sri Lanka?' he added, glancing at Alice.

She nodded. 'Tea would be great, thanks, Mum.'

Marianne Brockley walked stiffly to the kettle and switched it on, and Freddie raised his eyebrows at Alice as she silently readied their cups on the worktop.

As much as Alice hated the circumstances that had brought her brother home, she was glad he was here. Freddie had always had her back, been in her corner, and she had a feeling that in a moment or two she was going to need him more than ever before.

'So.' Marianne put a mug of tea down on the counter in front of Alice. 'Come on, then – out with it.'

Alice took a deep breath, and then she told them how she had called Richard from Sri Lanka to end things, how she had done so because she was not happy and did not see a way to be happy with him, and finished by asking if it was all right for her to move back home – albeit temporarily. The words all came out in a rush, Alice keen to expel them before she lost her nerve, and as she spoke, she looked not at her mum but at her brother. Freddie nodded along as she told her story, his expression grave enough to make it clear that he appreciated how serious this all was, but not so severe that Alice felt concerned about his reaction. He was just as she had expected him to be – understanding and supportive. But when it came to her mother, Alice's expectations were markedly different – and quite rightly, too.

'And you just decided this, did you?' her mum demanded, making Alice wince. The anger she had anticipated was flowing out of Marianne like venom.

'It just occurred to you one day that you were miserable? I mean, for God's sake, Alice. Poor Richard. I wouldn't blame him if he never took you back.'

'I don't want him to take me back,' Alice said patiently.

Freddie had abandoned his cornflakes and was now sipping his tea, a thoughtful expression on his gaunt face.

'I think it's great,' he said, and both Alice and her mum turned to him in amazement.

'What?' he said. 'You know I love Dickie – he's a good bloke. But Alice always looks so on edge when she's around him, like she's a jack-in-the-box waiting to pop. You must have noticed it, Mum?'

'I have noticed no such thing,' Alice's mum said primly.

'Freds is right,' Alice said, wading back in to the uncomfortable discussion. 'I feel like I'm about to explode most of the time. Sometimes I get so anxious that I go to the water meadows and run and run until I can barely breathe, or I go to the pool and dive off the highest board, just so I can let some tension out.'

'Oh, for pity's sake, Alice.' Marianne Brockley was seriously unimpressed. 'You're not a child any more.'

'No, I know!' Alice put down her tea. 'That's the whole point, Mum – I'm not a child, so I can do those things without hurting myself. I had an accident – *once* – I can't live every day like I'm going to have another one.'

'You don't know what it was like for me!' her mother cried, and Alice braced herself. She had been expecting this, and she had her answer ready.

'I do know,' she said. 'I was there, remember. And so was Freddie. All our lives changed that day. We were all affected by it, by my mistake. I have had to live with that ever since, and the guilt of it, and all the worry, it turned me into someone I don't even recognise as me – a person who only exists to make everyone else happy. But I'm not happy, Mum. Not with Richard and not in my job and not even in my own skin.'

Her mum's eyes were wide now, her cheeks flushed with dismay.

'I just think,' Alice went on, 'that if I let myself do more of the things I want to do – that I need to do – then I won't have all this anxiety nibbling away at me constantly. It's not like I'm going to tightrope-walk over the Grand

Canyon or train to be an astronaut; I'm just talking about travelling a bit more, and having some more adventures.'

'I just want you to be safe,' her mum muttered. 'All I have ever wanted is for both of you to be safe. You were always such a handful growing up, Alice. I didn't know what to do with all that energy you had – and then you had your accident and got that dreadful scar and I blamed myself. I should have been better at controlling you. If I had, you would never have been up on that stupid roof in the first place.'

She took a breath, her own rhetoric exhausting her.

'Do you know how hard it is to see your child in pain?' she asked.

Alice shook her head.

'Well, I can tell you, there is nothing worse – nothing in the world. I made a promise to myself that day in the hospital that I would never let you hurt yourself again, even if it meant keeping you under house arrest. I couldn't stand all that pain, Alice, I just couldn't.'

'But I'm in pain now!' Alice exclaimed, exasperated but trying her hardest not to show it. 'Or I was, at least, until I met someone who made me realise there was another way.'

Freddie stood up from his stool and moved behind Alice, putting a hand on her shoulder.

'I was in pain, too, Mum,' he said, and Alice watched as Marianne's eyes filled with tears. 'Alice is right – both of us have been trying to make up for that accident ever since we were kids. You were so upset, then so angry with us all the time. I just wanted to do whatever I could to make you happy again.'

Alice watched as her mother took it all in, seeing the flicker of accountability register as the tears began to fall. It wasn't easy for her to hear any of this stuff, Alice knew that, but it was also too important to be glossed over any longer. Freddie looked sad now, too, but relieved, as if a huge weight had been lifted from his shoulders. He must have been trying to work out how to broach this subject for months now – maybe even years, ever since he took that job in the City that he didn't really want. Alice felt ashamed that she had not come to his aid sooner. It could have saved them a lot of heartache if she had.

'You both think I'm a terrible mother,' Marianne sobbed, using the bottom of her apron to wipe her eyes. 'All I have ever wanted was what was best for you both.'

'I know you do,' Alice soothed, stepping forwards and placing a cautious hand on her mum's arm. 'But you have to try not to worry so much. You *are* a good mother. You've raised two strong people, and you can trust us to look after ourselves.'

Freddie braved a small laugh. 'Well, you can now, in any case. A few weeks ago, I couldn't be trusted to go to the corner shop and back.'

Alice's mum managed a chuckle. 'Oh, stop,' she scolded. 'This is no time to be making jokes, Fred.'

'On the contrary,' Freddie said. 'There's no better medicine, if you ask me.'

The next thing Alice knew, he had pulled both her and their mother into a group hug, all three of them laughing and crying and exclaiming how sorry they all were. They stayed like that for some time, breaking apart only to fall back together again in earnest. It felt so good to have so much truth out in the open, and Alice kept catching Freddie's eye and laughing in disbelief. After all this time, and after so many mistakes, she and her brother had finally stood up for themselves, and it had not even been close to as painful as either of them had feared. It was liberating.

Eventually, Alice crossed the kitchen to make more tea, then dug through her backpack in search of the gifts she'd brought for them – an elephant-dung notepad and pen set for Freddie and a beautiful sarong for her mum – and she was given her own belated birthday present, a silver bangle engraved with a message that read: '*For our own Alice In Wonderland*'.

'You know, not being a neurotic mother is going to take some getting used to,' Marianne mused. 'Will you both forgive me if I revert back to old habits every now and then?'

Freddie rolled his eyes and Alice snorted with amusement – there was no way that either of them genuinely expected their mum to change overnight. Alice knew there would be tough days ahead, and that she would frequently need to remind her mother of the conversation they had just had, but she also knew that it was a challenge she was ready to take on. More than that, it was one that she relished.

'As long as you don't try to stop me working my way through my bucket list,' she warned, smiling as her mum wrung her hands in pretend despair, only for her look of genuine horror to give her away.

'I don't even want to know,' she said, cutting across Alice just as she was about to start listing activities. 'What

I don't know can't worry me. Just don't jump out of a plane, for God's sake.'

Alice bit her lip. Perhaps there were certain things that her mum never needed to know.

What she had yet to tell either of them was that she did have a plan that concerned her new to-do list, and that it was going to involve some very big changes indeed. All in good time, though, she thought, snapping out of her daydream as she heard the doorbell chime.

'I don't think we're expecting anyone,' her mum said, and Alice's mind lurched immediately and ridiculously towards Max. She knew that he and Jamal had got back to the UK, because Steph had received a message saying as much when they were still in Sri Lanka, but it had been frustratingly lacking in details. When Steph asked if everything was OK, Jamal had merely responded by saying that he would call her once the girls were home. Alice had scoured Max and Jamal's social media accounts looking for clues that he was over the fever that had struck him down so forcibly in Sri Lanka, but so far, she had drawn a blank, comforting herself with the knowledge that if there had been any bad news, she would have heard about it by now. Talking to Max was the very first thing on her to-do list – she wanted to see him so much that she could barely keep still with the thought of it. She only hoped that he would give her the chance to explain why she had been so idiotically dismissive of his feelings that fateful night on Tangalle beach, and to tell him she was sorry.

'Maybe it's Maureen,' she said to Freddie. 'She did say she would be round to visit you as soon as she could.'

'She did?' Freddie said, sitting up straighter, and Alice grinned at him. If anyone was going to put a smile back on her brother's face, then it would be Maur. Ever since Alice had told her friend to go for it with Freddie, Maur had been busy formulating a plan. Alice would have put money on her brother being out of the singles' market for good by the time summer began, and it was a bet she would be very happy to win.

'Alice,' her mum called from the hall. 'It's for you.'

Alice made her way along the carpeted corridor to find Steph hovering in the open doorway, looking unsure of herself.

'What is it – did I pack your pants instead of mine?' Alice asked, grinning at her own terrible joke.

Steph didn't so much as flicker a smile, and Alice realised she had been crying.

'What's the matter?' she asked, drawing her into the lounge. There was a photo of a young Alice framed on the wall beside them – the last one before she had got her scar.

'I . . .' Steph began, staring at the carpet. She seemed unable to meet Alice's eyes.

'What is it?' Alice asked, still grasping on to the possibility that this might all be nothing, even though she knew, and could feel, that it was something bad. 'You're scaring me.'

Steph looked up, her face collapsing into misery.

'It's Max,' she said. 'I'm afraid I have some bad news.'

## 52

'All Saints Hospital,' shouted Alice, slamming the door of the black cab behind her.

The driver looked at her in his rear-view mirror, his eyebrow lifting in surprise when he took in her dishevelled state. Alice had not had time to change out of the dust-covered leggings and oversized T-shirt that she had worn on the flight home from Sri Lanka, and her hair was wild where she'd run her hands through it and tugged with despair during the train journey from Suffolk to London.

'Quickly, please!' she begged, tossing her bag on to the seat and grasping the plastic bar to steady herself as they zoomed up the ramp away from Liverpool Street Station. Her first thought had been to drive, but when she reached her battered Mini, parked down the road from the flat she had, until that day, shared with Richard, she had found the battery completely flat.

Sitting in the taxi, she went over what Steph had heard from Jamal. 'It's not looking good.' The infection was worse than he had thought, and the last he had heard, Max was going into surgery.

'Can you go any faster?' Alice said, an image of Max covered in tubes and wires making her feel faint. The driver turned briefly and shook his head.

'Sorry, love – it's the time of day. It's pretty much grid-lock all the way along here.'

'Fuck!' she said with feeling, and the cabbie switched on his intercom again.

'I know a short cut,' he said. 'Sometimes there are delivery vans parked down there, and we might get stuck worse than we are here, but I'm happy to try if you like?'

'Please!' Alice thought she might scream soon. 'Try whatever you can.'

She stared out with unseeing eyes at the blur of the capital, unjustified rage rising in her chest every time she saw a person meandering along – not desperately on their way to hospital, not filled with fear, not doubting their survival. Why Max? Why had it happened to him? She could have wept with the unfairness of it all.

After Steph had told her what was going on, she had only one thought – that she should be by Max's side, the very place she should have been already. She had been an idiot in Sri Lanka – a coward and a fool – but she had known even before Max collapsed on the beach in Tangalle that she did not want to spend another minute, another moment, another breath, without him. But she had not been ready to accept her feelings then; nor had she been brave enough to admit as much – not even to herself. Then she had got Max's poem, and as she read it, Alice had wept tears not only of regret, but also of recognition, because he had put into words everything that she was feeling. She, too, had sought his love unconsciously, but unlike Max, her hope was no longer blind, because his words had renewed it. They had provided her with the strength she needed to break up with Richard, and finally face down the suffocating and misguided love of her mother. When it came to Max, Alice had realised too late how much he meant to her, how much she wanted to be with him, and now she was afraid that she would be too late again.

'All Saints is just up there,' the driver said, rousing Alice from her thoughts. He was pointing through the windscreen towards where a vast, grey building loomed. They were on yet another busy road where the traffic was lined up bumper to boot, and Alice immediately saw his meaning – it would be quicker for her to get out and run.

Shoving a twenty-pound note through the partition, she yelled out her thanks and bolted along the pavement, knocking into passers-by as she went. One woman screamed obscenities as Alice accidentally kicked her shopping bag, causing it to split and spill its contents, but still she didn't stop. She did not hesitate, even for a second. Ever since Steph had uttered those awful words, all Alice had been able to think was that she must be with Max. She did not know if he was still in surgery or not, but it didn't matter. All she knew was that he wasn't well, that he was in pain, and that was enough to spur her into action. She needed to see him. She needed to know that he was all right.

Racing through the automatic doors of the hospital entrance, Alice saw a large queue at the main reception area and felt a surge of panic. She didn't want to wait – she didn't think she could wait. Images of Max were assaulting her – his amused grin when she jumped up and down with excitement at the skydiving centre, the pressure of his warm thigh against hers as the train rocked and lurched, the sadness in his eyes when she told him that she didn't believe his feelings, that she could not accept his love.

Scanning the signs on a nearby wall, she spotted an arrow for the lifts and hurled herself around the corner, her dirty trainers squeaking as her feet skidded across the polished floor. There were three lifts, and Alice pressed the call button for each of them, before running a finger down the hospital plan that was displayed nearby. If he was having an operation, then surely he would be in the intensive care unit? Alice had not been in a hospital more than a handful of times since her accident twenty years ago, and she cursed her own lack of knowledge. She would start in the ICU, then come back to reception if necessary.

The lift pinged and the doors slid neatly aside, but Alice had to wait while a young family filed out past her. The mother was being pushed in a wheelchair by someone in a blue hospital uniform, while a proud-looking father carried a car seat bearing a tiny baby. He smiled at Alice as he passed, but she barely mustered a response. Max was here, in this building, in one of the hundreds of rooms in the vast structure above her. There was nothing else that mattered right now.

The lift spewed her out on the fifth floor, and Alice immediately found herself thwarted yet again – this time by a set of locked doors. There was an intercom to the right, and she pressed it several times.

There was a crackling sound.

'Yes?'

'I'm looking for Max. Max Davis.'

Silence.

'Can you help? I'm here to visit Max Davis. Is he here? I need to see him!'

'Hold on,' said the voice. Whoever it was sounded stern but bored, and Alice bit her fingers to stop herself pressing the intercom button again. Where the hell was their sense of urgency? Didn't they understand what was at stake here?

She was just about to say to hell with it and try again, when a kind-looking nurse with blonde hair approached her on the other side of the doors, her face immediately softening when she saw Alice's stricken look.

'Do you need to get in?' she asked, once she had opened the door.

'Yes! Thank God. Thank you!' Alice rushed through the gap. It was deathly quiet now that she was inside, and the silence stilled her for a moment. Taking a deep breath, she walked along to a deserted reception area, telling herself to remain calm. Someone would be along in a minute, all she had to do was wait.

She drummed her fingers on the desk, then began to tap her foot. There was no sign of anyone, and all of the doors in the unit were closed. Green curtains had been pulled across where Alice guessed the open wards began, and she itched with the knowledge that Max was most likely lying on a bed behind one of them.

It had been five minutes now. Alice coughed, as loudly as she dared, but still nobody came. There was no bell in the reception area to attract attention, and the blonde nurse who had let her in was nowhere to be seen. Alice leaned over the counter, wondering if the call button might have been put there, out of reach, and as she stood back up she saw it through a part-open doorway – the corner of a white board with a list scribbled on it. Taking one last look around to make sure she was alone, she walked around behind the desk, scooting past the office wheelie chair and through the door beyond. Max's name was there, third from the top. She had found him.

She almost fell over in her haste to get back out to the main corridor, and she jogged all the way along until she reached room number three. Giving herself only a second to catch her breath and swallow the huge lump in her throat, Alice pushed open the door.

## 53

The empty bed stared back at Alice, its flat, sterile lines so at odds with the fierce tangle of emotions that were rushing through her. She stood paralysed, her mind racing to finish the story before her heart was ready to comprehend its truth.

'No,' she murmured. Her voice sounded far away, as if it had become detached. She imagined the word breaking off from the mooring of her consciousness and floating away, a lost particle in space, destined to orbit without purpose.

She tried to take in what she could see. Sheets folded neatly in a pile on the bed. A television screen attached to a retractable arm, which had been pushed against the wall. There were no flowers, no cards, no sign that any living person had ever inhabited the space. The sludgy green-grey walls were bare, while the floor was clean enough that she could see the overhead strips of light reflected in it. It hurt her to look at it for too long, just like it hurt her to be here.

She made it to the bed before her knees gave way and she crumpled to the floor. Pressing her face against the bedframe, she felt the cool metal digging into the soft part of her cheek and neck. She brought up her hands and knotted her fingers together, digging in her nails until the flesh below them turned pink, then red. She could not feel them. She could not feel anything.

He was gone. Max was gone. She was too late.

Alice felt the wail surge up and through her, but when her mouth opened to release it there was no sound. She wanted to run and she wanted to curl up into a ball and she wanted to pull out her hair and bite her lip, harder and harder, until she tasted blood.

After everything that Max had already endured and overcome, surviving an explosion that had killed two of his friends, going to the darkest of places in his bid to walk again, battling with PTSD and gritting his teeth through the pain and mess and mayhem of it all to find himself again – and to find her, too. How could he be gone now, after all of that?

She crammed her hands over her ears and closed her eyes until they were slits, squeezing out the world. Images flooded into her mind, unbidden. Images of Max, his hand holding hers, the hint of laughter on his lips, the reflection of stars, thousands of stars, in his deep-set eyes, always kind, always searching out her own. She would never look into those eyes again, never feel the warmth of his fingers, never bask in the glow of his strength, never have the chance to tell him how much she loved him. She loved him. She loved him. She loved him.

'I loved him.'

She let herself slip into the blackness now, static ringing in her ears, her face pressed against the floor.

She didn't know how long she lay there, until there was a sound behind her, hands on her back.

'There now,' said a voice, sweet as honey. 'Let's get you up. Come on, now.'

Alice gripped the bedframe harder. She did not want to open her eyes. Reality was too cruel a game, and it had played her its hardest hand.

The honeyed voice left her, but seconds later it was back, and this time strong arms lifted her, rolled her back until she was lying sideways on top of the bed. His bed, she thought, and shuddered herself upright.

'There you are.'

The blonde nurse peered at her.

'You gave me such a fright,' she said, gently stroking Alice's hair out of her eyes.

'I . . .' Alice stopped, waiting for the world to cease its spinning.

'Max is . . . gone,' she choked out, tears running from her eyes into her open mouth.

The nurse was crouching down in front of her now.

'Are you a friend of Max's?' she asked. 'Max Davis?'

Alice could not speak, so she nodded, closing her eyes again so that she could avoid seeing this kind woman's pity.

'Do you want to see him?' the nurse asked, and her tone was so upbeat that Alice opened her eyes again in shock.

'I don't think that I . . .' she began, then blinked, looking at the nurse properly for the first time.

'What do you mean, see him?'

'I mean, come and see him,' she said cheerfully. 'He's doing well after his surgery yesterday, so we moved him down to a ward. I can take you there, if you like?'

Alice waited, staring into the eyes of this woman, urging the pieces of herself that had splintered into smithereens to find their way back together and get her on her feet. She took a deep breath in, then another.

'I would like that very much,' she said.

# 54

The curtain had been pulled closed around Max's bed at the far end of his ward, and Alice found that she could not move her hand to push it aside. She had been nervous up on the intensive care ward, but now she was petrified. She could hear voices coming from behind it – not his, but a woman's, and another man whose tone was deeper than the one she had become so accustomed to hearing in Sri Lanka. She would have known Max's voice anywhere.

The blonde-haired nurse, who was standing right beside her, smiled encouragingly.

'I'm sure he'll be thrilled to see you now that he's feeling better,' she told her quietly. Alice looked at her name badge. Lucy Dunmore, she read, repeating it silently in her head. She wanted to remember this woman – this kind soul who had picked her up off the floor, brought her back from the teetering edge of despair, and helped her wash the tears from her face.

Alice gestured towards the cubicle beyond the curtain.

'He's obviously busy,' she murmured back. 'Maybe I should come back later?'

'Nonsense!' Lucy lifted her eyebrows at Alice. 'You love him, right?'

Alice nodded, still too dumbstruck by the whole situation to articulate her feelings. All the way to the hospital, she had pictured herself charging up to Max's bedside and pouring her heart out, but now she felt as if all her words had abandoned her, and her feet were fastened to the floor.

'Well, then,' Lucy said. 'That bumps you right up the queue.'

Before Alice could say anything in reply or even turn to flee, the nurse had poked a quick head around the curtain and then pulled it to one side with a happy sort of flourish. Alice froze, colour rushing up to fill her cheeks as her eyes searched the faces of the four people who were now all staring at her. When she found the one she was looking for, the face she had been dreaming about, Alice let out a high, strangled sob and brought her hand up over her mouth.

For a moment, nobody spoke, and then the woman sitting beside the bed stood up and smiled at her.

'You must be Alice.'

She felt Nurse Dunmore's warm hand in the small of her back, urging her forwards, but Alice resisted. Max was there, right in front of her, close enough to touch if she could only make herself step across the space that divided them. But it was too much, the emotions were coursing through her again, tears building behind the dam of her eyes.

'I need to . . .' she said, and then she turned and hurried away.

'Alice!'

Someone was following her. Alice made it to the end of the ward before he caught up with her. She recognised him from Max's Instagram posts. He looked like Max, only bigger and broader with coarser hair and more weathered skin.

'Alice,' he said again, and when she looked at him she saw nothing but delight in his expression.

'I'm Ant.' He held out a hand. 'Max's brother. I'm so glad you're here, he's talked about nothing else since he woke up. I was beginning to think about venturing out on to the London streets in search of you, just to shut him up.'

Alice smiled. A laugh still felt like too much. Not ten minutes ago, she had been huddled on the floor in grief, believing Max to be dead.

'Will you come back in?' Ant asked. 'Please say yes. Only, we've been here since before lunchtime and I'm bloody starving. Now that you're here, Mum will finally agree to pop out for a few hours. Go on, you'd be doing us a huge favour.'

Alice felt shy around this man, who was so large and confident and relaxed in his own skin. She remembered what Max had told her about his brother being the big tough guy, and how he had wanted to be just like him. She could understand why.

'Chop-chop.' Ant beckoned her with a hand, and Alice moved forwards, timidly at first, and the two of them headed back through the ward towards the end cubicle.

'Come on, you lot,' he bossed, going back around the curtain and leaving Alice on the other side. 'We're going for some grub and no arguments. Alice is going to keep an eye on Max, Mum, so don't pull that face at me.'

Alice cringed inwardly, staring down at herself and only now remembering how dreadful she looked, with Sri

Lankan red dust all over her trainers and leggings, and spots of blood on her T-shirt. She didn't know how they had got there, until she registered how swollen her lip was and realised she'd bitten through it on the hospital floor upstairs. No wonder Mrs Davis was reluctant to leave her son alone with such a wild-looking creature. Alice was surprised, then, when Max's parents emerged and his mum – who was tall and willowy with striking grey eyes – pulled her into an unexpected hug.

'Thank you for coming,' she said, and Alice was again forced to bite her sore lip to stem the flow of tears. She felt as if she had been turned inside out and had all the energy wrung out of her body. The phone call with Richard, the long journey home, the showdown with her mum and the race to get here – it all felt like it had happened a lifetime ago, to someone else. There was a wonderful clarity in Alice's mind now – she knew what to do next.

She waited until Max's family were out of sight, and then, wishing she could steady the pounding of her heart, Alice pushed aside the curtain.

## 55

## Max

For the first few moments, they simply stared at each other.

Max was overwhelmed with an urge to get up off the bed and comfort her, but there was no arguing with the drip in his arm, or the heavy swaddle of bandages around his stump. Alice looked so small standing there in front of him, and so delicate. He was afraid that if he touched her, she would come apart in his hands, like a dandelion in the wind. He could see that she had been crying, and she was covered in dirt, too, as if she had crawled through a field to reach him. Her brown hair was tangled and a small rucksack hung limp in her hands, but when he looked again at her face, into the eyes that he had learned so effortlessly off by heart, he saw hope reflected back at him.

'You're alive,' she said at last, and Max found his smile.

'Afraid so.'

'I thought you were . . .' She stopped, unable to bring herself to say the final word. 'Jamal told Steph that things weren't looking good, and then I got here and went to the intensive care ward, and I found your empty room and I . . .'

She stopped again. Max could almost taste her anguish, so raw that it pained him.

'It's OK,' he said, needing to reassure her. 'I'm definitely not dead, and I don't plan on being dead any time soon.'

She nodded, fighting yet more tears.

'I gave Jamal quite a fright on the flight home,' he told her lightly. 'Passed out cold. I'll spare you the gory details, but let's just say it was touch and go for a while. My leg was infected, and the nasties got into my bloodstream, but it's all been cleaned up now. I should never have ignored that pain I was having. I'm an idiot.'

'That makes two of us, then,' she said. She still hadn't moved from her spot just inside the curtain, and Max heaved himself up into a better sitting position and patted the bed.

'Come and sit with me,' he offered, and then, when she hesitated, 'Please.'

Alice came towards him, still gazing at him as if she could not quite believe he was there, that this was happening, that the two of them were together again. She looked down at the bandaged end of his stump, which was resting on top of the covers.

'Does it hurt?' she asked, her eyes solemn.

'Probably,' he allowed. 'But I'm on far too many drugs to notice.'

Alice smiled at that, and this time it felt like a genuine one. Max lifted his hand and touched her arm just once, very gently.

'I'm glad you're here,' he said. 'I missed you.'

Alice looked at his hand, swallowed.

'I have missed you, too,' she said. 'So much. I was so worried after you left Sri Lanka, I just wanted the holiday to be over so I could come home, so I could find you and tell you that I . . .'

Max waited, taking her in as she fumbled for the words she wanted to say. She was perched up on the bed now, facing him – so close that he could see the freckles on her cheeks and her Mickey Mouse earrings. He yearned to pull her down against him.

'That you what?' he prompted quietly, and Alice made herself look at him.

'That I'm sorry. Sorry for what I said to you at the beach, sorry for being such a coward and a fool and sorry for letting you go believing that I didn't care about you, when I did. I do. I really do.'

Max let go of a breath that he had not known he was holding.

'I got your poem,' she said then, picking up her bag from where she had dropped it on the floor and unzipping the front pocket. Max recognised the piece of folded paper, and felt the heat in his cheeks.

'Jamal must have found it,' he said. 'I wrote it right before I came to find you, that night on the beach in Tangalle. I guess I was just trying to make sense of what I was feeling, but I never planned on showing it to anyone – least of all you.'

Alice smiled. 'I'm very glad it found its way to me,' she said.

Max chuckled. 'Bit late to worry about it now,' he said. 'By the time I'd got back to the room that night, I was out of it. The doctor who came gave me something that got me through the airport the next morning and on to the plane, but I don't remember much after that. The next thing I knew, I was here, and my mum was here, telling me that I was going to be all right.'

'It must have been awful,' Alice said, and Max reached out the hand not attached to the drip to comfort her.

'Not just for me,' he said. 'For you guys, too. I'm so sorry I scared you like that.'

She smiled. 'I think we both say sorry too much,' she said, and Max laughed.

'I think you might be right.'

'I broke up with Richard.'

She had blurted it out so quickly that at first Max thought he had misheard.

'You did what?'

'It's over,' she confirmed. 'You were right. The truth is, I didn't want to marry him. I realised that he could never make me happy, and I could never make him happy, either. The old Alice would have made it work, but she's long gone now. I left her behind in Sri Lanka.'

Max was forced to quell a huge smile. He was proud of her, he realised, but nervous, too. Just because she and Richard were no longer together didn't mean she would automatically want to be with him.

'Honestly,' she went on, 'I have been like a new person these past few days. I even stood up to my mum – me! And it was nowhere near as scary as I thought it would be. I think she might even change, although it's going to take a while yet.'

Max grunted in amusement. 'You'll have to give me some pointers,' he said. 'Once I'm back on my feet – my foot,' he corrected, and Alice rolled her eyes in good humour. 'Then me and my mum are going to have a proper chat. It's time for me to move away from home now, and do something that makes me happy.'

'I've just had to move back home!' Alice exclaimed, and they looked at one another and laughed, relieved to be able to do so.

'Thank you,' he said, and she inclined her head, confusion on her face.

'For what?'

'For making me realise that I was in danger of settling, and for helping me believe that I can have everything I want when it comes to being with someone – and I mean really being with them. Sri Lanka proved to me how much more I need from my life, and my work, but being there and meeting you was only a beginning. Now I know that I want to do all the things you want to, Alice. I want to go on adventures, and travel more, and I want to help people, too, people like me.'

She was nodding again, tears welling in eyes that were full of understanding.

'I don't think I will ever be able to say thank you enough to you,' she mumbled. 'I feel like my whole life, from the time I fell off that roof to the moment I met you in Habarana, has been on pause, and that now, my life can begin again. My true adventure can begin – the one I was always supposed to go on.'

'Oh, Alice,' he said, so moved by her words that his voice cracked as he spoke. 'You have always been on an adventure – you just didn't realise it.'

For a few seconds, they gazed at each other, and again

Max felt the pull of a thread inside him – the same one that had fastened him to this woman, this wonderful, hopeful, daring and beautiful woman, the moment he first saw her, and which had never frayed. Lifting his hand, he reached across to stroke away the loose strands of hair from her face. Alice closed her eyes, pressing her cheek against his open palm, and smiled. For the first time since she had appeared in the hospital, like a tatty angel he had conjured from a dream, Alice looked at peace, and Max knew that this was it – the love he had been searching for. She was the future he had been waiting to find, while he was the adventure she had not even known existed.

Alice opened her eyes, and dropped a kiss on his hand.

'Can I ask you a question?' she said, a smile dancing on her lips like light across water.

Max dropped his hand to her shoulder.

'As long as it's an easy one.'

'Well, let's see,' she replied, moving forwards until Max could almost feel the beating of her heart, and running a shy hand through his hair. Her fingers felt cool and soft against the back of his neck, and Max shivered beneath them.

'It's a yes or no answer.'

He put his head on one side, his lips now a whisper from hers, and Alice leaned towards him, her eyes beginning to close. Max could feel the love between them, and it felt like coming home.

'I think you already know my answer, Alice,' he said.

And then he kissed her.

# Acknowledgements

It would not have been possible to write this book without a great amount of help, so I must begin with my thanks. First of all to Blesma, for putting me in touch with the brave and brilliant Matt Southwould, Linden Allen and Glynn McNary. It was an honour speaking to you all, and Max would not have become the darkly humorous and intricate soul he is without your incredible insight. Thank you for being so generous with your time and for answering all my no-doubt bizarre questions. I should say here that any errors concerning Max and his prosthetic limb, or any military terminology, are completely down to me.

Heartfelt thanks to Maureen Stapleton, who very kindly bid to have a character named after her in this book as part of the Authors For Grenfell auction. I hope you enjoy the antics of your namesake, and agree that she is every bit as bold and wonderful as you. Thanks also to SJ, for being the auction runner-up and for generally being one of the best, loveliest and most amazing ladies I have ever met.

I am so grateful to my wonderful friend Tamsin Carroll, who came out to Sri Lanka with me and also taught me the importance of a good pillow. Let us never forget bakery tuk-tuks, pelicans in trees, aftershave on cut knees and, of course, Captain Siri. Thanks also to Senura Dulanjith and friends, who gave up their seats on the Kandy to Hatton train for us and got us to Adam's Peak in one piece. You are all LEGENDS. I must thank Graeme Dunn, too – when I brought back slightly more from my Sri Lanka trip than elephant-dung notepaper and a tan, he was there in the hospital like a guardian angel. Never have I been so glad to see a friendly face (and a needle).

To my wonderful agent, Hannah Ferguson, the team at Hardman & Swainson and all those at The Marsh Agency, thank you for being so flawlessly supportive and infinitely wise. To my truly masterful and mind-bogglingly smart Road-Running marvel of an editor, Matilda McDonald, what a mission this one was! Thank you for being so unfailingly kind, clever, patient, and funny, too. Laughing is very important during editing, don't you know! To Sarah Harwood, Laura Nicol, Maxine Hitchcock, Maddy Marshall, Beatrix McIntyre, Sarah Bance and Jessica Hart and all the other p-p-p-perfect Penguins, THANK YOU for all you do and have done for me and for this book. It was a bold step forward for me, and I never felt anything but cheered on throughout the entire writing process. A huge round of applause must go to Eve Hall, who conjured up the incredible title of this book. When I saw it, I knew, just like Max and Alice did.

To the Book Camp crew, thanks for all the advice, all the laughs and all the biscuit cake. I look forward to sharing a hot tub and a secret love of Andrew with you all again soon. The book world is full to bursting of amazing and inspirational people, and to list every one of them here would require another 400 pages. You already know who you are, you brilliant bunch. Massive love to all the book bloggers and reviewers who read so tirelessly and with so much enthusiasm – I have nothing but awe and admiration for you all.

To Sadie Davies, Katie Marsh, Gemma Courage, Ranjit Dhillon, Sarah Beddingfield, Chad Higgins, Vicky Zimmerman, Ian Lawton, Carrie Wallder, Nina Pottell, Louise Candlish, Clare Frost, Fanny Blake, Alex Holbrook and Corrie Heale, thanks for being the best friends a Broom could ever wish for – and then some. I promise to work hard on my writing schedule next time around, so that you actually get to see me more often than once a year . . . between deadlines.

I was a hopelessly clumsy child – much like Alice in this book, in fact, only worse. I managed to crack my head open, break my nose multiple times, fall off roller boots and horses, drive a moped through a fence and swing a doll around my head in circles until it kicked me in the face. Despite all this, my mum still encouraged me to be myself, to be proud of myself and to explore as much of the world as I could. She also encouraged me to write, which is why this book – and, indeed, all my books – belongs to her and to every single member of my amazing family. I love the lot of you – mad dogs and all.

And finally to YOU, my cherished reader. Thank you for picking this book when there are so very many to choose from, and for coming on this journey with me. I really hope you enjoyed it. Do come and tell me what you thought on Twitter and/or Instagram (@isabelle_broom), or find me on Facebook under Isabelle Broom Author. To see location photos and read more about me, and my books, you can pop over to www.isabellebroom.com.

# Isabelle
# Broom

Follow Izzy on

@isabellebroomauthor

Follow Izzy on

@Isabelle_Broom

Follow Izzy on

@isabelle_broom

Sign up to Izzy's newsletter!

Visit www.penguin.co.uk/authors/isabelle-broom/126001/